The Valet's Witness

Rohn Hein

HISTORIUM PRESS

The Valet's Witness

More on this book and the time it is based in at:
www.rohnheinauthor.com

Cover design by White Rabbit Arts at
The Historical Fiction Company

Hardcover ISBN: 979-8-950078-93-4
Paperback ISBN: 979-8-950078-94-1
Ebook ISBN: 979-8-950078-95-8

Published by Historium Press USA

2026

This book is dedicated to my dear wife, Cheryl Dunican-Hein, and my daughter, Tahlia Kramarz Hein

Table of Contents

INTRODUCTION

The Declaration of Independence is one of the most sacred documents of the United States of America. When asked, less than half of Americans know why the Declaration was adopted. Fewer Americans know that the document wasn't signed until August 2, 1776. Even fewer people know that two motions were adopted by the Second Continental Congress to achieve independence from the British. The first was a motion made by Richard Henry Lee of Virginia that was adopted July 2, 1776 and said,

"Resolved, that these United Colonies are, and of right ought to be, free and independent States, that they are absolved from all allegiance to the British Crown, and that all political connection between them and the State of Great Britain is, and ought to be, totally dissolved."

The second motion that was adopted was the Declaration of Independence on July 4, 1776.

If we know so little about the specifics of the official document, the fine specifics that took place in Philadelphia in 1775 and 1776 are much more difficult to cipher.

To assist the reader, I would like to offer some points that will make the story clearer.

- Edward Rutledge of South Carolina refers to those he enslaved as servants and not slaves.
- When the Declaration was signed, the delegates knew that they were taking an important step toward independence but did not refer to the document specifically as the Declaration of Independence. Throughout the book I refer to the document as the declaration on independence.
- Travel distances and time meant different things to the colonists than they do for us. During the 18th century, it would take 3-4 weeks to travel from Charleston, South Carolina to Philadelphia. A traveler would need to expect 3-4 weeks to travel from Philadelphia to London, but the return trip would take 6-12 weeks.

Philadelphia Beckons the Rutledges

The bell in the mansion's back room made a sharp, crisp ding, which meant that Pompey's master, Edward Rutledge, needed him in his downstairs study. Edward resided in his mansion with his new wife, Henrietta Middleton, daughter of one of the most influential and richest citizens in Charleston. Pompey dropped the button he was sewing on Master Edward's breeches, turned down the hall, and took the stairs to the first floor to discover what new task Edward needed him to perform. He could smell fruit pie baking in the kitchen as he passed through the dining room that was elegantly set with fine China, polished silverware, and crystal glasses for dinner. As he moved through the hall that had velvet top hats hanging on the wall and an oversized mirror, Pompey entered the booklined office and saw Master Edward at his nearly empty mahogany desk with a feather quill in his hand.

Edward Rutledge was of average height and had a slender physique. With ruddy skin and always wearing a powdered wig, he looked the patrician that he was, never to be mistaken for an outdoorsman.

"Pompey, I thought that I told you to purchase ink for me last week," said Edward. "I am in the middle of an important letter and find no ink in my well. Where did you put the new ink?"

Pompey thought, *Master Edward never asked me to purchase any ink last week*, but that was the last thing that he should tell him.

"I must have been busy with the clothes you wanted me to fix, sir. I am sorry, but I'll go right now to buy the ink, and it shouldn't take much time at all. Sir, should I buy it on your account, or do you want to pay cash?"

"Just put it on my account and be quick about it."

"Yes, sir." Pompey exited the study to the front door and into the busy streets of Charleston.

Outside the Rutledge mansion, Pompey saw a bustling colonial port city, where cobbled streets met the humid air of the South Carolina coast. Across Broad Street, the spire of St. Michael's Church rose above the rooftops, its bells marking time for merchants, lawyers, and enslaved laborers alike. Horse-drawn carriages clattered past storefronts and taverns, while the scent of sea salt mingled with tobacco and indigo from nearby warehouses.

Pompey, eighteen years old of average height, but strong and wiry, had been a valet for Edward Rutledge for the past two years. His close-cropped, curly hair, high cheek bones, broad nose, expressive eyes, and mahogany-colored skin was typical of a native of West Africa.

He didn't expect to be given money to pay for the ink because Rutledge was cash poor. He couldn't remember the last time that he had seen Rutledge pay cash for anything. Pompey also knew that, because Rutledge did not question him any more about the previous order. Pompey sensed that Rutledge never asked him to buy the ink in the first place.

Pompey's job as valet was a welcome task when faced with the prospect of working at one of the plantations that Rutledge owned with his business partner and friend, Charles Cotesworth Pinckney. By being efficient and quiet, Pompey had earned a position as valet which would keep him out of the fields, but it also didn't hurt that his father had once worked for Edward's father as his manservant many years ago. Even so, Pompey's future was now dependent on how well he pleased Master Edward.

As Pompey walked down Broad Street, just west of the Battery, he could see the neighboring two-story houses of clapboard, while the Rutledge abode was a Georgian, brick, three-floor structure. The scent of lemon balm and crushed magnolia drifted from the garden as the sun cast sharp shadows from the wrought-iron balconies and palmetto fronds that swayed lazily above the cobbled walk.

Pompey kept to the street so as not to encounter any white citizens, and he kept his eyes staring at the ground to conceal any hints of indiscretion. He made his way to James Poya's shop on East Bay Street, where the merchant offered a wide range of imported goods from England. Mr. Poya and his workers knew Pompey, so this should be an easy task. Pompey loved coming to this store and was often mesmerized by the lanterns and rope hanging from the ceiling, the barrels filled with flour and spices, and all manner of items behind the counter.

"Hello, Pompey. What does Edward need today?"

"Sir, he needs some ink for writing a letter."

"No problem at all. I'm sure that he wants this on his account."

"Yes, sir. That is what he told me."

"I'll bet that Edward and his brother are eager to head north for the new Continental Congress. When do you think they are leaving?"

Pompey was not sure how to respond. He had not heard Edward speak of returning to the Continental Congress at Philadelphia and had not seen Edward's brother for the past week. "I'm not sure," he said.

"Tell him to let me know if he needs any supplies before he leaves. The citizens of Charleston are counting on the two of them to represent South Carolina well."

"I will tell him that, sir." He took the ink and the receipt and ran back to the mansion wondering what another trip to Philadelphia would mean for him.

A carriage rumbled past, its wheels clattering against the uneven stones, driven by a liveried enslaved man in a faded blue coat. Inside, a powdered lady cooled herself with a lace-edged fan, her gaze fixed ahead, avoiding the gaze of passing tradesmen. Across the street, a group of gentlemen in linen coats and breeches stood beneath the shade of a portico, their voices low but urgent as they debated the latest news from the northern colonies. One gestured with a folded broadsheet, the South-Carolina Gazette, its ink still fresh with news of militias and petitions.

He opened the front door and dashed into the study where he found Edward talking with his brother, John.

"Haven't I told you not to come rushing into a room when I am speaking with someone?" Edward said.

"Gentle, Ned. I am sure he didn't mean any harm, and he knows me. It's not like you're having a meeting with John Adams. What do you have, Pompey?"

"Just some ink that Master Edward asked me to purchase, sir." Nervously, he said, "Mr. Poya said that if you need any items for your trip to Congress, you should let him know."

"How did he find out about this so soon?" said John. "News certainly travels quickly. What else did he say, boy?"

"He said he hoped that you would represent Charleston well."

"What do you think he meant by that, John?" Edward said.

"Probably exactly what the boy said, he wished us well and hoped that we would do a good job. That shouldn't be that hard for two Rutledges."

"But how did he find out about Congress meeting?" Edward asked.

"What difference does it make, Ned. We have much more important things to talk about before we leave."

The second trip to Philadelphia in one year was overwhelming to Pompey. Last year when they arrived by schooner, he was a stranger in a new city. This year he will have a better understanding of the place and his station. Looking forward to rekindling the friendship of other Black valets and the other delegates, he didn't think that Master Rutledge had ever noticed what Pompey did with his free time. The slaves had their own fraternity, and they shared the secrets they heard from the lips of their masters and their friends.

"Pompey, that will be all for now. My brother and I have a great deal to discuss before we leave. I will give you instructions when my brother leaves on how you can prepare for our journey."

Pompey left the study, passed by more pleasing kitchen aromas, and returned to his work of fixing Mr. Rutledge's breeches. He looked forward to seeing the other Black Valets: Cato, Bob, and Caesar again. The attendance of the valets with the other South Carolina delegates, Cicero who belonged to John Rutledge, Peter who worked for Henry Middleton, and Sam who toiled for John Lynch, would also be a fine distraction.

From the harbor, the salt breeze began mingling with the scent of horses and tobacco, and the distant creaking of the wooden ship hulls could be heard. The city was poised, elegant but uneasy, on the cusp of revolution.

John and Edward Rutledge knew that Congress had decided the previous fall to meet in May, but both were surprised that it had become gossip in Charleston. "We need to protect the interests of South Carolina if the King continues to block any accommodation toward us," said John. "I am concerned that our desire for reconciliation may fall on the deaf ears of King George."

"I wonder if something else has happened to which we are not privy. I fear we may need to take more drastic action if the King does not respond kindly," said Edward.

"I have no fear about these events. As leaders of South Carolina, we need to stand strong and protect our interests, no matter what events may follow. Our job is to delay and deny, so that good decisions can be made. We will delay until the course of action is clear, and we shall deny that we seek special treatment for South Carolina. If the fight with Britain occurs, we will take up our share of the responsibility, but we should focus solely on independence and not allow ourselves or the other delegates to be sidetracked by other issues, such as our planter society."

"Do you think that the other colonies will try to stop our slavery policy, even when we are trying to fight for independence?"

"I pray that it does not happen, but we must take initiative. Whenever this issue arises, we need to quench the flames before they turn into an inferno. I think that is what Mr. Poya meant when he told Pompey that he hoped we would protect the interests of South Carolina."

"You are probably right, as usual, big brother. I think I will go down to Gadsden Dock and arrange for a schooner we can take to reach Philadelphia in the next two weeks."

"Good idea, Ned. We can talk more over dinner tonight as we are hoping that you and Henrietta will join us."

"That would be splendid. Sunset?"

"Very good. See you later."

Edward started to turn over in his mind how the Second Continental Congress would be different than the First. He had a good opportunity to meet the delegates last year, so his level of comfort would be increased, even though he always felt that he stood in the shadow of his brother. Edward wished to make a mark for himself among the delegates and hoped he could receive some more key committee work, unlike the previous year when only John had been assigned to the significant committees. Maybe the more important task was to plant the seed in the delegate's minds that they were really assembled for a discussion on independence and not to regulate slavery.

In the meantime, Pompey looked forward to seeing his friends.

THE RUTLEDGES RETURN TO PHILADELPHIA

A vast array of emotions stirred a delegate's yearnings for independence as events cascaded upon this gathering of men who were bound together with the responsibility of responding to Britain. Only six months earlier, the delegates had left Philadelphia with a desire to hear a whiff of understanding from England, but the pain of rejection and the atrocities of war were too obvious to ignore. On April 19, 1775, British troops, who marched to Lexington, Massachusetts to capture a trove of powder and rifles, were met by colonial patriots who resisted. The conflict that followed the redcoats back to Boston through Lexington brought death to both sides and thus changed everything.

The delegates representing South Carolina at the Second Continental Congress were the same as the first session, and with news about the fighting at Lexington and Concord, the case for reconciliation, which they'd strongly supported in September, was harder to justify. Armed combat between redcoats and patriots had driven the radicals to make their voices heard. The conservatives led by John Dickinson recognized the importance of winning favor of the Rutledges, while the radicals felt compelled to direct their favor toward liberty and independence. Once again, John Rutledge was named to important committees, and Edward would be left with more mundane assignments.

Edward Rutledge, at just twenty-six years old, was the youngest delegate in the Second Continental Congress—a fact that weighed heavily on him as he arrived in Philadelphia alongside other men of towering reputation and experience. Surrounded by elder statesmen like Benjamin Franklin, John Dickinson, and Samuel Adams, Rutledge felt pressure to prove his worth not only to his fellow delegates, but to the political establishment of South Carolina that had entrusted him with such a consequential role. His legal training in London and successful practice back home gave him confidence, yet the gravity of the debates over war, independence, and the fate of thirteen colonies, had stirred in him a deep sense of caution. He often aligned with conservative voices, opposing premature moves toward independence, which suggested a young man keenly aware of the risks of bold action and the need to earn credibility through restraint and deliberation.

At the same time, Rutledge's youth may have fueled a quiet ambition and a desire to shape the course of history. He was energetic, articulate, and politically savvy, and Edward did not shy away from leadership, working to delay the vote on independence until South Carolina was ready to support it. That balancing act between youthful drive and political prudence likely created an internal tension. Edward would speak boldly with the knowledge that he should have the wisdom to listen. In a Congress where age often conferred authority, Rutledge had to navigate not only the issues of the day but the perception of his own legitimacy.

In the summer of 1775, Charleston Harbor at Gadsden's Pier pulsed with revolutionary tension and mercantile energy. Christopher Gadsden's newly completed wharf, an 840-foot marvel stretching along the Cooper River, stood as a bold symbol of patriotic ambition, though it had been built by enslaved labor to serve the colony's expanding trade and political aspirations. Ships bobbed at anchor, some laden with rice, indigo, and naval stores, while others faced scrutiny under the Continental Association's import bans. The air was thick with both salt and uncertainty, as rumors of British troop movements mingled with the clamor of dockworkers, merchants, and militiamen drilling nearby. Gadsden's Pier was no longer just a commercial hub—it had become a stage for rebellion, where Charleston's future was being loaded, debated, and declared.

When Edward and John Rutledge and the other South Carolina delegates, Henry Middleton, Thomas Lynch, and Christopher Gadsden, left the dock in Charleston on a clear June day with not a cloud in the sky and seagulls squawking, they had no idea that the Revolutionary War had already begun. Just before they sailed into Philadelphia harbor, they received more information, via a messenger ship sent from Philadelphia harbor, that blood had been shed in New England, thus making the weight of their potential deliberations even heavier. Soon the schooner glided into a berth and was lashed to the moorings to allow the passengers to touch firm ground. Standing on a wharf made of aged pine and cedar, they were welcomed by a trio of other delegates: Thomas Stone of Maryland, Samuel Ward of Rhode Island, and James Wilson of Pennsylvania.

The schooner bearing South Carolina's delegation eased into Philadelphia Harbor as the city was bracing for war. The five delegates stepped ashore into a city alive with militia drills, political pamphlets, and the scent of fresh ink from presses churning out revolutionary rhetoric. Their arrival was both ceremonial and strategic: Middleton, a former president of the First Congress, lent gravitas; Gadsden, the radical merchant, carried Charleston's firebrand spirit; and the Rutledges and Lynch brought legal acumen and generational continuity. Dockworkers paused, recognizing the Southern gentlemen whose presence signaled unity across colonial lines. As carriages rattled toward the Pennsylvania Statehouse, the delegation's arrival underscored South Carolina's commitment to the Continental cause—rice planters and revolutionaries alike were now bound to the fate of thirteen colonies.

The South Carolina delegates shuffled down the gangway that groaned under their weight and led them to waiting carriages for the ride to the Statehouse, while separate wagons would carry their belongings to their lodgings in Philadelphia. A tense atmosphere hung over the wharf because of the recent deaths of patriots in Massachusetts, and the rejection of reconciliation by the King that resulted in a mind-spinning catharsis. The work of the Congress had suddenly become a deliberate and serious struggle. This was no theoretical debate, and the stakes for all the delegates had been suddenly raised to a much higher level.

"Good to see you again," John Rutledge said to James Wilson. "What is the overall morale of the delegates? We heard more details earlier onboard our schooner about the tragedy in Massachusetts. Do you have any additional information?"

"We have received a good deal of correspondence from people in Lexington, Concord, and Boston," said Wilson. "The more difficult factor is trying to get into the minds of the British. I am sure that they received considerably more resistance than they expected."

"Do you have any reports on the injured?" asked John.

"We have some preliminary reports showing that about fifty patriots were killed, but the British lost almost twice as many, and our injuries were considerably less than the British received. I heard a bulletin that 200 lobster backs were shot but survived. We certainly gave them a whipping, but this battle will only be the prelude to a much greater conflict.

"That is why we are here. When does Congress meet next?"

"We will convene tomorrow morning at 9AM sharp. We are glad you are here, safe and ready to debate. It's good to see the South Carolinians hale and hearty."

"I'll let you know how hearty I am," Christopher Gadsden said, "as soon as I get some good food and drink in me."

Everyone laughed as they looked for their carriages, while the manservants, including Pompey and Caesar, began the chore of handling the luggage.

The atmosphere on the Philadelphia wharf bristled with heat and tension as the schooner from Charleston moored alongside crates of gunpowder and barrels of flour destined for the Continental Army. Dockhands paused mid-haul as Pompey and Cicero began unloading the personal effects of South Carolina's elite delegates—trunks of polished mahogany, saddle cases, crates marked with initials in bold script, and a caged songbird chirping above the din. Silks and silver glinted in the sun, hinting at the planter wealth behind the patriot cause. The carriages waited nearby, their wheels freshly oiled, while curious onlookers, Quaker merchants, apprentices, and militia officers watched the Southern gentlemen approach their carriages with measured grace. The scent of river brine was mingled with pipe smoke and horse sweat, as Philadelphia absorbed not just their belongings, but also their ambitions.

The carriages were on a higher level than the wharf and could be reached by a short walk along the dock and then up a staircase of twelve steps. The carriage sounds of the wheels running over the cobblestones, with the squeaking of circling seagulls, and the barking of the drivers of the freight wagons were mixed in a symphony of the seaport.

"Pompey, we will be at the City Tavern," said Edward. "After you finish with the luggage, please return there so I can give you more instruction."

The warm, dry afternoon made for easy work, pulling the crates and boxes off the schooner, dividing them among the wagons, and delivering them to the residences whose addresses the masters had already provided. Jack, Christopher Gadsden's valet, Peter, Henry

Middleton's manservant, and Sam, John Lynch's valet, had the more demanding jobs because Middleton always traveled with the most accompaniments, and Lynch had more medical issues to address. As the carriages full of the South Carolina delegation moved up the hill from the dock toward the city center, the five Black valets began to unpack the schooner and divide the crates among the available wagons.

Sam and Peter opened the hatch and began to place the crates stored below on deck so it would be easier to move them to the wagons. Jack moved the crates from the deck to the pier. Pompey and Cicero would move the cargo to the wagons.

"I didn't think that war would be arriving so soon. For all the loud talk we hear, I thought that they would smooth things out before they started killing one another," said Pompey.

"That caught me by surprise, also. I wonder if they started fighting in South Carolina, too, after we left."

Cicero usually deferred to Pompey even though they were the same age and Cicero's master was Edward's older brother. Pompey had a commanding voice with other slaves, and a presence that Cicero admired. "You know these things better than I, Pomp. Master John seemed to be greatly concerned about the news of colonists' deaths."

"As well he should. That is what makes a good leader. Did you notice that Master Edward didn't say a word and held his tongue as soon as his brother was on the scene?"

The local livery man had backed down two open flatbed drays to the dock so that the crates and luggage would be delivered to the Shippen House and Mrs. Yard's boardinghouse. Sam and Peter had finished bringing the crates to the deck of the schooner, while Jack was now helping Pompey and Cicero in dividing the cargo accordingly.

The Philadelphia Harbor, in the lull between arriving schooners, settled into a rhythm of anticipation beneath the summer sun. The wharf creaked under emptied barrels and stacked crates, some marked with initials denoting Southern shippers, others already claimed by porters in dusty waistcoats. Ropes lay slack on the cobbles, and gulls wheeled overhead, their cries mingling with the distant clang of a blacksmith's hammer and the murmur of merchants tallying goods. A faint breeze stirred the river, carrying the scent of molasses, tar, and tobacco. Dockhands leaned against bollards, wiping sweat from their faces and scanning the horizon for the next mast to rise. The harbor, momentarily still, was a canvas of readiness—its people, its planks, its politics all braced for the next arrival, whether laden with cargo or consequence.

After loading the drays, Sam, Peter, and Jack went on the wagon to the Shippen house, while Pompey and Cicero rode on the dray toward Mrs. Yard's boardinghouse. The wagons began the uphill slope to the city with a great deal of jostling as the driver negotiated the cobblestone avenue.

Pompey said, "I wonder if Cato, Caesar, and Bob have arrived. They probably have more information about the war."

"How do you keep up with the information? I have a hard enough time just minding the things that Master John gives me to do. You have a rare talent for putting things in order."

"My father was a valet for the father of Masters Edward and John. When I was young, he would tell me stories about how he managed to work with Master Dr. John. When I started with Master Edward, I had a vision of what my responsibilities would be and so my life has been mostly simple, except when Master Ned forgets what he told me to do. I have learned to observe and hear much and to say and do as little as possible."

The wagon stopped on Second Street in front of Mrs. Yard's boardinghouse.

The driver of the wagon said, "Hurry up and unload this wagon, as I have another pick-up to do."

"Yes, sir. We will be quick about it." Pompey bounded off the cart and pulled the first piece of luggage to the street. Cicero also jumped off the dray and then turned around to lift a huge crate.

"Cicero, do you think you have the strength of ten?"

"The man said he wanted us to be quick, and you know how I want to please."

In short order, all the cargo was in the street and Pompey went to the front door and knocked to see who was at home. After a moment, the door opened so that Pompey could see the smiling face of Mrs. Yard.

"Pompey, I was expecting you later today," Mrs. Yard said. "I have rooms for Edward and John upstairs already prepared. It looks like you have plenty of clothes and wares packed. I am so glad to see you and Cicero."

"Thank you, ma'am. We'll have these upstairs in a flash."

Pompey found a rock to keep the front door open, and they moved the eight pieces of luggage from the street into the house. Carrying the pieces upstairs and into the room only took a few minutes, such that Pompey and Cicero could now spend a few minutes at the city market on High Street before arriving at The City Tavern to receive more orders.

Pompey wondered what news Cato and Bob might bring.

THE COLONISTS GIRD FOR WAR

On a crisp morning, delegates from every colony were congregating at the Pennsylvania Statehouse to begin the next session of the Second Continental Congress. The delegates appeared clad in the style of the many regions of the colonies. They filled Chestnut Street and were milling around in conversational circles of three or four men, discussing the recent attack on American patriots and debating how the colonies should respond. Various carriages brought the leaders of the Congress but also those whose names were foreign to most in the crowd.

A crowd of at least fifty citizens lined the sidewalks in front of the Statehouse and spoke among themselves in hushed tones. They pointed at various delegates as they disembarked from their carriages and wished them good luck in the work that they soon would undertake.

The city, already humming with revolutionary fervor, received George Washington of Virginia with a mix of admiration and expectation. Dockworkers and townspeople paused as his carriage rolled past the cobbled streets toward the Pennsylvania State House, where the Second Continental Congress was convening amid the thunder of distant skirmishes and the ink of fresh petitions. Though not yet formally appointed, Washington's bearing and reputation preceded him. He was the man many already saw as the colonies' military standard-bearer.

As Washington exited his chariot, wearing a buff and blue military uniform connoting his rank of colonel in the Virginia militia which accentuated his height, he towered over most of the delegates. John Adams of Massachusetts, and Richard Henry Lee of Virginia wore formal colonial garb, while Edward and John Rutledge sported silk breeches, waistcoats of colorful embroidery, silk ascots, and shoes with buckles that reflected the morning sun. The crowd of colonial patriots were soon entering the hall to discuss the next steps that needed to be taken after the battle at Lexington and Concord.

Delegates were eager to begin, but administrative details needed to be agreed to for the proper order of business. Delegations were identified and accepted, an agreement to keep Congress's activities secret was adopted, rules of debate were decided, and they elected a President - Peyton Randolph of Virginia. However, he needed to resign within three weeks when his services were needed in the Virginia colony and, consequently, John Hancock of Massachusetts, would lead the Congress after Randolph.

During these first few weeks of Congress, reports from the siege of Boston revealed how the colonial patriots had trapped the British forces by surrounding the city and leaving only sea access to support the Redcoats. Congress was also advised that patriots from Connecticut and Vermont had attacked and won Fort Ticonderoga at the base of Lake Champlain in New York, and delegates debated approaching the residents of Canada to join with the patriots. Canada had only come under British rule in 1763 as spoils of French and Indian War. She had become a preoccupation with some of the patriots after the Quebec Act of 1774 that extended the colony's boundary south to the Ohio River. The Act also preserved French civil law and feudal land tenure, which angered American colonists who saw the Quebec Act as well as the Boston Port Act, the Quartering Act, the Massachusetts Governing Act, and the Administration of Justice Act as the Intolerable Acts. Colonists saw them as a direct assault on their rights and self-government, and a threat to their territorial and political ambitions.

As news was reported, Congress knew that local militias in Massachusetts and other New England colonies were carrying the fight to the British, and a unified military response was required. On June 15, 1775, Congress created a Continental Army consisting of all patriot militias. Just days after Washington's arrival, John Adams nominated Washington to lead the newly formed Continental Army by a motion that passed unanimously. Washington, rising with characteristic restraint, accepted the command with solemn humility, refusing any salary beyond expenses. His presence transformed the Congress from a political gathering into the nucleus of a war effort. The Virginia planter had become the embodiment of continental resolve, and as he departed shortly thereafter for Boston, the Congress had not only chosen a general but had taken its first irrevocable step toward revolution. A command structure was established with major generals and brigadier general's posts created as well as other positions such as adjunct general, commissary general, paymaster, engineer, and other positions to prosecute the enemy. Articles of war were agreed upon for the care of soldiers, how prisoners of war were to be handled, and many other rules of engagement.

The unanimous vote to install George Washington as the leader of the military to fight the British was a unifying act that provided a much-needed sectional realignment. This showed that a Southern colony, Virginia, would come to the aid of a northern colony, Massachusetts. More importantly, the selection of Washington showed that an alliance developing amongst the colonies was not just idle talk but was demonstrated by right action.

Washington said, "Though I am truly sensible of the high Honor done me in this appointment, yet I feel great distress, from a consciousness that my abilities and military experience may not be equal to the extensive and important trust. However, as the Congress desire it, I will enter upon the momentous duty and exert every power I possess in their service and for the support of the glorious cause. I beg they will accept my most cordial thanks for this distinguished testimony of their approbation.

"But lest some unlucky event should happen unfavorable to my reputation, I beg it may be remembered by every gentleman in the room, that I this day declare with the utmost sincerity, I do not think myself equal to the command I am honored with."

Five days later, Thomas Jefferson brought his credentials to Congress from Virginia designating him as a delegate from Virginia. Less than one month later, Jefferson wrote the first draft of the "Declaration of the Causes and Necessity of Taking Up Arms." The declaration was a forceful yet measured justification for colonial resistance against British military aggression. Drafted primarily by Jefferson and revised by John Dickinson, the document laid out a decade's worth of grievances from taxation without representation to the coercive acts and expanded vice-admiralty courts, while emphasizing that the colonies did not yet seek independence. Instead, it asserted that Americans had taken up arms "in defense of the Freedom that is our Birthright," and would lay them down once British hostilities ceased. The declaration blended Enlightenment ideals with urgent political rhetoric, framing the conflict, not as rebellion, but as a last resort against unconstitutional domination.

In the ensuing weeks, a strategy for engaging the citizens of Canada was prepared, and Congress appointed General Phillip Schuyler to lead Continental Army troops from the New York colony that would be supplemented by the militias earlier sent from Connecticut and Vermont that had taken the strategic Fort Ticonderoga on Lake Champlain from the British.

The Second Continental Congress struggled with organizing a military infrastructure to manage the ever-widening conflict with Britain. As summer turned into fall, the notion of a brief confrontation had succumbed to the reality that the conflict would be long, bloody, and expensive. Congress requested that colonies initiate a draft for eligible men to fight, and form Committees of Safety to oversee defense and security. Colonial leaders faced a complex and urgent dilemma in terms of navigating relations with indigenous nations whose allegiances could tip the balance of frontier warfare. The British had long cultivated ties with powerful confederacies like the Iroquois, and by mid-June, several nations—including the Mohawk, Seneca, Cayuga, and Onondaga—had declared support for the Crown, drawn by promises to uphold the Proclamation of 1763 to protect native lands from colonial encroachment. In response, the Congress debated how to secure alliances or neutrality from other tribes, recognizing that indigenous warriors could either defend frontier settlements or devastate them. The issue was not merely military, but diplomatic, cultural, and territorial, requiring emissaries and interpreters who needed to strike a delicate balance between revolutionary ideals and expansionist ambitions.

The important economic policy of non-exportation established at the First Continental Congress in 1774, was scheduled to go into effect by the colonies in July 1775. Parliament had recently passed a resolution attempting to divide the Congressional delegates by exempting four colonies from an English ban on sales to countries outside the English Empire. John and Edward Rutledge were at the center of the debate to limit non-exports equally among the colonies so that each would share the burden of less export income. The discussion of allowing British ships into American ports led to an examination of the current state of the American Navy. Gadsden supported the build-up of a navy but, John and Edward Rutledge saw this as an affront to the British. In the end, Congress decided to build a navy. The debate was both spirited and strategic as some delegates feared provoking Britain further, while others, like John Adams, argued that without a naval force, the colonies would remain vulnerable to blockades and unable to intercept British supply ships. Rhode Island had already urged action, recognizing that coastal defense required more than local patrols. In October 1775, Congress authorized the fitting out of two armed vessels to capture enemy transports, an event which marked the birth of the Continental Navy. Though modest in scale, the decision signaled a shift from protest to organized resistance and laid the groundwork for a maritime campaign that would harass British commerce and bolster colonial morale.

A Massachusetts convention asked Congress for guidance on forming a government to replace the Royal assemblies. John Rutledge chaired a committee that recommended the colony design an assembly that did not interfere with their colonial charter, which John Adams saw as an attempt to preserve obedience to the King. A few months later, John Rutledge must have changed his mind, when New Hampshire approached Congress about the same issue and Rutledges committee encouraged them to follow their own ideas of governance. Rutledge quickly asked his committee to allow New Hampshire, as well as South Carolina, to go forward with developing an independent colonial government structures.

As royal governors fled or were ousted amid rising revolutionary fervor, the American colonies faced the daunting task of constructing local governments from the ground up. Most colonies had operated under royal or proprietary charters, with executive authority stemming from appointed English officials, and local leaders left with limited control over their colonies. With the collapse of imperial oversight, colonial leaders scrambled to establish provisional congresses, committees of safety, and ad hoc councils to manage defense, finance, and law. The challenge was not merely administrative but ideological. Colonists had to reconcile Enlightenment principles with practical governance, often without legal precedent or consensus. Deep divisions over representation, executive power, and the role of property qualifications complicated efforts, and in some regions, loyalist resistance further destabilized the transition. The vacuum left by royal authority demanded swift innovation, but it also exposed the fragility and diversity of colonial political traditions.

With Washington as General, a wary group of delegates came to the realization that much work remained while the delegates were reassembling. Not only were the selected delegates looking forward to meeting again and making decisions, the Black valets of some of the delegates would be holding their own reunion.

Valets Become Reacquainted

The change of meeting site for Congress, from the smaller Carpenter's Hall the previous year to the larger Statehouse chamber gave delegates more room to confer, but did not affect the lives of Pompey or the other Black valets who assisted their masters in day-to-day chores. The meeting of the delegates provided the opportunity for the valets to become reacquainted with each other.

In June 1775, the Pennsylvania Statehouse stood at the heart of Philadelphia, a bustling colonial city poised on the edge of revolution. The Georgian-style building, with its symmetrical brick facade and modest cupola, housed the Second Continental Congress in its Assembly Room, where delegates from thirteen colonies gathered amid rising tensions. Outside, the cobbled streets echoed with the footsteps of messengers and murmurs of townspeople, while inside, the plain wooden furnishings and open fireplaces bore witness to the birth of a rebellion that would reshape a continent.

In the heat of the day, Pompey and Cicero were at their posts near the rear door of the Statehouse awaiting any orders that Master Edward or John might have for them. They could see across the courtyard that Cato and Caesar were quietly awaiting any messages from their masters, while Peter and Jack were busy making small talk while they waited. Suddenly Bob exited the rear door.

"Bob, where have you been? I have been awaiting your arrival?" said Pompey.

"We arrived from Maryland late last night. It's good to see everyone. Did I miss anything?"

"We are waiting for what you have to say. Things have been moving as swiftly as thought. George Washington was named General of the Army, and I'm sure you must have heard about the battles in Massachusetts. People are on edge."

"Master Thomas was talking about the battles in Lexington. It sounds like a lot of people died."

"Apparently, the British had the worst of it. People are worrying about what is going to happen next. They think the King will retaliate because he is so mad."

Cicero said, "Has your master been talking about anything else?"

"He received a report from Boston that explained what happened during the battle. He said to one of the other delegates that if the British are going to fight the colonies like they did in Concord, then this should be a short war."

"What did he mean by that," asked Cicero.

"The report he received made the British look very foolish in how they conducted themselves. After being surprised by the strength of the patriots in Lexington, they just continued to Concord like they owned the place. What happened next was even more stunning than the greeting they received in Lexington. Finally, they retreated twenty miles back to Boston with the patriots chasing them the entire way. They did not seem to put up much of a fight."

"Thanks for the information, Bob," said Pompey. "We had only heard that there was a battle, but we had no idea how strong the resistance was and how inept the British were. Did you hear anything else?"

"Mostly he seems to be worried about how long this struggle is going to take. He is concerned about money as he is sure that the policies adopted at the last Congress will harm his finances."

"Well, I don't know much about money, but I think Master Thomas isn't the only one worried about it. They either feel the pain now, or they will lose to the British and hurt worse, but I am sure that Master Edward will not ask me for my opinion."

"Maybe he should. They need some fresh ideas on how to make sure they don't become slaves like us."

Pompey and Cicero laughed. "Bob, you got a lot to learn about how these things work. The last thing that any master will ever do is ask a slave for his opinion. He doesn't even know that we have opinions, and if he did, he would never admit that he could learn something from us. Just shine those boots, fix my socks, fetch some supplies, get me something to eat. You know the routine."

"Do you think that will ever change?"

"Yeah," said Cicero. "When horses climb trees."

As they all started laughing, Peter and Jack looked up to see if anything was wrong. When they saw that it was just Pompey, Bob, and Cicero having a chuckle, they too joined in.

The sunlight spilled across the red brick walls and dappled the packed earth with shifting shadows cast by the tall elms and chestnut trees. A few horses were tethered near the carriage house, their tails flicking lazily at flies, while messengers in dusty boots strode purposefully toward the back entrance, clutching folded dispatches. The scent of fresh-cut grass mingled with the faint aroma of ink and parchment wafting from open windows above, where the voices of Congressmen rose and fell in heated debate. Nearby, a printer's apprentice leaned against a barrel, catching his breath before returning to the press, while two young boys chased each other past the well, their laughter piercing the solemn air. The scene hummed with quiet tension as ordinary tasks unfolded in the shadow of extraordinary decisions.

Just then, a messenger came out of the door of the Statehouse and called Cato, who responded by walking directly toward him. Cato brushed past Cicero and Pompey and entered the Statehouse as the messenger told him that Richard Henry Lee had something to say to him. The valets went back to their positions because laughing out loud could cause a problem for some of the everyday people on the sidewalks. Valets were to serve and not have fun according to the residents who the valets called 'wanna be' masters.

Cato exited the door shortly and said, "Master Richard has a need for some snuff. He forgot to bring his silver snuffbox and somehow, that became my fault. I'll be back in a little while."

"I am always reminded that I am moved by another's pleasure," said Pompey. "I would like to deny it, but it is a fact of life. The less I try to fight it, the easier my life becomes."

Caesar strolled over the courtyard toward Pompey, Bob, and Cicero and asked, "Is everyone staying in the same house that you did last year?"

"We remain at Mrs. Yard's," said Pompey who was also speaking for Cicero.

"We continue to have the pleasure of staying with the Shippen family," said Peter for Jack.

"We have a new residence," said Caesar. "We're at the home of Mr. Richard Penn, who is the grandson of William Penn, the founder of Pennsylvania. He is most supportive of the Congress, even though he owes his political office to his relationship with the King."

"That sounds like a dangerous game to play. Do Master Francis and Richard Henry trust him?"

"They must or we wouldn't be sleeping under his roof. I have listened to him when he speaks with the masters, and he sounds as sympathetic as any of the other delegates who share dinner with us."

"I wonder what clues white folk use to tell if they should fully trust another white person. I know it's not so easy for us."

Black valets sought trust among strangers through quiet observation, careful speech, and the subtle codes of deference and dignity. In a society where their status was often precarious, they relied on reputation, mutual acquaintances, and shared labor networks to gauge safety and sincerity. A valet might study a man's posture, his tone when addressing tradesmen, or the company he kept before risking a conversation or helping. In taverns, stables, and behind the grand homes of Chestnut Street, they exchanged whispered warnings and quiet endorsements, building fragile webs of trust in a city where liberty was loudly debated but unevenly doled out.

"How did the masters react to the elevation of George Washington to be general of the army?"

"As Master Francis said, 'It was the pinnacle of achievement.' Both are from Virginia, and I wasn't surprised by their reaction. The Virginians stick together."

"Master John spoke about Washington's experience in the French and Indian War. I don't know what that French and Indian War was. Were the French fighting the Indians?"

"No. The English describe that war as a fight against both at the same time. Washington must have been a young soldier then."

Just then, Cato came around the corner and knocked on the door to get the attention of the messenger boy to whom he gave the snuffbox so it could be delivered to Richard Henry Lee.

"Next time he'll probably ask me to hold his handkerchief as he tends to his nose."

The valets laughed at the thought of Cato holding the kerchief to Mr. Lee's nose.

A Black valet would likely know with quiet certainty whether his master was good-hearted or a hard taskmaster, not through grand gestures, but by the daily rhythms of call and response. He would read the tone behind orders, the patience shown in moments of error, and the respect, or lack thereof, offered in private as well as in public. A good master might grant small liberties, speak a name rather than a title, or offer protection in tense situations. A harsh one might wield silence like a whip, demand perfection without praise, and treat loyalty as entitlement. The valet, ever observant, would learn to interpret these signs not just for his own survival, but to navigate the delicate social terrain between servitude and self-respect.

Cato then said, "I heard you talking about Mr. Washington. Master Richard said he is one of the biggest slaveowners in the colony. That just doesn't look right."

"What kind of a master is he to his slaves?"

"What difference does that make. He owns people and won't let them go free."

"I can't argue with you about that, Pomp. Good masters. Bad masters. They are all masters. I wonder what kind of general that will make him?"

"He better not treat his soldiers like his slaves," said Bob. "I wonder if he will allow any Africans to be in his army. Maybe he will offer them freedom if they serve in the war and survive."

"I don't see that happening. First off, they would have to give guns to Black men. Do you think that is going to happen? And then they would need to work with the other soldiers who are white and hate Africans. That looks like trouble brewing."

"I would be very surprised if they ever allow Africans in the army. As fearful the whites are afraid of a slave revolt, that will happen when the James River runs backward."

As the valets were finishing their conversation, the rear door opened and some of the delegates walked out, it appeared they were pausing for the afternoon dinner break. All the valets scurried to their appointed places from where they were to accompany their masters. As usual, a steady stream of delegates was heading for the City Tavern. The morning session had gone quickly, but from the looks on the delegates' faces and their quiet demeanor, it was obvious that difficult topics had been discussed.

The sun had risen higher in the early afternoon sky, and the air had grown warmer than at the start of the session. Pompey spied Edward Rutledge talking with Thomas Stone as they exited the hall and he also caught the eye of Bob. They fell behind Rutledge and Stone to discover where they would go for dinner and planned to wait outside until their masters needed help. Maybe if they went to the City

Tavern, Pompey thought to himself, they would be able to get some food at the kitchen door.

The Rutledges Were Born to Privilege

Edward Rutledge was born on November 23, 1749, in a Charleston brick mansion that his mother, Sara Hext Rutledge, inherited. She was married at age fourteen to Dr. John Rutledge and they had seven children. Edward was the youngest. Edward's oldest brother, John Rutledge, the oldest child of Dr. John and Sara, was born in 1740, when Sara Hext Rutledge was fifteen years old. Dr. John Rutledges brother, Andrew, was the first Rutledge to settle in South Carolina from England and established himself as a successful attorney and prominent landowner. He had married Sara Hext, the widow of Captain Hugh Hext, and introduced his brother, Dr. John Rutledge, to his stepchild. These overlapping ancestral families resulted in an estate that included a Charleston mansion, three plantations, more than 100 slaves, various other properties, and considerable debts.

Edward was only a one-year-old when his father died, and his mother never remarried. His oldest brother, John, became his surrogate father. He grew up in a mansion in Charleston with Black servants and never wanted for anything. John Rutledge left for London to study to become an attorney in 1758 and Edward probably believed that his life would follow a similar trajectory.

From the day he was born, Edward Rutledge stood in the shadow of his oldest sibling. Growing up in the Rutledge family meant following the success of his older brothers, John, Andrew, Thomas, and Hugh, as well as his two sisters, Sarah and Mary. By the time Edward was fifteen, John had already started his own family with the first of ten children, of which eight grew into adulthood.

Edward left for London in 1769 to attend Middle Temple, was called to the English bar in 1772, and rode the circuit with local barristers which would make him more familiar with the work upon his return to South Carolina in 1773 when he was admitted to the South Carolina bar. John Rutledge paid for his expenses and provided guidance about navigating the educational requirements based upon his own experience as a barrister.

Sara Rutledge bequeathed to Edward land titles to a plantation that made him eligible for election to the Commons House of Assembly upon his return from London.

Edward, who aspired to politics early in life, was elected to the Assembly upon his return from London but turned down that position so he could first build a career as an attorney. He sought cases that could increase his income, but also to give him better exposure to the business community, so that clients might seek him out for legal work. Because of the active public life that John Rutledge pursued, the Rutledge name had already started opening doors for Edward.

In March 1774, Edward Rutledge and Henrietta Middleton, the oldest daughter of Henry Middleton, one of the wealthiest citizens in Charleston, were married. Shortly thereafter, Charles Cotesworth Pinckney, who was to become Edward's law partner, married Henrietta's sister, Sally. The joining of these Charleston political powers – Middleton, Rutledge, Gadsden, Heyward, Lynch, and Pinckney – would echo through the history of South Carolina for many years to come.

In the months preceding the First Continental Congress, Edward had increased his profile through the works of the court, but also in the political arena. As an attorney, he had represented a man who was arrested for breach of privilege for printing a document without permission. The highly publicized accounts in the newspapers found a sympathetic judge who declared his client innocent and cemented community praise for young Edward.

John Rutledge had been elected in 1761 to the South Carolina Commons House of Assembly, that shared legislative authority with the Royal Governor and his appointed council. He became a leader in Commons House the next year when he led a struggle with Royal Governor Thomas Boone over the sitting of Christopher Gadsden in the Commons House. In 1764, the Stamp Act roiled the colonies over the issue of taxation without representation. South Carolina was one of the first colonies to respond to a call from the Massachusetts House of Representatives to meet in New York to discuss a common strategy against the act. John Rutledge, Christopher Gadsden, and Thomas Lynch, a wealthy planter, represented South Carolina in what would be called the Stamp Act Congress. They met and became acquainted with delegates from nine colonies who would become the vanguard of the American patriots. The Congress adjourned on October 25, 1765, as Edward was turning sixteen years of age, while John Rutledge returned to South Carolina to lead the Commons House in how to respond to the Act which was soon to be repealed in 1766.

Between the time the Stamp Act was repealed and the meeting of the first Continental Congress in September 1774, South Carolina was engaged in a power struggle between the Royal Governor and the Commons House, and it was here, John Rutledge played a key role. Establishment of a militia to confront the uprising of Cherokee in the west, appointment of judges and customs officers, the housing of Royal troops in Charleston, and financial wrangling were some of the issues that John Rutledge attempted to form a consensus around, while among the Carolinians. By 1769, colonists were in constant disagreement with the Royal Governor over directives from London on expenditure of colonial funds. By 1773, the latest Royal governor of South Carolina sailed for London and never returned. Edward returned with his law degree from London and was immediately engaged in representing people involved in political arguments that roiled the colony. Edward Rutledge received greater visibility and opportunity to exhibit leadership.

In 1773, Parliament passed the Tea Act that resulted in the Boston Tea Party. When South Carolina learned of the Tea Party and the decision of the Boston patriots to cut off trade with London, leaders called for a provincial meeting to discuss how to proceed collectively. At a general meeting that attracted roughly 400 citizens from throughout South Carolina, there was unanimous support for aiding the people of Boston. However, considerable concern was raised on the matter of boycotting imports and exports. After much discussion about supporting the boycott or not, John Rutledge offered a compromise that passed unanimously suggesting that the issue should be left to the Continental Congress that was to be held in Philadelphia in the spring. The delegates elected to the First Continental Congress were John Rutledge, Henry Middleton, Christopher Gadsden, John Lynch, and Edward Rutledge.

Henry Middleton was representative of the original founders of the colony of South Carolina and was one of its richest plantation owners. His grandfather, also named Henry Middleton, had emigrated from England to Barbados to the Carolina province in 1678. For Edward Rutledge, marrying into this prestigious family made his entry into the world of colonial power much easier.

Sailing from Charleston for the First Continental Congress, the Rutledges brought their wives and servants and arrived in Philadelphia early so that they could become acquainted with the various delegates. John's participation in the earlier Stamp Act Congress allowed him to mingle easily with their compatriots. John and Edward Rutledge and Christopher Gadsden made significant impressions on some delegates. Pennsylvania delegate Joseph Galloway thought John Rutledge supported reconciliation with Britain and was correct in his judgements. John Adams was less enthralled with the South Carolina delegation calling John "Nothing of the profound, sagacious, brilliant or sparkling." Describing Edward, Adams also wrote, "This is a young, smart, spirited body…sprightly but not deep." It was noted that John was a conservative, Edward moderate, and Gadsden radical.

Edward agreed with his brother on almost all issues, although he was occasionally heard exploring a more radical point of view, closer to Gadsden's. The Congress decided they needed to be focused on drafting a statement of American rights, grievances, and a plan of redress. Two delegates were selected from each colony to draft the document and South Carolina selected John Rutledge and Christopher Gadsden. Thus, a pattern developed that when committee assignments were doled out, John would be named to important committees, while Edward would only be asked to serve on lesser ones.

Through the debates in Congress, many of the delegate's observations about Rutledges were noticed. When discussing American rights, John protested the inclusion of the law of nature, that holds that every person is born with inherent rights to life, liberty, and self-preservation, independent of any government, yet it was included. Regarding grievances, Virginia delegates were directed not to include actions prior to 1763 that John Rutledge opposed, but once again, this provision was included. The Rutledges argued for a reconciliation with Britain that was encouraged by a proposition by Joseph Galloway which Edward called "almost a perfect plan." Even so, this was also defeated.

The most difficult issue to resolve was the non-import and non-export trade resolutions. Edward's statements on ancillary issues evolved, as evidenced by his swing from conservative to radical positions. He was supportive of a total non-export measure and then opposed it as being too punitive to South Carolina. Near the end of the session, the Rutledges, Middleton, and Lynch walked out of a meeting in protest of a total non-export action that they thought would unfairly harm rice and indigo farmers in South Carolina. Seeking unanimity, the other delegates in Congress asked for their return and granted an exemption for rice export, while the indigo remained banned. The document to the King was approved, and they adjourned to meet again on May 10, 1775. In his diary, John Adams, in exasperation, wrote "Young Ned Rutledge is a perfect Bob o' Lincoln… excessively vain, excessively weak, and excessively variable and unsteady – jejune, inane, and puerile."

Upon return to South Carolina, John Rutledge and the other delegates reported to the South Carolina organizing committee, and a general meeting of the entire colony was called to explain the proposals decided during the Congress. To soften the exemption of rice for non-export while not for indigo, John Rutledge offered a compromise that rice farmers would subsidize the indigo farmers for their losses. After much discussion the compromise was adopted by the newly formed First Provincial Congress that would eventually replace the Commons House.

Slaves Debate What Masters Discuss

Pompey and Cicero arrived at the Statehouse on a sunny summer day in June with Edward and John Rutledge and were waiting in the courtyard behind the hall where the delegates were meeting. While Congress deliberated, the valets of some of the Southern colony's delegates gathered either in the courtyard or outside the hallway that led into the main hall. Pompey and Cicero were the first to arrive on this day, but shortly, they were joined by Bob, Cato, and Caesar.

Congregating in groups of no more than two was considered appropriate, but if three or more were joined in conversation, slaves were at risk of being viewed as plotting some horrendous deed. The Black valets always adhered to this unwritten rule while out in public.

Black valets whose work put them in position where they could observe the private lives and whispered anxieties of their masters, would have recognized the fear of slave revolt as both vulnerability and contradiction. They saw how men who spoke of liberty and rights in Congress flinched at rumors of insurrection, locking doors, and lowering voices when discussing uprisings in the Caribbean. For the valet, this fear revealed a truth: that power rested not solely in law or lineage, but also in the fragile trust between master and servant. Some may have quietly resented the hypocrisy, others may have used it to negotiate small freedoms or protections, knowing that a fearful master might be more cautious, more watchful, and occasionally more generous in the name of self-preservation.

Pompey casually walked away from Cicero and approached Cato who was standing by himself near the entrance to the Statehouse.

"Beautiful morning for a game of dice. I don't think the delegates would mind," he said jokingly.

"Sometimes I think that the delegates are playing a game of dice with the King. How could they object, if we would do the same with real dice?"

"You are a merry fellow. Have you heard anything interesting at the Shippen House?"

"The mood seems to follow the most recent courier that arrives at the house. I did hear one rich story though that you might find interesting."

"Pray, tell me."

"Apparently, they created a committee. What else is new? It's to write a letter to be sent to the Indians."

Slaves held a range of views about Indigenous peoples, shaped less by formal ideology and more by lived experience, rumors, and the shifting alliances of colonial life. Some may have seen native people as fellow outsiders beyond the dominant white order, communities dispossessed, surveilled, and spoken of with fear or disdain by white elites. Others, especially those who had witnessed frontier violence or heard tales of raids and reprisals, might have regarded indigenous groups with wary respect or pragmatic caution. In taverns and stables, they may have overheard debates about land, treaties, and rebellion, sensing that native resistance mirrored their own quiet hopes for autonomy. Yet, valets were kept close to the colonial hearth, where indigenous people were often discussed as abstractions, figures of threat, pity, or political leverage, rather than as neighbors or kin. In that gap between rumor and reality, valets navigated their own judgments, shaped by survival and the subtle calculus of trust.

"How are they going to read a letter? Hardly any Indians speak English."

"They must have a way to translate it because the letter was six pages long. Those men certainly do like to talk and write. Well, the letter is asking the Indians to stay out of the conflict between the colonies and England. The Indians are told how nice the colonists are, and this conflict is between family members and has nothing to do with the Indians."

"Do they think that the Indians are going to agree with that rubbish? I'm not sure, but they are trying to make the natives believe it. How can they say that the colonies have been nice, when the Indians know full well that killings and pillaging have been going on ever since the English arrived?"

"They must think the Indians are either stupid or have a short memory. What must the Indians be thinking when they see this letter? The English will force them out of more territory if they win, and the colonists will force them out of more territory if the colonists win. This offer is a poor bargain for the Indians."

"Indians thinking that the English would treat them fairly is as ludicrous as Africans thinking that the English would treat us as equals."

Cato edged away from the door and made an approach to Bob who was standing alone next to a tree across the courtyard. "How do you fare, my dear friend?"

"Good morrow, Cato. You are looking well this morning. Any news that you bring from the big house?"

"Big house, is it? The house is not big, but some of the delegates think they are."

"You have a real turn of humor. Master Thomas was complaining about the bed in his room last night, and I was thinking that he had it better than the bare corner of the scullery I slept in."

"Masters have no sense of proportion when it comes to meeting their needs. Have you heard any news from the dining room table lately?"

Black valets often endured their masters' trivial complaints with a practiced blend of restraint, quiet endurance, and subtle emotional detachment. Whether it was a misplaced wig, a lukewarm cup of tea, or the creak of a carriage door, they learned to absorb petty grievances without reaction, knowing that dignity lay in composure. Behind the bowed head or the softly spoken "yes, sir," there was often a sharp awareness of the imbalance of men who preached liberty while fretting over lace cuffs. Some valets may have found private humor in these moments, exchanging knowing glances with fellow servants or venting in hushed tones behind the stables. Others used the predictability of such complaints to navigate their day, anticipating whims and smoothing irritations before they surfaced. In this quiet choreography of service, they preserved their own sense of self, even as they moved within the narrow expectations of other men's comfort.

"The longest conversation I heard was about George Washington being named General for the Continental Army. The delegates seem happy with designating a Virginian and thought it a wise choice considering his experience in the British army during the French and Indian War."

"It didn't hurt his image much by dressing the part in waistcoat, breeches, and brass buttons especially since no one else came in a uniform. He does have a commanding presence, but I am not sure how that translates into being a good general. At least they didn't name John Adams, for I believe that would have been a disaster."

"I hope you never try to jest with your master as you do with us slaves, because I think you would get in trouble."

"I keep my thoughts to myself when I'm with the master or other white people, but you have no idea what goes on in my head. It's a good thing no one can read my mind, because if they could, I'd be in for a big whipping and probably sent to the fields to work my fingers to the bone."

"If I were you, I'd keep my mouth shut."

"That's fair advice," said Bob who moved across the courtyard to strike up a conversation with Caesar.

"I am glad to see you. Cato told me about the delegates choosing Washington as general. Have you heard anything else of interest?"

"Did he tell you about the other big battle near Boston?"

"No, what happened?"

"After the Redcoats took a licking from the Sons of Liberty in Lexington and Concord, Britain thought they would teach them a lesson, so they picked another fight on Bunker Hill, and they were in for a big surprise. The British believed they could use brute strength to overcome the patriots, and they tried two frontal attacks to take control of this hill overlooking Boston and were pushed back both times. The British losses were huge, but they tried a third time and won because the Sons of Liberty ran low on ammunition and needed to withdraw.

"That sounds like it was an English victory."

"It may appear that way, but the British army was embarrassed by the colonial militia, because the British took losses of over 1,000 men while the patriots only lost less than 500. If there was any doubt that the colonists could stand toe-to-toe with the British, Bunker Hill was a symbolic victory for the colonists."

"That sound remarkable. Was General Washington there to direct this battle?"

"No, that is one of the astonishing facts. Washington was named General of the Continental Army on June 15th in Philadelphia, and the Battle of Bunker Hill took place on June 17th in Boston."

"It sounds like the British have already received some decisive information about how the colonists will resist. I doubt if they'll walk away though, because they will need to show resilience to protect their honor."

In another corner of the courtyard, Cicero approached Jack, the Black valet of Christopher Gadsden and said, "Must have been some lively conversation at the Shippen House last night with a group of rich Virginia and South Carolina delegates."

And Jack replied, "They made a parade of themselves. One might think that they had an audience with the King. I am not sure who they were trying to impress. The amount of money they must spend on being finely dressed probably is more than they spend on their soldiers. Much of the discussion was about the cost of the conflict and how it would affect their plantations. Those fellows are full of wind and pride."

"Money is at the center of almost every conversation. How much is tobacco selling for today? How much does a barrel of rice bring? What will I lose if this fight drags on for months? I wish someone would ask, how much does it cost you to pay your slaves who bring you your tobacco and rice?"

"Cicero, you better be careful about that kind of conversation. You keep it up, and we'll all be in trouble."

"I don't talk like this except to other slaves. Master John lets me speak my mind to him alone and I value that. His brother, Edward, is not as lenient with Pompey, but we look out for each other. How is Master Christopher treating you?"

"He treats me just fine. I have been his valet for only a year, and I already know this was the best opportunity for me. I was afraid he was going to put me out in the fields, but I think he knew that I would be of more use to him inside with my skills."

"Skills? What sort of skills do you have?"

In 1775, a Black valet's path to literacy was often quiet, cautious, and deeply personal—an act of self-preservation as much as self-advancement. Though laws and customs discouraged Black education, some valets, especially those serving in elite households or in Quaker circles, found discreet opportunities to learn. A sympathetic master might leave a Bible or ledger within reach, or a fellow servant might share whispered lessons by candlelight. The Pennsylvania Abolition Society, founded that same year, began laying groundwork for Black education, though its efforts would grow more formal in later decades. For a valet, mastering letters meant more than reading orders. It meant decoding contracts, writing petitions, and conceiving of a life beyond servitude. Each word learned was a quiet rebellion, a step toward autonomy in a world that rarely granted it.

"One of the cooks has started teaching me how to read and write. We use the recipes she works from and the Bible. Master has no idea that I am learning, but I think he senses it is good for him to have someone with knowledge to get the things done the way he wants."

"I'd be very careful how you use that knowledge. You don't want to find yourself in a situation where you are accused of something you didn't do, just because you could read or write. Never believe that the master can't find something out because he does have all the power."

"Thanks for the advice. I never looked at it that way."

A messenger appeared at the door of the Statehouse and motioned for Pompey to follow him as they disappeared into the Statehouse. The valets deduced that Edward Rutledge had called Pompey for some tasks.

Two minutes later, Pompey came through the Statehouse doors, turned to his left and exited toward the market on High Street. The other valets stirred, and Cato could be seen moving to the Statehouse door in case another messenger appeared.

After about ten minutes, Pompey was rounding the corner and going to the rear entrance of the Statehouse. He knocked on the door and as a messenger came forward Pompey handed him a small package.

"It's obvious to me that the delegates are arguing about getting to the marrow of some issue today," said Pompey.

"What are you talking about?" asked Jack.

"Master Rutledge was in a need of his toothpick holder. We certainly don't want the mighty Edward to be caught with food between his teeth."

They all laughed and enjoyed yet one more example of their masters' fragility.

SLAVERY: THE TABOO TOPIC

From the first settlement, slavery and South Carolina were always spoken of in the same sentence. The first governor of South Carolina, William Sayle, brought a small contingent of slaves in 1670 to the founding of Charles Town that would later be known as Charleston. The first constitution of the colony made references to slavery when plantation owners from Barbados arrived. They brought slaves with them, as well as a plantation mentality and business model based on the use of forced labor.

By 1708, South Carolina was the first British colony in America to have a Black majority population. By 1720, Blacks represented 65% of the total population, and in 1776, Black slaves represented 56% of the inhabitants.

The multitude of African slaves amid white settlers engendered fear of an organized revolt. In 1739, those nightmares became reality when the Stono Rebellion exploded in South Carolina. Led by a single man near the Stono River, only thirty-five miles from Charleston, initially twenty slaves broke into a gun store, stole weapons, and turned them against white residents. Eventually their numbers grew to sixty and they killed twenty white residents. A white militia was formed and hunted down the rioters, executed most of them, and sold the survivors to West Indian plantations.

In response to the Stono Rebellion, the South Carolina Provincial Assembly adopted the Negro Act of 1740 which created strict laws to restrict slave movements, prohibit their ownership of firearms, ban education, eliminate the right to carry money, and make it illegal for Blacks to congregate in groups.

By 1776, Charleston was the wealthiest city in the south. In all the colonies, Philadelphia was the wealthiest, followed by Boston and New York, and all had more diverse economies than Charleston. The plantations of rice and indigo in Charleston provided significant wealth through sales to England, the West Indies, and the northern colonies.

Slavery was not the only thing to add to the success of the Carolina colony. Shipbuilding and related industries needed to support slavery were located primarily in Rhode Island, Connecticut, and

Boston. The Triangle Slave Trade thrived in Rhode Island, supported by Newport and Providence distilleries that boosted import/export activities. Ships built in Newport were filled with barrels of rum distilled in Rhode Island that were exported to Africa and traded for slaves. Those ships, filled with kidnapped Africans, sailed to the West Indies and exchanged Africans for sugar products, then sailed back to Newport where the sugar products were sold to distillers who made more rum for the next trip. All while money traded hands at each port.

In 1776, South Carolina was a slave majority state. Virginia, Maryland, North Carolina, and Georgia each had more than 27% of their populations enslaved. With 533,000 slaves in a total population of 2,622,000 in the British colonies, the average percentage of enslaved Africans in each of the colonies was 20%.

While South Carolina had its Stono Rebellion, other slave revolts took place in colonial America. The earliest revolt happened in 1663 in Gloucester County, Virginia. New York had two incidents, first in 1712 and another in 1740, while Maryland experienced the Chesapeake Rebellion in 1730. Each time slaves rebelled, whites formed militias, some white residents were killed, the slave leaders and other slaves were executed, and stricter laws were adopted to punish Black slaves and deter them from rising again. The Negro Act of 1740 in South Carolina mandated that slaves were property (chattel), and all African blacks were treated as slaves unless they could prove otherwise. Additionally, slaves were prohibited from learning how to read or write, prohibited from growing their own food, could not congregate, earn money, own property, and could not travel without specific documentation from their masters.

Just as South Carolina instituted draconian laws to restrict slaves in response to Stono, all colonies adopted measures that were based on the South Carolina act. In response to the Bacon's Rebellion in Virginia in 1676, the Virginia Slave Laws were adapted from those enforced in another British slave colony, Barbados. Maryland adopted slave laws as early at 1664 that declared slavery for life for all African slaves, which was reinforced by an act in 1671 that disallowed Christian baptism to free slaves. In 1708, the New York Colonial Assembly passed a law which required the death sentence for any slave who murdered or attempted to murder his or her master. In addition, New York established other harsh controls that were like the South Carolina laws.

Free Blacks resided in all colonies, but limitations on their activities were tightly restricted. "Freed man" status for Blacks, usually took one of three forms: those who willingly settled in the American colonies, manumission from their previous owner, or the purchase of freedom from a master.

Blacks who willingly came to the colonies represented the smallest slice of freedmen. During the period ending in 1720, a few individuals came from Africa or Britain as indentured servants. After completing their contract, they gained their freedom and sometimes property. Colonial laws later changed the rules that had previously kept their descendants free.

Manumission provided the largest number of freedmen. Mostly occurring in the northern colonies and Virginia, masters would grant freedom to slaves for services provided. Upon the death of an owner, slaves were sometimes given immediate freedom or freedom with strings attached. Slaves were considered property, and heirs had the power to ensure that manumission would take place, or not, particularly in states with more restrictive slave laws.

Self-purchasing was available to some slaves, but only for those who resided in the colonies that allowed slaves to earn money from work with their master's permission. While earning money was possible, it was always under the control of the enslaver and never a protected right.

As more colonies instituted stricter slave laws, freedmen saw what freedom they had before was severely limited. Often, slaves and free Blacks were treated much the same, but freed men always suffered the risk of being kidnapped and sold into slavery once again, with little protection from colonial governments.

Before Africans became the primary enslaved population, Native Americans were enslaved in large numbers, especially in New England and the Carolinas. The aftermath of conflicts like the Pequot War saw entire tribes captured and sold as slaves.

In the early 1600s, some enslaved Africans could own land, sue in court, and even gain freedom. But as racial ideologies hardened, laws were rewritten to strip these rights away. The shift from indentured servitude to racialized chattel slavery was gradual but inexorable.

Colonial laws established that a slave's child's status followed that of the mother, not the father. This legal twist ensured that children born to enslaved women—regardless of the father's status—remained enslaved, reinforcing generational bondage on the mother's side.

While Quakers are known for their abolitionist stance, many owned slaves in the 1600s and early 1700s. It wasn't until the mid-18th century that Quaker meetings began formally disowning members who refused to free their slaves.

In 1772, a judge in London authored the Somerset Decision, citing that a fugitive slave could sue for freedom when his master tried to sell him to owners in Jamaica. The court ruled in favor of the slave because there was no law in Britain at that time that sanctioned slavery. The impact on the American colonies was profound. Southern plantation owners feared that the crown would extend this interpretation of the law to cover them. Northern states capitalized on the ruling to support their efforts to abolish slavery in their colonies. Throughout the colonies, patriots viewed the rulings as one more instance of royal overreach that was tightening the restraints around them.

A manservant worked indoors and performed domestic duties like serving meals, dressing the master, or maintaining the household, often under closer scrutiny but with slightly better clothing and living conditions. A field worker, by contrast, endured grueling physical labor from sunrise to sunset, often in extreme weather, with little rest and constant oversight. Their tasks—planting, harvesting, clearing land—were punishing and impersonal, and they were typically housed in communal quarters far from the main house. While both roles were dehumanizing, the manservant's proximity to white families sometimes offered marginal privileges—as well as heightened vulnerability to personal abuse.

The Name I Know

The breeze from the river helped make the July afternoon bearable to Pompey and Cicero who were waiting in the courtyard of the Philadelphia Statehouse where the delegates were meeting. They could see Cato and Bob across the courtyard as the Black valets were biding their time while Congress was discussing how to fix the broken relationship of the American colonies and Britain.

"Cicero. How long have I known you?" asked Pompey suddenly.

"I guess it's been almost two years. Why do you ask ?"

"I was thinking last night when I finished shining Master Edward's boots that I never heard you talk about your African family."

"Maybe the reason is that there is nothing to talk about."

"I can't believe that. Our slavers stole our families from Africa, but they can't steal the memories of those who came before us."

"What are you talking about, Pomp? I think you've been standing in the sun too long. You need to ease up."

"I assure you, on my honor, I am being very serious. My folks were probably from the same part of Africa as yours. I have been truly fortunate that many generations of my family have been owned by Rutledges. My ancestors have related stories that tell us that we descended from the hills of Gambia and brought with them experience growing rice. They also told my family that my name is not Pompey. That is what the slavers called me. The masters want us to forget that we had a rich life before we were kidnapped and brought here."

"What do you mean by "Pompey" is not your name? I have known you for two years. I remember you with your mother when I was a little boy. If you're not Pompey, then what is your name?"

"If I tell you, you must promise that you will never say my African name in front of any white person because they don't want me to know it and they don't want any other slave to know theirs, either. Do you promise?"

"I promise, Pompey, or whatever your name is."

"My African name is Tomba Adebisi. Adebisi means royalty. Tomba is the name of my great-grandfather. He was a proud man who was revered in his village because he was a good farmer who helped increase rice production for the entire village. Why do you think that our masters wanted to steal us away from our families? They not only wanted our bodies, but they wanted to learn how to make rice grow fast and easy."

"I've never heard you talk about this before. How did you learn all this?"

"My mother told me stories that her mother told her. The slavers can steal our bodies, but they cannot steal our minds. Hasn't anyone you know told your story?"

"Why is it that the people with the stories are women? My mother tried to tell me about her family, but my father told me not to listen to women talk because we need to concentrate on staying alive."

"I understand that your father was teaching you an important lesson, but my mother gave me the strongest reason to survive when she told me about my family. No master will ever take that away from me, and when I start a family, I will make sure that my children know exactly where they came from. My master may call me Pompey, but I know that I am Tomba Adebisi."

As Pompey was finishing his story, he had not noticed Cato cross the plaza and head right for him. "You got a serious look on your face. Is everything okay?" said Cato.

"Good to see you this cool afternoon."

"Are you touched in the brain?" said Cato.

"That's just like you, Cato. You always have a way to make everything funny, even when you don't know what you're talking about. I was just asking Cicero if he knew what his real name was, as opposed to what the Rutledges told him his name was."

"Pompey, next you're going to tell me that your name isn't really Pompey."

"As far as anybody who employs me, I remain Pompey, but in my heart, I know that my African name is Tomba Adebisi. I am sure that if I ever tried to get Rutledges to call me that, I would be out in the fields in short order. But that doesn't change the fact that Tomba is my real name. How about you?"

"I'm not sure what to say. How did you learn that your name is not your name?"

"There you go again try to make a joke out of everything. I learned this because my mother told me a story about how I was named after my great-grandfather. My African name is Tonga Adebisi. My mother thinks we may have royalty in our family line."

"I guess we can start calling you Prince Pompey, now."

"Cato, you're a wag."

"It's not every day that I get to meet and mingle with royalty."

"I understand better than you, Cato, why this would not lighten your worries since you don't even know who your mother and father are. I didn't mean to ridicule you ."

"Pomp, we are good friends, and my joking is just my way of dealing with how lonely I get, when other people are talking about their families. It's my problem not yours."

"Cato, I think of you as a brother. I don't want to do anything that might hurt your feelings or your person."

"I hope you know that I feel the same way. Do you think I'll ever know who my mother and father are?" asked Cato.

"That's a hard question. All I know is that we come from Africa. Hey, we might be brothers after all!"

Cicero and Cato broke out into wide smiles and all of them started patting each other on their backs.

"I was just telling Cicero the same thing. Brothers, we need to stand up for each other and help each other. I hate being a slave, but meeting all of you has been one of the best things that ever happened to me."

EDWARD MEETS SAMUEL WARD

Edward was lingering in the Statehouse after a brief morning session of Congress when he was approached by Christopher Gadsden, a fellow South Carolina delegate. With Gadsden was Samuel Ward, a delegate from Rhode Island. Gadsden was a highly successful merchant and the only Carolinian delegate who was an avid supporter of independence. He would become well known as the originator of a flag later called the Gadsden Flag of a coiled rattlesnake with the motto, 'Don't Tread on Me.' Samuel Ward was a farmer and a Rhode Island Supreme Court Justice.

"Mr. Rutledge, I would like to introduce you to a friend of mine, Samuel Ward, delegate from Rhode Island. Were he a resident of South Carolina, he would own the greatest plantation in the colony."

"I am glad to have your acquaintance. I saw you in the sessions, but we have never shared the same committees. I did not have much opportunity to get to know you. Christopher has told me that you are an attorney and a plantation owner. I am a farmer who's been honored with representing my colony at many gatherings, but none so important as the one we are currently in the midst of."

"The honor is mine, Mr. Ward. I do own a plantation, but my law office takes up the bulk of my time. Being on the Committee of Correspondence has allowed me to hear from delegates, but I would be interested in knowing more about your business. I understand that your colony helps extensively with providing ships for transport. Is this commerce part of your livelihood?"

"No. I am a farmer at heart, and I do raise cattle and dabbled in breeding racehorses. The shipbuilding business in Rhode Island is very prosperous, and I understand that many of the merchants around Newport, earn their wealth from the various other businesses connected to the maritime trade."

"Gentlemen, I would suggest that we retire to the City Tavern where we can find something good to eat and carry on this conversation further," said Gadsden.

Walking to the City Tavern in Philadelphia on a warm June day in 1775 meant weaving through the lively pulse of a city bracing for revolution. The cobbled streets echoed with the clatter of carts and the chatter of merchants, while the scent of fresh bread and pipe smoke drifted out of open windows. As one passed the brick facades of Walnut and Second Streets, the tavern came into view, a stately three-story building bustling with activity. Delegates from the Continental Congress, tradesmen, and curious townsfolk mingled at its entrance, where polished boots met dusty hems and whispered news from Boston passed between tankards. Inside, the air was thick with debate and the aroma of roast meats, but even before stepping through the door, one could feel the weight of history gathering like a storm cloud —one pint, one argument, one decision at a time.

Christopher Gadsden reached the entrance first and pulled the heavy wood door open. "It appears we have beat the crowd today. We have a choice of tables. Let's take this one close to the hearth."

Stepping into the City Tavern was like crossing a threshold between the clamor of the street and the charged intimacy of revolutionary discourse. The door opened onto a polished interior of paneled walls and flickering candlelight, while the mingled aromas of roast meats, sweat, and rum punch filled the air. Delegates, merchants, and officers gathered in clusters beneath the high ceilings, their voices rising in debate or laughter, while their boots clacked on the wide-plank floors. A server might slip through with a tray, dodging elbows and glances, as a newcomer paused to remove his hat and scan the room for familiar faces. The tavern's entryway was not just physical, it was social and political, a gateway into the ferment of ideas and alliances that would soon shape a nation.

Samuel Ward led the way, followed by Rutledge. Edward thought that their trifecta made an interesting scene: Rutledge in his silk coat and crisp silken breeches, embroidered waistcoat, and buckled shoes, Gadsden in a faded woolen coat, plain waistcoat, well-worn breeches, and heavy unadorned brown leather shoes, with Ward in a woolen coat, modest waistcoat, tailored breeches, and black leather shoes with no buckles. Amid the noise of the City Tavern, they made their way to a table, caught the eye of a server, and ordered some food and drink.

Edward said, "I attended Middle Temple in London and was admitted to the English bar before returning to Charleston to start my law career. My family owns a few plantations in South Carolina where we grow rice primarily and a small plot of indigo."

"From everything that I have heard about the Southern colonies, you must use a fair number of slaves to maintain a prosperous business," Ward commented. "Don't you worry about revolts among your slaves?"

"A few instances in other areas have occurred, but we've never had any major problems. We treat our servants fairly, and they react well to the care we provide. I have come to understand that some of the ships built in your colony have provided Negroes to our colony."

"That would not surprise me, sir. Our shipyards are busy every day making vessels to serve the various needs of the colonies. We have Negroes working to cut down trees, making pitch to caulk the ships, and helping to fashion nails and bolts. Your plantations support our economy quite well."

Shipbuilding in Newport, Rhode Island, thrived as both a commercial enterprise and a strategic necessity, shaped by the mounting tensions of revolution. Newport's skilled craftsmen and bustling waterfront yards produced a range of vessels, from merchant sloops to armed schooners, designed for speed, maneuverability, and resilience in the contested waters of Narragansett Bay.

Samuel Ward and Christopher Gadsden were both ardent patriots with deep ties to maritime commerce. They had found common cause in naval shaping policy and trade restrictions. Ward, representing a colony heavily reliant on shipping and coastal trade, served on committees addressing non-importation and export regulations, while Gadsden, a wealthy merchant and shipowner, was instrumental in outfitting the nascent Continental Navy.

"I know from my wharf traffic that those ships that come to Charleston filled with servants and goods keep my business going strong," said Gadsden. "That is why we each need to be together in dealing with the King and Parliament. They don't understand what a strong and successful enterprise we have, and they want to stifle our freedom. My sentiments for the American cause, since the Stamp Act , have not changed. I am still of the opinion that it is the cause of liberty and of human nature."

"Well said. Let's drink a toast to liberty and human nature," said Ward. Gadsden and Ward joyously clinked their tankards together while Rutledge meekly joined in. "Where is your resolve young man?"

"I sense that the two of you are more radical than my sense allows me to be. I hear your words, but my heart remains attached to the way of life we have enjoyed for many years. Do you think that the King will ever change his attitude toward us?"

"My friend, we are not the oldest delegates at Congress. Look at Dr. Franklin, or Roger Sherman or my compatriot from Rhode Island, Steven Hopkins."

"Or your father-in-law Middleton, Ned!" shouted Christopher.

Ward said, "We, the American colonists, have seen the bloodshed at Lexington. We have been mistreated with the Stamp Act and the Tea Tax. We have endured blockages at our ports and shelling in our cities. They fired the first shots on what was once their family. What kind of family shoots and kills its own? I, for one, am resolved to fight for independence like my life depends on it."

"Edward, this is why we're here," said Gadsden. "You are young and will have the opportunity to enjoy the fruits of the work we are destined to complete. This is only a step, but it is a necessary step. We need to find the strength and determination to stand up and say we are at the end of our tethers."

Edward had become comfortable coexisting with radicals and conservatives in a daily exercise in restraint, frustration, and strategic silence. The city, alive with revolutionary fervor, was a crucible where radicals like John Adams and Christopher Gadsen pushed for sweeping change, while conservatives, men like John Dickinson and Henry Middleton, clung to the faint hope of reconciliation with Britain and the preservation of social order. In taverns, assembly halls, and even family parlors, conversations could turn volatile, with radicals accusing conservatives of cowardice or betrayal, and conservatives viewing radicals as reckless agitators threatening the fragile fabric of colonial society.

"Mr. Gadsden, I have always known you as a man of strong belief who is never afraid to act when others shy away," said Rutledge. "The more I talk with the delegates, the more I hear that the independence you speak about yearns to be embraced.

"And I believe that you will embrace it in time. I recognize that you are worried about drawing up a plan for confederation, and I am sure that will be done, but we need to stand up stoutly to the King and declare we'll have no more of it."

"I agree with Christopher. What will it take for you to become comfortable with independence, Edward?" said Ward.

"If I may speak bluntly with you."

"Why, of course. That is why we are here."

Rutledge said, "I have one concern that has not been debated, but I fear that may make it impossible for me to agree to independence.

"Let us talk through this issue and maybe we can find some benefit for our friendship," said Ward.

"During the last Continental Congress, we delegates adopted the Continental Association."

"I remember well. I was one of the signatories."

"Very good. Then, you probably remember as part of the non-import section of the association, we agreed to a ban on the slave trade. Although it has not been suggested that a ban should be part of any declaration that is adopted, I want to make sure that colonies see that it would be imprudent to attach such a provision to the goal of independence."

"I understand your concern. As we spoke at the start of our conversation, many colonies have an interest in the slave trade, and I agree that if we were to have that conversation today, it would not be a gentlemanly discourse. If all you need is an assurance that the slave trade issue will not be attached to the efforts for independence, I would support that."

"Thank you, Mr. Ward. I am not saying that is the only issue I have which prevents me from calling for independence, but I will say that knowing that others support the idea of separating these issues soothes my concerns greatly."

"Let's toast to unity and success."

"To unity and success."

They emptied their tankards, and Gadsden asked the server for another round while Edward and Samuel shook hands and settled back into their chairs.

Later after their meal, the three delegates left the City Tavern and were met by cool early summer breezes blown off the river and trees in bloom with flowers of white and red. A few children playing with a hoop and stick filled the street, while others were playing with marbles in an alleyway. The muffled voices of men at work, men in carriages, and the clopping of horses' hooves engendered a symphony of sounds as the three men walked down Chestnut Street toward their residences.

THE CONTINENTAL ASSOCIATION

The Continental Association, formally known as the Articles of Association, was adopted by the First Continental Congress on October 20, 1774 in response to the British Parliament's punitive measures known to the patriots as the Intolerable Acts. These acts, passed after the Boston Tea Party, were designed to punish Massachusetts and reassert imperial control over the colonies. The Continental Association represented a unified colonial strategy to resist British oppression through economic means. It called for a comprehensive boycott of British goods—banning imports, halting exports, and discouraging consumption of British products—as a peaceful yet forceful method of protest.

The document was drafted by delegates from twelve colonies (with Georgia abstaining) convened to deliberate on a collective response. Drawing inspiration from earlier local agreements like the Virginia Association of 1769, the Continental Association was largely shaped by the ideas of Richard Henry Lee and George Mason. Though Thomas Jefferson was not yet a delegate, his political circle influenced the statement's tone and structure. The final draft opened with a declaration of loyalty to King George III, a strategic move to frame the boycott not as rebellion but as a demand for redress. This rhetorical balancing act allowed the colonies to assert their rights while avoiding outright treason— at least for the moment.

The document outlined specific resolutions, including the cessation of trade with Britain beginning December 1, 1774, and a ban on the slave trade. It also included moral prescriptions for colonial conduct during the boycott, discouraging extravagance, gambling, and public entertainment. These provisions reflected the belief that political virtue required personal discipline and communal solidarity. Enforcement was delegated to local committees, which sprang up across the colonies to monitor compliance and to shame violators. These committees became early instruments of revolutionary governance, foreshadowing the more radical steps to come.

As part of the economic pressure on England, the colonies agreed to a total ban on the importation of slaves in America. This allowed the colonies to assert economic independence from Britain, since the transatlantic slave trade was heavily dominated by British merchants.

What may seem to be a radical agreement is less extreme when viewed as an economic tool to apply pressure on England. Regardless, all twelve colonies (less Georgia who did not send any delegates) agreed "that we will neither import nor purchase any Slave imported after the first Day of December next, after which Time we will wholly discontinue the Slave Trade, and will neither be concerned in it ourselves, nor will we hire our Vessels, nor sell our Commodities or Manufactures, to those who are concerned in it."

The delegates to the First Continental Congress agreed to these provisions, although none viewed this as a burden to their colonies. South Carolina was more concerned about allowing exportation of their rice for economic reasons, probably decided to save the battle over the slave trade for another time. The walk-out of the entire South Carolina delegation, except Christopher Gadsden, almost scuttled the Association's measure unless it included the rice exception. Gadsden's refusal to agree to the rice exception created a permanent rift between him and the Rutledge family.

Ultimately, the Continental Association was more than a trade agreement. It was a declaration of intercolonial unity and resolve. Though the boycott was short-lived, overtaken by the outbreak of war in April 1775, the Association marked a turning point in colonial resistance. It demonstrated that the colonies could act in concert, enforce collective decisions, and articulate a shared political identity. In crafting and signing the document, the delegates laid the groundwork for future declarations and institutions, including the Second Continental Congress and, eventually, the Declaration of Independence.

When the British fired on the Massachusetts colonists in Lexington and Concord, the political landscape changed dramatically. The American colonies no longer needed the Continental Association to convince citizens to avoid exporting and importing items to and from England, and the slave trade ban provision drifted out of the public discussion.

As the Second Continental Congress convened, the issue of the slave trade was a topic that was not openly discussed through the Fall of 1775 to the Spring of 1776. However, delegates from South

Carolina were concerned that some anti-slavery delegates might try to attach a similar provision to their complaints with the King.

Indigenous People and Slaves

The back room off the kitchen at Mrs. Yard's boardinghouse was a comfortable place to shine Master Edward's boots. Bins of flour and cornmeal as well as gunny bags of lentils, beans, and peas were the obvious clue that Pompey's hideout was the cook's larder. The mingling of scents coming from these foodstuffs, tickled his nose and made him wonder when dinner was to be served.

Pompey was sitting on a wooden stool buffing and polishing Rutledges boots. Edward always avoided puddles and was very careful in his walking, so he did not scuff his favorite footwear, making Pompey's job easier. Just as he was finishing the second boot, Cicero came through the kitchen door unexpectedly and said, "Masters Edward and John asked me to fetch you up because they want us to do something."

"I have just completed this job, so I wonder what he has in mind."

"I heard Masters John and Edward were talking about going for a ride today, and I think it has something to do with that."

Pompey delicately picked up the boots so Rutledge would be able to see his good work, and he walked through the kitchen where the preparation of dinner was already under way. Cicero took the lead because Pompey had no idea where the brothers were having their conversation and he steered the two of them to the den off the dining room.

"Pompey and Cicero. I need you to go the livery and bring back two horses so Edward and I may take a ride together this afternoon," said John Rutledge.

"Would you like us to ride with you?" asked Pompey.

"It's Sunday, so I think that we will be fine without you today."

"Pompey. Make sure that my clothes for tomorrow are pressed while we are out," said Edward.

Cicero and Pompey bowed their heads slightly, turned and walked out of the room, making sure that the masters did not see them run and cheer each other. Now they knew the afternoon would be for their own amusement. The two valets were outside when the door closed with a thump.

As Cicero and Pompey walked slowly up Second Street toward the livery, Cicero said, "I had a dream last night about some Indians chasing us through the forest."

"That sounds exciting. Did they catch us?"

"I woke up when they started to grab my shoulder from behind."

"Why would some Indians be chasing us. We hardly ever see Indians."

Cicero said, "I don't know, but they seemed scary to me. Don't you ever dream about Indians?"

"I can't recall any dreams like that. I usually dream about running into the forest, and I'm glad that I am no longer a slave," said Pompey.

"I'd trade dreams with you in a second."

"Dreams are strange, Cicero. Usually, I can recall things I have done or a thought that has crossed my mind that becomes the start of a dream. Where it goes after that, I'm muddled."

"Pompey, are you afraid of Indians?"

"I don't know about scared, so much as I am cautious. In some ways, the Indians are in just as bad a spot as us slaves. The white man hates Black people, and he also hates the red people. We should be on the same side, but it just doesn't seem to feel right."

"Master John talks about Indians as being a big problem, yet I can't remember ever seeing any Indians that look dangerous. I think all my impressions of Indians have come from what Rutledge has told me."

Pompey said, "You have got me thinking about Indians and believing whatever comes out of the master's mouth as the truth. The only way for us to know something as the truth is to experience it ourselves. If I can't see it happen, how do I know that it's the truth? Why do we always believe everything that the master says? I think the answer is easy. We believe it because he has all the power over us. He tells about the Indians, and since we have little or no contact with Indians, we believe the master. I think that gives us a warped way of looking at our existence. Why should we believe their stories when all they want from us is work with no pay?"

"Pompey, sometimes I think you think too much. Of course, we need to believe the master because he has a wider access to information than we do."

"But how do we know if he is lying? Everybody lies sometimes. Have you ever heard about the Yamasee War?"

"No, what was that?"

"That war happened sixty years ago, if you believe Master Edward. When the British first came to South Carolina, many Indian tribes had been living in these areas for many generations. When the colonists started pushing the Indians away and settling in the lands the indigenous used for hunting and farming, the natives fought back. The battles were called the Yamasee War, and many tribes combined forces, killed many white settlers, and pushed all the colonists back to Charleston. Only by receiving aid from the colonies in North Carolina, Virginia, and Massachusetts were the Carolinians able to survive. Once the colonists had gained control again, the Yamasee and all its ally tribes were forced to leave the Low Country. The losses were tremendous. The colonists lost over 500 lives, and the Indian losses were in the thousands when you include not only the war casualties but also the deaths caused by distemper."

"What's distemper? Is it some kind of weapon?" Cicero asked.

"It's not like a gun or a knife. Pestilence are things that make you sick. Sometimes, you get so sick that you die. That's what happened to thousands of Indians."

"How do you know anything about this?"

"Like everything else, we learn from our masters talking among themselves," said Pompey.

"It's no wonder why the colonists only tell us bad stories about the Indians."

"Because they won the war, they get to write the history."

"Master John was talking with Mr. Gadsden the other day. That got me thinking, and now it fits in better."

"What was he talking about?"

"He was talking about the Cherokee tribe and how they could not be trusted because they say one thing and do another," said Cicero. "Mr. Gadsden was worried that if South Carolina joins with the colonies to the north to fight King George, we would be defenseless against the Cherokee, who he thinks support the King."

"I've never had any problems with the natives, but if they see slaves as being allied with the colonists, then they'll start to think that we must be their enemy also. I never volunteered to be a slave, and I never volunteered to be an enemy of the indigenous."

"We are tainted by our company," said Cicero.

"If the past can tell us about the future, I guess that the colonists will get the upper hand on the Cherokees soon unless they can exhaust the colonists. Every time the colonists fight the natives, the natives lose, and their homes and hunting fields are pushed farther away."

"I wonder if natives wrote the history of these events how different it would be from the ones we hear from our masters?"

"I am sure that they would see things differently," Pompey said. "The stories about the Yamasee and the Cherokee makes me feel that we cannot take sides against our masters in this fight, but it also means that we should not be too obvious about supporting them, either."

The valets had arrived at the livery and began a short conversation with Samuel Garrigues' employees to lease two horses for the afternoon. As usual, the livery accepted a signed credit that Cicero had received from John Rutledge before they left the boardinghouse. As they returned, Pompey and Cicero traded stories they had been told about the indigenous and were joking about how many of them were true or false.

SOUTH CAROLINA GOES HOME

The cool evenings of November had brought a chill to the air. John and Edward Rutledge trudged down Fourth Street toward the red brick mansion of Dr. William Shippen to have dinner with Christopher Gadsden and Henry Middleton. After finishing a long day at Congress, the two brothers spoke intently about the situation in South Carolina and the proceedings in Philadelphia.

The Shippen House, with its refined colonial architecture, was a symbol of wealth and influence, and was nestled near South Second Street and Pine. Originally built around 1695 and later expanded, it was the residence of the prominent Shippen family, which included Dr. William Shippen, a leading physician and early advocate of anatomical study.

The impassioned politics in South Carolina might have been one of the reasons why John Rutledges position on provincial self-government was evolving. Back home, a Council of Safety had been formed to provide for the common defense of the colony, and rumors had begun to circulate about a possible slave revolt.

"Henry and I have already decided to participate in the establishment of a new government structure by and for the people," said John. "These are exciting times, but filled with stress, while everyone is trying to make sure the best decisions are made."

"Your ability to have the Continental Congress approve of the creation of a colonial government for South Carolina was exquisite," said Edward.

"It was fortuitous that New Hampshire made their request. All I did was to ask that South Carolina should also be given the same authorization. Often, leadership shows up when timing and preparation meet at an appropriate setting."

The Shippen Home featured a classic Georgian layout with a front parlor, central stairway, and rear drawing room, each adorned with paneled walls, polished wood floors, and tall shuttered windows that filtered the city's light. The furnishings were elegant but tempered by mahogany chairs, carved sideboards, and imported rugs, balanced by shelves of medical texts and philosophical treatises that spoke to the Shippen family's scholarly pursuits, while the scent of beeswax and ink lingered in the study. It was a house where science, politics, and genteel society converged, hosting figures like John Adams, Henry Middleton, and Richard Henry Lee amid quiet conversations and the distant hum of revolution.

As Edward reached the front door and was ready to knock, the door suddenly opened and a welcoming house servant led them to the dining room where Henry Middleton and Christopher Gadsden were already engaged in conversation

"John and Edward," said Henry Middleton who was wearing his customary white powdered wig that always gave off a scent of lavender. "Christopher and I are glad that you can join us for dinner this evening."

"We appreciate the invitation, and, as everyone knows, there is a great deal we need to discuss."

"John, can't you just take a night to relax a little?" chided Gadsden. "You are among friends here, so let's have a good dinner without the business we argue about all day. Please join me in a madeira."

"Christopher thinks he's back in Charleston. He believes that on a Friday night we should take our time and relax after a hard work week."

"Well, at least I'm not returning to South Carolina for the good life," said Christopher.

Middleton appeared a little sheepish and shrugged his shoulders.

"Henry, I did not know you chose to tell Christopher so soon," said John. "I haven't told Edward, yet."

"Told me what?" asked Edward.

Middleton and John Rutledge shared a bemused smile.

"I thought we were to have this conversation over dinner, but I guess now is as good as time as any," John started. "Edward, Henry and I have decided to leave for South Carolina on Sunday, where activity is rising to a fever pitch, as we believe we can be of more service to our Carolinian neighbors if we return now. We feel confident about this decision because of the experience you have gained over the last year in Congress."

"I appreciate the confidence that you have in me, but your departure seems very sudden."

"It may appear that way to you, yet, Henry and I have discussed our departure over the past week and believe that it is in everyone's best interest. You and I were talking just a few minutes ago about how Congress has given South Carolina the authorization to form a new provincial government. In addition, if you remember, Congress also gave us the ability to name leadership in the militia and to be recognized by the Continental Army. These are positive factors that will give us the strength to deal with the happenings at home."

John Rutledge said, "the colony is gripped by escalating political turmoil as tensions between patriots and loyalists erupted into open conflict in the backcountry. The colony is deeply divided. The South Carolina Provincial Congress is a shadow government challenging royal authority, but Loyalist resistance remains strong in frontier regions, like Ninety-Six and Camden."

Henry continued, "This past month marked the beginning of the Snow Campaign, a patriot-led military effort under Colonel Richard Richardson to suppress Loyalist forces and secure control of the interior. We have received reports of skirmishes that reveal the depth of civil strife with neighbors turning against one another and militias mobilizing amid rumors of British support from Cherokee alliances.

"We believe that our presence in South Carolina now is more valuable than our time spent here," said John Rutledge. "The political landscape is no longer a matter of debate, it has become a battleground, with South Carolina's future hanging in the balance.

"I heard about the new Governor that was appointed," said Gadsden. "It appears he couldn't handle the Assembly, and now he resides on a ship in Charleston Harbor. Now, there's real leadership!"

"Let's move to the dining room," said Middleton. "We can continue this conversation over our meal."

"But who will take your place on your committees?" asked Edward.

"Most of my committees have made their reports, and I asked John Hancock to consider you more often for committee openings."

The four men moved to their dining room seats, and Henry gently rang a bell. He sat at the head of the table while John sat to his right and Christopher to his left. Edward took the seat next to John. Jack, Gadsden's Black valet, appearing silently through the kitchen door, brought a tureen of soup and circled the table offering ladles of soup to each diner, followed by Pompey, who offered the diners sweet potato biscuits and French rolls. After placing the soup tureen and breadbasket on the table, both sidled inconspicuously to a corner of the room.

"Who will replace you?" Edward asked.

"Edward, my first order of business when I reach Charleston is to discuss with the other leaders who our replacements will be," said Henry. "I am not sure if they will allow this, but I have hopes that my son, Arthur, would take my seat."

John added, "The other matter that can be delicately addressed is a replacement for Thomas Lynch, Sr. His health continues to be an issue, and we do need a replacement for him. Christopher will continue for a period until a replacement can take his place."

****

Thomas Lynch Sr. was in declining health, having suffered a stroke that left him partially paralyzed and unable to continue his duties in the Continental Congress. Within five months, his condition was so grave that his son, Thomas Lynch Jr., was appointed to succeed him as delegate, despite the younger Lynch himself battling a debilitating illness at the time. The probable cause was malaria that he contracted during the humid, tropical summer months that were common in South Carolina.

****

Gadsden said, "You'll find me here for a while."

"Gentlemen, why don't we defer the balance of this conversation," said Henry, "until after dinner? I understand that the cook has outdone himself tonight offering us roasted duck and pork tenderloin medallions. I hope you have brought your appetites."

Cicero poured claret into the crystal goblets of each man, placed the decanter on the table, and then retreated to a corner. Henry raised his glass and said, "Here's to the success of South Carolina." Each gently clinked their goblets and took a polite swallow. Finally, Edward raised his goblet again and said, "Here's to everyone's health and the success of the Continental Congress."

"Do you think that the Provincial Congress will wait for your return till they begin?" asked Edward

"I think that the Provincial Congress is scheduled to begin on December 1, but who knows? With the pace of activity, your guess is as good as mine. When things move too fast, details and understandings are hard to differentiate."

A small chime that came from the kitchen was a cue for the servants to retreat and prepare to serve the next course. All the servants quietly moved to the kitchen.

"I have come to appreciate the workings of the Shippen House. It's offers fine food and service, but I can't wait to return to Middleton Place."

"We will miss you here, Henry," said Christopher.

"I'm not sure I am willing to accept that gratitude, Christopher. You and your radical friends in Congress will probably cheer when they see my phaeton roll out of Philadelphia."

"Now Henry, you know that I meant that sorrow deeply. I can't speak for the others who support my thirst for independence, but for me, I will miss your logical approach to solving problems on the floor of Congress and on the various committees you have led."

"Thank you, Christopher. If there is going to be a fight in South Carolina, I trust that you will be there to lend your experience and leadership."

"I've never walked away from a fight in my life that I believed worth fighting for. If Congress does vote for independence, I doubt if the British will loosen their grip without applying some more pain. I know a thing or two about pain, and I want to be in front, leading the charge."

"We could never be more confident in your steadfastness," said John.

"Here, here," said Henry and Edward simultaneously as they raised their glasses and again clinked them in support of one another.

As if on cue, the kitchen door opened as the aroma of the prepared meal wafted into the room The servants had plates of food that were ready to be served. Peter carried a platter of roasted duck, Pompey brought another platter of pork tenderloin medallions, Cicero had a bowlful of butter-glazed carrots, while Jack placed smaller bowls of mushrooms, onions, and pickled beets on the table. Without saying a word, the servants followed each other in offering the various foods to their masters. Each diner would nod silently or raise an eyebrow to direct the servant to apportion the proper amount of food. The only conversation originated from the diners who commented on the quality of the food or its variety. The parade of servers circled around the table and finally left the unallocated portions at the end of the table while returning to their respective corners.

After an hour and a half of eating and conversation, the men finished supper and sampled truffles and tarts for dessert. When the dinner was completed, the servants cleared the table and repaired to the kitchen for clean-up.

"Did you know," began Pompey, "that the masters were returning to South Carolina?

"No," said Cicero. "That was the first that I heard about it. I guess I know what work I must do tomorrow to get the household ready for travel."

"That was first I heard of anything," said Peter. "I won't mind returning to regular chores once we get home."

"As much as we think we know what is happening in Congress, we discover that we understand less. We'll miss you, Cicero."

"It won't be long before Master Edward finds a way to return to Charleston."

"We better help clean up as much as we can before the masters leave," said Pompey.

Peter and Jack were pleased that Pompey and Cicero aided them in cleaning up in the kitchen. Peter thought to himself that he would miss listening to Pompey, as he was always good to have around.

Back in the dining room, John and Edward had retrieved their coats with the aid of one of Mrs. Shippen's staff.

"We'll be leaving Sunday," said John, "and need to make a stop in North Carolina to deliver instructions about support for their militia. Our plan is to arrive in Charleston by November 28th."

"Have a safe trip," said Christopher. "I'm sure we won't be apart for long. Please save me a seat in the Provincial Assembly."

"Give my love to Henrietta and tell her I will be with her as soon as possible."

The Rutledges shook hands with their hosts and started back to the boardinghouse. Pompey and Cicero followed five yards behind walking silently.

Soon, Edward himself would get his marching orders.

BROTHERLY ADVICE

John and Edward Rutledge walked back slowly to Mrs. Yard's boardinghouse after a sumptuous dinner with Henry Middleton and Christopher Gadsden. The walk from the Shippen House near Second and Pine unfolded under a canopy of stars and the faint glow of lanterns hung from iron brackets. The air carried the scent of woodsmoke and damp leaves, and the cobbled streets, slick with frost, echoed with the occasional clatter of a carriage or the distant call of a watchman. Passing through Society Hill, people were strolling past stately brick homes with shuttered windows and quiet gardens, their silhouettes softened by the flickering light of hearths within. St. Peter's Church loomed in quiet dignity, its graveyard still and shadowed, while the murmurs of late conversation drifted from behind closed doors, hinting at the political tensions that simmered beneath Philadelphia's genteel surface.

Pompey and Cicero trailed their masters quietly at a distance.

As the route turned westward toward Fourth Street, the city grew more animated. A tavern door might swing open to release a burst of laughter and the scent of ale, while a printer's apprentice hurried past with ink-stained hands and a bundle of broadsheets. The Statehouse stood solemn and dark, its windows reflecting moonlight, a silent witness to the day's debates. For a delegate or visitor, the walk was more than a passage through the city streets. As they quietly strolled by the plain clapboard homes, the brothers knew that the meeting of the delegates from throughout the American colonies would result in more than a realignment of the relationship with the King of England. In the past three months, John and Edward had worked in tandem and solo to protect the people of South Carolina. John believed his best efforts could be used in Charleston and Edward was unsure if he could carry the load in Philadelphia alone.

"I guess that it will be desirable to get an early start on Sunday?" Edward asked.

"Of course, if the weather stays as pleasant as it has been over the last few days, we should reach Charleston before the end of the month. I need to stop in New Bern, North Carolina before reaching home as I have some letters for John Harvey of the North Carolina

Burgesses regarding what he can expect from the Continental Congress."

"If you can keep to that schedule, you should be able to attend the next session of the Provincial Congress."

"That is the plan for now, but always remember that the plans we make are not always the plan that God has for us. For me, I will be happy to make a good start of it early Sunday."

"Ned, I want to talk with you about your place in the Congress when Henry and I leave. With John Lynch remaining with precarious health, Christopher Gadsden and you will be the only South Carolina delegates until we can decide upon and send replacements for us."

"Who do you think will be your replacements?"

"That doesn't really matter now for I want to talk to you tonight about issues for you to remember," John said. "The reason that I wanted to have this conversation is to make sure we agree about how South Carolina will be represented after I leave. We both know that the assignments that you have been given since we were members of Congress have not been the important ones you desired. I trust that my departure will present opportunities for you to be heard since I will not be here to draw attention away from you. I have spoken to Mr. Hancock and Mr. Adams to explain why I am leaving, and they were most accommodating to me as they understand the need for each of our colonies to depend upon strong voices and structures to withstand the adversity we may have when independence is declared."

Edward stopped mid-stride with his arm restraining his brother from walking any further.

"Excuse me, but do you think that independence is that close to happening?"

"I would not leave Philadelphia if I didn't believe that you and the others on the South Carolina delegation did not have the ability and best interests of the colony foremost in mind. The Crown has already said "No" to us in a loud rejection of our Olive Branch Petition. Blood has already been drawn on both sides in Boston, and I don't expect that the end of the bloodshed will happen anytime soon. However, there are many details that we must address to give us the best opportunity for our actions to be successful. We are proud Carolinians. We have a healthy economy that we have worked to develop over many generations, and we can't see that effort wasted. While I am away helping to form a strong government for South Carolina, you need to be working diligently to assure that our interests are protected. Whatever happens in this Congress, South Carolina can look back in the future and proudly say that we were at the forefront of history, and were proud of our efforts."

"You're sounding like Mr. Gadsden."

The pair picked up their pace as the wind at their backs seemed to increase.

"That is one of the points that I want to make to you," John continued. "Christopher Gadsden is a great man, and I hold him in high esteem. He has succeeded in most things that he has put his mind to. But Christopher can also go a little half-cocked on some matters. He has identified with the radicals in Congress from the very first day we arrived. I respect his opinion, but I also think that a vast number of people in South Carolina would like to move at a slower pace. After I leave, I am sure that Mr. Gadsden will attempt to influence you to move closer to his view on matters before the Congress. Don't! You have a fine mind and an excellent ability to express yourself. The need for some reconciliation remains on the table. If we blunder about with independence without taking care of the details for self-government and seeking outside allies, we may fail before we can prosper. Regardless, I believe that Christopher may decide, as Henry and I have, to leave for Charleston when he sees that his role in South Carolina is more valuable than his time spent here."

Edward said, "You can be assured that I will speak my own mind and not be swayed unnecessarily by Mr. Gadsden. I am curious why you are certain that the call for independence will come so soon."

John said, "When we left South Carolina for this Second Continental Congress, I was a staunch conservative, favoring reconciliation with Britain and viewing independence as premature and destabilizing. However, as military threats intensified and moderate positions eroded, I have gradually accepted the necessity of independence, not out of ideological fervor, but as a pragmatic response to the collapse of royal authority and the need to preserve South Carolina's autonomy.

He continued, "I think that the process has become more clear to see. The King has decided to bring us to heel at any cost. The embarrassment of Lexington and Concord followed by their great losses at Bunker Hill has forced him into either fighting us or letting us go. Their honor will not allow them to merely surrender, and the alternative is that they will fight until the outcome is clear. Britain is a mighty and proud nation, and the strength of their army and navy will be a major factor in the final success or failure of our war efforts."

"If the results in the field are any indication of how well our patriots may fare, I would wager that we will be triumphant," said Edward.

"Yes, but before we sign a peace agreement with the King, there are other matters that you need to keep in mind. There are issues which South Carolina must have settled, such as how the colonies are to relate to one another, and our ability to maintain our plantation system. Regarding the first matter, we must be clear on how that relationship is defined, or we will find ourselves facing exactly the same dilemma as we are now, in which the King wants one thing and the colonies want another. South Carolina is one of the richest colonies in America. We may not have the size or population, but wealth is power, and we should not be ashamed to make that fact clear. If we expect to survive as a colony within a larger association, we cannot afford to have any sort of central authority legislating to us about our business."

Edward said, "I have had some conversations with John Jay of New York and Thomas Stone of Maryland about the need for us to have a confederation agreement that would be accepted by the colonies before we call for independence."

"That is the right direction, but Edward we must have other delegates with greater influence in the Congress to say those things out loud. All we hear are speeches about independence and nothing regarding how we are going to govern."

"Along those same lines, we need to start talking about developing relationships with other countries who will see it in their self-interest to weaken Britain. I am sure that France and Spain would love to see King George harmed by an upstart colonial movement. However, we must guard against making ourselves servants to a new master just so that we can dispose of our previous one. If either of those powers join our side, I believe the road to liberty will be considerably shorter."

John added, "The French may become our main ally if we approach them carefully. I had a conversation with Dr. Franklin, who has had experience in speaking with citizens and royalty on the continent, and he suggested that some quiet diplomacy may garner great returns. I am not convinced that this assistance is fully understood by most delegates. Our experience obtaining a law degree in London gives the two of us a greater appreciation of the wider picture of the world that Congress must learn to understand.

"I think that I have had conversations with a few delegates who have also studied in England, and that experience is helpful in having this kind of talk."

"Well put, Ned. Those are the connections that could be valuable in casual conversations over dinner or the City Taven for establishing an atmosphere of unity around sound advice. Edward, these northern men may speak with different accents and hold different views, but if we are to preserve South Carolina's interests, we must earn their respect and trust. A firm hand in debate is useful, but a warm hand in friendship will carry our cause further than any solitary conviction."

The winds had increased gradually, and John and Edward pulled their collars up to stay warm. The chill pressed through their woolen coats and lingered on their breath as they proceeded down the uneven cobblestones, their conversation slowed by the quiet hush of the hour. The crisp air sharpened their senses, drawing their eyes to the flicker of lanterns, as if the city itself were holding its breath in the shadow of revolution.

John began, "The other matter which we need to discuss relates to the success of our plantation system in maintaining a wealthy and successful colony. Virginia and South Carolina bring to the united association of colonies a history of progress and power. The mechanisms of financial wealth that will transform America are the great plantations of the South, and what fosters that strength is the importation of workers from Africa. One cannot escape the fact that there are certain delegates in Congress who would argue for the termination of this arrangement. We can never remain silent on these matters, nor can we allow an incremental erosion of this practice. The issue is not the center of our debates thus far, but I see a time in the not-too-distant future when we will need to stand up for our rights. May I remind you that the document we agreed to during the First

Continental Congress creating an association stated, as part of the non-importation ban, that the delegates agreed to 'neither import nor purchase any slaves.' I fear that some anti-slavery delegates will eventually use our own words to punish our plantation system.

"If those words are included in the Association document, how do we prevent the issue to being raised again?"

John said, "You need to be vigilant. During the First Congress so much business was being discussed, and the non-importation issue was seen as a strong measure we could use to apply economic pressure. If we stopped buying goods from London, they would feel the pain. No one thought that we would see the day when the slave trade would end. Also, the inclusion of that statement was just a negotiating term that would continue while we seek reconciliation with the Crown. Now that British and American blood has been spilled and the idea of a united Colonies is conceivable, we need to watch our steps carefully. In addition, it is incumbent on you and our South Carolinian replacements to take the initiative discussing these topics with the delegates, so that our colleagues from the north will not simply adopt this item into any proposal that may be put forth."

"I understand that we may have allies in the northern colonies with shipbuilding interests who also prosper from the slave trade," said Edward.

"I am pleased that you have made that deduction. Over the past weeks, I have been gently reminding our fellow delegates to protect that interest, and you should do the same. We need to remind them of that point, although I would not be surprised that they know this fact, even if they may not be comfortable uttering the words. We should take nothing for granted on this matter. The entire South Carolina colony depends on us to protect their interests. Need I remind you, during the last session, the northern colonies thought nothing of sacrificing our interests when they wanted to ban the export of our rice and indigo production? If they were ready and eager to sacrifice our interests six months ago, we should be prepared to fight for our rights again before they are lost."

Edward said, "Brother, I have not heard you state these facts in open debate during any of the sessions. Why haven't you raised these valid points before so everyone would hear our pleas?"

"Ned, private diplomacy often works better when attempting to influence the judgements of persons who think they are sagacious and experienced. I have spoken with delegates during time spent outside Congressional sessions about how South Carolina's interests need to be protected. I would suggest that you should continue this effort. The most effective strategy is to provide enough information for a person to decide so that when they vote, they think that it was their idea. There may be more northern states with few slaves, but they know their value to our overall economy. We need to persist in reminding them."

"I will miss this conversation when you leave. Please notify me regarding progress in protecting our colony from the antics of the Royal governors who can't seem to hold onto their positions long before they take their leave in disgrace."

"Henry and I will have plenty of work when we return. Our first order of business will be to recommend a new form of government that will be accountable to its citizens. Second, we will need to strengthen our military capabilities because the British will eventually try to isolate us from the rest of the colonies, and we need to be prepared. Edward, I am confident that you will be able to represent our interests in my absence, and soon you will have other younger delegates to support your efforts. Choose your words carefully, and hold your friends closely. Good luck."

"I know that I will heed your advice. With your wise counsel, my job is made easier."

The Rutledge pair had reached Mrs. Yard's house and gently knocked on the door. In an instant the door swung open to reveal a servant who sat waiting for their tenants.

"Good evening, sirs. I trust you had a fine dinner."

"Thank you, we did."

John went up the stairs thinking about everything he needed to do prior to his departure on Sunday, while Edward's head was spinning with his new responsibilities in Philadelphia.

AN ELDER SHARES HIS WISDOM

Dinner at the Shippen House in Philadelphia was very similar to the Middleton Place, home to Henry Middleton. Here, supper was an event, combining good food, sumptuous surroundings and more than a hint of arrogance. In attendance tonight were Henry and his wife, Lady Mary Mackenzie, Edward Rutledge, and three of Henrietta's sisters, Sara, May, and Susannah.

The dining room of the Shippen House offered a refined, yet intimate, setting for conversation amid the growing tensions of revolution. Beneath its high ceiling and paneled walls, a long mahogany table stood polished and set with pewter, porcelain dishes, and cut crystal glasses that caught the flicker of candlelight from brass sconces. The hearth glowed steadily, warming the room against the autumn chill, while portraits of ancestors and botanical prints adorned the walls, reflecting the Shippen family's blend of Quaker heritage and scientific curiosity. The scent of roasted meats and spiced apples lingered in the air, and voices rose in measured tones over wine and politics. It was a space where civility masked uncertainty, and where each meal unfolded in the shadow of a nation being born.

Through the five courses of soup, poultry, veal, breads, and nuts at a family dinner like tonight, participants were encouraged to speak about their daily accomplishments. The dinner staff of slaves was discreet and held chairs for the diners, brought beverages of choice, offered options of each course, removed plates and silverware between courses, refilled glasses, and were generally available to perform any tasks that the host ordered them to do. Peter and Pompey were part of the slave staff.

After dinner was completed, Henry asked the ladies for some privacy and bade them retire to the parlor so Edward and he might have the opportunity for conversation. The following day the Middletons would leave for Charleston. In addition to Henry's role as delegate at the Second Continental Congress, he was the largest landholding plantation owner in South Carolina and owned hundreds of slaves.

Edward was always uncertain about his standing with his father-in-law, who had consented to Rutledges marriage to his eldest daughter, Henrietta, two years earlier. Her health had been fragile for a long time and became more of a concern after the birth of their first child in 1775. Edward's rapid rise in the political affairs of the colony, his care and concern toward his wife, and his budding career as an attorney, allowed him to feel satisfied that Henrietta's father held him in high regard.

"Edward," said Henry, who never used the more familiar "Ned" that his close friends called him. "We will be leaving for South Carolina tomorrow, and I want to inform you of how I believe the Congress is proceeding in our relationship with the Crown."

Edward fidgeted inside but knew not to show his reaction outwardly. He knew that Middleton was the most conservative delegate of the South Carolina team. Had he not been chosen as a delegate to the Congress, Rutledge believed Middleton would be very comfortable with the Loyalist business owners in Charleston. He leaned forward in his chair and was prepared to hear every word that Henry was about to say so that he had a good chance of pleasing his father-in-law. Henry straightened into his chair and looked deeply into the eyes of Edward.

Henry Middleton's conservative nature stood in quiet contrast to the rising fervor for independence that gripped the halls of the Continental Congress. A wealthy South Carolina planter and former president of the First Continental Congress, Middleton had long opposed British overreach but remained deeply committed to reconciliation and the preservation of colonial order. As more radical voices, like those of John Adams and Christopher Gadsden pressed for decisive action, Middleton grew increasingly wary of the social upheaval and economic disruption that full independence might unleash.

"Affairs of state are deteriorating quickly in the colonies, and you must keep a steady view on the importance of the matters directly in front of you," he began, gesturing with his right hand. "My father and grandfather came to South Carolina to grow a business, establish a family, and participate in the government to bring harmony among the inhabitants. The success we achieved was in concert with the Royal officers of the colony. I know that times have brought changes to South Carolina and that some of the actions of Parliament have made uncomfortable feelings among our neighbors. The call for independence by the northern colonies, however, should not drown out our experience which has provided our family with wealth and a good life. I urge you to heed my call and to press for reconciliation with the British before it is too late." Henry leaned back in his chair and said, "I shudder to think what would be the result of continued defiance to the King, and I fear that those of us who have been blessed will be at gravest risk if the Crown decides to use their immense strength to bring the radical demagogues to heel."

Edward pushed back his chair while Henry continued, "I know that many delegates at the Continental Congress are ready to break the ties that bind us to our ancestors, and I know that one of our own delegates, Christopher Gadsden, supports some of these more outlandish ideas, but I pray that you will see this through my lens of the unparalleled growth that I have been able to achieve and which I hope that you and Henrietta will enjoy in your future, long after these misunderstandings between decision makers are resolved."

Edward leaned forward in his chair and gently said, "Thank you, sir, for reminding me of how our family history has shaped South Carolina." Warily, Rutledge added, "I believe that the circumstances we face today are more than just 'misunderstandings.' Over the past few years, settlers from north to south have felt hurt and alarmed by what happens in London, because it seems that we are viewed as children, and not adults, and that our economies are owned by Parliament. Serious disregard for our work, your work, has forced us to take measures that may seem extreme in your eyes."

A smile crept onto Middleton's face. "I am thankful that you are Henrietta's husband. I see your point of view and this is the reason that I agreed to be a delegate in the first place. I am not confident that our united colonies are ready to make this leap so soon. We don't know what kind of government we might have that would please all colonies. How will the colonies relate to one another? How will justice be adjudicated in our colony and within the united colonies? Can this effort survive if we don't have the support of other countries to balance the great might of the British forces? These are questions that must be answered before we ride down a path of no return."

Rutledge wanted to assure his father-in-law that he agreed wholeheartedly with Henry's desires. "I have some of those very same concerns," Edward said. "I will continue to advocate for a document of confederation among our fellow colonies before we are to publicly announce that we strive for independence."

Middleton shook his head slowly and said, "I am not sold yet on the idea of independence as the only route for better relations with the King. Your brother and I are returning to South Carolina primarily to aid our fellow Carolinians building a structure that can exist alongside the Royal government. The colonies need to be systematic about how we strive for a fair relationship with Britain and should not take steps hastily that we may regret in the future."

Henry said, "I have profound concerns that northern delegates, many of whom came from colonies with declining slave economies and growing abolitionist sentiment, might use the revolutionary moment to challenge slavery in the South. Though the Congress is primarily focused on resisting British authority, I understand that the language of liberty and natural rights, championed by men like John Adams and Benjamin Franklin, carry implications that could unsettle the foundations of South Carolina's plantation society.

Henry picked up a silver bread knife that was left by the servants and pointed it toward the table. "These are serious times we are facing, and I want you to remain strong," Henry continued. "I have heard from some of the delegates of the northern colonies that they want to use this conflict with the Crown to abolish slavery in America. I have heard whispers in the statehouse and loud chatter at the City Tavern where some of these men believe that they can interject their prejudices into our lives. Let me be clear," Henry slashed the air with the knife. "South Carolina will never give up the right to use slaves so that we can make our economy strong and prosperous. Idle conversation about abolition should not be tolerated. I would rather see us form our own separate government than to submit like slaves to please some Yankee's version of righteousness for our dear South Carolina."

"Sir, I could not be more in agreement with those statements," Edward said. "I don't see that happening during these deliberations and certainly not as long as I am a representative of South Carolina."

"But that is the reason that you should be more attentive to the motives of these delegates from colonies who have few servants in their midst," Middleton said. "I fear for some of our own colonies, specifically Virginia, as I have heard Richard Henry Lee and others spout off about our labor practices. Often, it is the people closest to you that you must worry about most."

"Rest assured, dear father, that I will never let those words of abolition infest the conversation about independence or reconciliation," Edward said, confidently.

"Beware, my good boy. Since the Somerset decision a few years ago set Britain on a course to abolish slavery, this disease of abolition has infected many souls," Henry replied. "We must be diligent to head off any feint that might be a canard for weakening our position. Power has a way of polluting the best instincts of those who speak of higher virtue yet are seeking to exercise domination over the unsuspecting. If we had never used the art of slavery to tame this colony, the colonies would never have been able to hold this Continental Congress."

Edward sat up in his chair and said, "You are a wise man, and I am honored to be a member of your family. Henrietta always reminds me of how she always looked to you for strength and guidance. I truly appreciate this conversation, and I shall remember your advice whenever I am a delegate from South Carolina doing the business of the Congress."

"Edward, we are counting on you to represent us as the primary delegate from South Carolina until replacements can be appointed," Middleton said. "Use that God-given talent of yours to make good decisions, speak with authority, and guide our hopes and dreams here in Philadelphia. I am sure that you will live out your responsibility."

Middleton stood up from his chair and opened his arms to his son-in-law. Edward stood up and said, "Thank you, sir. Your support and guidance will be an inspiration in all the work that will fill my hours in your absence." Rutledge and Middleton embraced and then shook hands.

"I will not disappoint you, sir." Edward finally added.

Edward had never received a hug from Henry Middleton, and it took a long time for him to extract its meaning. Has something changed in their relationship? Was he now fully accepted into the Middleton family? It would take him years to determine the answer to these questions.

Edward Rutledge Matures

As the carriages carrying John Rutledge and Henry Middleton began their trek for the Carolina colony on a cool fall morning, Edward Rutledge stood alone on a Philadelphia cobblestone street. He waved farewell and sighed with the knowledge that the burden of representing the interests of South Carolina rested squarely on his shoulders. As the road changed to gravel, the carriage creaked forward, its iron-rimmed wheels crunching through frost-laden stones as pale morning light broke over the rooftops of Philadelphia. Breath from the horses rose in quiet plumes, and the driver, cloaked against the chill, snapped the reins with resolve as the city stirred faintly behind him. The vacuum left by his brother's departure marked the next chapter in his life. Edward needed to be accepted on his own terms, even though many would continue to view him beneath his brother's lingering shadow. He was determined to learn from his experiences in the Continental Congress while charting his own future. The cool morning air induced a breathy cloud at every exhale, a cloud that disappeared into the emerging daylight. He relished the notion of representing his colony's needs but was concerned that his youthful exuberance would remain an obstacle to gaining support as the first session had already demonstrated.

Down the lane, the haze of dust caused by the carriage wheels slowly dissipated as Edward returned to the boarding house for breakfast. A mild breeze rustled the fallen leaves against his shoes while the street began to awaken with men and horses moving wares to their shops as the city came to life again. He reached for the latch of the brick building and pondered that in only a few hours, he and fellow delegates would decide the next steps to take in determining how the freedom of colonists to live in peace and harmony would proceed.

Edward had been part of a five-person delegation representing South Carolina. Now, Christopher Gadsden and he would be the last two remaining representatives of his native state until replacements were named and arrived in Philadelphia. Keeping in mind the admonitions of his brother, John, and his father-in-law, Henry Middleton, Rutledge was determined to speak forcefully and clearly for the interest of his colony. Knowing that his wife was safe at home, and having already formed some close relationships with delegates from other colonies, Rutledge was confident that he could manage the growing spirit of independence without losing track of what he knew his fellow Carolinians desired. However, the departure of both his brother and his political benefactor from Philadelphia left Rutledge apprehensive.

When Edward first arrived in Philadelphia in June of 1774 with his wife, Henrietta, and his father-in-law, Henry Middleton, he'd had his brother, John, as a guide and mentor. John Adams, the firebrand leader of the Massachusetts delegation, had labeled Edward at their first meeting as "a young and smart spirited body and very high for liberty," although his opinion after a few months of interaction had changed. A later comment from Adams was that Edward was "excessively" variable and "unsteady." From Adams' perspective, the South Carolina delegation needed to be convinced to move to a more radical stance if independence was to be achieved.

Edward pondered some of the advice that his brother John had left for him. The parting words of the elder Rutledge to Edward led him to believe that independence and not reconciliation was the future that the colonists were facing. This gap between working for reconciliation and preparing for independence caused Edward's discomfort, and John had left mixed messages about how he should provide leadership. Maybe that was the test that John had left for him to discern. Edward knew that John felt passionate about the use of slavery on the plantation and how important it was to maintain what he regarded as their economic backbone for the colony and America. The lack of any specific list of delegates that he should contact in support of the slave trade was also puzzling. John had expected that Edward would need to speak to delegates outside of the deliberations of Congress to enlist their support to keep the slave issue from being on any final document.

Who had John spoken to about striking references to slavery from the Continental Association? Edward was perplexed by that point but thought that he should merely decide who needed to be encouraged to support Carolina's agenda, and if John had cajoled them previously, it should make his life easier.

Edward knew that his brother John viewed slavery as an essential pillar of his colony's social and economic order. Edward grew up knowing that John was a wealthy planter deeply embedded in the elite class that depended on enslaved labor to sustain rice and indigo production.

Through his long years in building up the South Carolia colony, John Rutledges political philosophy emphasized stability, property rights, and cautious reform, and, within that framework, slavery was not merely tolerated, it was protected. Edward had already learned that any disruption to the institution of slavery would threaten the cohesion of South Carolina's society and undermine the very foundations of its prosperity. The political balancing act Edward needed to project was how to weigh British overreach and the need to protect the institution of slavery, viewing their bondage as a local matter beyond the scope of national debate.

John and Edward agreed on many of the issues that were faced by Congress, from the non-export of goods, the need for a better equipped Navy, and for each colony to establish new governance to protect the rights of the people. Edward also knew that John trusted him to do the job in a manner that South Carolina would be proud of. John had been the conservative among the delegation, and Christopher Gadsden had been the radical. Now the burden that Edward had chosen was to balance these ideas in the opportunities that would be offered to him. Before he left for Charleston, John had confided that he rejected Parliament's ability to wield power over the colonies, and it became Edward's obligation to express this belief at the proper time.

How did the other delegates feel about slavery? This was something Edward would soon discover.

Who Had What Power in Philadelphia

John Adams and Richard Henry Lee found a meeting place in the Statehouse on the top floor where an extra committee room gave delegates some privacy. After the afternoon session concluded, they moved to the committee room to talk about strategy.

"Richard," began John Adams, "I think it would be helpful for us to review how the various delegates make decisions so we can achieve the independence we both desire."

"That's a tall order to put down in writing," commented Lee.

"Oh, I don't think that we should put this in writing," said Adams, "but I think we can review the various players in Congress and make educated guesses about how delegates may make their decisions.

"I have already seen how your lawyer experience has helped the Congress to pursue certain items, but now I am beginning to appreciate your aptitude for planning even better," responded Richard Henry.

"Let's first examine how colonies have exercised their political power in relation to Britain. Each colony could be rated on a scale from independence to reconciliation."

"That seems a reasonable place to start," said Lee.

"This may be the easiest gauge to discern," said Adams. "The northern colonies, including Massachusetts, New Hampshire, Rhode Island, and Connecticut have already made clear their preference in severing the ties with Britain."

"I would agree," said Lee, "but what should we make of New York, Pennsylvania, New Jersey, and Delaware?"

"Let's set them aside for now, as other powers that they have may be utilized later to move their delegates toward independence." said Adams.

"Virginia is in a class of its own," said Lee. "I think the majority of the delegation is ready to cry out for independence."

Adams responded, "I couldn't have chosen more apt language. But things get more difficult when we look at the remainder of the southern colonies of South Carolina, North Carolina, and Georgia."

"My assessment of their delegates leads me to believe that as South Carolina goes, so will the remainder of the southern colonies go," said Lee. "It's too bad that John Rutledge has returned to South Carolina because I felt that he was coming to see our point of view and he is a leader for the South."

"I am not so sure of his little brother, Edward," said Adams. "He is like a chameleon who will change his mind at the least provocation."

"I don't disagree with you on that analysis, but I sense that without his brother and Middleton keeping him still, he might grow into the man we need."

"I have been informed that young Rutledge has been insinuating himself into conversations to push for the delegates to not talk about slavery here," said Adams. "The issue of slavery is another one of the power centers that I would like to discuss."

"John, you have really been thinking deeply about the delegates."

"Richard, I am an attorney. When the jurors are selected in a matter before the courts, I make it my business to understand the behavior of not only the jurors but also the judge."

"I would like to commend you for your work on the Boston Massacre," said Lee. "How did you actually have the jurors find those soldiers not guilty in killing those Massachusetts patriots?" asked Lee with incredulity.

"By using this analysis," said Adams. "Let's apply it here. We know that southern delegates all want their peculiar institution of slavery not disturbed. That would include South and North Carolina, Georgia, Virginia, and Maryland. We also know that they are the important votes that we will need to have unanimity in declaring independence."

"Do you see that the process of achieving independence is to assuage the fears of southern delegates about slavery?" Lee asked.

"I doubt if this will or should be a quid pro quo." remarked Adams. "It will be interesting as we go forward to see how people will become more comfortable with the inevitability of independence. As the agenda for our meetings move toward freedom from British control, we should be cognizant of the traits of the delegates that we can predict."

"Thank you for these illustrations." Richard Henry said. "What other thoughts do you have?"

"One of the primary reasons why Massachusetts is ready for independence is that we have had blood spilled on our soil," Adams said. "When the Stamp Act roiled the colonies, we received support from every colony that was being taxed. If a colony is attacked, they will scream for independence, but if it's the other guy's problem, neighbors may not be so quick to respond."

"I have said it once and I'll say it as often as necessary if Norfolk or Charleston is attacked like Boston, there will be a parade of delegates voting for independence," said Lee.

"That is precisely what I believe," said Adams. "We need to be ready at all times to press the different delegates to act when they see events affecting or limiting their power."

"Let's talk a little bit about New York, Pennsylvania, New Jersey, and Delaware," said Lee.

"Delaware seems to be the easiest of the group," said Adams "I have had conversations with the Delaware delegate Thomas McKean, and he has assured me that when the vote is critical, we should be able to count on Delaware's support. New Jersey is very difficult to parse. The Colonial Governor is Benjamin Franklin's son, and the colony's delegates seem to go slow on independence. I understand that southern plantation owners are appreciated by New Jersey elite.

"I don't understand it, but it seems to be a fact. New York is another story. New York City seems to have strong British support. Their economy is highly dependent on trade with Britain. The New York colony ranks just slightly behind Virginia and South Carolina in wealth because of the trade with Britain," Adams concluded.

"What other factors do you think we should look at?" asked Lee.

Adams answered, "The other major issues all seem to be not as conclusive. We all have our legacies with the indigenous natives. Religion does not seem to be a decisive factor in differentiating among the colonies. The different nationalities of the colonies don't seem to be a deciding issue."

"It appears to me that the main issues that should help us understand the delegation are their views on independence, slavery, wealth, and the impact of the conflict on individual colonies," said Lee. "I think that our job is to keep our ears perked to concerns that delegates raise when we speak of independence. Then, we need to be able to coax them toward our point of view by knowing what motivates each of the colonial delegates."

"This conversation may help us to make our work better organized," said Adams. "I think we should meet like this on some sort of regular basis so we can compare notes on reaching the goal of independence from Britain."

"I like that idea," said Lee. "We may look back on this date years from now and understand that this analysis helped the colonies to break the binds with England.

THE OTHER CENTER OF POWER IN PHILADELPHIA

As Edward Rutledge left Mrs. Yard's boardinghouse for dinner at the City Tavern, he could see the lamp lighter pushing his ladder up the lamp pole to help light the way. Rutledge had first observed these watchmen ignite the numerous lights in London while studying law, but Charleston had only a few private lights. From back home, he could remember the strong scent of fish oil as a gentle breeze blew through the almost bare trees. Why couldn't Charleston decide to turn its dangerous dark streets into well-lit ones, as Philadelphia had done? Edward watched the worker on the ladder play with the wick, light the flame, and close the little glass door, then move on down the block to repeat his useful task.

The city was quieter now, though not asleep: the distant clatter of a carriage wheel, the murmur of voices behind shuttered windows, and the occasional bark of a dog punctuated the evening calm. Rutledge passed neighbors huddled in cloaks, tradesmen locking up their shops, and a printer's apprentice rushing a last-minute dispatch to a printshop. Congress had adjourned for the day, but tension lingered in the air like smoke while news from Boston, rumors of British troop movements, and talk of independence swirled in every tavern and parlor.

The City Tavern had been built in 1773 by a consortium of over fifty wealthy Philadelphians to serve as a grand and commodious meeting place for what was then the largest city in the American colonies. On May 20, 1774, more than two hundred city dwellers met at The City Tavern in response to the Boston Port Bill, forming a committee of correspondence to support Boston. This marked its emergence as a political rallying point.

As he turned onto Walnut Street, the glow from the City Tavern spilled into the night like a beacon. The building loomed sturdily, its windows lit with candles and hearth fires, casting golden light onto the street. Inside, voices rose in spirited debate. Delegates, merchants, and officers gathered over punch and roast duck, their breath steaming from the cold. A servant might swing open the door just long enough for a burst of laughter and pipe smoke to escape. The tavern yard was active even at this hour with horses being watered, messages being exchanged, and boots being scraped clean of mud. One stepped through the threshold into warmth and noise, where the scent of mulled cider and the hum of revolutionary conversation wrapped around one like a cloak. This was no ordinary evening. It was the heartbeat of a city on the edge of transformation.

Rutledge was to meet Silas Deane, a delegate from Connecticut, and John Jay from New York for dinner. Deane was a wealthy merchant and an attorney who served with Edward on the Board of War and Ordnance. Jay was born to a wealthy merchant family and was a fellow attorney, and also one of the few delegates about the same age as Rutledge.

Rutledge caught sight of Jay as he approached the entrance to the tavern. "Mr. Jay, it is good to see you this evening. Have you seen Mr. Deane yet?"

"No. He is always prompt, and I would wager that he is already sitting at a table waiting for us. Let us go in and find out."

Though he had known Jay since May, Edward naturally followed Jay's lead on many issues and had developed a strong relationship with the experienced lawyer and noted participant in the First Continental Congress.

The heavy oak door swung open to reveal a warm, golden glow spilling from candlelit sconces and roaring hearths that cast flickering shadows. The scent of roast goose, pipe smoke, and mulled cider mingled in the air as voices rose in spirited debate. Delegates, merchants, and officers gathered around tables strewn with papers and pewter mugs. A servant in livery hurried past with a tray, and for a moment, the tavern felt less like a public house and more like the nerve center of a nation being born.

The tavern was packed with people, at the bar and at tables. Jay spotted their eating companion, and Deane waved to Edward to join him at the table against the far wall just opposite a large fireplace.

"Good to see you, gentlemen," Deane remarked over the din. "I think the crowd is going to be larger as the night wears on. I don't want to stay too late as the morning Congress will come soon upon the morrow."

Edward had found that John Jay was a good listener who had keen insights into how delegates reacted to the latest news about the growing rebellion.

"I heard that your brother and Mr. Middleton left this morning to return to Carolina. Is anything wrong?" asked Jay.

"Nothing that a fifteen-day trip to the motherland won't cure. We're starting to write a new constitution and reforming our Provincial Assembly, and they wanted to be back home to be part of the process."

"That's not a problem that we have," said Deane. "We've been using the same Assembly we have had for years now. I'm just waiting for instructions that give me a little more room to speak more forcefully on independence."

Connecticut faced no urgent pressure to draft a new constitution because it continued to operate under its colonial Charter of 1662, which was broadly accepted by both patriots and moderates. Unlike other colonies grappling with legal voids after rejecting royal authority, Connecticut's charter was flexible enough to support self-governance without immediate revision. This continuity, however, masked deeper tensions—loyalist sympathies lingered in some towns, and debates over representation and religious establishment simmered beneath the surface. The absence of constitutional reform reflected both political conservatism and a pragmatic desire to maintain stability during wartime upheaval.

New York, on the other hand, faced a constitutional dilemma as its colonial assembly remained loyal to the Crown and refused to support the Continental Congress, leaving patriots without a legitimate legislative body. The newly formed Provincial Congress, created as an extralegal alternative, lacked clear authority and struggled to unify the state's fragmented political factions. War with Britain was escalating, yet New York had no formal framework for self-governance and debates raged over whether to declare independence before drafting a constitution. Amid this uncertainty, the colony operated in a legal limbo—caught between royal allegiance and revolutionary necessity, with no consensus on how to proceed.

Jay interjected "Not so fast, my friend. We cannot act too precipitously without knowing how we are to govern ourselves as a separate country."

"I didn't know we were already talking about independence here," Rutledge protested.

"There you go again about taking it slowly, Rutledge. You'll get there sure enough when the redcoats show up in Charleston," said Jay.

The three laughed uncomfortably, their conversation blending into the Tavern's buzz of liberty, no taxation, and independence. Soon, tankards of ale and fine fish, cornbread, and bowls of stew were at the table, and the talk went on for hours about revolution, government, and unity.

"Mr. Rutledge, why do you remain unable to bring yourself to our view that it is time to say goodbye to our British masters?"

"Mr. Deane, I am glad you ask such a fundamental question," he replied. First, my Assembly in South Carolina has only given me authority to seek a resolution with Britain, not to declare independence. Secondly, I do not agree with your opinion that we are in a master relationship with our Mother Country. We have the freedom to manage our own affairs without interference from the Royal Governor. Yes, we have differences occasionally, but we try hard to work out amiable ends."

"Now Mr. Rutledge, would you not agree that declaring independence is one avenue that could be described as seeking a resolution?" said Silas. "And, whether or not you agree with my statement about Britain being your master, I will give you wider berth on the question as you are far more experienced in dealing with slaves than I.

"Touche," interjected Jay. "I don't think it proper here to speak of slaves when the real issue is whether the English will treat us with the respect we deserve and that the three of us shall endeavor to maintain. I believe that independence may be our only option if they do not respect our point of view, but until we see specific rejection of all our entreaties, we should continue to seek common ground."

John Jay said, "Privately I oppose slavery on moral grounds. I think it is inconsistent with the ideals of liberty the colonies are fighting to uphold. However, I do not advocate for immediate abolition, and I will continue to own slaves

Rutledge fidgeted and then asked Silas, "Mr. Deane, I wanted to thank you for the great deed you performed at the First Continental Congress where you authored the first draft of the Continental Association. However, I have some concern that somehow the topic of the slave trade that was mentioned in the Association document might be brought up again for inclusion in the work we are doing now. As circumstances have changed dramatically since the adoption of the Association, I would ask that it not be included now."

Silas Deane did not publicly express strong views on slavery. His political writings from the period focused more on colonial governance and revolutionary strategy than on moral or social reform. Like many of his Connecticut contemporaries, he operated within a system that tolerated slavery.

"I just had a similar conversation with your brother about this same issue less than a week ago," said Silas. "I'll tell you precisely what I said to him. My goal here is to prepare our colonies to unite and throw the British out. I don't have any time for discussing or limiting the slavery that is practiced in your colony."

"I do not take offense at Mr. Deane's analogy," responded Edward, "but I do believe that we owe our brethren the obligation to articulate and make offerings to the Crown so that we cannot be accused of being ungrateful for the bountiful support that we have received over the last one-hundred and fifty years. But thank you for your support, Silas. My brother did not inform me that you had this conversation. It just proves that brothers can sometimes work at cross purposes. But I am sure that he also added that reconciliation remains a concern of our family and colony."

Silas Deane could hardly restrain himself. "Mr. Rutledge, the British have murdered innocent people, they have told us not to settle in parts of our own lands, they have tried to impose taxes without any consultation with us, they have engaged our Sons of Liberty and killed our people. What will it take before they arrest us and hang us for treason?"

"Now gentlemen, let's not spoil a perfectly good dinner by trying to solve all of our problems," Jay interjected.

"Please accept my apologies if I sounded a little blunt, Silas explained. "As Connecticut is like family to our friends in Massachusetts, I can react shortly at times. However, we must bear these actions in the context in which we engage in these solemn deliberations. As for me, I am comfortable with facing the hard facts that the Crown has pushed us to the point where liberty is our only route."

****

Connecticut and Massachusetts shared a close political alliance rooted in mutual support for the patriot cause and resistance to British authority. Connecticut's leaders expressed strong sympathy for Massachusetts following the Coercive Acts and the closure of Boston's port, with many towns forming committees of correspondence and passing resolutions in solidarity. When fighting broke out at Lexington and Concord, Connecticut swiftly mobilized over 3,000 militiamen to aid Massachusetts, underscoring their shared revolutionary commitment. Though Connecticut maintained its colonial charter and Massachusetts moved toward drafting a new constitution, both colonies coordinated military efforts and political messaging through the Continental Congress.

****

Rutledge paused as he gathered his thoughts to be as clear as he could with his friends. He said, "I recognize that my family and compatriots have not suffered the pain that you have. I pray that this will never be the case. Were redcoats to suddenly appear on the streets of Charleston, I would probably have a different reaction. I want to collaborate with you and the other delegates to find a path that will allow us to live in harmony with one another and Britain. Whatever that course may demand, I am comfortable to be a part of that solution."

"Hear, hear," Jay chimed in as the three friends raised their mugs and took long swigs of grog.

The delegates laughed among themselves about some of the idiosyncrasies of their fellow delegates and agreed that these meetings in Congress would be their fondest memories many years from then.

The City Tavern had become a central meeting place to find decent food, meet fellow delegates, and to relax after a long day at Congress. Tonight, the customers were of great cheer and boisterous. Even the meeting rooms on the second floor were filled with diners and revelers. Edward thought that he might find a use for them in the future.

A Frank Conversation About Slavery

Adjournment was near after another long debate on various expenses for the troops and munitions, when Edward heard a remark made by the Maryland delegate, Thomas Stone, that perked his ears. As the discussion hovered around the need for more powder to be provided for the Continental Army in Massachusetts, the Maryland delegate commented that the colonies should not be so bold in their actions such that the Crown would only conclude that they were acting as independent from the King. Those words appealed to Rutledge as the South Carolina delegates had been part of the more conservative faction urging Congress to go slow in causing a permanent rift with Britain. Edward mused that he and Stone, a delegate who was much closer to his age, might become kindred spirits. A dinner with Mr. Stone might begin to foster a closer relationship with the representative of Maryland.

When the gavel had been struck marking the end of the day's session, Edward moved to engage Stone as the delegates filed out. "Sir, I rather thought that your entreaty to the body today imploring more patience, and less ferocity was well said."

"Why thank you, Mr. Rutledge. It appears that some of our brethren are partial to sharp language, though, I believe more can be conveyed with a softer tone."

"I don't think we have had the opportunity to become well acquainted, and I would most enjoy your company for dinner this evening at the Tun Tavern so that we can discuss the matters of the day and see what else we have in common."

"I would be pleased to dine with you tonight. I shall meet you as soon as I write to my dear wife a letter to inform her of the deeds we have discussed over the last week."

"That sounds like a good idea. Regular correspondence with one's wife is a proposition that more gentlemen might endeavor to pursue. I find it helps to put into perspective the earnest work we perform. I will join you soon at the tavern." Rutledge bowed his head in recognition of the acceptance of his offer and turned to the door.

The grey skies of Philadelphia with the lingering daylight of late afternoon made for a somber walk to Mrs. Yard's boardinghouse.

Rutledge pressed the wrought iron thumb latch, went up to his room, and found his ink, pen, and paper to compose a message for Henrietta. He missed seeing his wife and would suggest to her that if her health improved, maybe in the spring she could join him. As he started to write, he thought about sharing with her some of the drudgery of the past week but decided instead to relate how much he missed Henrietta. Her fragile health had kept her in South Carolina, and the cold Pennsylvania weather would not help her now, but maybe when the weather improved, they could reunite.

After finishing the letter, Edward trudged down the stairs out to the street to meet his dinner companion. A November dusk had settled over Philadelphia like a woolen shawl, damp and heavy with river mist. Leaving Mrs. Yard's boardinghouse on Second Street, just above Walnut, the cobblestones glistened faintly under the flicker of oil lamps, and the air carried the mingled scents of hearth smoke, horse sweat, and distant brine. Rutledge passed the Pennsylvania Packet office, its windows aglow with lamplight and the rustle of newsprint, while a few late pedestrians hurried past in cloaks and tricorns, their breath visible in the chill. Heading east toward the river, the streets grew quieter, the buildings lower and more utilitarian—warehouses, cooperages, and the occasional tavern with shuttered windows and a faint glow within. The sound of gulls and the creak of rigging from Carpenter's Wharf signaled one's approach to the waterfront.

Tun Tavern stood near Water Street and Tun Alley, its stout timber frame nestled close to the wharf, where barrels and crates were stacked showing the trade in the neighborhood. The tavern's windows spilled warm candlelight onto the street, and inside, the hum of conversation rose, as sailors, merchants, and militiamen gathered over ale and beefsteak. On this evening, the air was charged with pride, as just days earlier, the Continental Congress had commissioned Samuel Nicholas to raise the first battalions of Marines. A regular patron of the Tun Tavern, Nicholas could be found in the rear hall recruiting men to become the first American Marines. As Rutledge stepped through the door, the scent of roasted meat and pipe smoke enveloped him, and the clatter of tankards and boots on floorboards reminded him that revolutions were not only forged in Congress but in places like this—where men gathered, argued and dreamt of liberty.

One could hear the chatter of the tavern without opening the front door as local businessmen, sailors, and merchants, in addition to the delegates, shared stories and a tankard. Rutledge looked around to see if he could find Thomas Stone, but not locating him, he found a table against the interior wall. Rutledge was not accustomed to dining in such a public place, but he had become curious about the camaraderie he was witnessing. He waited patiently for his companion while watching the many men with loud voices and hearty laughter share the friendliness of the moment. The aroma of the open hearth mixed with the fragrant tobacco smoke eased his temperament as the conversations waxed and waned. His mind wandered back to the London coffeehouse he frequented while studying law when he noticed the broad brimmed hat of Thomas Stone.

Rutledge rose from his seat and casually waved to Stone who promptly acknowledged his invitation and weaved through the crowd to join him. "I am so glad that you could join me for some conversation. With all the noise, I hope we can hear each other, and enjoy some light nourishment."

Edward caught the eye of a server and asked for two mugs of cider.

"I am glad to join you, but I cannot expect that the victuals offered at this establishment will ever come to equal the fine gourmet that I am accustomed to at *Habre de Venture*, one of the finest plantations in Charles County, Maryland," replied Stone as he took a seat and sat ramrod straight. "You should come visit when events of the day return to normal."

"You are probably accurate in your dining appraisal, Mr. Stone. I was mildly surprised when I ate here on an earlier occasion with Messrs. Dickinson and Ward, although I would fully accept your premise that our home cooking is far better than any we will find in Philadelphia."

"Please call me Thomas. Such are the sacrifices we must embrace for continuing the essential work of the colonies. I have found it challenging to establish personal connections with many of our colleagues, thus I appreciate your invitation to dine."

"Thomas, it would please me if you would call me Edward. My brother John, who I am sure you heard during earlier deliberations, has just departed with the other South Carolina delegates to work on fashioning the new government we will employ in our colony at the behest of Congress. Since their departure, I have been seeking some other colleagues to engage."

Thomas Stone said, "We, in Maryland, have not yet developed a government separate from the Crown. Our assembly remains with the desire that we can find some accommodation with the King, although I daresay that the latest Royal proclamation which he has made has given me some pause."

Maryland patriots began building a government independent of British control by organizing extralegal conventions and committees that gradually assumed authority from the proprietary regime. Although the royal governor remained nominally in place, real power shifted to the Maryland Convention, which coordinated militia mobilization, enforced non-importation agreements, and managed civil affairs. Local observation and safety committees sprang up across the colony, linking towns and counties in a network of revolutionary governance. These bodies laid the foundation for Maryland's eventual declaration of independence.

Rutledge said, "South Carolinians have also been wary of acting too belligerently and, thus, ruining any chance at reconciliation. The amount of rancor that the Crown has caused troubles me also, but we continue to seek common, middle ground as I sense is agreeable to you. Personally, I would be happy to leave for our plantations, allow us to strengthen our colonies, build economically solid communities, and raise our children."

"I would like to buy us a drink to toast to that happy ending. I would be pleased to return to my law office, allow my brother to keep the plantation healthy, and support my children so they can learn the law and the farm and have a brighter future."

"Do you think this can occur in our lifetime, Edward?"

"If the King could just see that we are a financial asset for the realm as opposed to trying to rule every facet of our lives, I think our wishes could be fulfilled, but how do we get there? That is the issue."

Edward waved to a server to bring them more cider.

"I am curious about your plantation. Should I assume that you grow bountiful and choice harvests of tobacco? South Carolina plantations primarily raise rice and indigo. Our servants are made of good stock to plant and harvest our crops. I understand that many performed these same tasks before they came to us. I cannot remember hearing that tobacco was cultivated in Africa."

Edward greeted the server who brought them libations and took an order for food.

Stone eyed Rutledge carefully. No one at the Congress had ever raised the slave question so matter-of-factly in conversation or comments. "No. The natives of this new world many generations ago taught us about tobacco, but we have been the pioneers growing and refining it as a cash crop that has allowed us to build and maintain our fortunes. Over the years, we have improved our methods and produce a fine product for sale to our French merchants."

Edward paused and said, "Pardon my forwardness, but I did not intend my question to make you uncomfortable and certainly did not want to imply that slaves could teach you anything. Our slaves are just better suited to endure our humid and hot environment as their temperament and fitness are well suited for the hard hours of work to make our plantations work economically."

"I did not take offense. I was just surprised by the nature of your comments. My law practice dominates my time at home, and I leave the day-to-day work and supervision of the plantation to my brother. Sometimes, the conversation with delegates from Boston and, even Virginia, about slavery is often scented with the language of abolition. I don't appreciate being lured into conversations that have no business here," Stone said.

"I could not agree more strongly. I came here to talk about the relationship of our colonies to the Crown, and yet, I sense from the idle chatter that more items than liberty or reconciliation are on the agenda. The enormous task of uniting our colonies on a joint reply to the Crown on our rights should not be jeopardized by talk of slavery or the slave trade."

"Rutledge, we do have a lot in common. Your point of view on this issue is not only shared by me, but I have also spoken with other business leaders. They are from colonies who have few slaves but, nonetheless, profit from our business habits. I think you might be surprised how many delegates feel the same as us on these matters. Hancock, Ellery, Hopkins. They all profit, but they'll never talk about it openly"

The server brought the men food that included a thick soup with a basket of wheat bread and cornbread and refills for their tankards of cider.

"Thank you for your candor. That is good news to my ears, and I appreciate that this topic has made sense to more delegates than just us. Our economies make the colonies vibrant and attractive investments for England and us. Our mercantile exchanges will continue to make life comfortable if the other colonies reckon with the reality that the serene slave life, which people often miss, is only as strong as our oversight to make sure that slave rebellions do not wreak havoc in our lives and against our women."

****

Slave revolts in Maryland prior to 1775 were rare and often suppressed before they could fully materialize, but they reflected deep resistance to bondage. One notable incident occurred in 1739 in Prince George's County, where a planned uprising involving over 200 enslaved individuals was uncovered before it could be carried out. It was thwarted by a loyal slave who informed his master. The plot's discovery led to heightened surveillance and harsher restrictions on enslaved people throughout the colony. While Maryland did not experience large-scale revolts like those in South Carolina or Virginia, these early conspiracies revealed the persistent undercurrent of defiance and the precarious balance of fear and control that defined slavery in the colony.

****

"We have been fortunate in Maryland that no uprisings have occurred at our plantations, but one cannot forget the death and fear that emerged many years ago at the Chesapeake Rebellion in Virginia. We are only one disgruntled black slave orator away from it happening again."

"I remember being told about that. The Stono Rebellion in South Carolina is my stark reminder of why we need to adopt strict measures to keep these events far from our homes. The economy of our colony rests on strict obedience to the law of God."

Thomas leaned forward in his chair and scooped up a mouthful of soup while holding a crust of bread in his hand and said "I am of the belief that no human process can elevate the black man to equality with a white man. And even if it could come to pass, would you want him at your table or mingling with you in a store? Would you trust them to serve on a town committee or to bear arms to protect our families? I doubt that you would, and I doubt if any of the other delegates here would welcome that eventuality or admit to it publicly. Slavery is not evil but a great good. A blessing creating a better life for Africans than they ever could aspire to in their homeland. So why should anyone be blamed? The slave traders should be thanked"

Edward said, "I think you have splendidly hit the core of the issue. In the South, we are willing to speak the truth out loud and to face facts as they are. Negroes were destined to be the engine of our economy because we are honest and know how to create a financially strong system that benefits our colony and our families."

Edward and Thomas settled back in the chairs as they continued to talk and savor the soup using the bread to mop the bottom of their bowls. The banter of family and plantation life filled the air as they enjoyed the next course of pan-seared brook trout and braised pork medallions, with cheese on the side. As the light from the fireplace and oil lamps continued to cut through the haze in the room, the atmosphere in the spacious room slowed down, and the crowd began to thin as people went home to their families.

"Thank you for a fine evening of conversation, Thomas. The next time we have dinner, maybe you could join me at Mrs. Yard's house. She makes a fine dinner."

Thomas said, "Miss Mary, at my boardinghouse, puts on a credible meal also. I trust you will join me soon in another fine evening of dinner and conversation, sir."

Stone and Rutledge had enjoyed the evening and retired to their respective lodgings. The next day would bring another session that would start at 9AM under the gavel of John Hancock from Massachusetts. Hancock was known to profit financially from the slave trade and to use the proceeds to support the patriots' efforts. Rutledge smiled as he walked slowly down dusty Second Street admiring the oil lampposts that cast a slight glow in the starry night.

As positive as Thomas Stone and Edward Rutledge were about slavery, not everyone agreed with their arguments.

What Does a Slave Know?

The alley behind Mrs. Yard's boardinghouse was littered with empty crates and a broken-down dray, but not a soul in sight. Next to the rear door was a Philadelphia cart that her indentured servant used to bring produce and grains from the market. Once night fell after sundown, Pompey exited the house and began a slow walk down to Market Street. As he moved, he peered at the backs of homes that were not so elegant as Mrs. Yard's. Pompey thought to himself that Master Rutledge had a very comfortable stay in Philadelphia compared to other homes, but none were even close to genteel living like Broad Street in Charleston.

Suddenly, a young man appeared from Market Street entering into the dark alley that caused him to swallow hard and tighten his jaw until he recognized the figure of Cato, the valet for Richard Henry Lee. Pompey raised his hands and motioned Cato to come closer, but he also put his finger to his lips indicating not to say a word out loud. The laws in Philadelphia were much more forgiving than in Charleston, but Pompey knew when he returned to South Carolina, he would need to change the habits he had acquired in Philadelphia.

"I thought that was you, Pompey. We got busy cleaning up after dinner that Master Lee had with John Adams. That man sure do like to talk. Seems to me that he thinks he is the smartest man in America!"

"After Master Rutledge had a meeting with him at your place, he came back muttering to himself about that Adams man. How long do you think we'll be here?" said Pompey.

"Hard telling. The way Mr. Lee talks to Mr. Adams I guess that we'll probably see the snow melt before we leave. "Have you heard of any other valets here but us? I heard that the delegates from Maryland, Chase and Stone, had hands here."

"Oh, yeah. The South Carolina men all came with black valets," said Pompey. "You know Caesar, and a few of the other men brought some. I do remember that Master Edward spoke with that Stone delegate from Maryland, and I know his valet, Bob. Maybe we need to do some more checking. I'm sure that you know about all the free men who have no masters."

In 1775, free black men in Philadelphia formed a small but resilient community within a city that was both a hub of revolutionary activity and a place where slavery persisted. Of the roughly one-thousand five hundred black residents at the time, only about one hundred were free, yet their presence was increasingly visible in trades, domestic service, and maritime labor. Some worked as skilled artisans, coopers, or sailmakers, contributing to the city's bustling economy, especially along the waterfront. Others found employment in taverns, stables, and households, navigating a society that offered limited rights but occasional opportunities for autonomy. Their lives were shaped by a precarious balance, free in name, yet subject to racial prejudice, legal restrictions, and the constant threat of being kidnapped or re-enslaved.

Despite these challenges, free black men in Philadelphia began to assert themselves socially and politically, often through church communities, mutual aid networks, and informal education. The city's significant Quaker population, many of whom opposed slavery on religious grounds, provided some support and moral advocacy, laying early groundwork for abolitionist efforts. In April 1775, the Pennsylvania Abolition Society was founded, the first of its kind in America, signaling a growing awareness of the contradiction between revolutionary ideals and the reality of bondage. Though their numbers were small, free black men in Philadelphia stood at the edge of a transformative era, poised between oppression and the promise of liberty, contributing quietly but meaningfully to the revolutionary spirit that surrounded them.

Cato said, "That idea of free Black men shocks me to my soul. They don't seem to be any different than us, yet they walk around like they own the place. How did they get that freedom? I heard Mr. Lee say that the day will come when all of us will have that freedom. Do you suppose that we will ever see that day?"

"I don't count on anything happening except the sun rising in the morning and setting at night," said Pompey. "They all talk about getting freedom from the King, while they don't say anything about freedom for us!"

Pompey continued, "I hear Master Edward, and his brother talk about the King making slaves of the colonies. I just shake my head because I think they have no idea about slavery like we do. No one is ever going to tell Master Edward when to get out of bed or fetch some water. These white folks don't have any idea how lucky they are. Can you imagine that Master Richard would ever clean out the privy? He wouldn't even know how to start or where to put the mess."

"I think the day will be far off in the future before we see any freedom. You are right about how well off these masters are. In the meantime, I'm keeping my head down and my mouth shut," said Cato.

"Good advice for staying alive and not get sold to someone who is mean. I was talking to a free man the other day, and he said that he one day saw two men just sneak up from behind a black man, threw a potato sack over his head, and hauled him away like he was a rug that needed a good beating."

"Didn't anyone try to help him?"

"Of course not," said Pompey. "Not a soul. There was hardly anyone else on the street when it happened, and they certainly were not going to ask a black man if I saw anything that was wrong. They just threw him into a wagon and drove off even though he was screaming. I guess people around here are not too concerned about how a black man is treated. Cato, white people don't even think that we are humans, and that is why it is so easy for them to think of us as property. They think that we are more stupid than the dumbest white person, that we have no morals, and that our temperaments make us well suited to be slaves. Heaven's sakes if we would have an original idea."

"Sometimes I wonder what goes through the heads of white people. They act like we don't exist except when they want something done. I don't understand how everything seems to be fine in Boston, and they have no slaves. Why can't the South do the same thing?

"How can you say that nothing is going wrong in Boston. The British are killing people in Massachusetts."

"I know that, Pomp. I was meaning that, before the British started to be hard on Boston, all the men and women there seemed to be living a good life. They didn't need slaves to tend their fields or wash their clothes or cook their dinners."

"They may not have black slaves to do their work for them, but they had other white people, who were almost treated like slaves, to serve food, clean the floors, and do the work for them."

"Why do some white people hate us black folks so much? I have never done any harm to them, yet even white folks who have never met me or tried to know who I am, feel like they can order me around or just be hard on me."

Most white men, north and south, harbored deep hostility toward African blacks, shaped by a plantation economy that depended on enslaved labor which engendered a pervasive fear of rebellion. South Carolina had tolerated a Black majority, especially in the rice-growing area close to the coast, which intensified white anxieties about control and survival. Memories of the 1739 Stono Rebellion, when enslaved Africans rose up violently, still haunted the white population, leading to harsh laws, slave patrols, and a culture of suspicion. This fear, combined with racist beliefs about African inferiority, and the desire to preserve economic dominance, fueled a climate where hatred was not just emotional but institutional, embedded in the very laws and customs of the plantation economy and colonial society.

"I think that most white people don't even like to think that us black people even exist. We are supposed to be invisible until called on to be at their service."

"I heard Master Rutledge talking about Dr. Franklin this morning. He must be a great man because people always have nice things to say about him."

"He must as old as Moses. Master Lee says he invented electricity. I don't even know what he is talking about. He says that he captured lightning in a bottle. What does that mean?"

In June 1752, Benjamin Franklin conducted his famous kite experiment in Philadelphia to prove that lightning was a form of electricity, a bold and dangerous endeavor that would become legendary. With his son, William, assisting, Franklin flew a silk kite during a thunderstorm, attaching a metal key to the wet hemp string and holding the dry silk portion to insulate himself. As the storm raged, the key attracted ambient electrical charge from the storm clouds, causing sparks to jump when Franklin touched it, thereby confirming the electrical nature of lightning. This experiment did not "discover" electricity, which was already known, but it demonstrated dramatically that lightning and electricity were manifestations of the same natural phenomenon, paving the way for the invention of the lightning rod and advancing the science of atmospheric electricity.

"I'm not sure, but it must be important. I don't know about you, but I am afraid of lightning. I once saw a tree bigger than a house split in half. Now that's power, but I can't see that fitting in a bottle.

"Maybe that's going to be a secret weapon that the patriots are going to use against the British," said Cato causing Pompey to laugh and pushing Cato into the darkness of the alley.

"I had better get back before the landlady locks me out. Always good talking with you, when we don't need to worry about what the master overhears.

"Sure is. Keep your ears open to any talk of the masters or if you see any black valets. We can expand our little group if no one knows. Good night."

EDWARD SEES JOHN ADAMS IN ACTION

Congress had created a committee of five consisting of Edward Rutledge, John Adams, George Wythe, Samuel Chase, and John Penn to discuss letters between General George Washington and General Phillip Schuyler. The subject matter was on the basic outline of the Northern Department military operation.

Edward viewed the committee as another avenue he could use to discuss his concerns about slavery with John Adams and George Wythe, two of the most powerful delegates in Congress. What Rutledge did not know was that Adams, Wythe, and Chase had been in communication on other matters and had a personal relationship with each other.

The meeting was called by John Adams to be held in one of the upstairs meeting places following the Congressional session that day. Edward, Wythe, Chase, and Penn arrived in the room at the same time.

"Mister Wythe and Mister Chase, it is good to work with you." said Rutledge.

"Likewise, Mr. Rutledge," said George Wythe.

"And I as well," said Samuel Chase.

"We have not been assigned together to any committees before today, and I am glad we are allowed that opportunity today," said Edward.

"I think we should wait for John before we start the meeting. I wonder what the cause of his lateness could be," said Wythe.

"While we are waiting for Mr. Adams, I would like to raise another subject with all of you," said Edward Rutledge.

"If it is not too lengthy, maybe we can make good use of this time," said Chase.

"Thank you, sir. I don't need to go into detail for you to understand that I am unsure about my readiness to declare independence. I believe that we need to have some agreement about how we shall govern the colonies as a collective association before we call for our independence. I am also concerned about the need to engage allies such as Spain and France to support our independence campaign."

American colonists had intensified diplomatic efforts to enlist France and Spain in their struggle against Britain, recognizing that foreign support was essential to sustain the revolution. The Continental Congress had already established the Committee of Secret Correspondence in late 1775 to initiate covert communications with sympathetic European powers. By early 1776, Silas Deane was dispatched to France to secure arms and supplies, laying the groundwork for broader alliances. John Adams, meanwhile, proposed a commercial treaty with France that would avoid entangling military commitments but offer mutual trade benefits, a concept later formalized in the Model Treaty. These overtures reflected a strategic shift: colonists were no longer merely resisting British policies but actively seeking international recognition and support for an independent American republic.

"I have been fully knowledgeable about your position, and I desire that you keep an open mind for the positions of others of us who feel the time is ripe now," said Wythe.

Chase added, "I recognize your concern. I have been speaking with another member of the Maryland delegation about this very point, and we have decided that we should be pushing for the establishment of a committee to make recommendations along those ideas."

"Thank you for your consideration. I believe this will address the point of view of other delegates."

"Well, that was direct and easy. I wonder what is wrong with John. It is not like him to be late."

"I am sure it is important business, however, there was one other matter that I wanted to discuss."

"Well, get to it young man," said Wythe.

"Yes, sir. My concern is that when the Continental Association was created at our first Continental Congress, we included some language about limiting the slave trade. I want to suggest to you that whatever declaration on independence may be proposed, we should not have similar language on slavery. Many things have changed since last year, and I believe that if we seek to have unanimity on a declaration, the language should be focused on changing our relationship with Britain and not on outside issues like the slave trade. I have spoken to many other delegates who believe as I that we need to remain focused. The southern colonies depend on the plantation economy to provide wealth to America, and if the slave trade issue should come up, I do not know how we could support such a document."

George Wythe said, "Mr. Rutledge, thank you for your candor. This is not an issue that we will resolve before John Adams arrives today, but I will say that many members in the Virginia delegation feel as strongly on this issue as you do. Candidly, other members, including myself, are supportive of the language from the Continental Association. Personally, I believe that under the law of nature, all men are born free, and yet, I own slaves and depend on them to provide me with the work necessary to maintain my circumstances. Frankly, the issue of the slave trade does not belong in the same conversation with independence, and trying to adjudicate one issue while being focused on another is a distraction that we cannot afford. I agree that we will need unanimity to succeed, but this will not come through a subcommittee meeting after a Congress session. I will take your thoughts under advisement when the time arrives where we shall have debate."

John Adams wearily entered the room and said, "I apologize for my tardiness, but every delegate seems to want a piece of me, either for advice or abuse."

"I doubt if you should receive much abuse that can harm you," said Wythe, "You have a thick skin. You will withstand many a man's hardest criticism."

"Has the group reviewed the correspondence, so I can continue to my next appointment?"

"I am sorry, Mr. Adams. I think that you have the letters. We have had nothing to review. In the meantime, we have had an interesting conversation that was led by young Edward Rutledge about the need for a committee to discuss how the colonies should relate to one another, if independence is declared."

"Well, Mr. Rutledge. I don't see you wasting any time in getting your viewpoint out in front of people," said Adams. "The point you raise has been discussed, and I believe that you will see action in that area soon."

"John, we were discussing the need for unanimity of the colonies to support independence, of which, I am sure you will agree," said George Wythe.

"Mr. Rutledge, I am so glad to hear that you are finally coming around to our logic. Thank you," said John Adams.

"Sir, I do not wish to be confusing, but Mr. Wythe pointed out one of the items that we discussed, but the other issue that I feel strongly about, he omitted. I remain firm in the belief that reconciliation should not be thrown out so easily," said Edward."

"Well, which way is it going to be? I hear that you stand with independence and then you wish to drag your feet. I don't think reconciliation was on our agenda for this afternoon, so why don't we focus on these letters that are the source of our meeting.

"Edward, we can talk about this other subject later."

"Why, of course."

Adams had a puzzled look on his face as they reviewed the correspondence back and forth between Washington to Schuyler. The meeting was adjourned in about one and a half hours as they sorted out whether Schuyler had responded meaningfully to the instructions he was given. Adams volunteered to write up a report for the committee, as it appeared no one else was ready to volunteer. The delegates embarked quickly into the night.

The opportunity to speak with Adams came and went before Edward had figured out how to approach him. In some ways, Adams reminded Edward of his brother, not in terms of his politics, but in his manner. Edward always deferred to John, not because he was asked, but because he thought that his contribution had already been represented. Adams was clearly more radical than John, but Adams had that quiet arrogance that he saw in his brother. The next time Ned has a chance to speak with John Adams, he needed to plan carefully to have more confidence.

THE KING SLAMS THE DOOR

The conservatives, led by John Dickinson of Pennsylvania, had advocated for reconciliation with Britain. He was supported by John and Edward Rutledge from South Carolina and John Jay of New York, as they aimed at finding a compromise between rebellion and loyalty to the Crown. After the agonizing bloodshed at Lexington and Concord and the brutal battles of Bunker Hill and Breed's Hill, the radicals had been more vociferous in their call for independence while the moderates argued that the new military arrangement might make King George and Parliament more open to reconciliation.

John Adams was adamant about the uselessness of another plea to the King. He spoke with passion and fierceness, "Powder and artillery are the efficacious, sure and infallible conciliatory measures we can adopt." John Adams and his allies in Congress remonstrated that the effort for reconciliation with the Crown was a waste of time, while the moderates readily approved a peace offering.

But Dickinson was cool and determined that another attempt should be made to engage the King and allow him to make a gentlemanly response to the earnest pleas of the colonists. Dickinson declared, "We, your Majesty's faithful subjects... beseech your Majesty to prevent the further destruction of your devoted subjects in North America."

Adams believed that to respond directly to Dickinson about how he disliked this approach to solving all the issues that the colonies were having with Britain would be a mistake. Adams knew not to insult him in person, as Dickinson was a more skilled orator than he, so Adams took his enmity home with him and decided to do what he did best, write a letter to lower his level of hostility by venting it through his pen.

Britain deployed spies in Philadelphia to monitor revolutionary sentiment and report on the activities of the Continental Congress and local patriot leaders. Merchants like Gilbert Barkly, who had ties to British commercial interests, secretly corresponded with officials in London, offering intelligence on colonial resistance and political developments. These agents blended into city life, using personal relationships and business dealings to gather information without drawing suspicion. Their reports helped the Crown assess colonial unity and plan countermeasures, though there was also a growing patriot surveillance network that made espionage increasingly risky.

Unfortunately for Adams, a private letter that he had written was intercepted by a Loyalist spy and disseminated to the delegates in hopes of causing havoc in the Congress. In the letter, Adams referred to Dickinson as "a piddling genius whose fame has been trumpeted so loudly, it has given a silly cast to our whole doings." The support that Dickinson received from the delegates after the disclosure of the letter temporarily embarrassed Adams, and the delegates decided to move forward with the reconciliation letter.

Congress created a committee of five members to draft the reconciliation document that became the Olive Branch Petition. After many objections over the wording of the document from the delegates, Thomas Jefferson and John Dickinson were added to the committee to revise the letter. Jefferson, known as an excellent wordsmith, produced a new draft which Dickinson thoroughly edited, much to the chagrin of Jefferson. Congress approved the final draft, and it was delivered to London by two emissaries, Arthur Lee and Richard Penn, the grandson of William Penn. Lee was the brother of Richard Henry Lee, delegate of Virginia, an agent for colonial affairs, living in London, and a business partner in the Lee family business selling tobacco raised in Virginia.

In part, the petition stated, "Your Majesty's Ministers, persevering in their measures, and proceeding to open hostilities for enforcing them, have compelled us to arm in our own defense, and have engaged us in a controversy so peculiarly abhorrent to the affections of your still faithful Colonists, that when we consider whom we must oppose in this contest, and if it continues, what may be the consequences, our own particular misfortunes are accounted by us only as parts of our distress."

The petition assured the King and Parliament that there was no intent to dissolve the union with Britain or to enforce separation by taking up arms. Finally, the petition stated that the colonists did not fight for glory or for conquest. Even though war preparations were underway, the petition allowed the colonies to claim they had exhausted peaceful options. This was crucial for gaining future international support, especially from France. By appealing directly to the King and blaming Parliament and his ministers, the petition positioned the colonies as loyal subjects seeking justice, not traitors.

The King's court in Britain functioned as the ceremonial and political nucleus of royal authority, centered around King George III and his advisors. While Parliament had adjourned in May, the royal court continued to operate through the Privy Council and various ministries, managing domestic affairs and responding to the escalating colonial rebellion. The King, increasingly resolute in his stance against the American insurgents, relied on ministers like Lord North to craft policy and coordinate military strategy, while court rituals and patronage networks reinforced loyalty among the aristocracy. Though largely symbolic in some respects, the court remained a vital engine of governance, diplomacy, and imperial command during a moment of growing crisis.

Unbeknownst to the patriots, King George had already begun to view the colonists as irksome and had decided to send an ultimatum to them. The Proclamation of Rebellion was drafted by the Colonial Secretary, Lord Dartmouth, and was ready for the King's review in August when the Olive Branch Petition landed in London. King George's proclamation was defiant. The colonists' petition would not be accepted, in fact, it was ignored, and King George did not intend to read it, let alone entertain any thoughts of compromise. The King declared the colonies were in open revolt against the British Crown because of their battles in Concord and Bunker Hill, and he directed the military to suppress them, using all available resources. In addition, he began planning for foreign mercenaries to be engaged in the colonies and told Parliament that he would accept any proposals to support military efforts to punish the colonies.

The Proclamation of 1775 stated that the colonies were fomented by a "desperate conspiracy" of leaders who claimed to be loyal to the King but were insincere. He believed that the goal of the colonies' leaders was to create an "independent empire". King George stated that these traitors to his country should be brought to justice, and that all loyal subjects of the King should aid and assist in bringing the colonists to the bar. Further, he wanted all loyal citizens of England to inform the Crown of all the conspiracies and attempts against Britain.

Two months later, Lord Fredrick North, the Prime Minister of England, drafted a statement for George III to be read at Parliament that drew heavily from the King's proclamation. After hours of debate, those members of Parliament who spoke up for the colonists warned the King that issuing such a proclamation would force the patriots to move toward independence.

Weeks later, the colonists learned that King George had rejected reconciliation. Support for the American colonies within Parliament was limited and deeply divided, with conciliatory proposals like Lord North's earlier resolution failing to gain traction amid rising calls for military suppression. Though a few members, including Edmund Burke and Charles James Fox, urged compromise and recognition of colonial grievances, the prevailing mood favored declaring Massachusetts in rebellion and preparing for war. The case for reconciliation was squashed.

None of the patriots rejoiced at the news of the Proclamation from King George, but the radicals could not hide their renewed enthusiasm to press the conservatives and moderates to reevaluate their position. Before the King responded to the Olive Branch Petition, Congress had adopted their own Declaration on the Causes and Necessity of Taking Up Arms that provided a rationale for arming the colonies against British coercion. The atmosphere in Congress had taken a decided turn toward independence and moderates and conservatives, like John and Edward Rutledge needed to reevaluate their positions.

Slaves Not Surprised by King George's Rejection

Bob was walking down the alley on a clear cool October night behind Second Street hoping that he might find Pompey because of the news he had just heard. Pompey wasn't at the back door to Mrs. Yard's house, and Bob did not want to linger much because he had no desire to court any trouble from the neighbors.

It was dangerous for black valets, many of whom were enslaved or indentured, to gather and converse at night due to the pervasive fear among white residents of insurrection and disorder. The memory of slave revolts had left a lasting imprint on the urban psyche, and any sign of organized communication among black individuals was viewed with suspicion. City ordinances and informal patrols often restricted the movement of enslaved people after dark, and gatherings could be interpreted as conspiratorial, leading to harsh punishment or imprisonment. Even free black men risked being accused of inciting rebellion or violating curfews, especially if they were seen speaking with slaves.

Bob kept moving down the alleyway and was almost to High Street when he heard his name, "Bob? Is that you?"

Recognizing Pompey's voice, he turned and casually walked back over to the door of Mrs. Yards past the barrels that lined the alleyway. "It's me, Mister Pompey. I thought that I wasn't going to see you, but I am glad you're here."

"What's the latest news? Did Mr. Stone give you the night off?"

"No, but I do have news. Mr. Lee was having dinner with Master Stone and Samuel Chase, and a courier came for Mr. Chase. He received a letter that said the King rejected the peace offering. He called it an Olive Tree or something."

"I think he was referring to the Olive Branch Petition."

"It matters not to me. Apparently, the King didn't even read what was sent. He was so mad that he had already made up his mind to call all of us criminals and was going to send foreigners to take us down a peg," said Bob.

"Master Rutledge is not going to like that news. I heard him talking to Mr. Stone recently that the Olive Branch Petition was the one last offer that the patriots would send, and if it wasn't accepted, it could change the fate for all the colonies. Did you hear anything else from Mr. Stone or Mr. Chase?"

"Mr. Chase said something like 'You now can see why I opposed this petition from the start' and he said that he wasn't surprised by the reaction of the King. Was this petition important, Pompey?"

"Important? That may be the last chance that the colonies had to prevent the King from sending his fiercest warriors over here and destroying us. I think that judgement day is coming soon."

****

The revolutionary fervor of 1775 heightened anxieties about loyalty, control, and social order. As white Philadelphians debated liberty and self-governance, many remained deeply committed to maintaining racial hierarchies and suppressing any perceived threat from the Black population. Valets, who often moved between elite households and political circles, were uniquely positioned to overhear sensitive conversations, making any nighttime interactions seem doubly dangerous to a society obsessed with secrecy and surveillance. In this climate, even casual conversations among black valets could be construed as subversive, prompting swift and often brutal responses from authorities or private citizens determined to preserve the status quo.

"Can you imagine what would be the masters' reaction if we pleaded with them to not work us so much? There would be a lot a whippings, I'm sure. And then they might make an example of one of those who did the asking. What do you mean when you said that judgement day was coming, Pomp?"

"Bob, the people who are our masters are on opposite sides of the question. Should we declare independence or do we ask for the King to understand our problems better? It looks like the King has indicated what side of the question he takes. I remember months ago, Master Edward and others spent a great deal of time writing, trying to put together the perfect letter to the King. It sounds like the King didn't like the letter."

"Didn't like it?" asked Bob. "He didn't even read it. The more we watch the masters meet and talk and plan, I think to myself, maybe we slaves should be planning for ourselves. We are accused of doing that sort of thing every day, and we get trouble from that. But maybe we should work to cooperate among ourselves."

"Bob, now you are talking crazy. I don't want to hear that again while we are here with our masters. Our families and friends are hundreds of miles from here. Even if we did do what you say, who do we know who could help us? The free men who nervously walk through the streets of Philadelphia? Bob, that is crazy, and I don't want you to mention it again because you'll get us all in trouble, and it won't improve anything for us.

"I'm sorry, Mr. Pompey. I just got carried away with the thoughts that the masters are using about their Olive Tree Petition. I promise not to do that again."

"A lot of unhappy people will not sleep well tonight. I am sure that the entire town will know this truth before the cock crows."

"What do you think is going to happen next?"

"That's one good thing about being a slave, it's not my problem to come up with that answer." said Pompey as they both had a good laugh.

"I don't think there will much laughing tomorrow," said Pompey. "We need to be on our best slave attitude, whatever they want, you do it, and smile. No back talk or opinions. Personally, this might not be bad for us because it looks like the die is cast, and that means there will probably be war which brings chaos and change. Who knows? Maybe that will create a situation when we can run free. Maybe the colonists will let us fight on their side and then free us when the battle is over. Whatever the circumstances, I can't imagine that it will be any worse off for us than we are now."

"You're such a wise man, Pompey. Why don't they make you a delegate!"

"And who would I represent? The Black Servants of America?"

They both had another laugh and decided it was probably better to be found at home, as opposed to being absent, when their masters learned the truth about the King.

Slaves Take A Shine to Knowing their Masters

The boots of Edward Rutledge were easy to keep shiny because Rutledge very seldom walked in places that would cause them to become blemished. Nonetheless, Pompey would always receive a pleasant smile and a lot of congratulations whenever Rutledge could see his face in the shine. Pompey was buffing the tops with a special rag that he had used for a long time when he started thinking of his friends, Cato and Caesar, who were the valets for Richard Henry and Francis Lightfoot Lee, respectively. He remembered a story that Caesar had told him back in August when the three were in the alley behind Mrs. Yard's boardinghouse.

They had traded stories of the latest gossip they heard, when Caesar told this story about Francis Lee, earlier that week.

"Mr. Lee was scolding me again on how his boots didn't shine as much as they should. 'I must have these boots reflect the beauty of my knowledge,' Francis said. 'They must be shined before I can go to Congress today,'"

Caesar started polishing his master's boots before dawn, working in a small, dimly lit room. He would carefully inspect the leather for scuffs and wear, then heat a mixture of tallow and wax over a low flame, applying it with a cloth in slow, circular motions until the boots gleamed with a deep, black sheen. His hands, calloused from daily labor, moved with practiced precision. buffing the toe, smoothing the heel, and ensuring the buckles or latchets were spotless and aligned. Though silent and deferential in his task, he was intimately familiar with the rhythms of his master Francis's life, preparing the boots not just for walking, but for riding, visiting, and commanding presence in the social world of Virginia's planter elite.

Caesar handed the boots over to his master, who smiled slightly and informed Caesar that, "I am making a speech today at Congress and I want to say that my boots reflect the light of liberty, and so our cause must be reflected. I will walk into Congress and people will say, 'There goes a man of distinction' and Caesar thought to himself, there goes a man who doesn't know how to shine his own boots.

They had a good laugh at their masters when they were not in earshot, and they all knew that they could not be too careful in this behavior.

In addition to the funny boot story, there was also the information they had heard about a failed negotiating ploy that the delegates had tried that landed with all the grace of a sinking stone.

"Mr. Rutledge was not very happy tonight," said Pompey. "The delegates are now forced to deal with a new reality. There will be no reconciliation. There will be only war."

Caesar chimed in by saying, "Mr. Rutledge and Mr. Dickinson were mentioned by Master Francis, but it would be impolite to report exactly what he said."

"Please do tell us the exact words they used so I won't forget."

"Mr. Francis Lee referred to Edward Rutledge as a muddle brained ninny hammer. And then went on to say that Mr. Dickinson was a walking catastrophe in breeches."

The three of them started laughing and could not stop.

"What's a ninny hammer?"

"I don't know, but no one was laughing at the table."

Black valets used humor as a subtle form of resistance and emotional survival within the rigid confines of elite white households. Their wit often took the form of quiet irony, coded remarks, or exaggerated politeness that masked deeper truths, allowing them to navigate power dynamics without overt defiance. In private moments, shared jokes and mimicry among valets could offer brief relief from the pressures of servitude, though such gatherings were risky and often discouraged by white overseers. Humor became a tool not only for bonding and endurance, but for preserving dignity in a world that denied their autonomy, revealing a quiet resilience beneath the surface of daily labor.

"These men should really try to find a sense of humor," said Cato. "Seriously, it sounds like they are really going to fight it out at this point. The petition was their last best hope to avoid total war. I think some of the delegates were not ready for the answer they received."

"I'm not sure how Master Rutledge views this, said Pompey. "Over dinner tonight, he almost sounded relieved that it was not accepted."

"I don't understand why masters don't say what they mean, when it comes to the fight with the British," said Cato. "There is little room for discussion when they think that we did something wrong. If they treated us like they do the British, maybe our plight might not be so bleak."

Many black valets came to believe their masters were not honest with them because they witnessed firsthand the contradictions between the rhetoric of liberty and the reality of bondage. These valets often overheard conversations about freedom, natural rights, and resistance to tyranny while serving men who denied those very principles to their slaves. Promises of fair treatment or eventual manumission were frequently vague or quietly abandoned, and the growing rumors of British offers of freedom to enslaved people further exposed the fragility of their masters' loyalty. In this climate of revolutionary upheaval, valets began to see that the ideals their masters espoused publicly were not extended to them privately, revealing a deep hypocrisy that bred mistrust and quiet resentment.

"Be careful what you wish for," said Caesar. "The Lees don't grasp that we understand better than them why their silly petition was ignored. The British have the upper hand, and they will slap the colonies down faster than wildfire on a windy day."

"Do you really think that Rutledge is going to start advocating for independence just because the petition was rejected?"

"Sometimes Mr. Rutledge is hard to understand. One minute he speaks forcefully for one idea in an argument, and instantly, he changes his opinions. I remember one evening at his mansion he said he wanted to wear a new set of clothes to a ball that some rich family was holding. I worked all day on the breeches, waistcoat, and coat to make sure everything was perfect and, almost right on the stroke, he changed his mind and orders an older suit of clothing to wear. Sometimes, I think his political life is not much different than his personal life."

"One thing that I can say about Master Richard Lee is that he always straightforward with me and never changes his mind about matters unless he states a very good reason."

"His brother is the same. Often, Francis goes along with the crowd and doesn't like to stand out or take any chances. That makes my life easier because I can predict most of the time how he will decide to handle most situations.

"Did anyone sense the direction the delegates will go now that reconciliation seems a dead end? I think Master Rutledge will start to move toward the talk of independence."

"I wonder how public he will go with that change. The Lees are full square behind the independence side and would love to hear that the Rutledges would support them."

"Now I didn't mean to include his brother John in this conversation. Master Edward remains firmly convinced that reconciliation is possible, but after the King's rejection, I don't know how long he can hold that position. It is interesting how young Edward tries to stay next to his brother on one hand, but he also wants to carve himself an independent point of view. It's strange how they are talking about independence from England, and I watch how a similar battle for independence goes on between John and Edward. Do you find a similar point of view from the Lee brothers?"

"The challenges between the two are different. Unlike Rutledges, only two years separate the Lee's in age. If I am not mistaken, John is considerably older than Edward."

"That is true. John is ten years older than Edward, and I think the age gap is a strong determinant in how they rate their points of view. Edward has deferred to John his entire life, and I doubt if that will change unless they are separated or John should die before Edward. Edward has always lamented how much he is in the shadow of his brother."

"I think that Richard Henry and Francis Lightfoot have been colleagues as much as brothers. Master Richard always seems to charge ahead, and Francis is close behind, providing political and brotherly support. Where Master Richard would be the fiery speaker, Francis would offer the political rationale for support."

Pompey reminded his friends that it was getting late, and they did not want to get caught all on their own without written explanations from their masters. Tomorrow will be another day of responding as black valets and listening for the latest news.

Virginia Feels the Pain

John Murray, a Scottish aristocrat, also known as the Earl of Dunmore, was named the Royal Governor of Virginia in 1771 after serving one year as Colonial Governor of New York. Shortly after his arrival, he launched a series of raids into the western part of the colony against the indigenous population and sought to extend the colony past the Appalachian Mountains, an adventure that was in direct opposition to the wishes of the Crown but supported by the colonists who had designs of land purchases.

This rebellious nature may have been obvious to any observer who knew that Murray's father in Scotland had sided with the rebellious Jacobite in opposition to King George II. For this decision, John Murray's father spent four years in the Tower of London until given a provisional pardon, while John, his mother, and siblings were under house arrest. After his father's release, John joined the British Army and became a captain but resigned his commission in 1760 to become the fourth Earl of Dunmore after his father's and uncle's deaths.

As Governor of Virginia, Lord Dunmore organized raids that led to a conflict, often referred to as Lord Dunmore's War, with the Shawnee Indians in the western part of Virginia, an attempt to expand the Virginia colony and his own political power. These actions were in direct defiance of King George who had issued his Proclamation of 1763, which came at the conclusion of the French and Indian War, and forbade settlement of white settlers west of the Appalachian Mountains on territory reserved for the indigenous population. Some Virginians, like George Washington and Richard Henry Lee, applauded these efforts because they were eager to purchase and then resell the land for profit. Although Virginia colonists were eager to move into this new land, Lord Dunmore attempted to accomplish this strategy without consulting with members of the House of Burgesses. The colonial assembly, that was dominated by Virginia's elites who also wished to extend their land titles, thought that the Governor had acted belligerently.

As the colonists continued to demand more autonomy over the authority of the colony, Lord Dunmore kept making decisions to curb the efforts of the House of Burgesses. In one instance, the British government issued a decree which mandated that prisoners in the colonies should be transported to London for trial. The government had acted because they felt that the justice meted out in provincial courts was too lenient and believed that proceedings in England would deliver better results. Non-importation associations began in 1765 to put economic pressure on England to treat the colonies fairly. Lord Dunmore derided the effectiveness of these associations without recognizing that this early form of inter-colony cooperation had become a steppingstone to the initial call for a Continental Congress.

The associations were a direct result of the edicts emanating from London such as the Intolerance Act, passed in London as the Coercive Act, the Stamp Act, and the Townsend Acts. Lord Dunmore tried to manage these edicts and the affairs of Virginia without consultation with the House of Burgesses, which could only meet when the Royal Governor called them into session. Lord Dunmore needed to consult with the Burgesses on financial matters so that revenue raised could be used to continue his assault on the indigenous population. When the colonists met, the first item on their agenda was to form a committee of correspondence with the other colonies. Dunmore immediately adjourned the meeting which set their relationship on a confrontational basis. The next year, Lord Dunmore reconvened the House and the colonial leaders called for a day of fasting and prayer that Dunmore despised and so he dissolved the House. The patriots reconvened that very day at the Raleigh Tavern in Williamsburg as the First Virginia Convention and issued a strong resolution of support for the Massachusetts colony and sent representatives to the First Continental Congress. Learning of these actions, Lord Dunmore became more strident in his opposition to the patriots which only fueled harsher reactions from the colonists.

One year later, the patriots convened the Second Virginia Convention and elected delegates to the Continental Congress that was to meet in Philadelphia. Dunmore tried to overrule their choices, which the patriots saw as an illegal intervention into their affairs. During the debate, Patrick Henry gave his "Give me liberty or give me death" speech. Immediately following the British attack on patriots in Lexington and Concord, Massachusetts, Lord Dunmore considered Henry's words as a statement of belligerence and ordered the seizure of gun powder in Williamsburg which the Royal Army did. At another impromptu meeting at the Raleigh Tavern, Patrick Henry raised the militia to confront the Governor and demanded the return of the powder or payment for it. Lord Dunmore backed down by making payment to the colonists for the powder.

In the months that followed, Lord Dunmore ordered British forces to plunder the plantations of the patriots and encouraged their slaves to join his cause. Patriot anger grew by the day and fighting back was their most effective tool. Publicizing the abominations that the patriots saw, various letters to the Virginia Gazette started to appear on its pages calling out the British for atrocities in Boston and other colonies. Solidarity with the other colonists was seen as vital to their cause so they reacted forcefully against the laws that were passed in London. In one of the tracts written by Thomas Jefferson, he declared, "The natural and legal rights of Americans have in frequent instances been invaded by the parliament of Great Britain." He added that Americans should make "common cause and exert their rightful powers which god has given us."

Dunmore threatened further retribution, including granting freedom to slaves who deserted their masters, which only infuriated the citizens. Angry protests erupted throughout Williamsburg, and the safety of the Governor was clearly at risk.

In November 1775, Lord Dunmore issued a proclamation that declared martial law, branding the patriots as traitors, and declaring freedom for all slaves in the colony if they would join the British army. The Virginia colonists had always feared a slave revolt and when the Governor's edict brought hundreds of slaves into the Crown's military, an explosive reaction followed in the colony and reverberated in other colonies. Yet, with the addition of nearly 1000 able-bodied, armed, former slaves on their side, Lord Dunmore faced a hopeless cause as the patriots grew in numbers and confidence. Realizing that he could no longer be safe on Virginia soil, he was forced to reside on a British frigate in nearby Yorktown harbor. After more conflict with the patriots in Hampton, Kemps Landing, and a decisive rout at Great Bridge, Lord Dunmore loaded the remaining British forces, Loyalists, and three hundred former slaves and retreated to New York.

SLAVES NOT SURPRISED BY DUNMORE'S ACTION

Pompey finished his early evening tasks for Master Rutledge and slipped quietly from the rear of the Richard Penn House, where Rutledge had shared dinner with Thomas Stone. To combat the autumn chill, he buttoned his coat tight. The streets of Society Hill were dimly lit, the cobblestones slick with mist from the Delaware River, and he moved with practiced caution, avoiding patrols, sidestepping drunken sailors, and nodding silently to other servants he passed. His route took him past shuttered shops and the faint glow of taverns until he reached the alley behind Mrs. Yard's boardinghouse near Second Street where whispers of Congress and revolution swirled in the air. In this narrow passage, hidden from polite society, valets exchanged news, mimicked their masters' speeches, and weighed the meaning of liberty spoken in drawing rooms but denied in their own lives.

"Cato, what are you doing over here at this hour? I thought you'd be asleep by now."

"Sleep? I couldn't get any sleep after hearing the news from Virginia."

"What are you talking about?"

"Haven't you heard? The governor in Virginia has just declared martial law and told the slaves that they would be freed if they run away from their masters and join the British Army."

"What the devil. Where did you hear this?"

"Master Lee was talking about it this evening over dinner with John Adams. Master Lee said a courier had just arrived from Williamsburg with the news. People are all excited," Cato said.

"Excited? That's an understatement! I wonder what kind of reaction the slaves will have."

"Master Lee said there were already some slaves who have left their plantations, but not many."

Pompey said, "Trading one master for another? I'm not sure that would be my choice. Are the British any better than our masters? It seems to me that our situation isn't any better one way or the other. I see the freemen here in Philadelphia, and they don't get much more respect from the white folks than we do."

"But to be free. Can you imagine what you would do if you didn't have to jump whenever the master wants you to fetch a blanket or get some snuff? I can almost smell freedom," said Cato.

Pompey said, "That smell you sense is the rotten promises of the British who are scared. I wonder what it might feel like to rise in the morning without waiting for a bell, without tying another man's cravat or polishing boots that will never be your own. I have heard the words "liberty" and "natural rights" echo through the halls of Philadelphia boardinghouses, spoken by men who debate rebellion over punch and pipe smoke. Yet none of them speak of my liberty. I watch free black men hauling crates at the docks or selling wares in the market and, though their lives are hard, they move with a kind of dignity I envy—a quiet ownership of time, labor, and breath."

"I imagine renting a room of my own, perhaps near Carpenter's Wharf, where I could earn wages and choose my own company," Cato continued. "Maybe I will learn to read or join the Free African Society if such a thing ever came to be. But beneath the hope lies fear: of being seized, accused, returned to bondage, or simply ignored by a world that sees me only as property. Still, the dream persists, freedom not as a speech or a parchment, but as a morning without orders and a night without fear."

"You better be careful what you wish for," Pompey added. "If our masters had been minding their own business and not talking about independence, do you think the British would be offering us freedom? It smacks me as fancy, not fact. How did Mr. Lee respond to the news."

"He and Mr. Adams didn't seem to be overly worried. Master Lee was concerned about how other slaves in Virginia were going to take the news. He says that he didn't think any of his slaves would take the offer, and I think he is probably right about that. Mr. Adams was more concerned about how slaves in other states may react and if other Royal Governors may get the idea that they should issue similar proclamations."

"It's strange that when our owners talk about their own freedom, the British start talking about freedom, too. A fine tale, if it were so."

"See, Cato, there's the rub. Our masters all get excited when they talk about freedom, when they talk about themselves, but as soon as we walk in the door at their request to perform a task or carry out an errand they want, suddenly they forget about freedom for us."

"You know some people will look at this and jump at the opportunity," said Cato.

"Take heed lest you stumble. Freedom is the bait that the English are using to attract us. If one would take the bait and then are shot by Americans, will the Brits bind your wounds? I suggest to you that they would rather watch us die, before they stop our bleeding. As far as defending our master's domains, we have no opinion on the taxes being levied on the colonies or any tax raised on the consumption of tea. Have you drunk much tea lately? We must ask ourselves, why are the British being so nice to us now? They come running to our rescue when they need our help, but they will cut us loose whenever the time of urgency is passed."

"Do you think that the colonists will make us the same offer?"

"Time will tell, but I am of the mind that if things get dangerous for the patriots, they'll make the same deal. I'd be as unsure of our owners' offer as I am of that the British. For me, the idea of freedom of body and soul is more important than tea and taxes."

"I have no doubt they will never treat as equals even if we join their army. More likely, they will give us the meanest jobs that the average British soldier would find disgusting, cleaning the privies, disposing of body parts, or carrying the wounded. I can't even imagine that they would give us rifles?"

"Heavens! Did you hear what you just said? They will never provide us with guns as they are too afraid of them being turned on them. I think the main purpose of this sleight of hand is to scare the colonists. White people know how to instigate fear, and we know that well. When was the last time you heard that a slave was to be chastised with a whip? They make a clean job of it."

"I am sure that they will dangle enticements in front of us, but what power will we have to enforce their promises? The master never does figure us out. Right now, I doubt if they even know that we are here in the shadows talking about them and freedom. The master is so smart he doesn't even see what is almost right in front of his face. Have you ever wondered what our masters think we are doing in our 'free' time?"

Pompey said, “I believe you are coming to understand this temptation for exactly what it is. I trust that few slaves will jump at the opportunity, but I am afraid some may take the prize while it remains in reach.”

“What would you do if Master Edward offered you a job in the South Carolina militia with the promise that you would be freed if you performed well”

“There are so many ifs in that offer, that I don’t think that I would take it. First, who gets to measure whether I performed ‘well’? Next, what kind of job in the militia would I be offered? Cleaning up for the dead or dying? Next, who would protect me from the other South Carolina ninny hammers who hate everything and everyone who is African? No, I don’t think that would be an attractive offer for me.

FRANKLIN HOLDS COURT

Edward opened the door of Mrs. Yard's boarding house and was greeted by a bright, shiny morning. With the door closing loudly behind him, he strode down Second Street to reach the building where the next session of Congress would be held. The birds were chirping from the trees, and a large black turkey buzzard floated high in the skies. He arrived early at the Statehouse to take his seat at the South Carolina table. A handful of the delegates were huddled in a few groups of conversations on three sides of the paneled room. Tables were arranged with the northern colonies on the right and southern colonies on the left with a small, raised table in the middle, where the chairman conducted the meetings. Surprisingly, Benjamin Franklin was not seated at his usual spot adjacent to the chair's table, but near the fireplace on the right front, leafing through a handful of papers and seemingly lost in thought. Edward had rarely had the opportunity to speak directly to the Doctor and thought that the timing this morning was propitious.

"Doctor Franklin, trying to keep warm near the fire, I see. Do ideas burn brighter in warmth?

"Only when the company provides a proper spark, Mr. Rutledge. And tell me, do your southern winds carry any warmth northward this winter?"

"You may jest, sir, but these winds carry caution. We tread carefully. Talk of independence flies faster than sense, and I fear its wings shall melt before the sun."

"A poetic caution, but time is not disposed to wait upon Southern patience. The Crown prepares for war, not reconciliation."

The Assembly Hall of the Pennsylvania Statehouse was a solemn, yet charged chamber, its Georgian symmetry lending a sense of order to the turbulent proceedings within. The room was lit by tall sash windows that admitted the pale winter light, casting long shadows across the polished wood floors and paneled walls. A huge crystal chandelier was lit with eight long candles that would last for hours. A central table, strewn with parchment, quills, and inkstands, anchored the space, surrounded by rows of simple wooden chairs occupied by delegates of the Second Continental Congress.

Franklin peered over his half-rimmed eyeglasses at Rutledge and said, "Your brother, John, I understand, has left for South Carolina. I enjoyed his manner of oration and the experience we need in these conversations of congress. Has the entire delegation departed?

"No, sir. Christopher Gadsden remains with me, and John informed me that replacements will be sent north in a short while to fill out our delegation. I hope that they arrive soon."

"Hope, young man, is a fine breakfast, but a poor supper. I have seen the King's ministers dismiss our pleas with the flick of a powdered wig. How many more declarations must we pen before we admit they are read only to be tossed upon the hearth, if read at all?"

"Then you would have us leap? Declare independence and unravel all that holds these colonies together?"

"No leap. A measured step toward a future we claim, or a chain we continue to polish. The longer we wait, the tighter it binds."

"Your wit is sharp, Doctor, but I must answer to men whose fortunes and lives are entangled in Britain's markets. They see rebellion not as liberty but as ruin."

The air was thick with the scent of wax and wool, and the quiet murmur of debate echoed beneath the high ceiling. At the front stood the Speaker's chair, later dubbed the "Rising Sun" chair, symbolizing cautious hope amid growing talk of independence. Though the furnishings were modest, the gravity of the moment imbued the room with a palpable intensity, as men weighed the future of a nation not yet born.

Franklin leaned forward in his seat and raised his right arm for emphasis and said, "Then let us show them it is not rebellion, but responsibility. The harder path, yes, but a righteous one. And perhaps even profitable, in time."

"Profitable rebellion? You sound like a merchant of revolution."

"Better a merchant of liberty than a subject of tyranny. But fear not, Mr. Rutledge, we shall debate, we shall wrangle, and in time, we shall decide. I only hope we do so before the King's soldiers do it for us."

"My brother mentioned to me that maybe, you and I, have something in common. I had no idea that your family was so large, and I certainly would not have known that you were the youngest, just like me. I have wondered if we are born to our places in family for some reason or that it shapes who we will become."

"It is true that I have many brothers and sisters, sixteen to be exact, and I am the youngest male among our menagerie. My dear sister, Jane, is younger than I, and one of my best friends. Regarding being one of the last on the tree of family life, I would say that it has its strengths and weaknesses. Mother and Father certainly had more experience in raising children by the time I became a family member, and I also was able to see how some of my siblings lived their lives and could choose to emulate or ignore. If I were only a single child, or even the oldest, no one is setting an example in the current of events and experiences in front of me."

"I've never considered it from that perspective."

"In some ways, we are alike. My next oldest brother was ten years older, which I understand is approximately the same difference you have with your brother. When I first set out on my own, my brother was the one who allowed me to become an apprentice in his print shop. I have no idea what I would have become if my brother had not influenced me. Truth be told, my relationship with my brother deteriorated while I was in Boston, and I made my escape to Philadelphia."

"Our paths are more similar than I had imagined. After I returned from Middle Temple law instruction in London, which my brother paid for, I worked in his office in Charleston to build a law practice."

"Well, I am not sure if your London-based education was equivalent to the apprenticeship I received in a small printing shop, but the outline of those events has some bearing. Since John's departure, I trust that you have others who will assist you in carrying out your duties as delegate from South Carolina."

"I have a coterie of delegates to speak with in addition to Christopher Gadsden."

"Ah, Mr. Gadsden!" Franklin began "There is a man who knows what he wants and then goes out to do the work. He strikes me as a model that could be followed. However, he does seem to be more radical than I have heard from your brother and yourself."

"Our colony has very different opinions on how to accomplish a task. They trust our delegates to interpret the climate of the conversation to be flexible in order to build a consensus."

The atmosphere in the Pennsylvania Statehouse on this brisk December morning was one of hushed anticipation and quiet urgency.

As more delegates trickled into the Assembly Room, the clatter of boots on polished floorboards mingled with murmured greetings and the rustle of woolen cloaks being shed. The fire in the two hearths crackled faintly, offering modest warmth against the chill seeping through the tall windows. Papers were exchanged, letters unfolded, and whispered conversations hinted at the gravity of the moment—news from Boston, troop movements, and the uncertain fate of reconciliation. Some men stood in clusters, their voices low but intense; others sat alone, reviewing notes or gazing thoughtfully at the high ceiling beams. Though the gavel had not yet struck, the room already pulsed with the weight of decisions to come, as the colonies edged ever closer to a break with the Crown. The voices increased, making it difficult to hear Dr. Franklin.

Rising from his chair and positioning his long, engraved cane in his left hand, Franklin said, "May I offer a small kernel of advice? When I was a boy, I thought truth was what I believed. As I grew older, I thought it was what I could prove. But now, at my age, I know it is what I seek. A few years ago, my viewpoint was not too different from where you view the world today. Having lived for a considerable time in London, as you did but under different terms, my thinking about our colonial life has evolved. The narrowness of mind, that was demonstrated to me when I was asked to answer Parliament, has convinced me that reconciliation is impossible. We have indulged ourselves in an expectation that the people of Great Britain would have preferred peace and a reconciliation, but when they were convinced that not be the case, the Crown reacted in open combat."

Franklin continued, "A leader needs to be flexible when the turn of events shapes our world in a fashion that we thought was not probable. As recently as last year, I would have supported the moderate's view of our relationship with England, however, after a brutal questioning from the Solicitor General of the Privy Council to the King of England, I have rethought my interpretation of our connection. As an agent for the colonies, I was abused and ridiculed for explaining the position of the colonies that was stated in non-threatening words. This lack of fairness and decorum has left me disillusioned for any mending of our bond. Rutledge, His Majesty is blind to our plight. He sees provinces, not people. Parliament sees revenue, not rights. I ask you, what is reconciliation worth if it chains us to injustice?"

"Is revolution the only path that we can take?"

"War is the bitter harvest of persistent contempt, yet it can yield liberty. Better a storm of our own making than silence under tyranny."

Franklin extended his hand to shake and Edward said, "Thank you for your time and wisdom. The start of the session is almost at hand. I truly pray that we shall have other opportunities to continue this conversation."

"Then let us proceed, Mr. Rutledge, not with haste, but with resolve. The cause is not yet ripe, but the fruit will not wait forever."

Slaves Speak About Freedom

On an unusually warm November Sunday morning, Pompey knew that he had the day off from attending to the needs of Edward Rutledge. Only a few big white clouds were over Philadelphia, and Pompey looked at them to see if they reminded him of the clouds in Charleston. To the Black valet standing outside the boardinghouse, the clouds hung low and heavy, like damp linen stretched across the sky that were gray with the weight of winter and war. He watched them drift above the steeples and rooftops, their slow procession mirroring the uncertain march of the men he served, whose talk of liberty rarely reached his own name. The trip to Philadelphia was so long, Pompey thought, they must be different clouds. Over time, Rutledge had allowed Pompey some free time on Sundays when official work of the Congress would not interfere with the freedom to explore Philadelphia. Of course, Pompey never had complete freedom to explore the city because he was a Black man in a white society.

When Pompey arrived in Philadelphia for the First Continental Congress, he was shocked to see Black men and women who walked with seemingly nonchalance on the streets of the city. Pompey saw an enslaved man hauling firewood along Walnut Street, then paused as a well-dressed Black man passed him, walking freely with a confident gait and no overseer in sight. Pompey's eyes followed him, struck by the quiet dignity in his bearing and the absence of deference in his posture. The free man nodded, briefly, respectfully, and continued, perhaps toward the carpenter's yard or to a Quaker meetinghouse. For Pompey, the moment was unsettling and electric, a glimpse of possibility that defied the daily rhythm of servitude. He had heard whispers of manumission, of northern laws and Quaker petitions, but never had liberty worn such a human face. That fleeting encounter planted a seed of curiosity, of longing, and of a question that would not easily be silenced. To his surprise, these people were not slaves at all but citizens, usually artisans and merchants, who knew a trade and could be part of the city's life. In Charleston, Negroes only walked the streets when their masters were close at hand. After living in Philadelphia for a while, Pompey learned from the local free men that there were certain informal guidelines that he had to maintain to walk the streets. First, never look into the eyes of any white person. Second, always make room for any white person who was in your vicinity. Third, when wearing a hat and passing a white person, always tip or take off your cap. Fourth, always carry some type of identification that connects you with your master. Fifth, never go out at night or form a group of three or more black people.

Pompey thought these rules were a terrible amount of work for any black man to remember and follow, even if you were a free man. If freedom means following all those rules, are you free?

Pompey, with the Rutledge family, lived in Philadelphia where the boundaries of bondage and liberty were unusually porous. The city was home to a small but visible population of free Black people, and the city's Quaker community had already begun to challenge the moral foundations of slavery. Pompey saw free men working as artisans or laborers, and witnessed the quiet dignity of a Black man walking unescorted through the streets. These glimpses, though fleeting, could stir questions: How did he come to be free? Who granted it? Was it earned, inherited, or stolen? In a city where liberty was debated daily in the halls of Congress and whispered in taverns, the idea of Black freedom was not abstract, it was embodied, visible, and unsettling.

Yet understanding freedom was not the same as grasping its mechanics or trusting its permanence. Pompey's world was shaped by the daily rituals of servitude, the constant surveillance of white authority, and the knowledge that even free Black men could be kidnapped or accused of being runaways. The founding of the Pennsylvania Abolition Society in 1775, though modest and Quaker-led, signaled that some white Philadelphians believed slavery was unlawful. Such beliefs were not yet law, and certainly not protection. Pompey viewed free Black men with a mix of awe and skepticism, wondering whether their liberty was secure or merely tolerated. To him, freedom seemed like a fragile garment, that was worn proudly, but always at risk of being torn away.

As he slipped out of the shadow in the alley behind Mrs. Yard's boarding house, Pompey began to walk down State Street toward the Delaware River where not a single person could be seen on the street. Pompey thought they must all be at church. Being accustomed to the waterways of Charleston, he was comfortable being close to the water, but the width of the Delaware River was foreign to him. Across the river, the shoreline was a forest with no buildings near the water's edge. Far south down the river, where Pompey and the other South Carolina group had sailed into Philadelphia, Pompey could see ships that were docked at a wharf nearly a mile away. He showed no interest in trekking that far as it might invite suspicion among the residents.

Pompey stood at the edge of the Delaware River, the mist rising in pale ribbons from the water's surface as merchant ships creaked in their moorings and gulls wheeled overhead. The river stretched wide and slow before him, its current indifferent to the quarrels of men, flowing past the wharves and warehouses with quiet authority. He had come in his free time and found himself lingering, drawn by the vastness and motion. The river was unlike the narrow lanes and crowded parlors he knew; it offered no commands, no claims of ownership. Here, no one called his name. In its breadth, Pompey saw something unclaimed, something that moved freely between colonies and coasts, beyond the reach of any master's hand.

Yet the feeling it stirred in him was not simple longing. Pompey felt a mixture of awe, ache, and quiet defiance. He knew the river carried goods and letters, soldiers and rumors, but it also carried the idea of elsewhere. Watching the sails drift until they disappeared, Pompey felt the sharp edge of possibility, that freedom might be real, not just whispered in taverns or glimpsed in the gait of a free black man. But he also felt the weight of his own tether, of his name not his own, his labor not his choice. The river did not promise escape, but it did offer a vision of movement, of lives unbound. At that moment, Pompey did not imagine running; he imagined knowing. Knowing what it meant to choose where to go, and when.

A tree was hanging precariously over the shoreline and Pompey found some branches that the water had deposited on the bank. He picked up one that was about a foot long and threw it as far as he could into the strong current of the river, then watched the piece of wood bobbing and flowing down the river until disappearing under a wave. The current was strong, and he took every precaution not to fall into the water as he had no experience of swimming. He looked north up the river, and all he saw was water and forests.

Pompey thought about the idea of making a raft and floating down the river but stopped thinking about it when he concluded that he might end up in the ocean with no possibility of being on land again. The river did not hold his interest, so he decided to retrace his steps up State Street to find something new. Being Sunday, all the shops were closed making the street very quiet, although a man leading a horse-drawn wagon could be heard by the clop-clop of the horse's shoes against the cobblestone road slowly moving up the incline away from the river.

As he strolled past Front Street, he squinted and recognized the silhouette of a Black man, his friend Cato, standing a block away.

"Cato. I'm surprised to see you out here so early," he said as he approached.

"I have been walking around since breakfast with nothing to do. Do you want me to show you a hiding place I found up the river?"

"That sounds interesting, but won't we be taking a chance if someone finds us?"

"That's what makes it so good. I don't know if anyone knows about it. I'm thinking the Indians used this place before the white men arrived. Let me show you, it's just a little way up the river."

Cato started walking along the shore, without checking if Pompey was behind him, so Pompey decided, "Why not?" and followed his friend into this adventure.

Cato was scrambling over the rocks between the trees and the river and said, "It's just around this next bend."

The river made a small eddy from the part of the shore that jutted out from the forest. Cato swung his arm around a willow tree branch that hung over the water and then disappeared.

"Cato! Where did you go? Are you in the water?"

"Don't be a simpleton. I told you it was a great hiding place. Just swing around that tree and you'll see me."

Pompey trusted Cato and knew that he hadn't fallen into the current, but the river looked awfully dangerous. He reached for the tree and looked upriver where he could see Cato smirking.

"Don't be a milk-livered knave," Cato said.

Pompey saw a landing spot just beyond the tree and now recognized how Cato had swung himself around. He grabbed the tree with both hands and swung his legs over next to Cato.

"How did you ever find this place."

"I get curious when I am walking about because I want to get away from people, and a hiding place like this is ideal."

Pompey looked around and now understood why Cato liked this spot. Not only was there a jut in the forest that they had just mastered, but twenty feet upriver another jut of land did the same thing, and this little clearing was completely isolated.

"Cato, you have found a wonderful hideaway."

"I'm not sure if it will be great when the winter comes, but for right now it's perfect for us."

Pompey looked around and saw a dense forest across the river and the city that lay behind. The shoreline offered a much better view of the other side of the river than what he had seen earlier. Looking intently, he could see the roof of a small building, close to the water. Further upriver was an island. Pompey's mind wondered whether Indians lived on the island and might they come at night and attack the city.

Cato sat on the ground near some large rocks that had been set in a half circle and said, "I told you this was a great hiding place. No one can see us, and I doubt they would come here to look for us unless they thought we were runaways.

"Don't talk like that, Cato. You start saying those kinds of things out loud and sooner than not they become the truth. But you were right. This is a great spot. How did you find it?"

"Master Lee came to the Congress many months ago, and he would often allow me my Sundays out, if I didn't get in trouble. One day I was further up the river than we are now and was tracing my way home, when I stumbled on this place. This place gives me a feeling of freedom like I have never known. No one to give me orders, no shoes to shine. No master to tell me what to do."

"I can see the appeal of this place straight away. I am looking up at the skies with the white puffy clouds racing across our view. I see the seabirds winging across the river in search of food. I see the hawks above the forest floating in the warm skies, circulating on a glide, and then a fish leaping in the air out in the middle of the river. I can see what you mean when you see this as freedom."

"Pompey, do you think we will ever be free?"

"I don't see it in my lifetime, but I can't believe God will allow this curious institution of slavery to exist forever. It's just not natural that one man should be allowed to own another person. I hear that slaves have always been here, but I was also told that when it began, the slaves were the losers in a war. What war were we ever in?"

"It just doesn't feel right. Why am I a slave? Why shouldn't white people be enslaved? They call themselves that when they talk about the King, even though they aren't. They forget completely about us in the next moment."

"I have learned here in Philadelphia that many colonies have no or few slaves. Look at the freemen here in Philadelphia, and I understand that there are more free men in Massachusetts where Mr. Adams lives. They are no worse off than we are in South Carolina, but we are enslaved, and up north, hardly anyone is enslaved. It makes no sense to me."

"The problem, Pomp, is that no one asked our opinion."

"Can you ever imagine one of the delegates saying, 'Now I think we should hear now from the wise delegate of Virginia, Mr. Cato."

"I don't see that happening ever too soon. What would be the crime in asking our opinion? We are closer to the problem than anyone else."

"Stop trying to sound logical, Cato. Slavery only makes sense to the masters. I think the only way they will ever give up the right to be slavers is if they are compelled by force of arms. The sooner they do it, the less blood will be spread."

Pompey had heard men whispering in taverns, boys in alleyways, black soldiers fighting for independence alongside whites. Could Blacks and whites ever carry muskets and march beneath the same flag? The thought stirred something fierce and fragile in him, a chance to be counted, to fight not just for a country but for a name of his own. Yet fear pressed close, reminding him that even in war, a Black man's courage might be used, but not honored, and freedom promised might never be given.

Slaves in Washington's Army

Edward Rutledge and Thomas Stone cultivated a collaborative relationship during their participation in the Second Continental Congress as they shared similar perspectives on independence and slavery. The two delegates, though representing different colonies, South Carolina and Maryland, found common ground in their cautious approach to independence, both favoring reconciliation before full separation from Britain. Their cooperation reflected a broader effort among moderate delegates to preserve unity within Congress while navigating the volatile path toward revolution.

During the fall of 1775, after the Congress received letters from General Washington, Rutledge offered a resolution that would require Washington to discharge all blacks, including free blacks, from the Continental Army.

"I rise today to address a simmering problem within the Continental Army," said Rutledge. "I am not talking about the supplying of uniforms, food, or powder, but the insidious way that we are arming Negroes to carry out our obligations. The American colonies should be relying on our own forces to fight our battles. Just because the Crown has seen fit to tempt our workers with the opportunity of freedom to join their side, why should we take the fatal step to provide arms and ammunitions to slaves who will inevitably turn those weapons on us to fight for their own freedom?"

"Mr. Rutledge makes a good point," echoed Thomas Stone, delegate from Maryland. "One of the biggest concerns my neighbors and I face in Maryland is the gnawing ache that our slaves will obtain arms and use them to violently kill our women and children. By arming them and teaching them how to be effective soldiers, we are creating a menace that we will rue to have unleashed. After the last slave revolt in Virginia, the Maryland provincial assembly adopted new legislation to limit firearms and powder, decreased their mobility during the day, and limited their freedom to roam after sunset. Inviting them into our Continental Army makes no sense to me."

William Hooper from North Carolina added, "We oppose the enlistment of enslaved men in the Continental Army because we fear it will disrupt the institution of slavery and encourage rebellion among the enslaved population. We also are extremely worried that arming black men, whether enslaved or free, will undermine white authority and threaten the social order that sustains our economic and political power."

John Adams rose to be recognized and remarked, "We are not in a position where we should turn away the resource of any confederate who is willing to help the separation of our colonies from Britain. Steps have been taken to limit the use of arms by these soldiers. Our main goal is to defend ourselves against the tyranny of the Crown, and we should accept the support offered to us."

John Dickerson, the leader of the conservative faction at the Congress, added, "General Washington should be responsible for cultivating the army he needs to win our liberty. He is not encouraging his commanding officers to actively recruit slaves to be part of our efforts. I don't think that we should interfere with his efforts to engage the British. He is a Virginian, and he personally knows the risks inherent in allowing Africans to be part of the army.

"May I remind our dear friends of South Carolina that less than two months ago, this body debated for many days about how we were to prepare an adequate fighting force for General Washington," said George Wythe, a noted attorney and delegate from Virginia. "The officers under General Washington are reliable in their ability to identify recruits. They know how to be careful to identify those who are suspicious and find personnel who would be fully committed to service in the Continental Army."

John Jay of New York said, "I am more inclined to support the enlistment of enslaved men in the Continental Army because officers know that it is a practical necessity to bolster troop numbers amid dwindling enlistments and rising casualties. I also view military service as a potential path to manumission, aligning with emerging anti-slavery sentiments in the colonies"

Button Gwinnett, delegate from Georgia rose and said, "I have known Georgia without slaves, and I have known Georgia with them, and I can assure you that having guns available to our Negroes would be a disaster. We should resolve to strengthen our army in all other ways before we employ these malcontents in our revolutionary army."

Delegate from North Carolina, John Penn said, "Just this past July, the good people of Wilmington, NC were forced to round up more than forty slaves who had planned to use the guns that they had stolen and were ready to mercilessly murder citizens of our community. To think that this body would knowingly give guns and ammunition to Negroes is against every fiber of my body, and I can't imagine supporting such an effort."

Edward thought that these personal pleas from fellow delegates could sway the opinion of the Congress. However, they were outnumbered by the bulk of the responses that came from mid-Atlantic and Northern delegates who wished to set the issue to the side. After thirty minutes of debate, the resolution was tabled.

****

Despite the constraints of slavery and racial prejudice, several Black individuals in the 1770s emerged as striking examples of success and resilience in the American colonies.

Crispus Attucks, a sailor of African and Native descent, became the first martyr of the Revolution when he was killed in the Boston Massacre in 1770, symbolizing Black patriotism and sacrifice.

Born into slavery in Massachusetts, Peter Salem was manumitted and later served as a soldier in the war for independence. Before 1776, he had already gained local recognition for his skill with arms and providing discipline. At the Battle of Breed's Hill, he was credited with shooting British Major John Pitcairn, a pivotal moment that elevated his status among patriot forces.

Another free Black man in Boston, Prince Hall, was a leatherworker and abolitionist who founded the first African American Masonic lodge, African Lodge No. 1, before the Declaration of Independence. His advocacy for black education and civil rights began in the early 1770s, when he petitioned the Massachusetts legislature for the abolition of slavery and the repatriation of freed blacks to Africa.

Born into slavery in Massachusetts, Salem Poor purchased his freedom in 1769 and became a celebrated soldier during the early Revolutionary battles. His bravery at Breed's Hill earned him formal commendation from fourteen officers, who petitioned the Massachusetts General Court to recognize his valor.

These individuals, though living under vastly different circumstances, demonstrated that Black Americans were not only present in the Revolutionary era but were actively shaping its course through courage, intellect, and strategic action

Washington's own personal feelings about slavery and Africans were conflicted. He owned slaves and kept a close watch over them, yet in the early months of the war, Washington saw Black soldiers in action, fighting alongside whites in the Continental Army. Within seven months of taking command of the army, Washington approved the enlistment of free Black soldiers, something he and other general officers had originally opposed.

During the war, Washington was in close contact with three idealistic young men who ardently opposed slavery and whose opinions he valued. John Laurens of South Carolina, Alexander Hamilton of West-Indian birth, and Marquis de Lafayette from France. They were three young officers who never flinched at making their thoughts known that Black individuals should have many of the rights as others. They believed that Africans had the same God-given qualities as white people.

During the war, Washington encountered Phillis Wheatley, a gifted young Black woman who became a noted poet. In October 1775, Wheatley sent a letter with a poem from her home in Providence, Rhode Island. Four months later, Washington sent both the letter and poem to his friend Joseph Reed in Philadelphia, and they were later published in at least two newspapers in the colonies. Washington also wrote directly to Ms. Wheatley, thanking her for her work and inviting her to his headquarters. He went on to say, "I shall be happy to see a person so favored by the muses and to whom nature has been so liberal and beneficent in her dispensations."

Debate about Black members of the Continental Army continued until the end of the war. Rutledge felt it was important that these issues be addressed by Congress so that actions by local militias would not set a precedent that other colonial assemblies might not be willing to support. It was a well-known fact that General Washington owned slaves and brought William Lee with him everywhere as his personal valet. Rutledge believed that Washington was aware of the potential for problems from having ex-slaves in his army, and might be influenced to limit African participation in the Army by limiting it to free men. In the heat of battle, Washington was probably more concerned about having able-bodied men available to fight than he was worried about the effect that Black soldiers would have on the colonies after the war.

Two months after the Rutledge motion was defeated, General Washington issued an order that forbade the recruitment of additional free Blacks into the army but made it clear that any free Blacks who were currently in the army could remain. Six weeks after this order, Washington had come to a different opinion of the need to include Blacks in the army, and he issued another order allowing recruiting officers to enlist additional free Blacks. The Continental Congress in January 1776 accepted the General's order, but Southern delegates insisted that only free Blacks should be accepted.

Obviously, the decisions that General Washington made regarding the use of Blacks in the Continental Army were irresolute and confusing.

Slaves Have Families Too

The kitchen in the City Tavern was noisy with waiters yelling at the chef, the chef bellowing at his assistant cook, and the serving staff pushing the house slaves away from the food. Whenever Edward Rutledge had dinner at the City Tavern, Pompey was most eager to attend as he knew that some tasty food would become available, and there was a good chance that he would see his friend, Cato.

Edward arrived early and told Pompey to stay near the kitchen entrance as he might need his services. Being acquainted with the staff at the City Tavern, Pompey was able to stay warm in the back of the kitchen or to spend his time in the basement if necessary. Tonight, the kitchen staff was harried with orders, so staying outside of the kitchen was the smart choice.

The kitchen of the City Tavern was a bustling, smoky heart of colonial hospitality, alive with the clang of iron pots and the hiss of roasting meat. Its wide hearth dominated one wall, where multiple spits turned slowly over open flames, tended by enslaved and hired cooks alike. Rough-hewn tables bore the weight of pewter platters, bundles of herbs, and barrels of ale, while shelves lined with crockery and copper kettles gleamed dully in the firelight. The air was thick with the mingled scents of onion, mutton, and nutmeg, and the floor of flagged stone was worn smooth by countless hurried footsteps. Amid the chaos, there was rhythm: a practiced choreography of chopping, stirring, and shouting, all driving toward the moment when steaming dishes would ascend to the tavern's genteel dining room.

Pompey loved to watch the chef work the pan, spinning the food and causing more juices, flipping the food in the air without losing a single morsel. Another person, with a long ladle in one hand and a wooden bowl in the other, reached down into a giant pot and served up a hot serving of soup. Pompey's eyes could not hide his appetite for the soup he desired, but his mind told him to stand back and be patient. Just last week, he had been here, and without even asking, a cook poured him a bowl full of potato leek soup that warmed his entire body. Maybe similar good luck would also prevail tonight.

At the back door, Pompey heard a soft knock, and he could see through the window the face of Cato. Pompey put his fingers to his lips to quiet Cato's knocks and with his other hand grabbed the latch, opening the door slightly so he could slip out to join Cato.

"Why don't you just let me in? It's cold out here," Cato said.

Pompey gently pushed Cato against the outside wall with his forearm and said, "If you want some of the great food, we need to be patient. When did Master Lee bring you here?"

"I came straight here after he entered the tavern," Cato said. "How do we get something from the kitchen if we're standing out here in the cold?"

"I have learned that the orders come in waves. That makes the cooks work hard, then it calms down before the next orders come in. We need to enter when its active, and then when it slows down, we might get lucky," said Pompey.

"I like how your mind works. Where did you learn how to do this? I'm sure no master taught you this trick."

"You are right about that. I had an older brother who once showed me how to use the white folks to get what I needed. White people want to think that they are always in control, and for the big things, like where I work, they are in control. But for the rest of my life, I got to figure out how to survive."

Cato's stomach clenched with hunger, but more than that, with the ache of invisibility. The tavern fed congressmen and merchants, men who spoke of liberty over steaming plates, yet he remained nameless, his labor unseen, his hunger unacknowledged. Each passing servant might offer a crust or a glance, but the feast within was not his to claim. He peered into the window and saw that the hustle in the kitchen had slowed. He said, "I guess we need to wait some more. After a moment of silence. Cato asked, "How many brothers do you have?"

"I have three older brothers and two sisters," Pompey said. "We have been fortunate about two things. Our family has been kept together, and we are all house slaves, just like my mother and father, so I guess we have just been lucky."

As Cato waited outside the kitchen, he said, "Sounds like your family led an easier life, long before you came around. I don't even know who my mother and father are. Long as I can recall, Master Lee and the cook are as close as I get to family."

"That's hard, Cato. Do you have any recollection of your mother and father at all?"

Cato, looking down and kicking his boots at imaginary rocks replied, "My earliest thoughts are with Miss Betty, who is the cook in our kitchen, and Master Lee. They've always treated me right, and made sure I had good clothes, food to eat, and a place to sleep. All I was expected to do was to not talk back to any of the whites in the house and to never look anyone in the eye. That's not hard if I just lower my eyes and listen instead of talking."

And yet, in that moment of waiting, Cato felt something more than hunger, something like defiance. The warmth spilling from the kitchen was not just physical; it was symbolic, a reminder of the world divided by walls and status. He watched the bustle and imagined what it might be to serve oneself, to choose when and what to eat, to be more than a shadow at the edge of comfort. The tavern's kitchen was a place of sustenance, but also of hierarchy, and he stood at its margins, not just hoping for food but yearning for recognition. The clatter of dishes became music he could not join but could not ignore. In the quiet between footsteps, he wondered if liberty, like bread, might someday be offered to him not as charity, but as a right.

"It's strange that we come from completely different places, but we're at the same place right now," said Pompey. "Let's go inside, I think work is picking up again."

Pompey slowly opened the door, and Cato followed closely as they slipped inside quietly, shut the door, and stood silently against the outside wall. One could hear the sounds in the kitchen rise as the pans clinked, the plates jangled, and the voices crescendo.

"It looks like you have been around here often. Have you ever left unfed?"

"Once or twice, but I usually get something to eat. See that server with the white shirt, red scarf, and brown hair? He helps me out regularly."

"So, you don't have any uncles or aunts to help you out? That doesn't seem fair."

"Fair! Since when is slavery fair? I talked to some of the field hands and their stories are much worse than mine. They regularly get whipped just because they sneeze. If they look at the overseer in anything like a cross way, they get whipped. I once saw the biggest slave Master Lee owned, just whipped until he died. Do you think that was fair?"

"I heard stories at the plantation about things like that, but I have never seen them. Did you know the man?"

"No, didn't matter because it could have been done to any of us. That's why Master Lee forced us to watch. He wanted this to be a lesson to all his slaves that if you didn't do exactly what you are told to do, you could be the next one whipped."

The kitchen was reaching a high-pitched noise, and the men could see the waiters piling food on plates and ladling up the soup. Soon the frenzy began to die down again.

"Get ready, Cato. I think I see our path to food," said Cato.

As the last of the servers left through the door to the main dining area, Pompey stepped closer to the sorting table that separated the kitchen from the back.

"Mr. Brown, do you think you could help feed a couple of day workers some bread and such?"

The man in the white shirt and red scarf turned and grinned. Pompey knew that look of acknowledgement. "Who is your friend, Pompey? I never seen him here before."

"His name is Cato, and he works for Mr. Richard Henry Lee. Do you think you could help us out?"

"You work for Mr. Lee? I have heard a great deal about that man. He seems to be ready for liberty. For that, I will gladly give you some bread."

Brown turned quickly to a worktable, grabbed plates and bowls, poured some steaming soup in a bowl, and then put the bread on the plate pouring some gravy over it.

"Now get outside, and have a good meal."

The boys grabbed the food and turned toward the door.

"Thanks, Mr. Brown. You are a good man," said Pompey as they slipped outside.

The cook at the City Tavern, weary from a day of preparing meals for congressmen and merchants, felt a quiet sense of duty, or perhaps defiance, in slipping scraps to Pompey and Cato who lingered near the kitchen door. Though the tavern's hierarchy mirrored the social order of the streets, the kitchen was its own world, ruled less by politics than by necessity and rhythm. Feeding the valets, whether enslaved or free, was not an act of rebellion, but of recognition. With a nod to shared labor, the cook and the valets could identify with the long hours and silent endurance that bound them more closely than the dining room's polished speeches ever could. The cook knew the rules, but he also knew hunger, and in the flickering firelight, a ladle of stew or a heel of bread became a quiet gesture of humanity, passed hand to hand in the shadows.

The boys did not go far before they leaned up against another building and wolfed down the gravy-soaked bread and drank the hot potato soup.

Cato said, "Now that's a satisfying meal. It's just damn terrible though that our masters come in here to sit down and be waited on, but we must enter the back door and beg.

"I been wondering about what you told me about your mother and father, and it got me thinking. Did you ever give it a thought that Master Lee and your cook might be your actual mother and father?" asked Pompey.

"I been teased about that endlessly by some of the field slaves, and I just try to forget the question. All I know is I'm black and a slave. Even if it were true, what good is it for me? I'm still black. I see how free blacks are treated, and I doubt if it would be any different than how I am treated now. No. I am a slave, and I am black. That's all I need to know."

Pompey said, "There's been rumors for years about the Rutledge family and newborn slaves on their plantations. All I know is that they have all power, and we slaves must follow their demands. The womenfolk in South Carolina have a tight bond, but nothing is going to stop what the master wants to do when he gets it into his head that he wants something. It makes you wonder what the white women are thinking when they see little babies being born on their plantations from dark black mothers who create soft brown skin babies. They can't run from the truth, but they don't do anything about it. White women almost act as slaves to the masters. I guess that the overseers don't see any difference in abusing their own womenfolk as much as they abuse us."

Pompey took the empty plates and bowls back to the kitchen that once again was bustling with activity. He made a wave at Mr. Brown, but the cook was too busy to notice. At least, he will see the tongue licked plates and bowl when things are quiet.

Rutledge and Sam Adams Work Together

Edward knew that Sam Adams was one of the most powerful leaders of the radical delegates during the Second Continental Congress, calling immediately for independence from Britain. When he first met Adams, and his cousin, John, during the First Continental Congress in 1775, John Adams quickly developed a negative image of Rutledge and his brother, John. John Adams exuded a condescending approach to both, criticizing their demeanor, political views and the way they spoke, while Sam was more compassionate and focused on action. Edward realized that the relationship with Sam and John Adams was as different as Edward's disposition between his brother John and himself.

Before January 1776, Edward had little committee work with Sam or John Adams. This all changed when he was surprised to be on a committee to create a War Office. It was the first committee of substance that Rutledge had been nominated to serve on with Samuel Adams, Thomas Lynch (who would soon leave for South Carolina because of a stroke), Benjamin Harrison of Virginia, his friend, Samuel Ward from Rhode Island, and Robert Morris from Pennsylvania. As usual, Edward found himself, age twenty-six, on a committee where the average age was about fifty-five.

While John Rutledges reputation preceded him, Edward had to earn his influence through careful speech, strategic alliances, and a posture of deference that masked his ambition. The younger Rutledge may have felt the sting of comparison, but also the drive to distinguish himself, not merely as a brother, but as a delegate with his own convictions. In the candlelit halls of Congress, he listened, learned, and waited for the strategic moments to speak, knowing that history rarely favors the second name unless it announces itself with clarity and force.

Following an afternoon of business at the Congress, the committee met in a second floor room at the State House. Benjamin Harrison, who had been presiding at the earlier Congress session, called the meeting to order.

"We are gathered here this afternoon gentlemen to discuss how best to organize a War Office to better assist General Washington and to facilitate the best flow of information and decision making," stated Harrison.

"How is it to be presumed that we can make decisions for the General when we are not even close to the battlefield, with little firsthand information to make educated judgements?" asked Samuel Ward.

Sam Adams replied, "Our role is not to make decisions for General Washington but to improve information flow about maneuvers, armaments, materials, and guns. We often discuss these topics in Congress, but they are better decided by those closer to the action."

"Gentlemen, it is my belief that we should concentrate on how best, in the long run, we can manage the affairs of the War effort, but to leave the military decisions to our Generals," said Robert Morris.

Morris, the pragmatic financier from Pennsylvania, and Adams, the fiery radical from Massachusetts, represented contrasting but influential strains of revolutionary thought. For Edward Rutledge, a young delegate from conservative South Carolina, working with them may have felt both daunting and instructive as it offered a chance to observe power in motion and to assert Southern interests amid growing calls for independence.

Edward had never had any relationship with Robert Morris, although he knew from comments by his brother that Morris was managing the finances for the Revolution from his vast experience as a merchant and investor. Edward had frequently encountered individuals in South Carolina of substantial wealth, but Morris appeared to reside in a significantly more elevated economic tier. Nearly every day, when financial resources were required for gunpowder or uniforms, Morris procured the necessary funds.

Though he often favored moderation, Rutledge understood the importance of unity. Serving on a committee to consider the establishment of a war office placed him at the heart of the Congress's evolving military strategy. In the company of Morris and Adams, he felt the tension between youthful deference and the need to shape the future, not just of the colonies, but of his own political identity.

Benjamin Harrison said, "Please excuse me if I missed some of the debate on this matter, but I heard that the critical decision we should undertake is whether we have the propriety to establish such an office. For all the reasons already suggested, we should tread lightly on rushing forward with a plan before we even know what the latitude of such a body should have."

"Thank you, Benjamin for this sage advice," said Adams. "We should wonder no small amount why your experience has been added to this committee."

"I am in concert with this advice, but Congress has taken the time and effort to form this committee, and they only want to know how the office should be formed and what the power of a War Office should be."

Harrison asked, "Young Rutledge. What say you on this matter?"

Edward was surprised by the question. It reminded him of law school in London when a professor asked for details of a case that was on the reading list, but he had not read. Edward had started to describe the circumstances of the case, but he could not remember the outcome. His professor cut him off in mid-sentence and asked another student to answer the question. He must not fail this test.

Edward said, "I agree that we should examine the propriety of our recommendation to create such an office before we decide what powers should be given to such a department. Currently, Congress receives information almost daily about how best to finance and run the war effort. I see the new committee to be the repository for the questions asked. The committee will take a broader view of this coordination and make referrals to the full Congress on an as-needed basis. General Washington seems to be managing situations quite well without our interference so I am not sure if creating another committee or office will improve his progress."

"I agree with young Rutledge," said Adams. "I think our work could be better understood if we look at both issues before us. Should we establish such an office, and if so, what power should it possess?

"Our committee would not have been established unless a considerable number of our delegates thought that a War Office should be created," offered Harrison. "I believe that we should form two subcommittees to examine both issues. Should an office be established, and what authority would it possess? Mr. Morris, would you be so kind to lead the first subcommittee on the efficacy of such an office? I would be glad to see that the other group meets."

"I accept this responsibility if the other members assembled here agree," responded Morris.

Being in agreement, Ward would join the Morris group while Rutledge and Adams would work with Harrison. The group decided to get together in a week so that each subgroup could meet before making recommendations.

"I think we should go to the City Tavern, order some food, and find a private room where we can eat and work," said Adams. "I talked to the proprietor the other night, and he said it should be easy to find a study room for us to use."

The three patriots bounded out of the State House with their overcoats pulled snugly around their throats and turned south toward the City Tavern. The late afternoon sky was overcast, and it felt like snow would be in the air soon.

Stepping into the City Tavern was like crossing a threshold into warmth, noise, and revolution. The air inside was thick with pipe smoke and the scent of roast beef, ale, and spiced pudding. Delegates from Congress, merchants, and officers crowded the tables, their voices rising in debate and laughter, cloaks draped over chairs and boots drying near the hearth. On this night, a fiddler played in the corner, half-drown out by the clatter of dishes and the bark of orders from the kitchen. Amid the din, one could catch fragments of conversation about news from Boston, rumors of French interest, and the ever-present question of independence.

As they reached the tavern, Adams opened the wooden door and made his way to the bar where he hailed the bartender with a great "Hello!"

"Aye, Mr. Adams. Back so soon? What is your pleasure this afternoon? asked the burly bartender with a clipped beard, a tousle of black hair, an apron hung loosely on his body, and a rag in his hand.

"Ebeneezer, dear friend," cried Adams. "We're in need of a room upstairs for some food and a meeting. Can you help us?"

"Sure! Go upstairs and the second door on the left should be open for you. I'll send up one of the servant boys with an order in a minute or two. Do you gentlemen want a drink to take with you?"

"How about three ciders for us to get started."

"Coming right up for you, gents." The drinks were on the bar in a flash, and each grabbed a full mug, and made their way to the stairs, an oasis from the bedlam on the main floor.

At the top of the stairs, one could see the bodies below moving around, arms being waved in every direction. The smoke from the tobacco pipes mixed with the smell of burning wood in the fireplace and filled the giant room like a blanket on the heads of the revelers.

Ascending the narrow staircase to the second-floor meeting room of the City Tavern brought a sudden shift from the clamor of the public dining hall below to a quieter, more deliberate hum of conversation. The room was lit by clusters of candles set in brass sconces and pewter holders, casting flickering shadows across the paneled walls and polished floorboards This was no ordinary supper gathering. It was a crucible of ideas, where whispers of independence mingled with logistical talk of supplies, troop movements, and alliances. The room felt charged, not with celebration, but with the weight of decisions that might soon reshape the world.

"Here's the room, gentlemen," Adams said. "We can get some quiet if we shut the door, but for me, I like the camaraderie from downstairs. I'll leave it to you."

Sam had already found a chair before Edward was hardly in the room. Harrison grabbed a chair across from Adams, and Rutledges seat was the only chair with a high back.

"I reckon that you will sit in the throne, Ned," said Sam.

Benjamin smiled and said, "Have a seat, young man."

Harrison opened a pouch that he was carrying with paper, pen and ink. "Our job is to make a recommendation about the powers of the War Office," he said.

Adams said, "We should create a system to provide the necessary supplies for the strategies that General Washington requests. Our focus should be on information and how Congress can translate this into action. The committee should be the place where General Washington will know his requests for the everyday needs of battle can be communicated and know that he will be heard."

Harrison was trying to catch all the words from Adams which were often difficult to hear as his mouth was in constant motion. Rutledge noted that Sam Adams was a man of action.

Edward began, "We have been asked to establish an office to monitor the war and to provide provisions so that it will be successful. The large distance from Massachusetts to the Carolinas means that, even if General Washington is busy with troops in one colony, it is probable that the British Army will be attacking elsewhere. The office should be knowledgeable about military reconnaissance, troop movements, uniforms and ordnance, leadership and officers, and military correspondence and letters."

"That's a good start, Rutledge," said Harrison. "I am not sure if the delegates were chosen to manage these tasks as this will be a great deal of information to follow."

"But we are doing a great deal of this now as requests for additional men and arms are constantly on our agenda," said Adams. "Just within the last week requests for powder, clothing and arms have all been discussed during the Congress meetings. If we can establish a standing committee that could monitor these details, we would have more time to speak about strategy and support."

Rutledge said, "The terms of enlistments seem to be a problem as noted in the correspondence from General Washington, and the pay schedule is connected to enlistment also. Furthermore, some of the colonies, like South Carolina, have militia, that might be confused with the Continental Army. Clear distinctions need to be made lest conflicts between commanding officers could spiral into blurred lines of authority."

"What should be done about captured soldiers, prisoners of war?" asked Adams. "As the battles become more intense, POWs will naturally occur. We need to develop a policy on how prisoners are handled, not to mention the exchange of prisoners' process. Where do we house them in the meantime?"

"Gentlemen, I am trying to reduce all these ideas into writing, so please go a little more slowly. I think I have the gist of the conversation, so why don't we order some food so that we can chew on our thoughts?" said Harrison.

Adams moved to the open door and yelled to a waiter who came in and took orders for food and refills for drink. Harrison sat back in his chair and reviewed the document filled with notes of the meeting and sighed, "I think we have the start of an excellent report. Let's have some drink and the rest of our work will go easy."

Noting a break from the discussion about developing a War Office, Rutledge had been mulling over the notion of discussing with Harrison and Adams his concern about the language that was included in the Continental Association document regarding the slave trade. He stood up and walked near the door where Adams was waiting for the food to be delivered,

"Mr. Adams, I wanted to discuss with you something we agreed upon at the First Continental Congress and how that action may affect our work in Philadelphia today."

"What's on your mind, young man?"

Rutledge said, "I would like your understanding of the Continental Association we adopted and sent to the colonies specifically about the non-importation of slaves. Do you believe that it is in our self-interest to pursue the suggestions made in the Association since the King has ignored our Olive Branch Petition and has attacked and killed colonists?"

Edward continued, "That was over a year ago, and I think the strategies and actions we need to take today are completely different than those we agreed to before. The King has shown his colors, and I doubt if he has any interest in appreciating our concerns. I don't think the slave trade is part of the discussion that we have here today,"

"I am not too sure if I would agree with that position, Mr. Rutledge," Benjamin Harrison said. "The dual purpose of that section in our Association was to put economic pressure on the King, and to put us on a path toward curbing the slave trade in the colonies. I am sure that is not the answer that pleases your ear, Edward, but I have concluded that slavery, in a long view, will be an issue that either tears us apart or fades from our memories. The clause regarding the slave trade in the Continental Association was a message to the colonies, that we need to repair our own houses if we wish to be truly independent."

Approaching the table to answer Harrison, who remained seated at the table, Rutledge said, "Sir, I am not in agreement with your position. As I am sure you know, Virginia and South Carolina are the wealthiest of the American colonies and the source of that wealth has been the successful plantation system we utilize. I would not say that independence is more important than our plantation economy, but I know that many of my fellow Carolinians would think twice about losing life and fortune if it meant that we could not continue to run our own economy."

At this point the food had arrived, and Sam Adams said, "Why don't we get something to eat and maybe we can postpone discussion on this matter another time. Our job is to create a War Office and not to tackle such a tough issue as slavery."

Rutledge thought to himself, "*I don't know if I have an appetite for dinner now.*"

"Please sit down, Ned," said Sam Adams. "The three of us will not settle this matter in a meeting room on the second floor of the City Tavern. That conversation deserves the attention of a larger group of delegates than us.

"I apologize, Edward, for my bluntness," said Harrison. "My wife always reminds me I should have someone check my choice of words before I get myself into trouble. We are here to discuss the War Office and as we finish dinner, we will accomplish that end."

"Thank you, Sam, for that advice," Rutledge said. "I have been thinking that the establishment of the War Office is to act like an established nation. We desire to centralize our military coordination and improve our supply lines so that our troops don't move too far out from their supplies."

Harrison said, "Ned, I think you are heading down a good course. Having a War Office will demonstrate to foreign powers that we know how to prioritize our plans within the limits we have. Diplomatically, France and Spain may be more interested in siding with our cause if they see a serious effort on our part to govern and rule."

"We don't have the experience and expertise to handle this kind of organization," Sam Adams said. "The communication system we have is too slow to meet the needs of immediate war planning when strategies need to be altered in real time. We are looking at trying to build a country from Massachusetts to the Carolinas when it takes weeks to get information from one far point to another."

****

Sending information across long distances in 1776 was a slow, uncertain, and often perilous endeavor. Letters were the primary means of communication, but without a fully developed postal system, they relied on travelers, merchants, or trusted acquaintances to carry them, sometimes by horseback, wagon, or ship. A message sent a hundred miles could take two weeks to arrive, and there was no guarantee it had reached its destination unless a reply confirmed receipt. Roads were rough, weather unpredictable, and wartime conditions added the risk of interception or delay. Newspapers and broadsides helped spread news in urban centers, but rural areas remained isolated, and word of mouth was still a vital conduit. In a time when revolution depended on coordination, the fragility of communication was prone to espionage and interference, being both a logistical challenge and a constant source of anxiety.

"Everyone has that problem," said Harrison. "It's not like the British have a secret way to report from one place of their empire to another without encountering the problem of logistics. I am not worried as much about communication as I am about how we are going to be able to pay for guns, powder, uniforms, and meals. The list goes on further than I wish to think."

"Congress will be the place where those financial decisions need to take place, but the War Office should be the place to calculate what those costs will be," said Rutledge. "Congress must decide how the burden of finances will be shouldered by each colony."

"Rutledge, the more I hear you talk, the more I appreciate the value you add to this committee."

"Thank you for the kindness, Mr. Harrison."

"When you mention finances and Congress making the decisions on the sharing arrangements," said Adams, "I can predict easily that there will be howling when everyone understands that the public purse must be sustained by the equitable contributions of all who enjoy its protections."

"Political infighting has not hurt our efforts thus far, but I worry at some point each colony will desire to have their interests be paramount to another region," Edward said.

Harrison leaned back in his chair and said, "That is why we need the War Office. Congress has already realized the value of the committees that we utilize to handle problems as they arise. The War Office needs to be established so that we can handle the bulk of the work to organize the military effort on the ground."

Sam Adams said, "Let us not beat about the bush, but address plainly the point to Congress. We need to set down specific powers that the War Office should have, and we will report regularly to Congress on our progress and needs.

Benjamin Harrison said, "Gentlemen, I think we have an outline to bring to Congress. Why doesn't each of us volunteer to summarize these responsibilities, and then we will meet again tomorrow to combine them and bring a report to Congress?"

"I'll write the section on supplies and resources," said Rutledge.

"I can put together a draft on developing a centralized system for making decisions," Adams said.

"And I will develop recommendations for signaling to foreign governments that we can achieve independence," said Harrison.

Sam Adams said, "Let's finish this good food on the table and break until tomorrow."

The men joked about the quality of the food, the watered-down cider and the lack of heat in the room then left when they had finished eating. Little did they know that battles fought further away north of Massachusetts would soon dominate their attention.

The Failed Canada Entreaty

Patriots in New England and New York were fearful that, when the British troops started to engage the colonies at Concord, Lexington, and Breeds Hill, the King would send reinforcements from the north. The redcoats would menacingly march south along the Hudson River and severing the New England colonies from the balance of the colonies to the south. Of particular concern was the British stronghold at Fort Ticonderoga located at the southern tip of Lake Champlain that was armed with large cannons.

Taking control of the situation less than a month after the battles at Lexington and Concord, Ethan Allen and Benedict Arnold acted without the approval of the Continental Congress, marched in secret to Fort Ticonderoga, and captured the fort with almost no bloodshed. Allen and his Green Mountain Men of Vermont came from an area of New England that, due to conflicting survey work done when each colony was founded, was disputed by New York and New Hampshire. Forces under the command of Benedict Arnold of Connecticut organized fifty militia men and marched to Ticonderoga, only to find that Allen had reached the same conclusion about the fort. Together, they found it lightly defended with fewer than fifty soldiers. Allen and Arnold captured this major military position without the loss of a single man. In control of the fort and its battery of cannons, Allen and Arnold quickly decided to proceed north to capture another British possession at Crown Point on the northern shore of Lake Champlain.

The activities of these two headstrong leaders and their militias were completed without the knowledge of the Second Continental Congress, which was notified a week later. After hearing about the capture of the fort on Lake Champlain, Congress asked John Jay to write a leaflet that was to be distributed to the residents of Canada, stating that the American colonies were asking the Canadian people to join with the patriots to cast off the heavy hand of British control. The patriots believed that people in Quebec, which had been ceded to Britain after the French and Indian War, would be open to this request.

Congress authorized troops from Connecticut to proceed to Ticonderoga and Crown Point but specifically instructed all combatants to refrain from invading Canada so that the peace letter could have a chance at success. General Arnold did not wait for any instructions and followed the Richelieu River north into Canada to surprise the British Army at Fort St. Jean, immediately south of Montreal. However, he was unsuccessful in taking the fort and fell back to Crown Point.

Although Quebec was a recent addition to Britain as spoils from the French and Indian War, they had no deep loyalty to the British. To curry favor with the local residents, Parliament passed the Quebec Act of 1774. It granted to the French residents of Quebec City permission to follow their Catholic faith which it was hoped would elicit greater allegiance to King George. The Act also enlarged the Quebec colony to include all lands south to the Ohio River. The American colonies had miscalculated in thinking the shared grievances over the British domination would resonate and bring them over to the cause of the patriots.

The total armed forces of the colonists and the British army currently in Canada were not of great size. General Guy Carleton of the British Army had only 800 soldiers to call on to defend Montreal. The defense of the walled city of Quebec City contained an additional 800 militia members. The plan that was communicated with the Continental Congress was to direct the army of Benedict Arnold to approach Quebec City from the southeast via the heavily wooded regions of Maine that was part of the Massachusetts colony. Congress had recently named General Phillip Schuyler to lead the Northern Division of the Continental Army, and his regiments would travel north to the lightly protected fort at St. Jean and then proceed to Quebec City. The weather in Maine that November was dominated by an early snowfall that caused frostbite and disease which cut through Arnold's ranks, leaving only 675 out of 1,100 soldiers who had started the journey. The trip through Maine would take forty-five days, twice as long as expected. General Phillip Schuyler, named by Congress to lead this part of the Continental Army became ill before the attack began, and gave the control over the operations to General Richard Montgomery who commanded an army of 2,000 men.

In its third attempt, General Montgomery captured the Fort at St. Jean with its 400 cannons and took 500 prisoners. After weeks to read the letter that was distributed to Canadian residents from the Continental Congress, Montgomery sent Ethan Allen to recruit Canadians to become part of the Continental Army. After enlisting 350 men, Arnold, without orders from Montgomery, turned south to claim Montreal hoping that Major John Brown's troops from the Continental Army would support him. Unfortunately, Brown's reinforcements never arrived in Montreal. Disastrously, Arnold met strong forces, was defeated, and Allen was captured as a prisoner of war. After General Mongomery subdued St. Jeans, he sent a small cadre of soldiers to Montreal and easily subdued the Canadians there, but the British forces defending Montreal had already left for Quebec City, taking their prisoner Allen with them.

On November 18, 1775, General Montgomery, after securing St. Jean, took his decimated band of less than 400 patriots toward Quebec with hopes of seeing 2000 soldiers under Arnold's command. When he arrived at Quebec City on December 2, he met with Arnold, and the combined forces of their armies totaled only 1700 men.

On November 29, 1775, the Second Continental Congress received word by courier from General Phillip Schuyler that General Richard Montgomery had successfully conquered Montreal and was marching northeast to Quebec City to bring Canada under American control.

On December 23, Congress learned that General Schuyler needed more enlisted men as most of their tours of duty had been completed and additional troops would be needed to secure Crown Point and Ticonderoga. On December 25, Montgomery ordered an attack on the walled city of Quebec City and was repulsed by the British garrison leaving General Montgomery dead. By this time, General Arnold rallied his remaining 600 troops and began a tactical retreat to fight another day. The Second Continental Congress would not learn of General Montgomery's death and the complete debacle of the Canadian expedition until January 15, 1776.

Although Americans remained in control of Montreal and there was a Continental Army presence surrounding Quebec City, spring brought fresh British troops and new war ships. Congress sent a peace commission consisting of Benjamin Franklin, Samuel Chase, and Charles Carroll, but the American representatives were disappointed to learn that the Canadian territories would never become the 14th colony. By May 6, British reserves led by General John Burgoyne with Hessian mercenaries had arrived, and the fate of the Canadian adventure became clear. After more defeats by the British over colonist's forces, the long retreat to Crown Point began and it was met by reinforcements Congress sent too late to bring a different ending.

Congress Must Face The Cold Facts

The cold winds of January 1776 remained unfamiliar to Edward Rutledge as he stepped out of his 2nd Street boardinghouse heading for Congress. Wrapped in a fine woolen cloak against the biting January wind, he would walk the half-mile stretch to the Statehouse with a deliberate, measured pace befitting his station as a wealthy South Carolina planter and delegate. His boots struck the frozen cobblestones with crisp precision, and his powdered hair was tucked beneath a beaver-skinned tricorne hat, shielding him from the flurries drifting down from the gray sky. Though Philadelphia's streets bustled with tradesmen, porters, and errand boys, Rutledge moved with quiet authority, nodding curtly to acquaintances and avoiding the muck near the gutters where refuse and ice mingled. His thoughts likely churned with the day's debates, independence, military supply, and the fragile unity of the colonies, while his eyes scanned the brick facades and tavern signs that marked this northern capital of revolution. In that short walk, he carried not just the weight of Southern interests, but the burden of youth among elder statesmen, and the growing realization that history was being shaped with every step. The swirls of snow across the hard-beaten street swirled around his boots as he pulled his greatcoat tightly around his torso and trudged along. Rutledge kept a hand close to the brim of his hat to secure it from gusts that were prevalent. Heading to the Statehouse for the latest meeting of Congress, he was hopeful that fireplaces there would be roaring with toasty blazes.

The latest rumor among the delegates was that news had come from Canada about the expedition to enlist the support of the Canadians to the cause of the colonies. Edward was curious about how the Continental Army could make the Canadian settlements safe in the north when the southern border of the colonies, like South Carolina and Georgia felt vulnerable. At least to the north, patriots from Connecticut and New York had taken the initiative in capturing the British outpost at Ticonderoga, but Rutledges mind was concerned about how well The Continentals could withstand the inevitable counterattack from Britain.

The news throughout the summer had been favorable even though Congress had limited knowledge of encounters with the British on Canadian soil. The colonists hoped the Canadians would respond to the letter of invitation sent by Congress asking them to join in the colonies' offensive against The Crown. By fall, Congress had learned that the Fort at St. John's had fallen to the Continentals. Maybe this new letter would bring more good news on this decidedly cold morning.

"Good morning, Mr. Rutledge," Edward heard from behind. The voice of Thomas Stone was easily recognizable even as a noisy gust of wind penetrated his coat.

"I dare say that this torturous weather would never be referred to as good in my pleasant South Carolina. I'm looking forward to the warmer environment of our meeting space and a hot mug of tea."

"Did you hear the news from Canada?"

"I heard that a letter has been received but know not of its contents. We could tolerate the receipt of encouraging news on this biting, chilly morning."

"I heard a rumor that things have not gone as expected," said Stone. "It's my understanding that casualties have been unexpectedly high."

"I am not an expert on the geography of Canada, but if we are suffering from the early onslaught of winter extremes in these lands, what must it be like in Quebec?" If Quebec is as far north of Philadelphia as Charleston is to the South, those colonial troops had better have warm mittens and long underwear to survive the battles."

****

Quebec City endured bitter cold and deep snow, with temperatures often plunging below 5°F, isolating the city as the St. Lawrence River froze and sleighs replaced carts on snowbound streets. By contrast, Philadelphia experienced a more moderate winter, with occasional snow and freezing temperatures, but also intermittent thaws that turned its cobbled streets into a muddy, slushy mess.

Stone added, "Congress prepared a bulletin that was to be distributed among the residents to welcome them to our cause, and we have approved measures for Connecticut, New York, and

Massachusetts to send additional troops and support. I can't quite understand how Captain Allen could have been captured while we were able to take control of Montreal. Is it possible that we are not receiving a full picture of what is happening on the ground?"

Rutledge had been thinking along the same lines but felt unsure about saying it out loud lest appearing to be weak. "I have struggled with the same thoughts. Often weeks seem to pass before I am apprised of happenings in my own plantation when I am working here in Philadelphia. Maybe it is not just the weather that can change over great distances. It may also be the delivery of news."

Finally, the two delegates found the warmth of the Statehouse where many other delegates milled around with an anxious buzz in the chamber. Less than five minutes after their arrival, John Hancock, the President of the Congress, was wielding his gavel and calling for order among the delegates. "Delegates, please take your seats. I have a correspondence from General Schuyler with important information about the progress of the Northern Division in Canada."

Hancock then gave the letters received from General Schuyler, General Wooster, and General Arnold to Charles Thompson, the secretary, to read. In a slow and deliberate pace, the secretary read the ill news regarding the account of the unsuccessful attempt made to gain possession of Quebec on December 31, including the death of Brigadier General Richard Montgomery.

The delegates gasped for breath, and with solemn silence and deep unease, mourned a fallen hero while reckoning with the sobering reality of their military vulnerability.

The secretary read the ignominious details of the attack with the deaths, and other casualties suffered by the brave patriots who fought for the cause of liberty in Canada. A hush filled the room. General David Wooster's letter described the heroic death of Montgomery, which brought into focus the full force of the sacrifice by these men and galvanized the steely purpose of liberty in the atmosphere of the Statehouse. General Arnold's detailed diary of the long march to Canada through the wintery Maine forests and the desperate attempt to seize the walled fortress of Quebec, mesmerized the gathered delegates and brought into focus the long journey toward independence and the grave cost to prevail.

As the secretary finished reading, a quiet filled the room. For months, the delegates had been led to believe that the endeavor for Canada was going to be completed, and these frigid facts felt like a bath of ice water.

Hancock spoke, "I resolve that a committee of five be established to make a report on the correspondence and report to the Congress. Members of the committee will be George Wythe, Roger Sherman, Samuel Ward, Sam Adams, and Thomas Lynch."

Rutledge said to Stone, "I was afraid that such a tragedy could happen, but I am heartened to learn that we will have some idea of what the report will contain as we have a good friend in Samuel, although Lynch will not be up to the challenge because of his health."

"I am glad that some of our elders like Wythe and Sherman will be of great aid in this hour of reflection," Thomas added.

Edward Rutledge received the news of General Richard Montgomery's death at Quebec with a heavy heart and sharpened anxiety, recognizing not only the loss of a brave commander but the fragility of the Continental Army's northern campaign. As a delegate from South Carolina, his thoughts quickly turned southward to Charleston's exposed coastline and the growing threat of British retaliation. Montgomery's fall underscored the reality that patriot forces were not invincible. Rutledge, young, ambitious, and deeply protective of his home colony, felt the pressure to advocate for stronger defenses, more supplies, and clearer coordination. The death of a general in the snowbound north was a distant tragedy, but for Rutledge, it was also a warning that Charleston, with its wealth and strategic port, might soon face the same fate if Congress did not act swiftly and decisively.

To drive the point home that Quebec and South Carolina were connected in their fight for liberty, Congress heard a final item on the agenda for the day that called for seamen to be provided by Virginia to South Carolina following a request that the colony had submitted the previous week.

The session was gaveled to adjournment to be brought open again tomorrow at 10:00 AM.

Slaves Know The Language

Caesar left the bedroom of his master, Francis Lightfoot Lee, after he had completed his tasks for the evening and headed down to the kitchen to exit from the house at the rear. He had promised Pompey that he would meet with him this evening after they had completed their obligations with their owners so they could share the latest news. Caesar tried to remember all the conversations that he had overheard at supper where Francis, his brother Richard Henry, and George Wythe had dined discussing the latest affairs at Congress.

Pompey had become a good friend among the other valets who served at the side of their masters as they discussed freedom for the colonists who strove to avert enslavement by the King of England. Caesar shook his head often, when he thought of the fact that their masters could not see the irony in their fear of becoming slaves while they ordered their slaves to shine their master's boots. He could not imagine Francis Lightfoot Lee ever shining anyone's boots! What should a seventeen-year-old Negro slave man-child know about Congress or the King? Caesar did not mind the fact that his master had no idea that he could read or write or that he had any opinions about anything. The master liked it best when you didn't say anything unless asked and, heavens, didn't give your opinion. Caesar's job was to get his tasks done quickly with no fuss or pride.

The night was cold with the wind blowing off the river. The trees that lined Chestnut Street bent from the force of the gusts and their leafless limbs partially blocked the half-moon that was rising in the east. Caesar pulled the scarf he wore over his mouth to keep the heat close to his nose. He had no gloves, and he struggled to keep his hands warm. At least Master Francis had finally provided him a cap to cover his head with flaps that he could use to keep his ears warm. Caesar could see his breath turn into wisps of clouds in the frozen air as it was illuminated by the gas lights along the sidewalk which remained a mystery to him. He paused beneath the glow, eyes lifted in quiet awe, and marveled at how the flame burned without wick or lantern, casting a steady light across the cobbled street like something conjured from a gentleman's parlor tale. With a low whistle and a half-smile, he'd murmured to himself, "Well now, even the night's got company in this city." He headed for two blocks to find Pompey, who would be in the rear of Mrs. Yard's boardinghouse on Second Street.

As he turned the corner, he saw a black figure one hundred paces away. It was Pompey, and he was waving his arms to beckon his arrival.

"Pompey, I was hoping you were not going to forget me this evening. I had no idea it was going to be this cold tonight."

Caesar tugged his coat tighter and muttered, as the northern wind bit through his wool coat like it had a grudge, "We're not in Virginia or South Carolina tonight. I reckon you haven't been acquainted enough with the wintry climate of the north," Each breath puffed white in the air, and he'd shook his head, thinking how even the frost here seemed to carry itself with Yankee pride.

"Oh, and the winter and I are well acquainted. I just don't like being reminded about it so often and so rudely."

"Did you learn about anything today?"

"For the most part, they talked about Canada," said Caesar. "I don't see what that is all about, but they didn't like the news they received. It sounded like they were expecting one event, and they got the opposite. Neither Mr. Francis nor Mr. Richard were very happy."

"Previously, they received good news about defeating the British at a Fort Ticonderoga, and they thought they could capture Canada. It sounds to me that the results didn't work out so well."

While elite white society debated the boundaries of new states and foreign alliances, the valet's mental map was intimate, local, and often tied to survival, where danger lay, where kin might be found, and where freedom was rumored to exist.

"Where is Canada and why is it so important?" asked Caesar.

Pompey tried to explain as best he could. "I don't know all the details, but Canada is owned by the British, though the French owned it before a war twenty-five years ago. Our masters thought that the Canadians might remain angry at the British and join us against Britain now. I guess they weren't as mad as the colonists thought."

"It sounded from the conversations that our master's don't think the cause is completely lost. I heard them talking about sending some delegates to talk with someone about fixing the problem."

"Seems to me that the masters have enough to worry about with the redcoats in Boston and New York, but of course, no one asked my opinion."

"I think maybe they should. Did Master Edward speak his mind again about the many things he doesn't know?"

"Do I detect a measure of sarcasm in your voice, young man?"

"Your master acts like he knows everything even when he knows that he doesn't. Have you ever heard him say 'I don't know'?"

"You're a merry wag, you are, Caesar. Sometimes, I think you know my master better than your own."

Caeser knew he could sense his own master's temper when his boots struck the floor. Quick and sharp meant bad news, and slow and heavy meant whiskey had softened him. While the gentleman prided himself on mystery, Caesar could predict his moods, vices, and secrets with more accuracy than any friend at the dinner table.

"You can see into him like he's made of glass. He must have said something else that will tell us more about how the Congress is working."

"The talk about Canada dominated the conversations the last couple of nights with Mr. Rutledge and his friends. They seem to be fixated on Canada. Why would they have an interest in a colony further north than South Carolina is in the south? The native Indians were also on their mind, and I think they still don't have any idea about how to make them less of a threat."

"I don't know about you, but I think the Indians are a bigger problem than the British. We haven't had much of a problem with them near my home, but I hear that is not the case elsewhere."

Slaves often held complex and varied views of Native Americans, shaped less by direct contact and more by the stories, fears, and political rhetoric they overheard in elite households. Some may have seen Native peoples as fellow outsiders to white colonial society, groups resisting domination, navigating survival, and holding knowledge of the land that even powerful men respected or feared. Others, influenced by their masters' prejudices or wartime propaganda, might have viewed Native alliances with the British or violent frontier raids with apprehension. Yet for many valets, Native Americans represented a kind of freedom, unfamiliar, perhaps dangerous, but untethered to the rigid hierarchies of plantation life.

Their thoughts were likely a blend of curiosity, caution, and quiet admiration, filtered through the limited, but telling, glimpses they caught from the margins.

"It's a giant problem around Carolina. I understand that an enormous conflict happened about fifty years ago, and that's when they started to try to enslave Indians the same way as us. The Indians seemed to always just walk away and the masters would hardly chase after them."

"That sounds familiar to me. Virginia had a big war with them a long time ago, but they are as fearful of them returning as they are of Africans rebelling. In my estimation, Virginia colonists know as little about the Indians as they know about us. All they do is try to exploit both Indians and Africans for their own use."

"Pompey, you really know how to look at things honestly. The master has all the power but has more brawn than brain. Why wouldn't the Indians be mad at the colonists? England just came here and stole all the land that the Indians have used for a long time. Just look at us, they steal us from Africa, and the colonists think that we act the same as the natives. The masters just don't know anything about how to treat a human being like they should. They only want to dominate and make money."

"Caesar, I don't think that is the sort of comment you should make in front of Mr. Lee. I would agree with you about the lack of understanding by the colonists. They know nothing of our reverence for shamans or our honoring our ancestors. They think we are savages or pagans with witchcraft. They show us no respect."

"My father told me about the time when he was first a slave here in America," said Caesar. "An old man who was a revered spirit talker among the slaves was practicing an ancient ritual of bringing the essence of his long past grandmother to mind by starting a small fire, burning sage, and waving his body and hands to reach her soul in the afterlife. After an hour, he reported to his family the vision that he saw, and they attained peace knowing that the woman was well in the afterlife. Hiding behind a large tree, an overseer for the master witnessed the event and reported back to the master that the slaves were practicing witchcraft. The master told the overseer to bring the old man to him so he could punish the slave for causing a potential revolt. These white men have no idea how important our spiritual lives are, especially when we need to survive the horrors of being a slave."

"Caesar, that is so true. I remember two summers ago, a few of the older slaves decided that it would help us feel better about ourselves if they could perform a drum service for members of the family. The men hollowed out large limbs and then stretched animal skins over the logs and made drums. The men then waited for a night with a full moon and began their drumming. The overseer abruptly showed up after about an hour and told the old men that drumming was against the law and that they had better stop or everyone would be punished. They stopped but hid the drums for future use. Apparently, the law they broke was established after a slave revolt forty years earlier. Those white people do scare easily," said Pompey.

"Master Lee and his friends were talking about money again," said Caesar. "and how this person needed to be paid and the price of buying powder or uniforms. They act like they have a never-ending source of money. They certainly don't spend very much of that money on us."

"Sounds like things are about the same, except about that Canada business."

"I am chilled to the bone, my friend. I am going back to the warmth of the kitchen. I'm hoping there is a place next to the hearth where I can sleep tonight."

"If your place is like ours, you probably already lost your spot. Stay warm and tell Cato I said hello."

"Sure enough, Pompey. Be well, my friend," said Caesar as he turned up the alley and followed the few blocks walk into the chilly night toward his home. He wondered when the colonists would just use some common sense in their relations with the slaves and the British.

THOMAS PAINE BRINGS *COMMON SENSE*

The moderates at the Continental Congress had delayed endorsement due to the lack of consensus among most of the citizens they represented. When sent to Philadelphia, many of these men did not have the full endorsement from their colony's assemblies to support a declaration on independence. The political temperature had continued to rise with each reported transgression committed against the colonies by the King, whether it be the attack on Minutemen in Lexington, the Proclamation from the Virginia Governor citing an open rebellion and offering to free slaves who joined the British army, or the conscription of foreign mercenaries to help the British put down the American rebellion Yet, moderate delegates remained fixed in their conviction to work toward reconciliation rather than demanding separation from Britain.

From an unexpected source, though, delegates were confronted with a groundswell of momentum from a little-known author who had penned a document that caught fire in the minds of American colonists, convincing them that talking was insufficient and now was a time for action. Thomas Paine's pamphlet, innocently titled *Common Sense* would create a tidal wave of support to declare independence by the colonies from Massachusetts to South Carolina.

Thomas Paine was recently new to the colonies, having landed in Philadelphia in December 1774 aboard a schooner that had taken nine weeks to sail from England. While in London, Paine had not had an easy path in life. He went from job to job trying to find a niche He had a talent for writing that helped him in some of his positions, but most often he found himself living on the edge. His raw talent brought him into contact with people such as playwright Oliver Goldsmith, the author of "She Stoops to Conquer," historian Edward Gibbons, author Samuel Johnson, and Benjamin Franklin, colonial agent for the American colonies of Pennsylvania, Massachusetts, and Georgia. Franklin gave Paine a letter of introduction.

Paine's early life in London could barely hint at the success that awaited him in Philadelphia. He bounced around from job to job, first as a staymaker like his father, next as a sailor on a buccaneer ship, then a patron of the coffeehouses where he met noted philosophers and writers, and finally as an inspector of commodities also known as an excise officer. In this last position, Paine wrote a pamphlet about the meager pay of such an officer employed by the government, that brought considerable attention to their plight, although the pamphlet did not ultimately sway enough votes in Parliament to alter the pay scale. Paine wrote the pamphlet, "The Case of the Officers of Excise" and although his peers found the writing outstanding, the mood of the country, and thus Parliament, did not agree. After spending considerable time publicizing the pamphlet, he was terminated from his position. At a crossroads in his life, he returned to the coffeehouse circuit and made the acquaintance of Dr. Franklin. This unlikely meeting set a narrative that would see Paine emigrating to America and becoming a national hero while developing a lifelong relationship with Franklin.

Upon arrival in Philadelphia after a grueling nine-week voyage, Franklin's physician met Paine and nursed him back to good health. He contracted a mysterious illness on the long voyage that included passengers suffering from typhus. After regaining his health, Paine sought a position in the literary field. Although numerous people had launched new magazines, few of these publications were successful. Paine contributed two articles to the inaugural edition of Pennsylvania Magazine and within a month had been designated as its editor. Circulation soared and Paine contributed more articles, many with a political edge.

Along with his work on Pennsylvania Magazine, Paine was working on the political treatise that would be known as *Common Sense*. He circulated the article as a pamphlet among many printers. The highly charged political positions he took made it difficult for him to find a willing printer, as they might become a target for printing such a radical treatise. After a couple of false starts, two printers volunteered to take a chance and started to publish what became a runaway success. Writing *Common Sense* with editorial assistance from another friend of Franklin, Dr. Benjamin Rush, the pamphlet was printed in Philadelphia in January 1776. About 120,000 copies were printed and distributed in the following three months, and more than 500,000 copies had been purchased by the end of the Revolution, when the population of the colonies was only 2.5 million.

The work was so popular that translations were made in German and French.

In addition to the sales, word of mouth publicity of *Common Sense* also boosted awareness of his clarion call for independence. In clear and understandable terms, Paine states in his conclusion:

> "Let the names of Whig and Tory be extinct; and let none other be heard among us than those of a good citizen, an open and resolute friend, and a virtuous supporter of the RIGHTS of MANKIND and of the FREE AND INDEPENDENT STATES OF AMERICA."

His forty-seven-page tract stated in succinct language for all citizens to understand, that now was the time to reject reconciliation as Britain had shown its true nature. Britain had killed colonists and adopted measures such as the Tea Act and the Stamp Act that throttled economic development of the colonies. In long passages, Paine rejected the notion that the relationship could ever be fair and reasonable if the King could rule by edict.

He clearly stated, "in America THE LAW IS KING. For as in absolute governments the King is law, so in free countries the law ought to be King; and there ought to be no other."

"We have every opportunity and every encouragement before us, to form the noblest, purest constitution on the face of the earth," Paine wrote. "We have it in our power to begin the world over again."

For the radical contingent in Philadelphia, *Common Sense* was exactly the message that many delegates wanted to hear. For the moderates, Paine's tract gave them political protection to move closer to the radicals' position while the conservatives felt the ground under their feet begin to move. Delegates to Congress started receiving letters from their fellow colonists urging them to hasten their speed toward independence. Even a radical such as Adams was surprised to receive correspondence from countrymen asking, "Why delay action when the citizens support a call for independence?"

The impact of *Common Sense* was monumental, and the leading patriots recognized its value instantly. A Connecticut reader marveled that "you have declared the sentiments of millions. Your production may just be compared to a land-flood that sweeps all before it. We were blind, but on reading those enlightening works the scales have fallen from our eyes; even deep-rooted prejudices take to themselves and flee away…The doctrine of independence hath been in times past, greatly disgustful; we abhorred the principle- it has now become our delightful theme and commands our purest affection."

Paine's pamphlet shattered all complacency with its forceful clarity, arguing that monarchy was inherently corrupt and that America's destiny lay in self-governance. His accessible prose and moral urgency resonated with a wide audience, including members of Congress, by reframing independence as both a practical necessity and a moral imperative. Paine's clear, forceful prose and radical call for a republic resonated with ordinary colonists, not just intellectuals and politicians. While other pamphlets debated policy or defended colonial rights within the British system, *Common Sense* shattered that framework, urging Americans to break free entirely. It didn't just reflect revolutionary sentiment—it accelerated it, pushing the Continental Congress toward declaring independence later that year.

General Charles Lee wrote to his commanding officer, General George Washington that "I never saw such a masterly irresistible performance. It will, if I mistake not, in concurrence with the transcendent folly and wickedness of the Ministry, give the coup-de-grace to Great Britain."

General Washington responded in kind after reading *Common Sense*, that "the sound doctrine and unanswerable reasoning contained in the pamphlet *Common Sense* will not leave the members of Congress at a loss to decide upon the propriety of separation."

John Adams was less than moved upon initial reading, and labeled it as a "tolerable summary of the arguments I have been repeating again, and again in Congress for the last nine months." Later, Adams would write Thomas Jefferson that "History is to ascribe the American Revolution to Thomas Paine," while Jefferson wrote that "no writer has exceeded Paine in ease and familiarity of style, in perspicuity of expression, happiness of elucidation, and in simple and unassuming language."

Delegates such as John Adams and Richard Henry Lee found their calls for independence increasingly supported, not just by ideological allies but by constituents energized by Paine's arguments. The pamphlet helped delegitimize the authority of King George III in the eyes of many colonists, making the idea of a break from Britain politically viable. As delegates began to debate a resolution for independence, the ideological groundwork laid by *Common Sense* had already softened resistance and prepared the Congress to act. In this way, Paine's work served as both a rhetorical catalyst and a strategic accelerant, helping transform a divided assembly into a revolutionary body ready to declare a new nation.

Benjamin Franklin's reaction to *Common Sense* was largely supportive, though somewhat understated. Franklin's broader political stance aligned with Paine's arguments for independence. He later maintained a cordial relationship with Paine, exchanging letters and helping during Paine's diplomatic efforts. Franklin's mentorship and ideological alignment helped pave the way for Paine's influence, even if his public reaction remained measured.

Now that the rationale for the revolution was clearly stated, it was the responsibility of the delegates to put a plan of action into place.

Slavery Lost in Common Sense

Cato had finished his tasks for the evening and pulled on his worn woolen jacket to venture over to Second Street in hopes of finding Pompey. The cool winds blowing off the Delaware River discouraged him from making the trek on this cold February night, but he had heard some information at dinner that Pompey might find interesting. No one was on the street in the nighttime, and the only people who Cato saw were a lamplighter and a few men making their way home from the local taverns. As he turned the corner, Cato could see someone in the alley talking to another person. It must be Pompey with one of his other valet friends.

Halfway down the alley, Cato yelled, "Pompey. Is that you?"

Immediately he saw a person leap from the shadows, waving his arms. Cato heard a voice, "Are you trying to let the entire neighborhood know that we are out here? How many times do I have to tell you to keep your voice down?" said Pompey.

"I'm sorry, Pomp. I was just excited to see you out here. But haven't you noticed that hardly anyone else is out on this cold night except us?"

Cato then saw that the other person was Bob. "Good to see you, Bob. How's life in Maryland?"

Shyly, Bob said," I guess things are good. Master Stone let me out early tonight after his dinner with Samuel Chase."

"Did either of you hear anything about a new pamphlet that people are reading about common sense? said Cato.

"Now that you mention it, Master Edward was talking the other night with John Dickinson over dinner about it," Pompey said. "I am not sure who is the one with common sense. Is it the King or the patriots?"

"To hear it from Master Richard Lee," said Cato. "*Common Sense* is what the pamphlet is called, and its focus is on the citizens of the colonies."

Bob said, "I haven't heard Master Bob talk about it at all."

"I guess you could say that your master doesn't have common sense," said Pompey.

The three valets started laughing out loud, with Pompey's laughter drowning out the others.

"I thought we were supposed to keep the noise down," said Cato. "And anyway, why are you laughing at your own jokes the loudest, Pomp?"

"Sorry about that, friends," said Pompey. "I couldn't help myself.

"Did anyone hear what was in the pamphlet?" asked Cato. "Master Lee and Francis thought it was well done."

"Edward said that it was aimed directly at the average citizen trying to alarm them of the facts of why the colonies should demand independence. The person who wrote it said, "The sun never shined on a cause of greater worth than the conflict between the colonies and England," said Pompey.

"How does this man know about a war?" said Cato. "Where does he get his facts? Does he say anything about slavery?"

Pompey said, "Master Edward said that the pamphlet may finally get all the citizens excited about independence, especially since it didn't mention slavery at all."

Bob said, "Why should that surprise any of us. We are always the last to be considered, unless they have some task, they want us to do."

Cato said, "Master Richard also said that the cause of America is in a great measure the cause of all mankind. I have a feeling that he wasn't talking about us."

Pompey said, "Our masters must think we are fools or idiots. I doubt if they could conceive that we are having this conversation because they don't think we are smart enough. What they don't realize is that some of us are as smart as our masters, even though we never went to any school like they did."

"School?" said Bob. "Master Thomas don't even like it when I tell him that I want to learn how to read. Can you imagine giving us time off to attend school with their children? I won't hold my breath for that to happen."

Cato said, "Master Richard has been kind about education for me. I'm sure that he would never let me go to school with any of his kids, but he did allow me to be taught how to read and write with the assistance of our cook. When I get home, I am going to ask if she can teach me about numbers, too."

Pompey said, "The masters have got this all wrong. They don't quake about us learning about their religion, but heaven help us if we want to learn how to spell or add."

Bob said, "Religion was one area that Master Stone has always been right good about. He gives us time to go to church every Sunday and he allows one of the slave hands from the field to conduct the service. Of course, he sends his overseer to make sure that we don't get too much religion, though."

"It's odd how the masters want us to have religion so they can use the religion to justify why slavery should be allowed," said Pompey. "They cite chapter and verse about how God allowed slavery, but the verses were often taken out of context or applied to a system of chattel slavery that bore little resemblance to the Bible."

Cato said, "Master Lee counters these interpretations by emphasizing the Bible's themes of liberation, justice, and human dignity. He says that slavery one day will just shrivel up and die. I don't know what evidence he sees. It's not apparent to me."

"Master Edward has never pushed religion on any of the slaves. Besides, Sunday is the only day that us slaves get a break from work, and I don't want to be told that I have to go to a church instead of using my time to myself," said Pompey.

Bob said, "I'd trade my Sunday religion for a chance to go to school any day."

"Why should we have to choose between education and religion?" asked Pompey. "I think we should be able to do both, but I want to be free also. The chance of any of the three happening is remote."

Cato said, "Maybe Mr. Paine could write something about us the next time so our situation would change for the better."

"I'll keep an eye out for that, Cato," said Pompey. "But don't hold your breath!"

Unbeknownst to the slaves or the patriots, Thomas had published a treatise on slavery that was a powerful critique of slavery in the Pennsylvania Magazine, signing it "Justice and Humanity." In the essay, he called out the colonists to demand freedom from Britain while continuing to enslave others. As powerful as the essay was, nothing changed as the result of it.

ADAMS ON GOVERNANCE

Since their first meeting at the City Tavern in 1774, John Adams and Richard Henry Lee formed a warm alliance over their ambitions and dreams surrounding the American Cause. Raised in completely different environments, Adams and Lee instantly concluded that their primary mission in the Continental Congress was to be in mutual accord.

Adams, from Massachusetts, and Lee, from Virginia, arrived in Philadelphia as delegates united by a shared distrust of British authority and a growing commitment to colonial rights. Though they had contrasting temperaments, they quickly found common cause in resisting the Coercive Acts and shaping the early framework of intercolonial cooperation. Adams's legal precision and Lee's eloquence complemented each other in debates over petitions to the Crown and the formation of the Continental Association, a unified boycott of British goods. Their early collaboration laid the groundwork for a deeper alliance, culminating two years later when Lee introduced the resolution for independence and Adams seconded it, turning shared conviction into revolutionary action.

After the news of the military debacle in Quebec, the success of Thomas Paine's pamphlet "Common Sense," gave the independence argument more impact. Adams and Lee saw the need for the colonies to establish new governments independent from royal authority and to adopt a clear statement about independence. Sitting again at a table in the City Tavern, John and Richard Henry sat for a meal after a long day at Congress.

"John, I think the time is appropriate for us to urge our delegates to foster the establishment of independent assemblies in their colonies, if we are going to be able to govern ourselves when the final decision for independence is made. I believe that Virginia is prepared to act, and I don't think Massachusetts will be far behind. We should bring a resolution to the floor of the Congress soon for each colony to create new governments in the image of the people and to unite for independence as soon as possible."

"Virginia may be ready, but our circumstances are different as I believe that other colonies may be also. We adopted a Provisional Congress that runs Boston; however, we have no formal structure that includes the other towns in our colony."

"That is precisely why we should have a specific resolution to encourage all the colonies to act. Every colony will have its own histories and relationships with Britain within their colony that will advise them in the creation of a final decision, and we, as Congress, should not proscribe to them how to accomplish this end. What we do need to do is to make sure that the efforts begin and the colonies take full responsibility."

"Was it ever so easy for us to pass a resolution and everyone heed our call? We must get all the delegates to accept this passageway."

"As we have discussed before, this Congress acts when Massachusetts, Virginia, Pennsylvania, and South Carolina agree on a plan. We can make plans to influence Boston and Virginia, but what arrangements have Carolina taken?" asked Lee.

"My recollection is the departure of John Rutledge and the other South Carolina delegates was for the purpose of returning to Charleston to complete the work of creating an independent government as we've just discussed. Wouldn't it be ironic if the main obstacle to our independence plans was the first colony to set up the new government structure we are discussing? Those Rutledge boys are full of surprises."

"If I am not mistaken, I remember that New Hampshire had asked for permission to proceed, and then John Rutledge interjected his thought that South Carolina would like to do the same. For that reason, I think it would be suitable that we approach John Hancock with our proposal and have him appoint young Ned and the two of us to a committee to draft the letter to the colonies," said Richard Henry.

"I believe he will agree that this is a good process to follow."

Pennsylvania was late to form a provincial government separated from Britain largely due to internal divisions and the dominance of conservative factions within its colonial Assembly. Wealthy merchants, moderate Quakers, and loyalists in Philadelphia held significant sway and resisted the push for independence, favoring reconciliation with the Crown even as revolutionary fervor spread elsewhere. These moderates instructed Pennsylvania's delegates to the Continental Congress not to vote for independence, creating a political stalemate that delayed decisive action. It wasn't until June 1776, under mounting pressure from radical committees and the Continental Congress, that a Provincial Conference declared the existing Assembly unfit and called for a new convention to draft a state constitution. This shift marked Pennsylvania's reluctant but eventual embrace of revolutionary governance.

"John, what do you think about Pennsylvania? John Dickinson continues to ask for reconciliation even in the light of the King's refusal to even look at our petition."

"My reading is that Pennsylvania will not be the main deterrent in declaring independence. Dr. Franklin speaks with unbridled conviction for independence. He is well respected among those men, and I believe that they will come into the fold when the time comes."

Richard Henry Lee took a bite of food from his plate and said, "I'm not too sure how long it will take to find some good home-cooked meals around here."

Compared to Boston's austerity and Richmond's rustic abundance, Philadelphia's cuisine was more cosmopolitan and tavern-centered, reflecting its political energy and cultural diversity. Food at plantation mansions in Virginia always had better food to eat.

Richard Henry Lee said, "Philadelphia was not chosen to host the Continental Congress because of their superior cuisine, but the quality of the local fare is satisfactory for my tastes."

"When we have finally settled all of our affairs with Britain, I would be greatly honored if you would join me at my home on the Potomac and I will show you the finest dining in all of Virginia," said Lee.

"Another thought comes to mind. I am sure that you remember last year I asked you to put in writing your ideas about how colonies might build a model that works for themselves," Richard Henry said. "I was so appreciative of those thoughts you shared with me that I shared the tract with a few of my legislative friends in Virginia, and I understand that it has been shared with a wider group of delegates. I want to thank you again for this important work that you have provided and the clarity of your recommendations."

Adams bowed his head slightly toward Lee and said, "Thank you for those kind words. I seem to be better at speaking my mind than writing my thoughts for others to comprehend, so I am doubly appreciative of your praise. I do remember the interaction, and I want to thank you for encouraging me to put pen to paper. I opine that some of my best ideas are lost to me and the world because I don't take the time to record those thoughts contemporaneously. This is a perfect example of two men working well together, and I look forward to continuing these efforts until we see a time when these colonies will be a United Colonies."

"Your service to the colonies will forever be appreciated by our descendants when they write the history of these troubled times. If we seek to achieve a united America, we will need to say it clearly and out loud for every man and woman to hear. To this end, we need to continue reminding our delegates that independence is our goal and we will not be deterred from its achievement."

"All our activity should have as its premise, that independence is our goal. After the King unceremoniously rejected our last effort to reconcile, we need to make fertile the ground where we plant the liberty flag. Delegates need reminders that we will not shrink from our responsibilities and make freedom our motto no matter what the cost we must pay. The victory will be sweeter when we know that we persevered when times were tough and persisted until we won."

"I think that we need to plan for the future of this debate about independence," said Adams. "If the colonies agree to have governments separate from The Crown, what is the leap to declare ourselves independent?"

"We are so alike in our thinking that the leap you describe is easy for us to see," said Lee. "However, the delegates who cannot imagine a total separation and dream of reconciliation will not agree to such an outlandish resolution to announce independence."

"Maybe not today or this week or next month," said Adams. "We can visualize, though, that the day will come that it will be inevitable for every delegate. I don't know when that time will be, but certain events will transpire which prove indubitably that the King of England is unable to understand our needs and is treacherous in relating to our rights."

"The day will be upon us when we least expect it," replied Lee. "For that reason, we should start thinking about how we can introduce a resolution for independence and follow it with a declaration on our independence. We should remember this conversation when the time is ripe."

Adams and Lee, satisfied that they had a loose plan of action to encourage the colonies to adopt new governmental structures and unite for independence, proceeded to finish their dinner and toast themselves with some madeira generously provided by the Shippens.

UNDERSTANDING DICKINSON

The cold winds off the Delaware River of early winter were not the favorite weather for Edward Rutledge who longed for his Carolina home. Snug in his woolen overcoat with a felt hat, to protect his head from the cold, Edward was trudging toward the London Coffee House to meet Pennsylvania delegate, John Dickinson, the leader of the conservatives in Congress. The coffee shop was a favorite of Dickinson and Rutledge as it reminded them of their law training at The Temple where Rutledge had matriculated years earlier. Edward reached the front door as a blast of winter flurries brought the warning that more snow might arrive soon.

Edward closed the door behind him and felt the warmth from the hearth of the establishment where many tables were filled with local merchants enjoying their fresh coffee. Looking for Dickinson, he gazed at the people in their wintry clothing that ranged from overcoats to watch coats to various headgear. One man had a great coat with a muffler and a fur-lined hat, and Edward could see he also wore heavy boots with woolen stockings.

Rutledge had heard that the city of Norfolk, the largest in Virginia, had been attacked by the British and burnt to the ground. Rumors abounded that Lord Dunmore was responsible for the initial bombing, and patriots had joined in and burned houses of Loyalists, destroying more property so that the British could not reclaim the city for strategic purposes later.

Inside the coffeehouse, the air buzzed with the scent of roasted beans and the sharper edge of political tension, as merchants, mariners, pamphleteers, and patriots crowded around communal tables beneath flickering candlelight. The clink of porcelain cups mingled with heated debate, some men railing against British tyranny, others cautioning restraint while bills of exchange and shipping news passed hand to hand. These spaces doubled as auction blocks, insurance hubs, and informal press rooms where revolutionary ideas brewed up as strong as the coffee. In the corner, a printer might read Paine's latest lines aloud, while a Quaker quietly sipped and listened, and a young Black valet absorbed every word, knowing history was being stirred with every spoonful.

Just as Rutledge thought that he had arrived early, the door behind him opened with a rush of cold air and snow along with John Dickinson in a grey overcoat, tricorn hat lined in beaver, and shiny black boots that came up to his knee.

"I trust the weather is to your liking, Mr. Rutledge."

"I am sure that you are jesting. For a body that is conditioned for warmer winter days, it is not easy to accustom to the cold of the season."

"We shall sit close to the fire, order some tasteful coffee, and warm our bodies with good conversation."

Dickinson led Rutledge past the tables nearby and beyond the bar where coffee and tea were ordered and found a table in the rear that stood next to another hearth.

"Most people forget to look back here. I always find the table I like," said Dickinson.

Rutledge found a chair opposite the fire and removed his overcoat showing his finest linen shirt and embroidered waistcoat. Dickinson was also attired in similar fashion although his shiny black boots were not matched by anyone in the coffee house. These two patrician delegates certainly stood out from the rest of the customers. It was obvious to Rutledge why Dickinson had decided to sit in the rear.

"I wanted to speak with you about that pamphlet that has been circulating lately calling for independence," said Rutledge.

Dickinson said, "I assume you are speaking about that vile diatribe called *Common Sense* by a fellow by named Thomas Paine. This sort of demagoguery puts revolution in front of government and is dangerous to our cause."

"The word-of-mouth praise that it has caused in many quarters worries me. People who are unaware of the efforts that we are attempting are getting excited about a process that could lead into more trouble or worse," said Rutledge.

The citizens of Pennsylvania reacted to Thomas Paine's *Common Sense* with a mix of fervent enthusiasm and cautious resistance, reflecting the colony's deep political and religious diversity. Published in Philadelphia, the pamphlet had quickly gained traction among artisans, radicals, and members of local committees who saw in Paine's plainspoken call for independence a powerful validation of their revolutionary hopes. Its arguments electrified taverns and coffeehouses, where Paine's words were read aloud and debated with urgency. Yet, conservative Quakers, loyalists, and wealthy merchants, many of whom dominated the colonial Assembly, viewed the pamphlet with alarm, fearing its radicalism and the social upheaval it might unleash. Despite this tension, *Common Sense* helped galvanize popular support for independence in Pennsylvania, contributing to the eventual overthrow of the old Assembly and the drafting of a new state constitution later that summer.

A server, clothed in cotton leggings and a tattered linen shirt with rolled up sleeves and a towel slung over his shoulder, brought two mugs of hot brew to the table. Dickinson quickly gave him five pence.

"My belief is that the momentum, from that pamphlet being provided, may help the Crown and deflate our efforts to bring about a meaningful and long-lasting new relationship," said Dickinson.

"Richard Henry Lee has been rumored to be buying copies of the pamphlet and distributing them to all of the delegates," Rutledge said.

"That would not be a bad idea. If everyone is reading the same words, I believe that most of the delegates will see how this idea is half-cocked at best. The author has no idea what the military capacity of our colonial militias is, particularly when we are faced with meeting the most powerful armies in the world. His approach is fanciful at best. Does he have experience in waging war? Is he aware of the size and professionalism of the Redcoats? What is he personally willing to do in this battle that he thinks will be so easy? I don't think he has thought this through to any extent."

"In addition," Dickinson said, "he has absolutely no grasp of the subtleties in productive negotiation and constructive engagement. If people follow him down this path of destruction, we will never be able to salvage any sort of meaningful relationship with the Crown. He is only offering a blunt attack on the monarchy and no resolution to the problems that we, as delegates, have been trying to address. My greatest fear is that most people will see this as the perfect reaction to the pains that the Crown has delivered upon us," said Dickinson.

"And what if the other delegates see this as wind in their sails that will chart a course to independence?" said Edward.

"I pray that wiser souls will see this pamphlet as pure propaganda. Our colonies have called upon us to be instruments to debate and make measured, legal responses to the injustices that have been waged against us. There is no room for appeals grounded in tradition and constitutional rights."

"How do you believe we should act to counter this plebian writing when other delegates react to their colonists' pleadings?" asked Rutledge.

"This single pamphlet does not change anything in the relationship that we have with the King and our provincial governments. We cannot completely ignore this pamphlet, but we should call it out for what it is, an ill-conceived broadside that will not assist us in our negotiations with Britain to form a new relationship with the empire."

Edward said, "Won't delegates say that the King has shown us his cards by allowing the attacks on Lexington and Concord? We need to find a positive way to go forward or there may be a stampede toward independence among the delegates. Events like the burning of Norfolk certainly assist the call for independence and show the King in a bad light."

"Remember, Ned, most of the delegates do not have the authority to vote for independence because the colonies have not been in total agreement on this path. Correct me if I am wrong, but South Carolina at present could not vote for liberty even if citizens of the state desired it"

"Will the King listen and contemplate a plan for reconciliation if presented from the unified American colonies?"

Rutledge said, "I doubt it, and other events will probably not motivate him to do so, either. The recent battle in North Carolina to derail British plans to regain control of the colony does not bolster our cause for reconciliation. The British employed Loyalist militias, and Scottish Highlanders were armed with broadswords to confront patriot forces. The brief, but intense clash resulted in the death or capture of hundreds of Loyalists, including their commander."

Dickinson said, "I had not heard of this event, but if it is true, our efforts will be set back. As to the authority of voting for independence, South Carolina is not the only colony with no power to declare. My state, Pennsylvania, also has not signed on to independence. Delaware, New York and Georgia find themselves in a similar situation. We have time on our side, and we will need it to convince England that negotiations are the wise path to ameliorate our predicament."

"You are far more experienced in these matters and that is part of the reason why I wanted to speak with you," said Edward. "Our delegation, and particularly I, have found solace in the support you have given to a more reconciliatory arrangement with England. I expect that the new delegates will see this as we have discussed."

"When do you expect the new South Carolina delegates to arrive?" John asked.

"I thought they would have arrived by now, but I am resigned to the possibility that it may be spring before they arrive," said Rutledge.

"I am sure you already acknowledge this, but please know that my door is always open to you when issues like this arise."

"Thank you, Mr. Dickinson. Since our work on the Olive Branch Petition and reading your "Notes from a Farmer," I have felt a kinship toward you when governmental affairs were on the table."

"Thank you for those kind words," said Dickinson. "We are on this journey together, and I feel fortunate to have you as a companion. This calls for a toast: Here's to the future of the American colonies!"

They clinked their mugs together and started on a longer conversation about their personal lives and ambitions. Edward had not had this kind of conversation since his brother left for South Carolina.

Pompey Wants to Be a Person

In the spring of 1776, Philadelphia's gardens and commons stirred with color as crocuses and snowdrops broke through the thawing soil, heralding the season's arrival. The spring flowers in the front of the neat clapboard houses of Philadelphia were a welcome addition from the windswept days of winter. Tulips, imported from Dutch stock decades earlier, bloomed in orderly beds behind brick townhouses, their bold reds and yellows contrasting with the city's austere façades. Along the Schuylkill River, clusters of wild violets and bluebells softened the banks, mingling with the scent of damp earth and woodsmoke. Colonial ladies tended to jonquils and hyacinths in kitchen plots, their fragrances mingling with herbs like rosemary and sage. Apple and cherry trees burst into blossom in the orchards west of town, their petals drifting like confetti over the muddy lanes. Even amid the tension of revolution, nature's pageant unfolded with quiet insistence, reminding Philadelphians of renewal and continuity.

Pompey was enjoying the Sunday afternoon warmth and was whistling softly to himself as he viewed the storefronts that were closed for business this day but would be bustling with business on Monday morning. He strolled down High Street toward the waterfront, when he heard his friend Cato's voice interrupting his solitude.

"Pomp, you look lost in your thoughts this beautiful afternoon," said Cato as he sidled up next to his friend. "I hope all is well with you. You look awful solemn."

"I'm just fine," said Pompey as he picked up a stick that was laying along the street. "I was just thinking of my grandfather who died in the springtime, and when I see the flowers blooming, I miss his wit and support."

"You remember your grandfather?" Cato asked rhetorically. "How old was he when he passed?"

"I'm not sure but, I do remember that I was only four or five years old," said Pompey. "On Sundays, he would take us fishing or just walking in the woods near the big house where he was a valet once to one of the Rutledges."

"Did he teach you how to fish? Wow, that must be capital!" said Cato.

"It was rare, good," said Pompey. "I'm also reminded, though, that my grandfather always said that he wanted to be free. To be a real person. Not to be a piece of property to a master."

"Did he say that to you directly or did you overhear a conversation meant for someone else?" asked Cato.

"He said it directly to me, and he said it more than once," said Pompey. "Grandpappy would take me and my brother walking on Sunday, and it was almost like being in church. He was our preacher, and he told us things about this life as a slave for the Rutledges. I don't remember many of the stories except for one that I always think of when I see birds flying."

"He called me Pomp just like you do," said Pompey. "He would start, 'when I was your age, I used to stare out past the rice fields at dusk, watching the sun sink low behind the cypress trees, and I'd dream of walking beyond them—just walking, no chains, no overseer, no fear. I remember one spring, I saw a flock of geese flying north, and I thought, they don't answer to no man.' That stayed with me. I'd hum songs my mama taught me, songs older than this land, and I'd imagine them carrying me far off, maybe to the hills where folks say maroons live free. I didn't know if it was true, but I held on to it like a warm ember in my chest."

Pompey continued, "When he died, I just felt this emptiness and sadness in my soul, whatever that is. I will always remember that even though I am a slave today, maybe someday I will have the right to come and go as I please. Until then, I am nothing more than a piece of property to the Rutledges"

Cato said, "Pomp, I think that you are speaking for your grandfather right now. The message you give me is not from you, but you are a connection from your past given freely to me. I find it amazing that with all the talk about independence by our masters, they don't even take the time to think of us as anything but property."

"They been doing it so long, they don't know any better, and as long as no one is complaining, they'll just keep doing it," Pompey said. "But I know one other thing that he taught me was that I should reckon myself most fortunate. I do not want to ever be a field man working long hours in the heat and swamp. Grandpappy told me also about the beatings that he saw given to men for almost no other reason than the overseer was having a bad day. No. No matter what Master Edward asks me to do, I know where my favor lies."

"I am amazed every time that we get together, you make me think how I should remember to never bite the hand that fills my plate," said Cato.

"That reminds me that the last thing he told me was, now you wear livery and serve in the big house, but don't let that fool you into thinking you belong to it. Freedom ain't just a place, it's a knowing inside you, a whisper that says you were made for more than this. I've seen men break under the whip and others rise with nothing but hope in their eyes. You keep that hope, grandson. You carry it quiet, like a seed in your pocket, and when the time comes, you plant it where it'll grow strong," said Pompey.

"Pomp, let's take that stick you been waving around and go to our secret place on the river," said Cato. "If we get there, we can probably stay out of trouble."

"Sounds like a plan," Pompey said as they walked quickly down to the dock and found the pathway to their lair by the river.

JEFFERSON SPEAKS

On the surface, one could think that Edward Rutledge would have an easy time connecting with Thomas Jefferson as both were among the youngest delegates at the Second Continental Congress, and they were raised in a southern colony on plantations with slaves. However, when Edward became a polished speaker in large gatherings, Jefferson was an accomplished writer who preferred to sit back and listen. Jefferson found smaller conversations preferrable and was direct and terse in conversation, as though he wished not to waste a single word. During the first session of the Congress, they engaged in small talk about some of their common interests, primarily protecting the export businesses that provided wealth from their plantations.

Rutledge gleaned from Jefferson's writings for the Virginia House of Burgesses, that he was known for his philosophical distaste for slavery, even though he owned more than 150 servants. Rutledge had concluded that Jefferson was more aligned with John Adams on the issue of independence and slavery than he. Adams, a non-slaveowner, had been outspoken against slavery in the colonies. Jefferson, however, grew up in an environment with slaves and utilized them for his economic advantage. Edward was puzzled by this paradox.

Thomas Jefferson embodied one of the most profound contradictions in American history, a man who penned the immortal phrase "all men are created equal" while personally enslaving hundreds of people throughout his life. He publicly condemned slavery as a moral evil and even proposed gradual emancipation and the abolition of the transatlantic slave trade. Yet, Jefferson never freed the vast majority of those he enslaved, not even in his will, and continued to benefit from their labor at Monticello. He described slavery as holding "a wolf by the ears" a dangerous entanglement that could neither be safely kept nor easily released. This paradox reveals the tension between Jefferson's Enlightenment ideals and the entrenched economic and social realities of his time, casting a long shadow over the founding vision of liberty.

During a recess at Congress, Edward walked the few blocks to the City Tavern to find some nourishment. As he entered the usually crowded hall, Rutledge was surprised to find only a few patrons eating and drinking. To his astonishment, he saw Thomas Jefferson sitting alone at a table with his nose in a book.

"Excuse me, Mr. Jefferson. Would you mind if I join you?"

Jefferson lifted his head from his reading and peered over his glasses wondering who was disturbing him from his pleasure. "Mr. Rutledge, I thought you were attending the Congress this morning."

Rutledge edged closer to Jefferson's table. "The Congress has adjourned for a recess, and an afternoon meal, so I decided to visit The City Tavern during the recess and was surprised to see you alone here. I thought we might have the opportunity to converse on a matter that pertains to our business."

"Please sit down, Rutledge. I am not sure that I am interested in any food now, but I would enjoy the conversation."

Edward pulled over a chair and positioned it so he could see the entrance to the Tavern, but not too close to Jefferson who always seemed to keep his distance. Putting aside his own need to eat, Rutledge said, "I'm not hungry, either."

Confronting the paradox of Thomas Jefferson's anti-slavery rhetoric while still enslaving people was fraught with political and cultural peril. Even among revolutionaries championing liberty, the institution of slavery was a volatile subject, too entangled with economic survival and regional identity to be openly condemned. Jefferson's own position—morally uneasy yet materially complicit—mirrored the broader American dilemma. How does one reconcile the pursuit of freedom with the reality of bondage?

Edward struggled with how he might delicately open the conversation about Jefferson's attitude toward slavery. "Mr. Jefferson, I was hoping that you could enlighten me regarding what seems to me a paradox that you own slaves and, yet you are against slavery?"

"Mr. Rutledge, may I call you Edward?" Without a word of approval, Jefferson said, "I know that it may appear as a contradiction, but it is more complicated than you think. It is my studied opinion that slavery is morally wrong, and when the timing and the public support has changed, it will inevitably end. However, we have a long history of it that leaves the puzzling question of how change may occur while not causing massive unintended complications.

Listening carefully, Rutledge posed another question, "How is it morally wrong if we treat our servants satisfactorily and are able to grow our colonies?"

"I have no doubt that you treat your servants in a satisfactory manner, as I do. It's natural law, though, that we need to examine. How can one person own another person, regardless of their color? Natural law provides that we are all the same and that slavery is a mean and barbarous activity that should be banned."

Rutledge said, "Your rationale seems to me that you would give these brutes from Africa the rights that we have. Hasn't it been proved that people from Africa do not have the same brain capacity as you or me? These beasts do not have the least amount of discernment and character that we civilized planters possess. If they were set free, I am sure of one thing: they will act on the resentments that have built up all their years of enslavement, and they would seek revenge on ourselves, and the members of our families."

"I have never said or would defend that slaves from Africa have the same mental genius that European people possess, nor would I refer to them as brutes or beasts," said Jefferson. "I have held indentured servants from Ireland and slaves from Africa. I have found within their groups that some are hard workers and others are laggards. I dare say that I know there are also laggards among the general population. Has not that been your experience also, Edward?"

"The servants we engage in working on our plantations do not exhibit the grace and maturity that we maintain in civil society. I would not sleep comfortably at night knowing that slaves might be walking freely in our midst. I fear that they will resort to their baser instincts and rape our women and kill the overseers."

Many American colonists, particularly in the Southern colonies, feared that ending slavery would unravel the economic and social order on which their livelihoods depended. Plantation wealth was built on enslaved labor, and emancipation threatened not only financial ruin but also a radical shift in racial hierarchy and political power. Some worried that freed black people would demand equality, land, or retribution, disrupting the fragile colonial society. Even among revolutionaries who spoke of liberty, there was deep anxiety that abolition would fracture the unity needed to resist Britain. The fear wasn't just economic, it was existential. Colonists dreaded that the very foundations of colonial identity, property, and control would collapse if slavery were abolished.

"The disasters that you foretell may not be a certainty, Edward. Although I question the need for slavery in perpetuity, I suggest that we should begin a process that leads to their freedom. The long path will take time, but we should not delay and let years go by before we have the courage to begin."

Edward Rutledge stated, "For the last one-hundred and fifty years, we have developed a system of plantations in South Carolina that is economically beneficial for our colony and has helped to support the wealth of other colonies in America. Through those years, we have provided for the care of our servants and given them a better opportunity of living than they ever could have achieved in Africa. We have shared our Christianity; we have taught them how to live in a civilized society; we set a good example to achieve what little they can grasp given their native lack of aptitude. Look at our valets, Pompey and Robert. We have given them an opportunity to thrive in service to us, and all of us have benefited from this relationship."

"I am not sure that I can agree to your assessment of the ability to flourish without our aid. Given proper supervision and adequate training, some of our slaves have had great success in learning skills that could reward their efforts and help them to avoid being a burden in our towns," said Jefferson.

"I believe these are the exceptions to the rule. Sir, have you no fear of the baser instincts that many of these slaves have that may burst into our plantations in a heartbeat if given the opportunity to be free? The institution has greatly enhanced the life of our colonies. Carolina is a wealthy colony because of the successful operation of plantations that deliver food for our citizens and commerce in the world. If slavery had not been available to our early settlers, the fields of South Carolina and Virginia would have remained a swampy land with little chance of succeeding. Instead, we provide fertile ground for commerce to our governments and safety and peace of mind to our residents," said Rutledge.

"I do not argue with you that without slavery our colonies would not be as economically strong. However, we should heed our environment and not become victims of our own success. Let me offer my own Virginia soil as an example. For years we have profitably grown tobacco in our fields, but we came to understand that the continued use of it was detrimental to the health of the soil. Therefore, we have begun a transition to produce wheat, corn, and indigo to continue with a strong economic viable business. Maybe slavery will follow a similar path."

"I know a fair amount about indigo, as in South Carolina it has been one the main crops we grow with the assistance of servants. I don't see the end of the slave trade in America as the panacea you try to describe," said Edward.

Some abolitionists believed that slavery would gradually wither away through the natural progress of Enlightenment ideals and economic evolution. They argued that as republican values of liberty and equality took root, the moral contradiction of slavery would become untenable, prompting voluntary reforms. Gradual emancipation laws reflected this belief, freeing future generations while allowing the institution to fade without immediate upheaval. These reformers hoped that education, religious conviction, and shifting labor markets would make slavery obsolete, avoiding the social and political chaos of sudden abolition. Their optimism rested on the assumption that reason and conscience would triumph over entrenched interests, though history would prove that slavery's grip was far more resilient.

Jefferson said, "There are some things that cannot be changed in a twinkling. For over two centuries, our colonies have depended on slaves so that we are able meet in Congress and speak about independence. Our fathers and our father's fathers depended upon the backs of Black Africans to sustain our plantations and grow our families. Is it morally wrong to enslave another human being? I find it easy to answer that question in the affirmative. But after a long history of this, how do we change this matter without doing great harm?"

Rutledge countered, "I am not sure that I agree with your premise that our servant's relationship to us is immoral. Everyone knows that the Negro does not think with the lucidness as us. His predilection for violence and sloth is well documented. We are doing a service by allowing Negroes to live by our grace and learn that despite his heathen ways, a better life is available."

Jefferson said, "I would not be surprised if you believe that the Negro and the Indians in our midst are the same. When I was a young man, a Cherokee Indian chief visited my father in Williamsburg before he left for England on a speaking tour. The moon was in full splendor, and he seemed to address himself in his prayers for his safety on the voyage, and for the welfare of his people during his absence. His resounding voice, distinct articulation, animated action, and solemn silence of his people at their several fires filled me with awe and veneration, although he spoke his words in the Cherokee language, and I did not understand a word he uttered. His presence showed me that it is possible that I may not know everything about the souls of people who I don't understand."

Rutledge said, "That is an elegant story that you recall from your youth, but I must live in the present. I have experienced numerous times when the actions of my servants did not reflect the wisdom and welfare of our society."

"Yes, and we need to seek ways to better understand our responsibilities for our property and point to a future that erases this apparent paradox," Jefferson said. "I hope that I have helped you to understand my position on this matter better."

"I must take my leave now, sir. I have just learned that my wife is on her way to visit from Charleston and I look forward to seeing her soon. I want to thank you for this frank conversation and enlightenment of your beliefs."

"Give my best to your wife. I trust that her trip will be pleasant and safe. That is another way that links us closer together, as my wife has been in fragile health and I miss her dearly."

"I hope that your wife also finds good health and that you have the opportunity to see her soon," said Rutledge as he shook Jeffrerson's hand and turned toward the exit.

Edward left the City Tavern and headed directly to the livery house to pick up the phaeton and horse that he had asked Pompey to procure for his ride to meet his wife in Lancaster.

South Carolina Sends New Delegates

Edward was returning to Mrs. Yard's boarding house after a long afternoon of debate in Congress, and as he entered through the front door, he heard the high pitch voice of Mrs. Yard, "Mr. Rutledge? There were two posts delivered by courier earlier today. I have them here, sir."

As Mrs. Yard handed Edward the deliveries, he said "Thank you, Mrs. Yard."

Edward knew instantly from the splendid handwriting that the note dated last night was from his loving wife, Henrietta.

"Dearest Edward," the note began. "Arthur and I have recently arrived with Reverend Clitherall in Lancaster, Pennsylvania where we are staying with his colleague, Reverend Thomas Barton, at the St. James Episcopal church. We are eager to see you soon, Yours truly, Henrietta."

The other post came from Arthur Middleton, the brother of Henrietta and the oldest son of Henry Middleton, his father-in-law. The news from Arthur was that he carried new instructions from the South Carolina Provincial Congress, and new delegates had been selected to replace his brother and others. The new delegates were Arthur Middleton, Thomas Heyward Jr, and Thomas Lynch Jr, who were all about the same age as he. Edward thought that he could not have selected a finer group of cohorts.

Beaming, he informed his landlady, "I will be away for a couple of days. I need to go to Lancaster where my wife has just arrived," as he turned and ran up the stairs to his room. Edward rushed to find his baggage for clothes and select the items he would need for an overnight trip to Lancaster.

Edward called for his valet to retrieve the phaeton carriage from the livery and make the necessary preparations for the travel west. He sat down at his desk and penned short notes for Thomas Stone and John Dickinson explaining that he would be away for the next four days to be reunited with his wife. He also penned a short request to the owner of the rented house he had resided in with his father-in-law to see if lodging could be found for his family and the new members of the South Carolina delegation.

A traveler setting out from Philadelphia to Lancaster could hire a chaise, a light, two-wheeled carriage drawn by a single horse, or a phaeton that was four-wheeled and steadier in inclement weather—ideal for navigating the uneven colonial roads with relative speed and comfort. The roughly sixty-mile journey followed the well-worn Lancaster Road, a vital artery connecting the bustling port city to the inland market towns of Pennsylvania. Though the route was passable, spring rain could turn stretches into muddy quagmires, making the phaeton's suspension and maneuverability a welcome advantage over heavier wagons. A gentleman or merchant traveling to meet associates in Lancaster would likely stop at roadside taverns for rest and news, his phaeton signaling both status and purpose as he moved through the countryside during a season of revolutionary ferment.

As late afternoon sun began its arc to the west, Rutledges phaeton rolled out of Philadelphia along the Great Wagon Road, also called the Lancaster Road, with his valet at the reins. Edward would soon be reunited with his wife and receive new instructions from the Carolina Provincial Congress.

After an evening's layover at the Thomas Moore Tavern in Downingtown, Rutledge was early to rise and approached Lancaster by early afternoon. Stopping at the Revere Tavern just east of Lancaster, Rutledge obtained precise directions on finding St. James Episcopal Church.

With the sun warming the fields and woods, houses and buildings became more numerous. Smaller plots with farmers in the fields were prevalent, which was foreign to Edwards' eye, as his experiences were in great plantations with slaves toiling. The road had become smoother as the carriage passed more houses and an occasional church.

As the phaeton slowed and the houses were now closer together, Rutledge gave orders to his servant to look for a stone bell tower which would mark St. James Church at the intersection of Orange and Lime Street. A few other wagons and carriages were active on the gravel road that passed by as small businesses beckoned. Women in shawls carrying baskets, men on horseback, and children playing gave the streets of Lancaster an active atmosphere.

After making a left turn, the stone tower of St. James loomed a hundred yards away. When in front of the stone masonry church,

Edward spotted a small house next door that appeared to belong to the church. Rutledge approached the front door, knocked on the gray oak entrance and waited for a reply. The door opened wide to show a middle-aged woman with a cloth bonnet who asked, "May I help you, sir?"

"Yes, madam. My name is Edward Rutledge. I am a delegate to the Congress meetings now in Philadelphia. I received a note yesterday from my wife that I could find her at St. James under the care of Reverend Barton."

"Oh, Mr. Rutledge. We did not expect your presence for another day or so. Won't you please come in? I will immediately tell your wife that you are here."

In a blink, the woman was gone, and Edward could hear the chatter of voices in an adjoining room. Soon, through the passageway burst Arthur Middleton and Thomas Heyward Jr.

"Ned! It is so good to see you," said Arthur. "We thought that you would be so busy in Philadelphia that we wouldn't see you for a few days."

Heyward added, "You have been gone for so long, we weren't sure how you would look after all of the solemn business that attends to you."

Rutledge looked at both and deduced, "May I surmise that my friends have been designated as delegates from our worthy colony?"

Rutledge also noticed that Arthur had brought his Black valet, Hector, to accompany him.

"Why, of course, old man," his brother-in-law said. "We did not feel comfortable knowing that you should remain here without any family around to restrain you from your baser elements. That is why I brought my dear sister with us to accompany you in these northern climes."

From the same threshold where his two friends emerged, a slight, fair-skinned beauty, Henrietta Middleton Rutledge, stepped out of the hallway and offered a loving glance toward her husband.

"You grow more handsome every time I see you," Henrietta said. Stretching her arms to him, she said "Seeing you again, my heart is full."

Wrapping his arms around her, Edward responded "I traveled all last night so the distance between us would evaporate sooner. How was your trip?"

Henrietta replied, "It was long, and we had some troubles. But we have arrived here in good shape, and it was all worth it as now you are here."

"I hope that you have had adequate time to relax and recover from your long journey." said Arthur. "Why don't we repair to the den where we can speak of the happenings in Charleston and Philadelphia."

"Splendid idea," Heyward stated. "I think you will be excited as we bring good news from the Provisional Congress."

"I'll leave you men to the business of the colonies while I repair to the upstairs so you can speak of business," said Henrietta.

The study offered a rustic yet respectable retreat from the bustle of the public taproom. Tucked behind a paneled door, the study provided a quieter chamber for private conversation with its walls lined with shelves of pamphlets, ledgers, and a few volumes of Locke and Addison. A sturdy oak table stood at the center, surrounded by ladder-back chairs, with a pewter candlestick casting flickering light over maps, correspondence, and tankards of ale. This room served as a haven for merchants, landowners, and traveling gentlemen to discuss politics, trade, or local news away from the ears of tavern regulars and the clatter of passing coaches.

Off the study was the den which the three old friends entered. The den had a fireplace, a well-worn sofa and a couple of wingback upholstered chairs. Books were neatly stacked in a case, and a pile of wood was piled next to the andiron and poker.

Arthur Middleton was the older brother of Henrietta and the probable heir to the vast estate of his father, Henry Middleton. The Middleton family were scions of Charleston, one of five families dominating the economic and political life of the Low Country. The Rutledge family were not as rich as the Middletons, but hardly any Charleston family was closely equivalent. The joining of forces between these families amassed political clout in Carolina. Arthur studied law at Middle Temple in London, just like Edward. Upon Arthur's death in 1787, the State Gazette of South Carolina would describe him as a "planter and humane master."

Thomas Heyward, Jr., had also attended Middle Temple for training as an attorney. As part of the planter class in Charleston, he combined attorney work and management of the vast plantations his father had accumulated which also included more than 200 slaves.

As they settled in their chairs, Rutledge asked, "Tell me about the new instructions. The pressure in Philadelphia is growing every day for independence."

"My intuition tells me that you will be very pleased with the new language that has been adopted to allow us to be true delegates," Middleton said. "I believe that the salient section of our new instructions says we 'execute every measure, which together with the majority of the Congress shall judge necessary for the interest of South Carolina and America in general.'"

"It appears there will be a considerable amount of interpretation by us as we proceed," Heyward said. "I believe that the time has come for us to abandon all charades that the Crown is ready, or ever will be ready, to treat us with the respect we deserve."

Rutledge smiled and looked at his friends and said, "The various thoughts that you have shared are the sum of the arguments that I have heard over the last months in Philadelphia. Thomas, it sounds like you could have been a delegate from Virginia in the manner you express yourself. Almost every day, I hear from the radicals that the time is past for us to consider calling for independence. However, without a clear agreement on how the colonies should relate to each other, I am not sure that independence should be declared too quickly."

The new, younger South Carolina delegates felt the urgency of the revolutionary moment and saw themselves as the vanguard of a new political order. They respected their elders' caution but believed that bold action, such as signing a declaration on independence, was essential to secure liberty. Their youth gave them a sharper appetite for risk, and they viewed their ascent not merely as succession, but also as a transformation, carrying South Carolina's voice into a future their predecessors had only begun to imagine.

"That is precisely why we have been chosen to work with you on how and when we should vote for independence," said Arthur Middleton. "My father is not one who would quickly lift the restraints that the King has burdened us with."

"Edward, it sounds to me like you might have been talking to Christopher Gadsden before our arrival."

Thomas said, "Colonel Gadsden has seen a great deal in his years, and if he sees that independence is the proper way to go, who am I to challenge his experience?"

Rutledge said, "I trust that both of you have been speaking with my brother about his views on how matters are unfolding here in Philadelphia."

"I forgot to tell you that Lynch Jr. will also be a delegate and should be arriving any day in Philadelphia," said Middleton.

"You bring good news in all matters, my friends. I especially appreciate the fact that I will now have compatriots of similar age to pursue our obligations to South Carolina. Why don't we rest for the remainder of the day and start for Philadelphia tomorrow morning?"

"I think you should get reacquainted with my sister, Ned," Arthur said. "I am confident that she will appreciate you are finally reunited."

"Thanks, Arthur. I think I will begin that effort presently," said Edward as he bowed to his friends and walked up the stairs.

FRANKLIN AND WASHINGTON DINNER

Undeniably, Benjamin Franklin was the elder stateman of the Second Continental Congress, while George Washington literally had the greatest stature of all the delegates. Neither man was a great orator nor given to idle conversation. Throughout his long life, Benjamin Franklin had met more people of importance and traveled to many more destinations than anyone in Congress.

On May 24, 1776, General Washington, commander of the Continental Army, appeared before the Second Continental Congress and met with a small committee to discuss the war and make recommendations for the management of the war effort. Benjamin Franklin asked General Washington to join him at his home for supper that evening to be joined by John Adams and Richard Henry Lee.

Benjamin Franklin's Philadelphia residence reflected the modest elegance of a prosperous colonial tradesman and statesman. Situated on Market Street, the brick facade was ornate, its symmetry marked by shuttered sash windows and a central doorway framed with simple wood trim. A small stoop led to the entrance, and above it, a dormered roof hinted at the attic workspace where Franklin once tinkered with inventions and correspondence. The house stood among other merchant dwellings, its appearance unpretentious yet dignified, befitting a man who balanced Enlightenment ambition with practical republican virtues. Though not grand, it conveyed stability, industry, and a quiet confidence in the revolutionary age.

Sitting in the reading room of Franklin's home, Washington was relaxing, away from the bustle of the work in Congress and the Continental Army. Franklin shuffled in, slowed by a recurrence of gout, and sat to the right of Washington in a large red and brown upholstered chair.

Acting as a host, Franklin said, "I thought a little quiet from this afternoon's business of the Congress would suit you. Please sit down so we can share stories."

"Excuse me, dear Doctor," said Washington, "but I am not the liveliest conversationalist you will meet this evening."

"Do not be concerned, for I have also invited Richard Henry Lee and John Adams, and they will do enough talking for both of us."

A slight grin and a nod of the head was Washington's only visible reaction. "I am sure you are correct. I want to thank you for this honored invitation."

"The honor is all mine, General. I was thinking, that before we have dinner, we engage our reliable friends to speak to the thoughts and motivations of the delegates. These delegates know how to make speeches, but long-term planning is in short supply. However, as I have said before, glass, China, and reputations are easily cracked and never well mended."

"You are a wise man, Ben. I doubt if I will ever realize as much as you have achieved in a long and prosperous life."

"You flatter me, sir. We have a long way to go before we can celebrate any victory and, as far as now is concerned, I believe we must brace for a long struggle. However, when you are standing victoriously on the final battle of this revolution, your stature as a leader will outshine anything that I have accomplished.

A knock at the door was answered by a servant ushering in Richard Henry Lee and John Adams.

The foyer of Franklin's house, with understated colonial refinement, reflected both his status and practicality. Upon entering, one might find a narrow hall with polished wood floors and paneled walls, lit by a modest lantern or candle sconce. A simple coat rack or peg rail holds cloaks and tricorne hats, while a small side table bore correspondence or calling cards. The scent of beeswax and ink lingered, hinting at the scholarly activity within, and a staircase, plain but sturdy, rose toward the upper chambers where Franklin conducted his experiments and correspondence. The aroma emanating from the kitchen hinted that a meal was in preparation. Though not lavish, the space conveyed order, intellect, and the quiet dignity of a man deeply engaged in shaping a new republic

"We apologize for our lateness. Congress business," Lee said.

"The strength of our state rests upon the employment of wise and good men and the youth who make us think," said Franklin, who added, "We applaud your work, Mr. Lee. It is always good to see you. What progress has Congress reached in its resolve to cast off the Crown?"

"The momentum has changed in the past few months," said Lee. "The pamphlet that Thomas Paine wrote has stirred a passion in the countryside. In addition, the burning of Norfolk and the North Carolina battle should convince many that independence is the route for us to take. As you probably know, Virginia has given us the authority to declare independence, and I understand that Rhode Island has also recently voted in favor. We are counting on a few more states to give us the unanimity that would make a big difference."

"We think that independence is nearly in our reach," said Adams. "We are even hearing positive things from the delegates of South Carolina and Delaware, although some care and feeding of these representatives may be needed to assuage their distress in moving from reconciliation to independence."

"The delegates need to understand that if the King wishes to pursue fighting, as opposed to negotiations, the battle will be protracted," Washington said.

"Too many think that the British will just cut and run. However, the Crown has made a significant investment in the success of her colonies, and we are becoming more sophisticated and lucrative," Richard Henry said. "They will labor from sun to candle to keep us in the empire. Don't you agree, Dr. Franklin? You have been in London over the last months, and I am sure you have measured the Tories for what they are worth."

Franklin replied, "The King does not see straight when the American colonies are the subject. Most of the members of Parliament walk behind him with little opposition."

Adams said, "The King, in his obstinacy, has mistaken firmness for wisdom and vengeance for justice." Adams continued "The cause we serve is no mere quarrel over taxes or trade—it is about the birthright of liberty itself. The eyes of all America, and indeed of posterity, are fixed upon your command. The trials before you are grave with the want of powder for battle, the wavering of some colonies, and the specter of British reinforcements. General, your fortitude is the pillar upon which our hopes rest. Congress has entrusted you not merely with arms, but with the moral leadership of a people awakening to their own sovereignty. Let no doubt creep into our hearts, for the courage you inspire in your men is the very breath of this revolution.

"Doesn't the King understand that the more he levies taxes," said Richard Henry, "and sends his troops and foreign mercenaries, that we will be more likely to unite in rebellion. The southern colonies have slowly started to understand that independence is the only route that we can take. We will all be stronger for it. Let us stand on our own two feet to make the important decisions on how to rule America."

"Dr. Franklin, the die is cast," said General Washington. "His Majesty's forces gather with intent not to reconcile, but to subdue. I fear we must meet tyranny not with petitions, but with powder. Our men are brave, but ill-equipped. The cause is just, yet the path is perilous. I trust your wisdom will rally the minds abroad, as I endeavor to hold the line here."

The Continental Army remained critically short on armaments and gunpowder, despite months of desperate procurement efforts. General Washington had earlier discovered that his forces possessed only a fraction of the powder needed, barely enough for a few days of sustained fighting, and domestic production was hampered by a lack of saltpeter and skilled labor. Congress scrambled to fund powder mills, but accidents and British raids disrupted output. Relief began to trickle in through covert French support, as Silas Deane and Pierre-Augustin Caron de Beaumarchais orchestrated shipments of powder and arms via the West Indies, including high-quality gunpowder refined by Antoine Lavoisier. Still, in April, the army's supply lines were fragile, and the success of the revolution hung precariously on foreign aid and the illusion of readiness.

"General, if the Crown would rather send Hessians than hear reason," said Franklin, "then let them learn that liberty is not so easily extinguished. I shall do my part to fan its flame in France."

Adams said, "I have seen the spirit of independence swell in the breasts of farmers, merchants, and lawyers alike. In Philadelphia, the debates grow ever bolder, and the tide turns toward full separation. You must press on, not only with military resolve but with the conviction that Providence favors the just. You were chosen for this hour because you possess gravitas, patience, and virtue to carry it Let your sword be steady and your example still steadier. The republic we dream of depends on your perseverance."

Richard Henry Lee said, "Gentlemen, the Crown hath declared us in rebellion and sent foreign mercenaries to enforce its will. What further proof do we need that reconciliation is but a phantom? The time for pleas is past—the time for liberty is come."

"I have spoken with delegates in the last few days, and we are of the mind to place the resolution before the delegates very soon," said Lee. "In the last two weeks new instructions from provincial assemblies in North Carolina, South Carolina, Rhode Island and Virginia have arrived, allowing their delegates to authorize a vote for independence. Presently, I've heard a rumor that Maryland and Delaware have also voted to separate."

"All of this sounds good," said Washington, "but what will it take for delegates to stand up and vote yes?"

Franklin said, "They may delay, but time will not."

"General, Mr. Lee has also told me that the Virginia delegation is behind him, and my Massachusetts delegation is tired of waiting," said Adams. "I believe that within two weeks, we will have an independence resolution on the floor of Congress and a declaration to support it following shortly. I am convinced that the other colonies will march with us upon hearing this clarion call, and then we will be prepared to meet the King at all fronts."

A servant appeared at the door to the reading room to announce that food was ready to be served. The men stood up and made their way into the dining room.

After finishing their supper of fish and pork, with rice and potatoes on the side, and some strawberry jam with biscuits to accompany coffee and tea, the patriots sat around the table and forged a resolution among themselves.

"Gentlemen, one year hence, we should be delivered a fate of independence or else," said Adams.

"That is a promise that I might not be willing to digest," answered Washington. "We are in for a long struggle if the colonies declare independence, a fact that I expect, and one should disapprove himself to think that this conflict will last only a short moment."

"Freedom is not a gift bestowed upon us by other men, but a right that belongs to us by the laws of God and nature," said Franklin. "Our cause is the cause of all mankind. We are fighting for their liberty in defending our own."

Lee added, "we must guard against the use of centralized power and urge the states to maintain strong local governance. The

Revolution is not just a break from Britain but a chance to build a government rooted in liberty and virtue.

"Thank you for your time and conversation this evening," Franklin said as the men were gathering their overcoats and hats. "With youth and experience, we have the ingredients for success against mighty Britannia.

The three men left Franklin's home and returned to their different residences to begin planning what should happen in Congress the next day.

Edward Rutledge Meets William Ellery

A few weeks earlier, Edward Rutledge had learned, as had many other delegates, that Samuel Ward, delegate from Rhode Island, had died from smallpox at the age of fifty-one. Having only been sick less than two weeks, the delegates were reminded once again how lethal these infections could be and why people should take vaccination seriously, as Ward had postponed receiving his. Ward had been Rutledges connection to the Rhode Island delegation, and the pair had spent many hours together discussing farming, the law, and politics.

In 1776, smallpox posed a grave threat in Philadelphia, where its endemic presence and the influx of soldiers and refugees created ideal conditions for rapid spread. The disease claimed hundreds of lives, especially among American prisoners of war held by the British, and its high mortality and disfiguring effects made it one of the most feared epidemics of the Revolutionary era.

Edward learned that the delegate chosen to replace Samuel Ward was William Ellery. In early spring, one late afternoon after Congress adjourned for the day, Edward approached Ellery in conversation.

Ellery worked variously as a merchant, customs collector, and clerk of the Rhode Island General Assembly. He began practicing law at age forty-three and became an active member of the Rhode Island Sons of Liberty, aligning himself with the Patriot cause during the Stamp Act crisis.

"Mr. Ellery, I am Edward Rutledge, delegate from South Carolina, and I want to extend my hand to you and welcome you to the Continental Congress. In addition, I was heartbroken when I heard that Samuel Ward had passed on. I extend my sincere condolences to you."

"Thank you, sir, for those kind words. His passing came as such a shock to the entire colony, and I hope that I will be able, in any small way, to carry on the great work he has accomplished for Rhode Island in this august body."

"During the last year, Samuel and I have had many conversations about mutual interests including his desire to make the colonies safer on the high seas. He strongly supported the creation of a Continental

Navy, advocating for maritime defense and endorsing measures to outfit armed vessels for protecting American trade and coastlines.

"Yes, that was one of his passions. He had close relationships with the merchants in Newport and knew how important protecting the seaboard was. I hope that he will be remembered for that and more. I don't think I have had the pleasure of meeting any of the delegates from South Carolina, so I am glad that you have sought me out. Arriving late to the Congress, I am handicapped by the fact all the other delegates have had the opportunity to develop close relationships over time that I have not."

Rutledge continued, "I have found the assembled delegates quite open to bringing you up to speed. You will be impressed by the breadth of experience amassed here together for this important work. You will find delegates like me who seek to develop a working relationship with you.

Shipbuilding was the principal industry in Providence, Rhode Island, fueling both commercial trade and the colony's early naval ambitions. With tensions rising, Rhode Island quickly repurposed merchant vessels into warships, laying the groundwork for the Continental Navy and an opportunity for the colonies to assert their maritime independence.

Ellery said, "We do have a strong marine industry in Rhode Island, and I am proud to say that some of the finest ships in the colonies are built in Newport and Providence. I do remember Ward mentioning your name discussing your plantation and his own agricultural endeavors. He said that was a common bond between you."

"He flattered me knowing that we shared that piece of information. We spoke about how his farming and merchant skills assisted him in navigating the rivalries in the colony."

"If Samuel spoke of the rivalries, then I know that he trusted you. You can count on me to continue that work as best I can."

Rutledge hesitated and then decided to proceed. "One issue that Sam and I agreed about was my concern that some New England delegates might be interested in raising up the slave trade issues and insist they be included in any vote for independence. We both agreed that the slave trade issue was not what we were sent to Philadelphia to decide. Our main and only focus is to define a different relationship with England. I trust that we are of the same mind."

"Sam Ward never spoke to me about the slave trade, and I have no way of acknowledging those conversations. I do know that the shipbuilding industry in Rhode Island was built partially on the needs of people who brought African workers to this country. I also know that my main reason for representing Rhode Island is to see that our colonies are free and allowed to grow. We are living in a period in which, a few years ago, no human could have predicted that these colonies could shake off and declare themselves independent from England. I will diligently work to see this dream become a reality."

Rutledge continued, "The interests of Rhode Island and South Carolina are entwined together in the slave trade. Rhode Island's economy was strengthened by the construction of ships and the export of spirits while South Carolina benefited through the constructive use of crops produced by the plantation economy. When the time comes, the delegates might be asked whether they support independence, with or without the slave trade. I trust that I can count on your consideration of how our colonies benefit from this system."

Ellery said, "I appreciate your openness to discuss this matter freely with me. I will consult with the other delegates from Rhode Island, as I am sure Samuel would have done, and I will provide them with the substance of our conversation which I fully understand."

"It is my understanding that a vote on independence will take place within a few weeks," said Rutledge, "and I share the same sentiment about moving toward that goal. I look forward to working with you as we enter this significant period when the colonies take the necessary steps toward freedom. I will be at your disposal, if you have any concerns or questions."

"Thank you, Mr. Rutledge. I look forward to more discussions of our mutual interests."

Adams and Lee Cooperate

The temperaments of John Adams and Richard Henry Lee varied, though they did share a yearning for independence from Britain. John Adams thought like an attorney and was well organized while Richard Henry Lee was eloquent, radical, and bold. Their common desire to have the thirteen colonies declare independence from England was the glue that would make their relationship work.

Beginning in 1775, the relationship between the two men evolved from a cordial but largely professional relationship as fellow delegates to the First and Second Continental Congresses in a powerful alliance grounded in shared vision and complementary strengths. Both men recognized each other as ideological allies in the movement for independence, though their personal styles differed.

After committee work together and the flow of business on the floor of the Congress in sessions going back to 1774, Lee and Adams would find common ground and political acumen to organize the Second Continental Congress and stand up for independence.

Following their meeting at the First Continental Congress in Fall 1774, Adams and Lee served on some of the same committees and grew accustomed to each other's oratory skills while each depended on the other's power of observation. As the Second Congress began meeting starting on May 10, 1775, the increased oppression that colonial leaders felt being exerted by the British brought these two men together with a similar response of "No more!"

On the evening of May 6, 1776, Lee joined Adams for dinner at the Richard Penn House, a Georgian mansion on High Street, to discuss the work of the committee that would draft a document on how the colonies would relate to each other after independence was declared. They understood the need to create colonial governments that were independent of the Crown. Perhaps they could discuss how the individual colonies together would be independent of Britain. On a warm and cloudless early evening, Adams walked from his boardinghouse to the Richard Penn house where Lee was residing.

"Thank you for joining me for dinner this evening," said Richard Henry Lee, dressed in formal frock coat, white breeches, stockings, waistcoat, and shiny buckled shoes.

"I am honored that you would receive my invitation," said John Adams dressed in a plain, navy frockcoat, worn breeches, a somber waistcoat and shoes without buckles.

A house servant opened a door off the foyer that led to a dining room richly appointed with oil paintings, wainscoting, and a huge table that could hold twenty people, though tonight only two delegates would dine there.

Much discussion had already transpired about what form of government the colonies should adopt, but the formation of a committee with representatives from each of the colonies was the first organized effort to put those suggestions and sketchy designs into a concrete plan.

"Let's take our seats and have some dinner. We can continue on this conversation while we eat."

The scent of the food preparation drifted around the room as Adams took his seat at the head of the table and Richard Henry sat to his right. The dining room was trimmed in white with deep green wallpaper in a floral pattern. The fireplace with bright embers directly behind the head table provided heat to take the chill from the room.

A Black servant entered the room from the door leading to the kitchen carrying a tureen of soup. She was followed by another servant who had small baskets of wheat and corn bread. The servants ladled soup and offered bread to the men. Richard Henry immediately recognized the second servant as Cato, his own Black valet.

"Such an elegant dining room," said Richard Henry. "It reminds me of the dining room that my brother calls Stratford Hall on the Potomac."

"We don't have prestigious homes in Massachusetts like these. It has taken some time and effort to feel comfortable when these pleasures are not easily available to me at home."

The servants began serving the main course of roasted pork medallions. Another servant arrived and provided a basket of bread and a bowl of potatoes.

"Just as we had a first conversation about how each colony should establish their own constitutions, now we are faced with doing the same task making an agreement on confederation between all of the colonies," said Richard Henry.

"I am assuming that we are of similar minds with regard to where this effort will take us."

Richard Henry began to eat his soup and used a crust of bread to capture some of the overflow from the lip of his bowl to the white cotton tablecloth.

Lee said "I would hope that is the case. Would you like to share some of your ideas with me?"

Adams started, "The first issue to determine is the relationship of the central government to the colonies. From all the conversations that I have heard, people are desiring a weak central government, so it does not mandate tasks for the colonies to perform. I assume that states want to retain full control over their internal affairs."

"I would agree with that. Each colony should retain its sovereignty, freedom, and independence," Lee agreed.

"Where we draw the line between the power of the central government and the power of the colonies will be the difficult decision. If we err on the side of too much power for the colonies, then the central government may be disabled. On the other hand, if the central government has too much power, we could dissolve into a relationship that we know too well right now," Adams said.

"If we have a Congress in the central government, how should power be divided? Should each colony have the same representation, or should there be provisions for larger colonies versus smaller?"

"I anticipate conflicts arising on both sides of that issue. What provisions should be articulated to define power? Population? Economies? Geographic size? None, because each colony has equal say?"

"How do we handle future growth? The lands west of the Appalachian Mountains will inevitably be populated with settlers, and those people will desire to be equally involved in this new government. How will we accommodate this growth? Who decides how we evolve? The colonies or the central government?"

"Another aspect that needs to be discussed is foreign affairs. Should the central government have 100% control over affairs with foreign countries? Should colonies have any power to create their own alliances?"

Adams paused from his presentation to use his fork to spear a piece of pork and then pour some gravy on it. He fingered a roll and used it to sop up the gravy before he shoved it into his mouth and used a napkin to clean his chin.

Richard Henry used the interval of Adams savoring his food to say, "John, as usual, I knew that you would have a rough draft of these matters in your head. We need to delineate these points in a draft so the representatives of the colonies can begin an open discussion."

"It is far easier to identify the major points that need to be addressed than to discern the proper relationships on each of the points. One other point which will forever cause us problems is how we pay for government? Taxation is at the center of our dispute with Parliament, and I imagine that it will not be an easier issue once we are free."

"To be honest with you," said Adams, "These thoughts have been rolling around in my head over the last six months, and I believe this is the first time that I have presented the full abstract to anyone. It certainly is not written yet, but I thank you for prompting me to do so. I will put all these thoughts on paper over the next day or two. Then we can distribute them to the other members of the committee and begin a full conversation.

"I look forward to working with you in moving the Congress toward making a plan for governance," said Richard Henry. "The task in finding consensus on all the issues, I am sure, will not be resolved quickly. I believe the time for independence is within our grasp, but first we need to stiffen the spines of those assembled with us. If we work together toward that end, we shall succeed. We will free ourselves from British tyranny and govern as a republic.

"Sir, I could not agree more with you," said Adams.

Before the adoption of the Articles of Confederation in 1781, efforts to form a united government among the thirteen colonies were tentative and largely improvised. The Continental Congress, beginning in 1774, served as a de facto national body, but it operated without a formal legal framework, relying on voluntary cooperation and ad hoc agreements. Earlier attempts at unity, such as the Albany Plan of Union in 1754, had failed due to colonial reluctance to surrender autonomy. Even during the Revolutionary War, states zealously guarded their sovereignty. There was no executive branch, no judiciary, and no power to tax or enforce decisions—Congress could only request funds and troops, often with limited success. The urgency of war forced collaboration, but true structural unity remained elusive until the Articles codified a loose confederation, still marked by deep suspicion of centralized authority.

The conversation between Adams and Lee continued about family and farming while they finished eating and toasting to the progress made in Congress toward independence. With the end of dinner and the servants cleaning up the dining room, John Adams and Richard Henry Lee could tell that this moment was special. If two gentlemen from Virginia and Massachusetts could discuss such a plan without rancor, then the chances of forming a new nation were greatly enhanced.

Rutledge Learns What Cooperation Means to Adams and Lee

Edward Rutledge was to meet with John Adams and Richard Henry Lee on a committee assignment for drafting a document that would be sent to the colonies for the creation of "assemblies and conventions" to better represent the citizens. Rutledge recognized that this assignment was the sort that he had craved since he first joined the Continental Congress eighteen months earlier. Much of the work of the Continental Congress took place in the committees that were established to review issues and make recommendations to the full body. Massachusetts, New Hampshire, and South Carolina had asked for their colonies to develop new governance structures free from Royal power in June 1775. Although Rutledge was uncertain about his readiness to support independence, as he felt much of the Congress was, working with prominent figures like John Adams and Richard Henry Lee marked a significant opportunity for him.

Rutledge was not deluded to think that he would be the sole author, or even a significant contributor, of the important report, as Adams and Lee had made clear their thoughts and plans. Lee was known for his advocacy of a swift and total break from the Crown. Adams, the fiery leader of the Massachusetts delegation, spoke confidently that he saw total independence as the only outcome. The prospect of collaborating with these principal patriots was a meaningful leap in responsibility from his last session of reviewing a petition by a Loyalist from South Carolina.

Rutledge also believed that one of the reasons he was chosen for this assignment was that South Carolina had adopted their own state constitution less than two months ago. That process had begun four months after John Rutledge had asked and received permission from the Continental Congress to proceed with the creation of a new constitution that was based on citizen control of the government.

Rutledge had been told to meet his colleagues after dinner. He would have preferred to meet earlier and have their discussion while they ate. He believed that Adams and Lee would be meeting for dinner, and that he was excluded, as he had been before, but it would be impolite to suggest that he should join them for the meal. Instead, he simply said, "I look forward to our discussion."

Rutledge knew that the events of the past months were leading to a call for independence, but he was not prepared to jump in like Christopher Gadsden and support a full break with London. At times, he conceived that a full break was inevitable, and at other times he imagined that reconciliation remained a possibility. Back and forth, the positions became a tug of war in Rutledges mind between reconciliation and liberation. The new instructions from South Carolina gave the delegates a strong backing if they sensed independence was the will of the Congress. This confidence was battling the many conversations he had with his brother about the need to strive for reconciliation until the final moment, yet how would he know when that moment had arrived?

Edward strolled down to the Richard Penn House where Lee and Adams awaited him. He was familiar with the Georgian mansion, which resembled Thomas Heyward's mansion that had been completed in Charleston in 1772. Thomas had recently been appointed as one of the South Carolina delegates after John Rutledge returned home.

The front door opened for Edward to see a tall, thin black man dressed in fine satin clothes consisting of a red cutaway coat, a ruffled white shirt, and trim black trousers with shiny, buckled shoes. "I presume you are Mr. Rutledge, sir?" the man spoke with perfect diction. "Mister Lee told me you would be arriving soon. Please come in."

With this formal greeting, Edward thought that he could easily be back in Charleston. The doorman reminded him of Henry Middleton's butler who had been in his employ ever since Edward was young. Rutledge mused to himself that he didn't know that they had such servants in Philadelphia.

Edward was led down a short corridor with another large door that opened to the right where a fireplace with a gentle fire burned, and he could see his hosts stand up from their armchairs to greet him. The door closed quietly behind him.

The den of the Richard Penn House reflected the refined tastes of a proprietary governor steeped in both English tradition and colonial sophistication. Tucked within the stately brick residence on Market Street, the den featured polished wood paneling, a tiled fireplace, and tall windows draped in damask curtains to soften the city's bustle.

Shelves were lined with legal volumes, parliamentary records, and pamphlets from London and Philadelphia. A writing desk cluttered with correspondence, quills, and sealing wax stood against the outside wall. Three upholstered armchairs flanked the hearth, inviting quiet conversation or solitary reflection, while portraits of Penn family ancestors and maps of Pennsylvania adorned the walls.

"Welcome, Mr. Rutledge," said John Adams as he extended his right hand while his left hand gently squeezed Edward's right arm. "I was just saying to Richard that I believe you have grown in your role here at the Congress since your brother has been recalled to South Carolina."

As Rutledge shook Richard Henry Lee's hand, Adams guided Edward to the upholstered chair between the seats the two men were already occupying. Edward had forgotten that Lee usually carried a black handkerchief to conceal the four missing fingers on his left hand from a hunting accident he'd suffered eight years earlier. Tonight, he was wearing a black glove.

Rutledge said, "This is a beautiful house. It reminds me of being in Charleston. One of our new delegates from South Carolina has completed building a mansion for his family that is quite like this wonderful structure. You are fortunate to have such beautiful lodging."

"I would ordinarily request that you pass on your affections to the owner, the grandson of the founder, the late William Penn, but he has retreated to London, and although a friend of our cause, continues to reside in Britain to protect his longer-term interests. We appreciate Mr. Penn's contribution to our efforts by allowing some of the delegates to utilize his property while we deliberate," Lee said. "Mr. Penn continues to be revered by a majority of the inhabitants of Pennsylvania."

Adams said, "Edward, I meant what I earlier said about your maturity in Congress. That is one of the reasons why we wanted you to be a part of this committee to urge the other colonies to form their own state governmental structures that reflects the needs of the people."

"I hope that I can be an asset to these efforts."

"Mr. Rutledge, I have asked Mr. Adams to provide a first draft of the preamble to be sent to the colonies," said Lee. "We would like you to take your time and review the document then provide us with your scholarly comments on how we can improve our language. We know that your brother's and your experience in helping to achieve a new constitution for South Carolina could prove to be great aid in encouraging others to follow our lead."

Edward took a quick look at the three-paragraph preamble in John Adams' scrawl and concluded that they were asking for only a small amount of his participation. They had already agreed with each other that they were satisfied. His inclusion in this project seemed only to embellish the document.

"It appears to me that this preamble has already been completed," said Edward. Silence was in the air as Adams and Lee exchanged glances.

John Adams said, "The task in front of us is small compared to the bigger task of how the colonies will receive this. South Carolina is important because you have already taken the needed action to create a strong governing structure as we continue to endure the resolution of our disagreements with the Crown."

"I understand your brother has been named President of South Carolina in your new government." Lee said. "And I also heard that the powers given to your brother, I mean the President, are vast. I think a strong central government is important for our colonies."

"Please understand that our constitution is only provisional. When the differences that we now have with the King are resolved, we will revise the document," said Rutledge.

"If the King continues to disrespect us and makes no provisions for any reconciliation, I believe that the majority of delegates will be ready for independence," said Adams. "Please correct me if I am wrong," Adams continued as he pulled a paper out of his vest pocket and read, "I think your new instructions from the South Carolina Assembly state that you should execute every measure, which together with the majority of the Congress shall judge necessary for the interest of South Carolina and America in general.'"

"You are very well-informed Mr. Adams. I have been thinking along the same lines lately.

"That's good to hear. We need you to refine this preamble for us to strengthen it so that other delegates will come to the same conclusion. I knew we could count on you. Do you think you could give us some thoughts on the preamble by first thing in the morning before our session begins?"

"That should not be a problem."

With that settled, Adams and Lee stood up and ushered Rutledge from the room.

"See you tomorrow, Ned,"

The door closed. Adams and Lee smiled at each other and shook hands heartily.

"I knew he would come around. I think that South Carolina is finally in the fold."

Rutledge felt as though he had been blindsided in a fait accompli with no significant participation from him expected. Edward knew that he needed to speak to some of his allies from other states before the next morning.

RUTLEDGE ENGAGES WITH LIVINGSTON

Late one evening at the City Tavern, Edward Rutledge and Robert Livingston were seated together discussing the latest action in the Continental Congress and the meeting that Rutledge had had with John Adams and Richard Henry Lee. The constant noise from the patrons of the establishment chased Rutledge and Livingston to one of the meeting rooms at the top of the stairs.

The City Tavern pulsed with the clamor of revolution and commerce, its rooms thick with overlapping voices, clinking pewter, and the scrape of chairs on wooden floors. The taproom echoed with heated debates as delegates, merchants, and militia officers spilled in from Independence Hall, their conversations rising over the hum of fiddlers and the bark of orders to the kitchen. Outside, the rattle of carriage wheels and shouts of errand boys filtered through open windows, mingling with the scent of ale and roasted meat. Inside, the din was not disorderly but electric, an audible testament to a city on the cusp of transformation, where every toast, argument, and whispered deal carried the weight of a nation being born.

As he poured a modest drink from his flask of claret, Rutledge said, "John Adams grows louder by the day. He charges through sessions like a man who already commands a nation. Richard Henry Lee is right at his side, spurring him on to even broader appeals."

Livingston, adjusting his glasses, said, "It is not the volume of Adams that troubles me, it is the velocity. He advances independence as though the mere breath of enthusiasm could galvanize thirteen colonies into one heart."

Rutledge said, "He scarcely tolerates hesitation. Virginia inches forward; South Carolina hesitates. But to Adams, every caution is cowardice."

"He sees nuance as obstruction. I have respect for the man—he is tireless, passionate. But diplomacy cannot run on fever alone.

"South Carolina needs assurances," Edward said. "Let us not be swept away by the fervor of Massachusetts or the eloquence of Mr. Jefferson. Let us instead be deliberate, measured, and wise. Delay is not defeat; it is strategy. Give us time to persuade our assemblies, to build consensus, to ensure that when the break comes, it comes with the full weight of united resolve. I will not see this Congress rush headlong into history only to find itself divided and undone. Our planters fear a rupture with Britain more than they fear royal taxes. They believe their prosperity hangs by London's silk thread."

Robert Livingston said, "In New York, it is even more delicate. The provincial congress has yet to empower us to vote for independence. I was summoned to draft declarations, yet my hands are tied. I do not oppose the cause, I have long believed Britain was deaf to reason and blind to justice, but I oppose the haste. Let us not mistake fervor for readiness. A declaration made in division is no foundation for a republic. Better to wait, persuade, and bind our brethren with argument and assurance, then to force their hand with premature resolve.'

"We must manage him. Adams cannot be silenced but we must implement delay. Steady the march and temper the declarations."

"Do you propose we intervene directly? asked Livingston."

"Not confront, redirect. Encourage postponement, consensus. We should let Richard Henry speak, but urge a committee to slowly draft the terms, without forcing an immediate vote," Rutledge argued.

Livingston said, "A committee is the great solvent of urgency. Excellent. And the longer we discuss and delay, the more time for our colonies to align or dissent, without condemnation.

"And Adams? Will he abide such delay?"

"Edward, he respects procedure, even if he detests patience. If the Congress agrees to form a formal committee, his protest will be blunted. Especially if Franklin or Sherman supports it."

Edward said, "Yes. And Jefferson? He's quiet but firm. He aligns with Adams but cloaks his responses in philosophy."

"Jefferson's pen is his sword. He writes passionately but speaks with restraint. I can work with him—better him than Adams driving the debate, "Livingston said.

"The colonies must be coaxed toward liberty, not dragged. Independence will fracture before it binds," Edward added.

"Well said. Liberty should never resemble coercion. Let us suggest a resolution, not for separation, but for further deliberation. We should build consensus through parchment and pause.

Edward said, "Your phrasing rivals Jefferson's."

Livingston added as he lifted his glass in a toast, “Flattery is the currency of Philadelphia. What concerns me most is not Adam’s ambition. It is the force of his moral argument. When he speaks of tyranny, he speaks with the fire of a preacher.”

The men drank lustily from their mugs.

“And yet, he forgets that some among us see liberty through the prism of property. A man’s rights are not abstract. They are tangible: land, labor, legacy,” said Rutledge.

“Including labor held in bondage. Adams condemns royal oppression, yet his argument beckons broader rebellion. If liberty is indivisible, how long before our own institution of slavery comes under attack from those who oppose?”

Edward leaned toward Livingston and said, “You mean by enlivening advocates of abolition?”

“Indeed. New York trades in the slave trade but without creating any plantations. However, you Carolinians stake your fortune on it. Jefferson is silent, but Adams may not remain so.

“I fear that Mr. Jefferson will not remain silent on all issues and specifically the subject of slavery. Regardless, we must be careful in our pursuit of consensus, because once we claim liberty for all, some will ask who "all" truly includes.

“If Adams writes the answer, it may not suit Charleston, or New York.

The two men locked eyes pondering that each man knew this was a core issue of contention.

Rutledge started, “He believes the people will rise. That liberty once spoken cannot be denied. But people also fear. They fear war. They fear want. And they fear change.”

“Adams has no fear. That’s the paradox. His lack of fear inspires the bold but unsettles the cautious.

“Then we must manage him not by opposition—but by surrounding him. Let the voices of Congress swell, not to silence him, but to shape him.

“Shape the debate, shape the language, shape the timing,” Livingston said.

“Yes, precisely. Delay the vote. Form the committee. Craft the declaration not as Adams would, full of fire, but tempered, witty and wise as Franklin might.”

"Both of us should speak with Hancock. He trusts my moderation while your movement toward independence may make his cooperation easier," Livingston said.

"And I'll speak with Dickinson," said Rutledge, "though he quivers at even the word independence. If he supports deliberation, that gives us cover."

"You and I must hold the center. Adams will always ride the front, Jefferson the flank. But it is the center that holds the army firm."

As he stood, Rutledge said, "Then let's steady our columns. I have no quarrel with liberty—but let it arrive not with a shout, but with a signature.

Livingston extended his hand to Edward and firmly shook his hand saying, "To signatures, then. And the ink of reason."

RUTLEDGE SEEKS JOHN HANCOCK'S SUPPORT

Edward Rutledge feared that the contents of any declaration on independence would include language on the slave trade similar to words in the Continental Association. Edward dreaded such wording would do harm to South Carolina and poison the debate. He decided to have a conversation with the President of Congress in hopes of some courtesy that Hancock might offer. As Rutledge knew that a declaration would be completed before the Lee resolution could be debated, he sensed that the timetable for the debate and passage of the declaration would happen at about the same time. Edward had decided he needed a plan.

Edward Rutledge and John Hancock had shared a collegial and occasionally strategic relationship as fellow delegates to the Continental Congress. Hancock, as President of the Congress, presided over the debates and proceedings with a blend of formality and flair. Rutledge often worked behind the scenes to moderate radical impulses and build consensus, especially among Southern delegates, while Hancock managed the public face of Congress and signed official documents. Though the two men came from different regions and had contrasting temperaments, they were united by the shared goal of colonial rights.

John Hancock resided at the home of Thomas Willing, a prominent Philadelphia merchant and banker. Willing's residence was located on Market Street near Third Street, placing Hancock within easy walking distance of the Pennsylvania State House where Congress met.

This arrangement was typical for delegates, many of whom lodged with local families or in nearby taverns and boarding houses. Hancock, as President of Congress, was a high-profile guest, and his stay with Willing reflected both his status and the hospitality extended by Philadelphia's elite to revolutionary leaders.

Earlier in April, Edward was going to the City Tavern for supper and had the good fortune to meet John Hancock at the front door.

"Mr. Hancock. I don't remember seeing you here. Are you meeting anyone? If not, I would be greatly honored if you joined me for your meal."

"Why, thank you, Mr. Rutledge. You are correct that the City Tavern is not my first choice for dining, but I wanted a break in my routine and to relax. I would enjoy your company for dinner."

The two men entered the bustling City Tavern, a place where congressional business was frequently conducted even before the delegates reached the Pennsylvania Statehouse. Rutledge pointed to a table on the far-left wall where they could sit, eat, and discuss the news of the day. Rutledge knew what he wanted to discuss.

"Edward, you seem to be very well acquainted with this establishment."

"Mr. Hancock, I have discovered that our discourse is different from British parliamentary traditions, the lively debate found here is conducive to a broader conversation and a more relaxed atmosphere of give and take."

"I would hasten to add that a business like the City Tavern is well qualified to provide potables that, after a while, would make men's tongues looser and be more appreciative of collaboration or fights."

"I believe you have high regard for this sensible business."

A server appeared from a crowd of patrons and took a meal order of smoked salmon and corn chowder, in addition to beverages. He quickly turned and was lost in a sea of men.

"Mr. Hancock."

"Please call me John."

"John, I am sure you have heard that I am concerned about the possibility that any declaration for independence may include some language that will be a problem for South Carolinians."

"I have heard rumors. News travels quickly in Congress, and I had at least three gentlemen tell me of your concerns."

"I am not sure if your knowledge is a good thing or not."

"I am not sure what to say about my knowledge of your activities, but I will submit that one aspect of your argument, that our declaration should be tightly focused, has had an impact on me," said Hancock.

"Thank you. South Carolina wishes to do the right thing. Christopher Gadsden has influenced me sufficiently such that, after the King rejected our Olive Branch Petition, independence was probably a conclusion that all the colonies would embrace."

"Edward, those are words that gladden my heart."

"John, the timing of the resolution for independence and the declaration on independence is the issue I wish to discuss. I know that, with the addition of new delegates from South Carolina who strongly support independence, our delegation is united that no mention of the slave trade should be included in the declaration. The slave trade issue remains a stumbling block, and I would like to seek your support in assuring that it will not appear in a declaration and rushed through for adoption.

Hancock said, "I can't imagine a set of circumstances where a topic as important as the slave trade would be adopted without significant and diligent debate."

Rutledge responded, "I trust your judgement, but from my perspective, the timing of the resolution and the declaration on independence is thorny. It's probable that they will be on the floor of Congress at about the same time. I understand that the resolution of Mr. Lee needs to be passed before the declaration can be made. The Committee of Five to draft the declaration is currently working on a document that may be available for debate in less than two weeks. Both actions could occur on the same day. If the declaration includes a slave trade section, we might need to vote on the Lee resolution before discussing the declaration."

"I am beginning to understand your dilemma. What would you like to see occur?"

"The South Carolina delegation asks that if slave trade language appears in the declaration, that you, as the President, recognize me immediately following the reading of the declaration, so I can offer an amendment to strike the injurious language. Given the importance of the declaration, I would surmise that other less controversial issues may be raised, but I am just asking that the South Carolina motion be placed at the head of the line."

Hancock said "A great many assumptions must happen if the course of events is to be played out as you have described. Although your scenario sounds creditable, we have no way of knowing if those facts will visit our plans."

"I would agree. However, I would merely ask that you be aware of our concerns and work with us to see that the offensive language on the slave trade is not included in any declaration that we approve.

"As I have said to you, some of the delegates have told me that you have discussed this issue with them over the last months, but my question is why you believe that such language would suddenly appear. I have not heard a single voice raised upon this issue, and I have had many delegates approach me, as you have today. No one has mentioned the slave trade to me."

"I understand your puzzlement, but in the Continental Association adopted by the First Continental Congress, language about the slave trade, which I now find offensive, was included. I realize that circumstances have changed dramatically in the last nine months, but that doesn't erase the fact that delegates to Congress last year agreed to language on limiting the slave trade. No South Carolina delegate will ever sign a declaration in 1776 that carries such language."

"Thank you for the thoughtful presentation of your concerns, and I can now understand your problem more clearly. I have sympathy for your challenge, and I will work with you to provide you an opportunity to eliminate such language if necessary."

"Mr. Hancock, thank you for your time and understanding."

Hancock asked, "If I may inquire, other delegates have asked me, and I have not had a complete picture, how is the health of South Carolina delegate, Thomas Lynch?"

"Thank you for asking. Mr. Lynch has suffered a stroke that has not been completely debilitating but has slowed his concentration significantly. The South Carolina Provincial Assembly recognized the problem and has named, Thomas Jr., to take his father's place. He should be arriving any day."

"Please extend our concern for Thomas Sr. and wishes that he may have a quick recovery."

The server appeared through a crowd of people and brought food and drink to their table. Rutledge and Hancock continued their conversation about Congress business and family before they left.

Edward and Arthur Discuss Strategy

Edward Rutledge believed events were cascading rapidly toward a denouement. On June 7, 1776, Richard Henry Lee stood before the full Continental Congress and made a motion, that "these United Colonies are, and of right ought to be, free and independent States . . . and that all political connection between them and the State of Great Britain is, and ought to be, totally dissolved."

Edward knew this date was coming, but he had calculated that it would not come so soon. No provisions had been made to develop a formal union joining the colonies one to another, and no entreaties had been made to foreign powers to secure alliances. He felt to his core that now was not the time to declare independence without providing a cohesive framework between the colonies. In addition, he remained concerned that the declaration on independence may contain language that would affect the institution of slavery to the detriment of South Carolina.

In Mrs. Yard's boardinghouse, the study offered Edward Rutledge quiet refuge from the clamor of Congress and the bustle of Market Street. The room was modest but orderly, with a walnut writing desk positioned near a small-paned window that gave glimpse of the night sky in early summer. Shelves held pamphlets, inkpots, and political tracts, while a worn armchair and a brass candlestick suggested late hours of reflection and correspondence. Here, Rutledge could compose his letter to John Jay, his pen scratching across parchment as he weighed the fate of the fragile state of the colonies, a bold move toward independence, and the need for New York to be represented in the process. The air carried the scent of sealing wax and pipe smoke, and the ticking of a mantel clock marked time in a city on the brink of revolution.

After the Congress adjourned, Rutledge returned to Mrs. Yard's boardinghouse, had dinner with his wife and fellow delegate, Elbridge Gerry, and then dashed off a letter to John Jay, delegate from New York. Jay had returned home to help form the New York Provincial Congress. Edward stressed how the Continental Congress was careening toward independence without a clear unanimous direction declared. "The Congress sat until 7 o'clock this evening in consequence of a motion of R.H. Lee's resolving ourselves free and independent States. The sensible part of the House opposed the motion. They had no objection to forming a scheme of a treaty which they would send to France by proper persons, uniting this Continent by a Confederacy" he wrote.

Rutledge believed that South Carolina was not ready to take the irrevocable step without articles of confederation and direct contact with foreign powers for support. "Every Colony considers themselves at liberty to do as they please upon almost every occasion," Rutledge wrote. He added that it should not be assumed that every colony was prepared to take the same path. Many were not prepared to act yet. He continued by saying that on Monday, he would move that action be delayed for three weeks. In this way every colony would have ample time to poll their delegates and local provincial bodies to elicit support so that a united front could be achieved.

Edward Rutledge found himself navigating a political and moral tightrope. As a staunch defender of his colony's slaveholding economy, Rutledge was deeply concerned that any move toward independence might embolden Northern delegates to push for abolition or include anti-slavery language in foundational documents. The Lee Resolution called for a formal break from Britain, but Rutledge hesitated, fearing that premature action could fracture colonial unity and expose Southern interests to radical reform. He and other Southern delegates worked behind the scenes to ensure that any declaration of independence would omit direct condemnation of slavery and preserve the institution while aligning with the revolutionary cause.

On Sunday morning, Rutledge rose early and, with his wife, Henrietta, and Arthur and Mary Middleton, made their way to Christ Church. As they walked, Edward said to Arthur, "Today is a good day to pray to God that the Congress will be led toward the righteous path of liberty."

"God will lead us, but we must follow," Middleton replied.

"Easier said than done, my friend," Rutledge said. "I wrote to Jay last night that I am going to ask the Congress tomorrow to postpone taking the irrevocable step to independence with too much haste and see if they will agree to a three-week delay"

“Do you think that is enough time to get the support needed for action?” said Arthur.

“At least South Carolina has given us authority to respond to this quick pace of decisions.”

“The new instructions we received from the South Carolina House Assembly give us considerable latitude in supporting such a resolution as presented on Friday. Do you think we should take the lead?” asked Middleton.

“The main reason I wrote Mr. Jay last night is that the New York delegation does not have the authority to support independence. The delegates present do not yet have authorization as those of us from South Carolina do, and in his estimation, the New York delegates do not presently demonstrate much energy for independence. The latest instructions given them are more binding and state that they should work for ‘reconciliation and not separation.’ Jay is attending meetings of the New York Provincial Congress, and it is his intention to prod them gently in the direction of independence.”

“Your active urging of Mr. Jay toward independence sounds as though you have already concluded that is the proper course of action we should follow, said Arthur Middleton.

Rutledge said, “I can envision a time in the not-so-distant future that we will vote for independence, but we have some other issues that must be addressed before we can publicly declare our position. First, we need to know that a system of government between the colonies is established. Second, the colonies must establish a process for approaching Spain and France to provide support for our struggles. Lastly, we need to know that slavery is not threatened in any way as we establish our governments.

“I understand the first two points about government and allies, but I never heard any discussion about slavery. Why do you believe that it presents a problem at this date?” asked Middleton.

“My brother told me that, when the Continental Association was established at the First Continental Congress, the delegates agreed as part of the non-importation ban, that all colonies would neither import nor purchase any slave,” said Edward. “We cannot allow the same wording to be secreted into any documents that steer our future.”

“Have you heard any of the delegates mentioning these issues while you have been part of the Second Congress?”

"Not directly, but I have heard many other conversations among the New England delegates which tell me that our plantation system does not please them. Many of these delegates will not concede that their own colonies are prospering by the same trade that they admonish. We need to be thorough in reviewing all the documents presented to ensure that we are not surprised."

"Gentleman, we are almost at the church." Henrietta said. "Why don't we delay this congress discussion for another time, away from our true purpose here on a Sunday."

"You are correct, my dear Henrietta. No more talk of business for the entirety of the morning. Let us pray for the wisdom to lead us down a path of liberty."

After the church service, Edward addressed Arthur, "We need to talk about the session coming up on Monday. I have had a conversation with Robert Livingston and John Dickinson, and it is my desire that we have the colonies united on a delay to voting on independence for another three weeks. That will give the other delegations an opportunity to receive authorization from their provincial authorities."

"You have my support on the delay, and I am sure that Lynch and Heyward will agree," said Middleton. "Honestly, we have already been speaking about a vote, and we thought that we would need to encourage you to vote with us. There will be jubilation when Thomas and John hear the news.

The two couples leisurely strolled from the church back to Mrs. Yard's boardinghouse with the gentle breeze from the river and the birds busily winging their way to their nests. Edward and Henrietta would share a rare day with themselves even as Edward was busily filing through his memory of how each delegate affirmed to him how they would vote in reference to the slave trade.

Dickinson Connection Confirmed

The London Coffee House was, for John Dickinson, his favorite meeting place away from the Pennsylvania State House. On this early June 1776 day, Philadelphia was experiencing an unusually warm spell before summer officially arrived and the sky was full of birds looking to establish nests. Dickinson was waiting for Edward Rutledge to join him to discuss strategy for the upcoming meeting of Congress.

The London Coffee House stood prominently at the corner of Market and Front Streets, just a block from the Delaware River's bustling wharves. Its brick facade, weathered but stately, rose three stories above the cobbled street, with shuttered windows and a modest wooden sign swinging above the entrance. Horse-drawn carts and pedestrians crowded the intersection, where merchants, ship captains, and politicians gathered to exchange news, strike deals, and debate the rising tide of revolution. The building exuded colonial practicality, neither grand nor plain, with a wide stoop and iron railings that framed the doorway. The entrance was flanked by barrels, crates, and the occasional enslaved person awaiting his master's call. Though its exterior was unassuming, the London Coffee House was a crucible of commerce and politics, its walls echoing with the voices of a city on the brink of transformation.

"Good afternoon, Mr. Rutledge," Dickinson said.

"And a good afternoon to you also, Mr. Dickinson."

Rutledge and Dickinson eased through the door and looked for a place to sit at the rear. The House was a lively, smoke-filled chamber where the scent of coffee mingled with pipe tobacco and the salt of nearby wharves. The room was modest but well-used, with wooden beams overhead and long tables crowded by merchants, ship captains, and colonial officials deep in conversation. Walls bore notices of auctions, ship arrivals, and public events, while private booths tucked into corners allowed for discreet negotiations or political whispers. The clink of tankards and the scratch of quills filled the air, as deals were struck with handshakes and news passed faster than the post. Though the furnishings were plain, the atmosphere was highly charged, for this was a place where commerce met revolution, and where the future of the colonies was debated over steaming cups and strong spirits.

"I assume that you wanted to speak to me about the motion that Richard Henry Lee is prepared to present in the near future at one of our Congressional meetings."

"That's correct, John. I met with Robert Livingston yesterday, and we had a congenial meeting about how momentum is pushing the delegates to precipitously take up the topic of independence before all delegates feel ready to commit to such an action."

"All three of us have been witnessing this march to independence for many months now. The timing seems to be hastened for everyone. Did you come to some conclusion on how we might navigate these deep waters?"

Rutledge explained his conversation with Robert Livingston and said, "We can easily agree that John Adams and Richard Henry Lee are anxious to march hastily to call for independence. Our conclusion was to accept these events, but to delay as much as possible. Each colony should have the time to authorize their delegates to vote. A new structure of government for the united colonies should be established, and a process should be created to seek support from foreign sovereigns to support our cause."

"I couldn't agree more with the premise, but how are we to delay this river from surging over its banks?"

"Livingston believes we should approach John Hancock as President of the Congress to delay a vote on Lee's preamble for independence for three weeks. This provides time for the other colonies to authorize their delegates to vote. In the meantime, Hancock should appoint a committee to author the declaration on independence. This gives Adams the opportunity to move the process along, but at a slower pace."

"Excuse me for being blunt, but are you not conceding the point of independence by agreeing to this process?"

"Not at all. The timing for adopting the document of independence needs to be delayed until we have the other two aspects of governance and foreign support in place. I have already spoken to Hancock about a possible obstacle, and he assured me that he would cooperate. These tasks will take time. In addition, the document that they design for independence needs to be discussed by all the delegates in Congress. We, Livingston and I, believe that will give us a second opportunity to delay until such time as the other two documents have been agreed upon."

"I remain troubled that Congress is prepared to declare independence when all channels of reconciliation have not been exhausted," Dickinson declared. "It is premature and destabilizing for a call for independence to be declared without having all these other matters made agreeable and concluded among all the colonies. Declaring independence now would be like braving a storm in a skiff made of paper. Furthermore, the divisions between the colonies have not been resolved satisfactorily. Rushing into independence may result in civil strife."

"I agree with those thoughts, but I also realize that the colonies have been shifting their positions on independence under our feet. Consider my own position: When I arrived from South Carolina in the spring of 1775, my instructions were broad but did not give me the authority to vote for independence. In April 1776, my authority expanded to include such a declaration. If South Carolina can recognize such a shift of opinion, why shouldn't New York, Maryland, North Carolina, Delaware, or Pennsylvania? The earth is moving under our feet, and I am recognizing the need to be agile enough to demand various concessions while moving toward independence. I know that is not your current appraisal, but Robert and I would like you to know that we view you as a kindred spirit in this arena and look forward to your support in seeing these actions taken so we can assure the best possible solution."

"Mister Rutledge, I have concluded that events may overtake my position and influence. I am thankful that advocates who share the bulk of my disposition have taken the time and energy to include me in their final plots and plans. I will endeavor to support you in those aims if they do not conflict with my temperament or my responsibilities as I perceive them."

"I have learned so much by listening to your advice and manner, and I have become a better man. I hope, by connecting with you through our time together in Congress, I will never forget how you manage to stay true to your instincts, while instructing others to seek their own truth. I look forward to working with you as our united colonies move to the next page of history."

Dickinson said, "Please walk me through the gambit one more time. Livingston and you believe that you will be able to convince Hancock of a three-week delay in voting on Richard Henry Lee's resolution so that colonial delegations can receive proper instructions from their local bodies to vote for independence?"

"Yes, and during this period, we would ask a small committee of Congress to draft the declaration on independence. In the meantime, we will continue to convince delegates to disallow any wording to about the slave trade in the declaration," Rutledge explained.

"Your ambitious program seems like a tall order to fulfill. First, you need to convince Hancock of the need for a delay. If he sees that the votes are there for independence, why would he want to delay?"

Rutledge said. "Everyone talks about needing unanimity on the resolution. Without a delay, some colonial delegations will have their hands tied without specific guidance. Take Pennsylvania, your home colony. I don't think you have the authority as of now to vote for independence."

"You are correct about that, but will three weeks be enough time for the crucial delegates to be sworn in and authorized?

"If not, then the radicals will need to delay themselves if they wish a unanimous vote."

Dickinson said, "Let's agree for the sake of argument that enough votes come through to make it unanimous, how do you propose for the articles to bind the colonies together to be completed before the vote on independence? You certainly won't receive foreign support before the final independence vote takes place."

"The Continental Association document gives us a leg up on binding the colonies together," said Edward. "All of the discussion that has taken place indicates that everyone wants the least amount of executive power, and in that, we concur. Finding a final agreement between the colonies should not be that difficult, but it must be done."

"I do love your pluck and mettle, Ned. But those qualities are no guarantee that your plans can be realized. I've told you already that I will support you if language about the slave trade is somehow included in the declaration, but I am not so sure the balance of your agenda is achievable."

"John, ever since the writing and distribution of *Common Sense,* the tide has turned toward independence. Neither of us can deny that fact of our lives today. The determination that I see in Lee and Adams shows me that we are going to see independence on their terms alone if we don't try to make a reasonable stand. Robert and I believe this is worth the battle."

"Your analysis may very well be accurate. Talk to me after you receive assurance of the delay from Hancock. Then we will speak again."

Delegates Respond to Declaration of Independence Draft

June 28th, 1776, began as a usual day at the Second Continental Congress in Philadelphia with high clouds, a cool breeze off the Delaware River and delegates streaming into the Statehouse. The evening before, there was a buzz at City Tavern that the committee had drafted a declaration of independence and might have their first draft ready for circulation, but no official word had yet been given. Edward Rutledge had followed the same routine that he had used since his arrival in Philadelphia last summer—breakfast early, then left for the Statehouse by 8:45. Edward had completed his homework.

Philadelphia stirred to life beneath a clear sky, the golden light glinting off brick facades and cobbled streets as shopkeepers unlatched shutters and apprentices swept stoops. The scent of fresh bread drifted from bakeries near Market Street, mingling with the tang of horse sweat and pipe smoke as carriages rattled toward the State House. Merchants arranged wares in stalls, and printers hauled damp broadsides into the sun to dry, their presses already humming with news of Congress and war. Church bells marked the hour, and the air buzzed with anticipation, whispers of independence, troop movements, and distant battles threading through conversations at tavern doors and boardinghouse parlors. It was a morning of ordinary bustle shadowed by extraordinary change, as the city stood poised between colonial routine and revolutionary destiny.

Upon Edward's arrival, things started to happen that clearly indicated this would not be an ordinary day. Edward saw Arthur Middleton and asked him if he knew what was happening.

"Your information is probably better than any that I have at my disposal, but I overheard two of the delegates saying that the committee was prepared today to share their draft of the declaration."

"Who did you overhear?"

'I think it was Thomas Stone and Samuel Chase from Maryland."

Edward looked through the crowd that was standing near the steps of the Statehouse in search of Stone. Finally, he saw him, but Stone was entering the doors to the main hall. Edward eagerly moved between delegates who were talking and made his way to the entrance, followed closely by Pompey. He then saw that the delegate from Maryland had disappeared into the main chamber. After waiting for four other delegates to pass into the room, Edward found Thomas standing near the Maryland table.

"Thomas. I hear today may be the big day. What do you know?"

"Not a lot, but Samuel Chase told me he heard last night that the committee has a draft of the declaration, and they are ready to present it to Congress. Hopefully, there will be a handful of copies so that we can see what has been written."

"Did Chase have any information about what was included in the document?"

"No. Only that it is not very long, it has an opening declaring independence, and then a list of reasons why the colonies are making this decision. He didn't mention anything else, although he did say that he thought that the entire document will be read to the full Congress."

"Thanks, Thomas. If you do get to see the document, please let me know. You know the one item I would be most concerned about."

The fact that it was to be read was a relief for Rutledge who, starting at Middle Temple when he was studying law in London, had developed a process for writing quickly in a shorthand to capture the full texts of his teachers. He gained an advantage over students by having these accurate notes to refer to when studying for exams.

He directed Pompey to stand quietly against the back wall.

The Assembly Room filled up unusually quickly, and it was still fifteen minutes before the time they were scheduled to begin. All the South Carolina delegates were at their table to the right of the chamber. Everyone was excited to discover what the committee had produced, and they were also curious to learn who had done the writing. Benjamin Franklin, John Adams, Thomas Jefferson, Roger Sherman, and Robert Livingston were on the committee of five, but everyone suspected that someone among this group would probably have been assigned to write a first draft. Edward mused to himself that over the last few days he had not spoken with his friend Livingston. Was that a clue? If so, Edward was hopeful that this version would not include any passages about the slave trade. However, if the writer was Jefferson, Rutledge was nervous as he had heard Jefferson make comments from time to time that, even though he owned slaves, Jefferson found the practice a blemish on the colonies that should be eliminated.

Suddenly, from the door adjacent to the fireplace on the right in front of the chamber, the Committee of Five entered. John Adams led the way, with Thomas Jefferson following, and then, Roger Sherman, and Benjamin Franklin. Robert Livingston was also on the Committee but was absent this day while attending to business in Albany, NY. Adams whispered to John Hancock as he gave him the documents. After a minimal amount of conversation, the committee members turned and returned to their seats with their state's delegation.

John Hancock and Charles Thompson stood at the head table in the Assembly Room and were giving orders to workers to help with the flow of papers. Of the papers that Adams had given to Hancock, he kept one copy and gave the other to Thompson. The noise in the chamber was subdued when Hancock took his gavel and struck it twice on its stand.

"Gentlemen, I call this session of the Second Continental Congress to order. Will the secretary read the first order of business."

Thompson stood and said, "I report that the Committee on Claims to whom was referred the petition and accounts of Thomas Thomson, report…."

The mundane items on the agenda began, with no clear indication how long this minutia of business would continue. Payments for reimbursement of affairs in Canada, the seating of new delegates from New Jersey, a report from the Board of War, appointment of a new delegate to an existing committee, a petition to sell powder to a militia in Salem, New Jersey, and a report from the committee to prepare a declaration were to be read to the Congress.

The room became quiet again as there was a quiet discussion between Hancock and Thompson. The seated delegates held their breath in anticipation of an announcement.

The murmurs in the room became louder, and anxious shuffling of feet could be heard. This seminal moment had Rutledge on the edge of his seat. What would be included in the declaration? What was the tenor of the document? Was it argumentative or tactfully direct? What were the repercussions of this act? In just a few minutes, all the answers to these questions and many others would be answered.

Hancock tapped his gavel gently this time and said, "Could we have some quiet. The secretary will now read from the committee a draft declaration on independence."

The room was quiet with no motion detected by the delegates. The windows of the Assembly Hall were open to allow fresh air to circulate at this moment of expectation.

Thompson stood and in his deep baritone voice began, "A Declaration of the representatives of the United States of America in general congress assembled."

"When in the course of human events it becomes necessary for a people to advance from that subordination, in which they may have hitherto remained and to assume the powers of the earth, the equal and independent station to which the laws of nature and of nature's God entitles them a decent respect to the opinions of mankind, requires that they should declare the causes, which impel them to change. We hold these Truths to be self-evident; that all Men are created equal and independent; that from that equal Creation they derive Rights inherent and unalienable; among which are the Preservation of Life, Liberty, and the Pursuit of Happiness."

And so, the reading continued for twenty minutes without a word being said by any delegates. Certain portions of the text made a few people wince, while others were cheered quietly.

However, one section of particular concern to Rutledge came midway through the reading. The section began with, *"he has waged cruel war against human nature itself, violating its most sacred rights of life and liberty in the persons of a distant people, who never offended him, captivating & carrying them into slavery in another hemisphere, or to incur miserable death in their transportation thither. This piratical warfare, the opprobrium of infidel powers, is the warfare of the King of Great Britain determined to keep open a market where men should be bought & sold, and he has prostituted his negative for suppressing every legislative attempt to prohibit or to restrain this execrable commerce."*

Although the words, and purpose of the words, were different from those included in the Continental Association, Edward knew that the people of South Carolina would never forgive him if these words were in the final version adopted by the Congress. Rutledge continued to take his shorthand for the remainder of the reading, but he was sure that he had missed some of the finer points because he could not get the phrase "raged cruel war against human nature" out of his mind.

Rutledge thought to himself, *how could a fellow southerner write such language that might have been attributed to the most virulent anti-slavery activist? Was the section placed in the declaration as a negotiating ploy? The draft must delete this unacceptable language if Congress expected to have unanimity of all the colonies.*

After the final passages of the declaration had been read, Hancock told the delegates that the debate on the declaration would follow the vote on the Lee resolution regarding independence which was scheduled for Monday morning. Next, Congress had a few other administrative measures to address and then adjourned until July 1 at 9AM.

Rutledge turned toward Pompey, motioned him to come close, and handed him a letter to take to Henrietta.

The room descended into a cacophony of discussion. It would be difficult to hear anyone if they were not nearby. There was cheering and some jeering. The righteous words of the declaration were beautiful, but many other items seemed to hit nerves that made members of the body uncomfortable.

It was clear, by the look of the South Carolina delegates, that they were surprised and disappointed about the language on the slave trade. "How could they put nonsense about the slave trade in the same document where we declare independence," said Arthur Middleton.

"We have our work cut out for us to make sure that the declaration will be stripped of this diatribe," said Thomas Heyward.

Edward Rutledge said "Men, this was the problem that has concerned me since I returned to Philadelphia. If we have done our work well, there should be adequate numbers of delegates who will support our effort to see this section of the declaration be deleted. Our job from now through Monday is to double-back and check with the delegates whom we have already spoken to and remind them that the section about the slave trade does not belong in the declaration on independence. We have plenty of friends who will support us, but we need to connect with them to ensure that they see this through our lens of freedom. We will succeed."

Rutledge moved through the crowd of delegates to locate Thomas Stone, Robert Livingston, John Dickinson, and Eldridge Ellery. If these men of great stature could be reminded of the conversations they'd had, he thought they needn't worry about the slave trade section remaining in the declaration.

Thomas Stone was in conversation with Samuel Chase as Edward sidled to Stone's side to listen to their conversation and engage Stone in discussion.

"Masterful writing," said Chase. "The committee has produced a document, that with a few minor revisions, will clearly state our situation and view of the future."

Stone responded, "I would agree about the overall structure and strength of the declaration, but I sense there are certain parts about which some of the delegates will request changes."

Rutledge chimed in, "The text was soaring in some sections, and I believe it caught the essence of what we all agree on, but I agree with Thomas that certain sections need to be reworked or eliminated."

"My dear sir," Chase began. "I am not sure which sections you found objectionable, but the attack on the British people seemed to be unneeded to me."

"The language used seemed to be a bit on the harsh side, for my tastes."

"How would you describe the section attacking the King for forcing the slave trade on the colonies? That is the section that I found unconscionable," said Rutledge.

Stone said, "I would agree with Mr. Rutledge on that point. I believe their zeal outran their reason regarding the slave trade. I thought the declaration should be solely focused on independence and that bringing up the issue of slavery at this point was unnecessary."

"Thomas and Samuel, thank you for those words of support. Please excuse me, but I need to speak with a couple of the other delegates before they leave. Good afternoon."

Edward felt relieved by the encounter with the two Maryland delegates and now he hurriedly searched the chamber for John Dickinson, who he could not find. However, William Ellery appeared from behind a crowd of people near the Rhode Island table. Edward approached him as Ellery was gathering papers to put into his portmanteau.

"Mr. Ellery, what did you think about the reading of the declaration from the committee?"

"Edward. I thought they did a consummate job of articulating in precise wording what needed to be said. What are your thoughts?"

"William, I thought the language they used to press our point about the need for local control of our lives apart from Britain was rich and useful. However, I did think that in some points, our case was argued too emotionally."

"Pray tell"

"The language that was used to describe how we had 'waged cruel war against human nature' was histrionic, and the goal of that section seemed totally out of place with the remainder of the call for independence."

"That section did make me take a pause, although, I did understand the gist of it."

"As we have discussed before, and as I related to you about Samuel Ward, it is the position of the South Carolina delegation that the entire section should be eliminated so we can focus our efforts on independence and not get mired in an argument about the pros and cons of slavery."

"The last point that you made does resonate with me. I will discuss the topic with Mr. Hopkins, and I assume that he would see the matter the same way. Thank you for pointing this out. I am not sure I would have gathered the importance of this issue if you had not brought it to my attention."

"Thank you, Mr. Ellery. I look forward to working with you to see the declaration clarified and the long battle that we will have in enforcing this document.

Edward did some calculations in his head and could count six states, Maryland, Rhode Island, New York, Georgia, North Carolina, and South Carolina that he thought would be inclined to support a motion to delete the section on the slave trade from the declaration. More conversations were needed to ensure that those votes were solid, but if early indications meant anything, the prospects for supporting independence on the Lee Resolution looked better.

Edward Rutledge stood silently for a few moments as he thought about the conversations that he had over the last twenty minutes. Minutes that could shape the politics of the new United States of America for years to come.

ANOTHER VIEW FROM THE DECLARATIONS READING

Before congress met this morning to hear the first reading of the Declaration of Independence, Edward Rutledge made a decision that altered how the slaves in Philadelphia learned about this important event.

Pompey had finished preparing the fresh set of clothes and accessories for Rutledge and was ready to ask if he could leave to allow Master Edward some private time before he left for the Statehouse, when Edward surprised him.

"Pompey, I am going to give you the experience of a lifetime today," started Rutledge. "I want you to attend today's session of Congress with me inside the Statehouse."

Pompey was shocked and wondered whether this was a joke. He stared straight ahead making sure not to catch the eye of his master. Gradually, the idea of listening to the delegates speak to one another was exhilarating, but in fact, he could not even begin to imagine what it would be like.

"Yes, sir," Pompey stuttered. "Whatever your pleasure is, I will obey."

"Today, we will be debating about a declaration for independence, and I may need your services to pass notes to other delegates as the debate unfolds. This is an important job, and I need you to be discreet, available, and ready to take orders."

"I understand, Master Rutledge," Pompey said.

"Now go and find some clean breeches and a shirt instead of those rags that you have on."

"Yes, sir," said Pompey as he left and made his way down to his small pantry off the kitchen which served as his living quarters.

Pompey was unsure if any other valets had ever been present on the floor of the Statehouse, although he remembered months ago Billy Lee, George Washington's valet, was seen leaving the meeting hall, but that was Washington. He took Lee wherever he went. Rutledge had mentioned carrying messages. That sounded very important, but he wondered why he was asked to attend today. However, Pompey had decided long ago that he would never try to understand why Rutledge would do anything, because it was a waste of time. It would always be better just to respond to the order of the moment and act accordingly.

Pompey had a pile of clothes next to his makeshift bed on the floor of the pantry. In a wooden box, he found a clean pair of breeches, a clean, white linen shirt, a silk cravat, and a multi-color vest that Rutledge had always admired. His boots needed a cursory shining so not to offend Master Edward or the other delegates. He was the valet for an important South Carolina delegate and needed to put his best face forward. He quickly dusted off the clothes, put them on, and returned to the stairway leading to the main foyer.

"Now you look presentable," Rutledge judged. "It is time to leave."

Edward, dressed in his finest waistcoat and breeches and gripping a valise filled with papers, opened the front door. He strode into the warm sunlit street with Pompey following close behind. Pompey knew this day was certainly to be memorable.

As Pompey followed Rutledge into the courtyard that led to the entry of the Statehouse, Pompey could see Cato, Bob, and Cicero who were staring at the sight of Pompey approaching the entrance with his master. When they reached the door to the Statehouse, Rutledge muttered some words to the man inside the door. The person inside was the one who had called the valet's name when a delegate needed something from the black valets waiting in the courtyard. Pompey followed close behind Rutledge, avoiding eye contact with the doorman. The other black valets were stunned to see Pompey vanish into the Statehouse as the door closed.

Although Pompey had been inside the chamber to assist Rutledge with mundane chores, he looked at the hall with different eyes today. The entry hall ceilings were decorated with multipatterned metal at least twenty feet high, and the walls held arched windows with carved facial features around the edges that create deep shadows. The massive columns with intricately designed decorations added splendor with precise molding around the top of the room. The stairs that led to meeting rooms on the second floor had deep brown mahogany handrails that wound upward. The Assembly Room, where the delegates were casually discussing issues with others, held thirteen tables with pine green tablecloths, writers ink wells at each seat, and spindled chairs. Four windows set deep into the wall on the south of the room provided light late into the day and an additional two were on the north side. At the head of the room stood a single table on a raised platform with the green tablecloth, inkwell and feathered pen, a candle, a gavel and a decorative chair with a tall back of finely cut design. On the wall behind the center table were two large fireplaces and two doors, but the largest attraction was a twelve candle, crystal chandelier with glass bulbs on the top and bottom that hung from the ceiling with a shiny brass chain. Pompey needed to remind himself not to be overawed by the experience.

Rutledge instructed Pompey to stand against the back wall that was close to the table for the South Carolina delegation. Pompey discovered quickly that he was the only slave in the room. Many of these patriots, in their wildest accusations, thought that the King was trying to make them slaves. Pompey knew how wrong that was..

Pompey recognized many of the delegates whom he had seen around the Statehouse but also at the City Tavern. A few, such as John Adams, Richard Henry Lee, Thomas Stone, Francis Lee, John Dickinson, Robert Livingston, and Ben Franklin had conversations with Edward and were familiar with Pompey. Many of the others he had seen in the streets of Philadelphia.

Suddenly, the man in the front of the room hit his gavel and cried out, "Order. Order. We have a great deal of business today, could you please take your seats so we can get started?" Although the noise did subside, many of the men continued their conversations, and the man in front, who Pompey would come to know as John Hancock, was prepared to strike the gavel again when the noise ceased.

Pompey stood as erect as an oak tree, his hands behind his back, his back straightened up against the wall without touching it. All the white men who sat at the green tableclothed tables were wearing powdered wigs and an array of coats, shirts and breeches that reeked of aristocracy.

Pompey mused *I can see what is going on here. The man up front tells his second-in-command what needs to be decided, and then the delegates fight to try to be the first to speak about the item. Once the first person stops talking, another delegates yells to be recognized so he can tell everyone how smart he is and why everyone should do what he says. These men are far worse than Master Rutledge. One will choose his words carefully and speak in a voice that is quiet and then loud. They strut like peacocks trying to get the most attention. What a bunch of windbags!*

Pompey couldn't always understand the different items being debated. *The chairman strains to keep order in the room as the delegates want to speak and give lengthy speeches no matter what the subject.*

This process droned on for two hours, and Pompey began to wonder why Master Edward had asked him to be present on this day. Not once did Rutledge attempt to engage Pompey with any tasks, and he thought this event was just a waste of time.

Another report was presented to ask someone to help build a fort in Delaware, and New Jersey wanted to purchase gunpowder to defend their town. Pompey thought, *Is this the work the delegates are accomplishing every day? I could do this! How do these patriots think that they can stand up to the power of the King of England?*

Suddenly, there was a hush that settled in the hall and one of the doors behind the front table opened and five delegates quietly marched into the Hall and presented a scroll to John Hancock.

Pompey thought *that's Benjamin Franklin, John Adams, and Thomas Jefferson, but who are the other two men?.* The room was calm with a few people whispering to others. Pompey thought *something important is happening. Was this the reason Master Rutledge wanted me to attend?*

After some discussion around the front table, Franklin and the other men moved to their seats at the tables for the colonies. John Hancock gaveled the meeting back to order and in a stentorian voice said, "Will the secretary please read the work of the committee."

A hush fell from the ceiling as the room breathed with anticipation and the still air was punctured by the words of the secretary, "When in the course of human events, it becomes necessary for one people to dissolve the political bands which have connected them with another…".

Pompey was not sure what to think but knew that he should try to remember as much of the speech as possible. *We hold these truths to be self-evident that all men are created equal,,,,,,, unalienable rights of life, liberty, and the pursuit of happiness,,,,, the right to abolish government,,,,, ought to be free and independent states,,,,, He has waged cruel war against human nature itself, violating its most sacred rights of life & liberty and carrying them into slavery,,,,,, determined to keep open a market where MEN should be bought & sold, ,,,,, we mutually pledge to each other our lives, our fortunes and our sacred honor.*

Pompey's mind was spinning. *Are they talking about me? Is it possible that slavery will be ended? Will I know a freedom that I thought was impossible? How will this change my life? Can this really be happening?*

When the secretary finished reading, the room remained quiet. The delegates sat transfixed on the words the committee had crafted and were quiet as they contemplated the impact of the document that was just read. They responded with a mixture of solemnity and restrained intensity. Pompey thought, *The Declaration's ideal of all men are created equal should apply to me, but I can't believe that they are going to agree with that. Many of us are slaves, and even free Black men face severe restrictions in Philadelphia. This lofty rhetoric carries a bitter irony.*

Pompey looked over to Rutledge who had turned and motioned to him to come close. *At last, I was to receive a task.*

Edward reached inside his coat and pulled out an envelope. "Pompey, I want you to take this to Mrs. Rutledge. Tell her I will be home later. Stay there until I return."

Pompey turned and moved to the door where they arrived earlier. He saw Bob and Hector but waved to them as he headed toward Mr. Yard's boardinghouse to deliver the letter. He would catch up with his friends later.

Slaves Sense Declaration is Not For Them

The air was thick with heat and anticipation. Inside the Pennsylvania State House, the Continental Congress had just received the draft of a document that would alter the course of history. Outside, in the shaded alley behind the building, two men waited—not delegates, not statesmen, but Black valets. Bob and Hector were black men, enslaved, yet intimately close to the machinery of revolution. Through the communication among the black valets, they probably knew as much about this declaration as the delegates.

They had seen the parchment carried in, watched the Committee of Five whisper and gesture, and heard the murmurs ripple through the hall. But now, in the quiet time between their duties, they spoke in low tones, their conversation a blend of curiosity, skepticism, and hard-earned wisdom.

Bob leaned against the brick wall, his linen shirt damp with sweat. Earlier in the day he had polished Stone's boots and delivered a note to Thomas Jefferson's quarters. Hector sat on a crate, a folded waistcoat in his lap, his fingers idly tracing the embroidery.

"They brought it in like it was the Sacred Ark. It was still a mystery to them at that moment, but Jefferson's valet Robert had already told us that Jefferson is responsible for writing the draft. Mr. Stone said it's a declaration. A declaration on independence," said Bob.

"Independence for whom?"

Bob chuckled, not unkindly. "Not for us, I reckon."

Hector said, "What luck is it that Pompey is inside listening to the delegates. Whatever happens, we can be assured that Pompey will tell us the plain truth."

Hector's eyes narrowed. "Mr. Middleton says it's for 'all men created equal.' He said those words to himself last week. But I've seen how he looks through me when I bring his letters. Neither respect nor equity are shown. Equal doesn't mean the same to them."

Both men had served their masters for years. Bob had been with Stone in Maryland for the past three years, where he'd learned to read by listening to the young lawyer dictate briefs. Hector had grown up on the Middleton estate in South Carolina, taught to groom horses and recite Psalms. Their proximity to power gave them insight, but not agency.

They had watched the colonies inch toward rebellion. They had heard the speeches, the toasts, the prayers. But they had also seen the contradictions—men who spoke of liberty while owning dozens of souls.

"Mr. Middleton says South Carolina won't sign anything that touches on slavery," said Hector. "He's firm on it. He won't be happy if Jefferson puts any reference to the slave trade in the document. I heard him say, 'We will not be dictated to by Massachusetts fanatics.' Maybe he needs to be worried about Virginian fanatics?"

"No one mentioned the slave trade last night. Mr. Stone's more slippery. He talks of freedom like it's a river, but he won't say who gets to drink from it. I think he believes in liberty—but only for his own kind," said Bob.

Neither man had seen the full text, but they had heard fragments. "Life, liberty, and the pursuit of happiness." "Tyranny over these states." "Consent of the governed." Hector repeated the phrases like incantations, trying to parse their meaning.

Bob said, "Consent of the governed. That's a fine phrase. But who's doing the consent? Not me. Not you. The way they detest the King telling them what to do, how will it feel when one of their own kind tells them to do something?"

"I asked Mr. Middleton once—what if a man owns himself? He laughed. He said that's a contradiction, and that some men are born to serve. What makes him think that he is any more special than either one of us?" said Hector.

Bob looked away and said, "Then let them serve their own hypocrisy."

As the delegates debated inside, the valets bore witness outside. They carried messages, fetched ink, prepared meals. They were invisible, yet indispensable. They understood, perhaps better than the men they served what the stakes were of the moment.

"They think they're making history. And they are. But they don't see the whole picture," said Bob

Hector added, "Maybe that's our job. All they need to do is ask."

Bob and Hector spoke of Crispus Attucks, the Black hero who had died at Bunker Hill, of the rumors of Black soldiers fighting in New

England, of the whispers that Lord Dunmore had promised freedom to slaves who joined the British. They weighed their options, not in terms of allegiance, but of survival.

"If the British win, maybe we get free. If the Americans win, maybe we wait another hundred years."

"Either way, we're just forgettable"

Despite their cynicism, both men felt the tremor of possibility. The very act of declaring independence, of saying no to kings, was radical. And if ideas could shift that much, perhaps they could shift still further.

"I don't trust them. But I trust the words. Words have a way of outliving their authors."

"Maybe one day, someone will read that parchment and sees us in it."

They imagined a future where 'all men' really meant all men. Where liberty was not a possession but a birthright. Where their children might walk free in the streets of Philadelphia, not as valets but as citizens.

Inside, the hall was quiet and then a huge noise swelled up through the windows. The draft had been read. Some nodded. Others frowned. The debate would begin on Monday. But for now, the document lay on the table, ink drying in the summer heat.

Outside, Bob and Hector stood. The sun was setting. They would be called soon, to light lamps, to prepare supper, to fetch water. But for a moment, they lingered.

"Do you think they'll sign it?"

"They'll sign it. And history will remember their names."

Hector smiled, a quiet defiance in his eyes. "Our voices need to be heard also."

Bob and Hector are not mentioned in any history books, and their words are lost in the passages of time. But men like them existed—Black valets, grooms, cooks, and porters who stood at the edge of revolution. They heard the words before they were canonized. They saw the men before they were immortalized. And they understood, with painful clarity, the gap between ideals and reality.

Yet even in silence, they bore witness. And in imagining their conversation, we honor the full truth of that moment—the hope, hypocrisy, and the enduring human desire to be.

As the delegates filed out, Bob and Hector looked tirelessly for Pompey to discover what he had heard. Hector noticed Edward Rutledge, but Pompey was nowhere to be seen. Bob saw Thomas Stone and Arthur Middleton was with Mr. Rutledge. Where could Pompey be? They would need to be patient but were certain that he would have a story to tell.

Pompey Reports to His Friends

Standing in the alley behind Mrs. Yard's boardinghouse, the world was spinning in Pompey's head as he waited for the next meeting with the other black valets. Why did Master Edward invite him to listen to the reading of the declaration on independence. He was told his job was to deliver messages to the other delegates, yet the only message Master Edward gave to him was a note to his wife. But most importantly, Pompey was in the room when the document Thomas Jefferson had written about independence from England was read to the delegates. Could he remember the words that were read?

"Pompey," shouted Bob as he ran down the alley from High Street with Hector following close behind. "What is the news from inside the building? I can't believe they allowed you to listen. Tell us what happened."

"I was thunderstruck," Pompey replied. "I am trying to remember everything that happened. The events went by so fast, and then Master Rutledge asked me to deliver a note to his wife. Some of this just doesn't make any sense."

"What was it like to hear the delegates speak?" Bob asked. "Did anyone ask why you were there? Did they take any action? Did the delegates argue?"

"Hold off, boys," said Pompey. "I am trying to keep a clear mind of what I saw and heard, and your badgering questions cause me to ruin my train of thoughts."

"We're sorry," said Hector. "We are just supremely curious, especially since you were a firsthand witness to the events inside the Statehouse. Why don't you tell us what happened in a slow manner and we'll listen."

"Yeah, Pomp," said Bob. "We'll sit back and listen."

"Thanks, boys," Pompey began. "I remain confused by all the events of the morning and afternoon, and I am sure that I will forget to tell you all that I can."

"This morning, Master Rutledge told me that I was to be granted a great gift by attending with him on the floor of the Statehouse so I could pass notes to the various delegates while they were talking.

What really happened was that he only asked me to pass one message and that was to his wife back at the boardinghouse."

"Sounds like Mr. Rutledge," said Hector. "He tells you one thing and does another."

"But I don't think that he needed me to pass messages at all. He wanted me to hear the reading of the declaration on independence that Mr. Jefferson wrote," Pompey said. "I must say that the words Mr. Jefferson used were like a song that I was waiting to hear. He used a phrase, 'all men are created equal' and 'our rights include life, liberty, and the pursuit of happiness.' He also read about how bad the slave trade is and how the King of England was responsible for slavery."

"Are you sure you heard that?" asked Hector.

"Absolutely! I couldn't make something like that up," said Pompey. "The surprising thing, though, was the delegates heard these beautiful words, and when the reading was finished, they hardly said anything. It appeared to me that everyone was shocked that he had put into words all the things that most of them believed, and they were afraid that something bad was going to happen now that it was said out loud."

"I don't understand white people," said Bob. "I thought everyone would be happy and jump for joy."

"I was a little surprised by the lack of excitement," said Pompey. "The more I thought about it, though, Mr. Jefferson's document took a big swing at the slave trade and slavery in general. Not much support from South Carolina and Virginia should be expected in that language."

"What are you talking about?" asked Hector. "The declaration will let us be free also?"

"I'm not sure," said Pompey. "Master Edward hustled me out of the chamber before any debate took place, but the language I clearly recall was the colonies were angry at the King for pushing the slave trade on them and is now trying to attract slaves into the British Army."

Bob said, "I don't know who is at fault, but the colonies and England alike have always seemed to be eager to bring more of our kin over from Africa. Do you think that our status as slaves will change?"

Pompey said, "I doubt it. I don't think that the slave trade is the central issue between the colonies and the Crown. In addition, the Rutledge boys have made it their business to delete any mention of slavery from any document going forward."

"Master Middleton," said Hector, "has said openly in front of me and others that he would never agree to a document that limited slavery in South Carolina."

"I don't think we know how this will turn out, but I am sure that Edward, Arthur, and Thomas will be working hard to see that their interests are presented," said Pompey.

Bob said, "I feel a mix of disappointment and resignation. I am angry they don't see the ideals of equality. They compromise, right before our eyes, and I am resigned to the fact that we should never have expected anything else.'

Pompey added, "Our omission confirms that the revolution's bold words are not meant for us. We polish boots and pour wine for the men who proclaim themselves champions of freedom. I don't think they are able to see the hypocrisy in these actions."

Rutledge and Jefferson Meet

The previous twenty days were the shortest and the longest span of time that Edward Rutledge had ever experienced. The shortest period could be explained by the amount of work that was needed to receive commitments from key delegates that they would support South Carolina in eliminating the section on the slave trade for the declaration on independence. The longest period was the uneasy period waiting in expectation for the trust he placed in delegates to fulfill their commitment to support Rutledge on what he believed were the needed changes in the declaration.

Edward's dilemma was that the resolution authored by Richard Henry Lee needed a vote of support before the declaration, clearly penned by Thomas Jefferson, went through its final amending process and a vote to approve or deny support. This prospect looked daunting at the outset, and it did make things more complicated. However, with cooperation from some of the officers of Congress, they might well see a favorable end for the South Carolina colonists.

Rutledge knew that an additional day would allow more time for the New York and Delaware delegations to reach Philadelphia and vote on Lee's resolution. While Robert Livingston, John Jay, Lewis Morris, and Francis Lewis were serving in the New York Provincial Congress away from Philadelphia, William Floyd was the sole delegate representing the interests of the New York colony in Philadelphia. Rutledge wanted to arrange with John Hancock to hold debate as soon as possible on the exclusion of the slave trade section from the declaration.

The twenty-day delay on the resolution by Richard Henry Lee expired on July 1, 1776. Congress was prepared to vote, even though Lee was absent from the Statehouse because of urgent business in Virginia.

President Hancock called the session to order. Various letters and requests were addressed. Hancock then asked the secretary to read the Richard Henry Lee resolution on independence. A point of order was requested by Edward Rutledge, speaking for three different colonies, South Carolina, Pennsylvania, and Delaware. This being a non-debatable motion, the measure on independence was delayed until the next day when more supporters of the Rutledge point of view would be present.

Leaving the Statehouse conference room after the July 1 vote, Rutledge made it a point to catch the eye of Jefferson before he left the building. Jefferson possessed a brilliant mind and expressed his ideas with clarity and elegance in writing, crafting enduring texts. However, he was a notably poor public speaker, soft-spoken and uncomfortable before crowds, often relying on others to read his speeches aloud or publish them for broader impact.

Two key components of the declaration drew much opinion, the tone of the language castigating the British people in not fully supporting the American colonists, and the denunciation of the King of England for perpetrating the slave trade in the colonies.

John Dickinson of Pennsylvania led the conservative delegates, speaking against the adoption of the Lee resolution believing that it was politically wrong to chastise the British people and that the focus of the colony's disagreements should be aimed at the King and Parliament.

The section on the slave trade had been the prime concern of Edward Rutledge from the day that his brother left for South Carolina. John had warned Edward that the slave trade might be used against southern colonies to create a wedge in Congress for an all-out campaign against slavery. Edward had held various meetings over the last seven months with delegates who agreed with him that the Declaration was not the document to be used for this discussion. To Rutledges chagrin, Jefferson had managed to include a four-sentence diatribe against the King of England for foisting the slave trade on the colonies and "calling slavery a cruel war against human nature itself… that the King had kept open a market where Men should be bought & sold… and that he is now exciting those very people to rise in arms among us."

Rutledge approached Jefferson and extended his arm for a handshake saying, "Mr. Jefferson, I presume that your talent in the written language is unsurpassed by anyone I know and the reason for the splendid document presented to Congress. I thank you with utmost sincerity."

"Thank you for those kind words, Mr. Rutledge, but I cannot help but think there are portions of the document that do not meet your approval."

"That is true, but the overall language of the document sings to our aspirations and supports the goals upon which we can all agree. I have had many conversations with delegates about the undesirability of including outside issues that do not directly appeal for freedom and liberty. The words you have used about life, liberty, and the pursuit of happiness are music to my heart. However, blaming the slave trade on the King in the context of a declaration on independence seems to addle our wider purpose."

"What would you have us do, Mr. Rutledge? Act like slavery does not exist?"

"No, sir, and in the context of declaring independence from Britain, I believe, and I have heard this comment from many other delegates, from northern and southern colonies, that the topic does not belong in this document. There are too many sides to this issue which might consume the air of debate for independence. We might jeopardize our unity in calling for independence."

"While I am not sure what I should say next, I have heard, on good authority that, at the First Continental Congress, the South Carolina delegation threatened to walk out before an agreement was reached on the export ban. I would hope that mood is not to be played out here."

Rutledge said, "Your information is mostly correct. We did walk out. However, when cooler heads prevailed, a compromise was reached. The circumstances here are completely different. As I said, I have spoken with New England delegates who also feel strongly about this issue. South Carolina wants independence as much as Virginia, and we will fight beside all the other colonists. We also firmly believe that including those accusations about the King and the slave trade does not support our case for independence. Our cause is probably weakened by it. By the same token, eliminate that wording, and you will see the unwavering support of the South Carolina delegation."

"Thank you for your thoughts and consideration. I look forward to working with you on the adoption of the declaration."

"You can depend on that, sir"

Jefferson shook Edward's hand and briskly slipped by him and exited the rear door of the chamber. Ned knew that he couldn't change Jefferson's mind, but he felt it important to directly relate to Jefferson the concerns that he and many other southern colonists had.

Rutledge scanned the room for the other delegates remaining and noticed William Ellery completing a conversation with Roger Sherman. Edward moved to his left between Ellery and the exit door where he waited.

"Progress is being made, wouldn't you say Mr. Rutledge?"

"Things are moving fast these days, but I am trying to make sure that all of the details are addressed."

"And what are those details that concern you the most, Edward?"

"I just had a conversation with Thomas Jefferson about his declaration. What a tremendous document! However, one point gives me some apprehension."

"Excuse me, but are you referring to the clause on the slave trade? I remember a conversation I had with you upon my arrival in May about that very subject. Although I understand the point that Mr. Jefferson is attempting to make, I remain in agreement that the declaration is not the appropriate document for this discussion."

"Thank you, Mr. Ellery. "I appreciate your memory, and your support. I will be making a motion tomorrow to have those words struck from the declaration, and I am hoping you might provide a second. I believe it is important that Mr. Jefferson sees that the motion is supported by southern and northern colonies."

Rutledge and Ellery shook hands and then Ellery left the soon to be vacant chamber. In a corner in deep conversation were John Dickinson and Robert Morris with whom Edward wanted to share his concerns about the slave trade. He paused and stood next to the exit as three more delegates from Congress made their exit. The high temperature from the hot July day had brought a stifling heat to the hall and being outdoors provided some relief from the steamy chamber where fifty men had sat and debated for the past eight hours. He wanted to speak with both men, but not at the same time, so Edward decided to engage Dickinson when their parley was complete.

Both men started to walk in Edward's direction signaling that either they were taking the conversation elsewhere or were concluding it.

Rutledge approached them and said, "Mr. Dickinson and Mr. Morris. Forgive the interruption, but I should greatly value a moment alone with Mr. Dickinson."

"Edward, good afternoon," said Robert Morris. "We were just ending our conversation, and I will move on to another locale where it is cooler while you gentlemen continue to converse in this hot room."

"Thank you for your time this afternoon, Robert." As Morris exited through the main exit of the hall, Rutledge edged closer to Dickinson leaning against the railing in the Statehouse.

"Now, Mr. Rutledge, what is on your mind?"

"I was hoping we could revisit the conversation we had a few weeks ago about eliminating language regarding the slave trade from the declaration on independence," said Edward.

"I do remember that conversation, but I would like to have a different conversation with you about the entire document. I remain against the declaration because it is premature. The colonies don't have our own business arranged properly to survive. We have no formal ties with foreign powers. Many foreign powers see struggling colonies and may make us a target for attacking. We don't have a formal agreement between the colonies on how we should relate to each other. It is possible that disagreements between the colonies might create a civil war between colonies even before we have an opportunity to survive. Lastly, I continue to believe that we can find common ground for reconciliation with the King, a point that I thought we had in common."

"Mr. Dickinson, I thank you for your time and great felicity of breaking down the issues that confront us. You are correct in remembering that I once stood for many of the things you have stated. My perspective has changed as time and events have flowed over us. I have concluded that Britain will never recognize our concerns with any balance of virtue and that now is the time when we need to take the bold steps necessary to create our own nation."

Dickinson said, "I have heard that same message from many delegates. In fact, that is what Morris and I were discussing just before. I know I may seem like a melancholy fellow who fits to sour the feast. But I have my own honor and conscience to protect, and I will defend that obligation until I can no longer take a breath."

"I recognize your courage and strong beliefs. I come to you not to convince you to vote for the declaration, but to make it a stronger document if it is adopted, which is probable in the days to come. Mr. Jefferson has included language in his draft that speaks sharply about the King's responsibility in the slave trade, and as we have spoken before, I believe that this document is not the way that issue should be addressed. If the delegates prefer to declare independence, then let's make it clear and unambiguous. The document should be focused on independence with no sidetracks to slavery."

"Mr. Rutledge, I agree, the paragraph on the slave trade is inflammatory and unnecessary." Dickinson said.

"Thank you, Mr. Dickinson. Tomorrow, I plan to offer a motion to eliminate those statements, and I am hoping that you will support me. I have already heard from a northern colony who will support the exclusion of this language, and your additional support could be crucial."

"My standing within the Pennsylvania delegation is precarious because of my intention to persist in my beliefs, but I will follow your advice on this issue and see where it takes us."

"Thank you again. I value your friendship, support, and wisdom."

"Young man, you will go far in this world when you speak the truth as you see it, attempt to understand the truth as others see it, and seek consensus whenever possible," Dickinson said.

As Edward held the door for Dickinson to exit, he said "Thank you for being a wise man and sharing your experience."

Dickinson extended his hand to shake then used his other hand and gently grabbed Edward's forearm. He said, "You have a bright future, my good man. Keep your head up and speak the truth."

Dickinson quickly turned to the right toward the city livery to check on his horse, and Edward turned toward Second Street and the City Tavern.

As expected, the City Tavern was bustling, filled with delegates and Philadelphians. The noise in the main hall was so great that it was a struggle to hear someone across the table. More men were standing at the bar and alongside the tables than those who had found seats. The windows struggled to bring fresh air into the room, but the steady stream of customers and the excitement in the air prevented much relaxation.

Edward glanced over the sea of men in the room and caught sight of Arthur Middleton near the far wall as he gestured in a jovial manner speaking with Thomas Stone.

"Hello, Arthur. I am glad to see the two of you this afternoon. That was quite a session we had today."

"I was surprised how quietly Thomas Jefferson sat during the entire proceedings. He appeared to be perfectly satisfied with the flow of the discussion without uttering a single comment."

Edward said, "Mr. Jefferson is a bright and knowledgeable man. Looking at the breadth of the declaration, I must allow that he acquitted himself rather well. His humility showed his lack of defensiveness. Tomorrow will be the day when we see if we can improve on the perfection he created,"

"How can you call it perfection and remain committed to offering a major edit yourself?"

"I use the word perfection to describe the entire document with the needed edits. King George of England will know exactly where we stand on our ability to rule ourselves, once he reads this declaration. I hope he takes more time to read this than he did with the Olive Branch Petition."

The three fellows laughed and ordered another round of cider from a server who was passing by. With the thirsty crowd bellowing and gesturing, Edward mused to himself that they may wait an hour before they see that libation.

"I was surprised by your negative vote today, Ned," said Thomas.

Arthur said, "It's part of our plan. Didn't you talk to Thomas about our strategy, Ned."

"Not completely. Thomas, you know that we have talked before how South Carolinians need to have assurances that slavery should not be brought into the argument for independence. The declaration, as written now, has a series of chiding statements relating to how the King waged cruel war upon human nature. These are code words for our plantation system and represent an attack on our livelihood. They need to be excised from the declaration."

"How would you proceed to accomplish this goal?" asked Stone.

"Our first goal was to delay the vote, which we accomplished today. Next, we need to speak to as many delegates as we can advising them to be ready tomorrow when I will offer a motion for the elimination of the odious words."

"That seems like a tall task to complete," said Stone.

Arthur said, "Perhaps, but we have already started the process of enlisting supports to this venture. Ned has already spoken with Dickinson, Livingston, and Ellery. They represent three colonies whom we should count as our allies. We are also depending on others who may support us but don't want to be too public about it."

"That is an ambitious plan."

"We must be ambitious. Delaware, New Jersey, Rhode Island, and Connecticut all either have more than a fair amount of slaves, or they share in the wealth of supporting the plantation manner of commerce. Add South Carolina, North Carolina and Georgia to that list and we have a strong chance for success. Apparently, the New Jersey delegation has been replaced. We need to reach out to Richard Stockton or Francis Hopkinson."

"I will speak to Mr. Stockton," said Arthur. "We had a meaningful conversation just the other day when I welcomed him to Congress. I think he will be amenable to our cause as will his cohort Hopkinson. I learned in that first conversation that both are slaveholders."

"Thank you, Arthur. Great work. I think we will have the balance of the states supporting our efforts."

"Representing Maryland, I could be supportive also. I would imagine that the balance of the delegation will also be supportive, although I am not sure about Charles Carroll. I will speak to him this evening."

The waiter sat three large mugs on their table.

"Gentlemen, let's toast to good timing, a good cause, and independence."

The three clanked their mugs together and each pulled a strong draught to his lips. They lapsed into other conversations about the business of Congress and had huge smiles on their faces knowing that independence was near at hand. Rutledge was becoming more confident to vote in favor of Richard Henry Lee's resolution on independence as he envisioned that he had the support of delegates to remove the noxious comments about the slave trade.

DINNER AT MRS. YARD'S BOARDINGHOUSE

The dining room at Mrs. Yard's boardinghouse had tall sash windows dressed in damask curtains that filtered the afternoon light into a warm amber glow. The paneled walls were painted in a fashionable faint green, adorned with framed metal print plates of classical scenes. A polished mahogany table stretched the length of the room, flanked by Queen Anne chairs with gently curving legs and shell-carved crests. Beneath it lay a Brussels carpet imported from England, its floral pattern slightly faded but still elegant.

The smell of fried food wafted from the kitchen and filled the air in the dining room of the boardinghouse. The dining room table was set for fourteen people with stoneware plates, polished silverware, and crystal glasses. Salt and pepper plates were offered made from local pottery laid out with additional condiments ready in the kitchen.

Edward Rutledge entered the front door and was welcomed by Henrietta.

"How is my darling?" Edward said.

"Thank you, Ned," said Henrietta.

"I feel wonderful this evening," said Edward. "I hope you have not been bored waiting for my return."

Henrietta said, "I've been letter writing today, and doing embroidery. I've learned that some of the wives get together for tea and conversation. That will help to keep me busy."

Henrietta Rutledge spent her days in quiet domestic rhythm, shaped by her delicate health and her refined upbringing as a Middleton. Residing in a boardinghouse near Market Street, her southern manners and wealth afforded a degree of comfort, yet the uncertainty of war and her husband's political duties cast a shadow over daily life. She walked briefly in the garden or along the cobbled streets, listening to news from Charleston or updates from Congress, her thoughts divided between home, family, and the fragile birth of a new nation.

Edward said, "I am glad that you have found ways to fill your time. The affairs of Congress demand concentrating most of my time and energy in making decisions that will affect our lives for years. Just today, we heard a draft of a declaration on independence for the

American colonies. One day, we may look back on today and try to comprehend what it was like before today's events,"

"Oh darling, you know that I realize how important your work is. I apologize if I might have sounded demanding."

"I didn't want to sound like I was not paying attention to your needs," Edward explained. "We still have much work to do, but today I heard a document read that made me wonder if we could understand fully the impact of our actions. The Congress stands on the threshold of a new era, and we are all an instrument for that occasion. Much more work will be necessary to complete the course, but excellence is close to our fingertips"

"Ned, I am so proud of you," Henrietta said as she wrapped her arms around Edward. "What news do you have about my brother, Arthur?"

"We all met directly following the Congress session," Edward started, "and took assignments for the work we must complete before the next open discussion on Monday. I am sure that we will have our usual Sunday dinner at the Shippen home, where the conversation will swirl around independence. Speaking of which, who will be sitting at our table for dinner this evening?"

"As usual, we don't know until they arrive, but Mrs. Yard said that the Adams's would not be dining with us, and Mr. Gerry would."

"That sounds marvelous. Please permit me to wash and change before we sit down for supper. I promise not to be long," Edward added. "I'll be right back"

Edward, with a grin on his face, scampered up the staircase as nimble as a cat on a hot hearth.

Henrietta had not seen Edward so happy since they were married in March 1774. Maybe all the work that he labored during the previous months has suddenly come into alignment. She only wished for the day when they could return to South Carolina where her heart would always be.

Just then, the door opened again and Elbridge Gerry, with his usual cocked tricorn hat and shiny boots, entered the foyer. Gerry was a merchant who wore sober but respectable clothes. His long face and sharp eyes gave him the presence of an intelligent man. Not a tall man and rather thin, he handled himself as a well informed and deliberate man who was serious about his efforts.

"What cheer, Mrs. Rutledge? It is a fine afternoon, and I look forward to another abundant repast.

"Good cheer to you, Mr. Gerry, My husband just arrived and seems to be in good favor from news at Congress this afternoon. Do you share his pleasure?"

"I am pleased to hear that. Oftentimes, news can strike different individuals in a variant fashion. Your husband's good mood makes my joy heightened. I look forward to an excellent dinner."

To wash his hands and face before dinner, Gerry drifted to the staircase and slowly walked up the steps methodically, as though he were measuring his steps. As he reached the top, he disappeared down the hall.

Left alone, Henrietta found the door to the kitchen to see if there was any small task she might be able to assist with.

Thirty minutes later, Edward and Elbridge descended the stairs and were engrossed in a conversation about the day's events in Congress.

Rutledge said, "I am certain that Mr. Jefferson must have written the original draft. His ability to match words to inspiration, I find inspiring. Now, I may have some quibbling with some of the words, but I thought the overall tenor of the text to be impeccable."

Gerry answered, "I would agree with your overall description. I think you may be right about the author. If John Adams had written it, we would see a great deal of characterizations that were blunt, not to say that some of the accusations in the document didn't feel like a rapier at times."

Rutledge pointed out, "My reservation is with the diatribe against the King about the slave trade. I don't believe that the document is the proper place for this discussion. My brother and I have had numerous conversations with a lot of the delegates about this issue. We need language that everyone can agree with and that which our own colonies will support. Including language about the slave trade, I fear we will not have unanimity."

Elbridge said, "I understand your position, but you must look at the other side also. If we do not put some language in this document, where is the proper place to raise this concern? You realize that many of the delegates own slaves. Why, some even brought them to this venue, including yourself. But that does not mean that they and you are not struggling with the dilemma that slavery is amoral while continuing to own bodies. Highlighting the slave trade gives these men the possible solution to this vexing problem."

"Elbridge, it is not a problem if you see it through the lens of economic security for the colonies," said Rutledge. "The Southern colonies have made America the richest colony in the world by utilizing a successful plantation system that delivers true economic results in addition to making the lives of Africans better than they ever would have in their homelands."

Gerry said, "I am not sure that all delegates would agree with that thesis. You may be correct in your premise that the declaration may not be the correct document for settling this issue, but if not this, then what is and when?"

"I am not saying that I have all the answers to that question, but I know that the declaration is the wrong conveyance for this issue. We must have unity now so we can proceed with independence and not be distracted by other issues."

"I respect your opinions on the topic, and I welcome some additional conversation, but right now I am more interested in basking in the light of a wonderful new opportunity for us to proceed and have a great meal."

Mrs. Yard entered through the kitchen carrying a huge tureen with soup, and she was followed by Henrietta with a giant bowl of potatoes. Mrs. Hornsby, another tenant at the boardinghouse, brought a basket full of fresh bread, and Mrs. Smith, also a tenant, brought in a tray with various sauces. As soon as she had placed the food on the table, Mrs. Yard went back to the kitchen and returned with a plate of smoked pork, mutton, and chicken.

As everyone sat down, Henrietta suggested, "Gentlemen, we applaud the work that you are doing for all the colonies. But could we please tonight just talk about something else?"

"We'll do our best," said Edward, "but I wouldn't be surprised if we have a lapse of discernment."

Everyone sat down at the table, listened to a blessing by Elbridge, and then enjoyed a fine supper to cap this momentous day.

DECISION DAY HAS ARRIVED

Edward Rutledge awaited the Congress convening with a mix of caution, strategic concern, and youthful intensity regarding the vote on the resolution offered by Richard Henry Lee. He carried the weight of representing a deeply divided colony whose economy was dependent on servants to maintain his plantation, though personally he finally was inclined toward independence. Rutledge feared that a premature vote—without full consensus among the colonies—would fracture the fragile unity of Congress and undermine the legitimacy of any declaration. His reaction was marked by a desire to delay the vote until unanimity could be assured.

Rutledges instincts were shaped by both political calculation and regional sensitivities. Aware of these tensions, he feared that a divided vote would embolden Loyalists and weaken the revolutionary cause. He had spoken with urgency about not including any allusions to the slave trade and urging his fellow delegates to postpone the decision until the middle colonies, particularly Pennsylvania and New York, could be brought fully on board.

Rutledges plan consisted of tactical resistance—not opposition to independence itself, but to the timing of its formal adoption. He worked behind the scenes to coordinate with other cautious delegates and sought a delay that would allow for broader support.

Meanwhile, John Dickinson spoke on the resolution before Rutledge could ask for a delay of one day on the vote. According to notes that John Adams made later, Dickinson gave an impassioned and eloquent case against the resolution. He opposed immediate independence, arguing that it was premature and dangerous, and he feared it would alienate moderate colonists, provoke Britain into harsher retaliation, and jeopardize potential foreign alliances. Lastly, he emphasized the need for more time, unity, and a clearer path forward before severing ties.

The last section of Dickinson's speech was exactly what Edward Rutledge wanted to hear.

After Dickinson's speech that was equally ingenuous and eloquent and delivered with politeness and candor, the body seemed transfixed in their seats. John Adams rose and gave one of the most important speeches in his life. In his autobiography, he said about the speech, "This was the first time in my life that I had ever wished for the talents and eloquence of the ancient orators of Greece and Rome, for I was very sure that none of them ever had before him a question of more importance to his country and to the world." Adams defended the resolution with conviction, countering Dickinson's arguments and urging Congress to embrace independence. He acknowledged that the arguments had been rehearsed many times before but felt compelled to speak because no one else had risen to answer Dickinson.

After Adams had finished his speech, great turmoil was heard among the delegates. Edward moved to the front of the room to engage Benjamin Harrison in a discussion of delaying for one day the final vote on the Lee resolution. Rutledge urged the delay because of the problems that faced New York, Pennsylvania, and Delaware, and he also added that in its present form he would not be able to deliver the South Carolina delegation's full support. Standing to the side of this discussion was John Hancock who looked at Benjamin Harrison with a look of silent request of what should be the path forward.

Hancock, as the presiding officer, stood down from the chair, walked directly to John Adams and had a brief conversation. After forty-five seconds of conversation, Hancock returned to the chair and spoke to Harrison.

Hancock gaveled the session back to order and called on Harrison, who looked at Adams, and then in his deep baritone voice said, "The resolution agreed to by committee of the whole being read, is postponed, at the request of a colony, till tomorrow."

"So ordered," said Hancock and then the room returned to noise and confusion. However, John Adams and Edward Rutledge could be noticed exchanging nods of approval. Adams later recalled that Rutledge "had a great deal of sense and eloquence," and that he was active in the debates surrounding independence, remarks that were far different from some of the earlier comments that had been made about Edward.

Tomorrow will be a big day. Would those delegates who Rutledge and his South Carolinian delegates had approached live up to their thoughts about erasing the slave trade section from the declaration on independence, and would the other state delegations be able to adopt the Lee resolution unanimously?

Decision Day Two

By the end of the morning, delegates at the Second Continental Congress had disposed of numerous letters including a request from General Washington, a letter from a Massachusetts Bay assembly, a letter from the Governor of Connecticut, a weekly account from the Board of Treasury, and a letter from the paymaster. The vote on the Richard Henry Lee resolution to dissolve the relationship with Great Britain would be taken soon. The most important conversation for South Carolina, about eliminating the language on the slave trade was to be discussed next.

As the delegates took their seats for the afternoon session, suddenly, Caesar Rodney, a delegate from Delaware, strode into the chamber with his cloak and boots smeared with mud, his spurs remaining on his feet after riding his horse overnight, traveling eighty miles to cast his vote for independence. Before his arrival, Delaware had only two men who disagreed on supporting the Lee resolution.

"I trust that I am in time to vote," said Rodney with his hat casually cast off and his cloak covering a chair at the Delaware table. "That was quite a storm last night with lightning, thunder and heavy rain. I am glad that my horse was rested and knew the way."

Edward Rutledge exhaled a sigh of relief.

Presiding officer John Hancock pounded his gavel to reconvene the meeting and asked the secretary, Charles Thompson, to read the resolution offered by Richard Henry Lee for independence. Hancock then asked the delegates to caucus and vote their colonies' vote. After a fifteen-minute caucus of colonial delegates, the secretary was ready to ask for one vote from each delegation.

Hancock gaveled the session back to order and asked to tabulate the votes.

Charles Thompson said, "How does each colony vote for the Lee resolution?

Connecticut – Roger Sherman said, "Aye."

Delaware – Caesar Rodney said "Aye

Georgia – Button Gwinnett said "Aye."

Maryland – Charles Carroll said "Aye,"

Massachusetts – John Adams said, Aye."

New Hampshire – Josiah Bartlett said "Aye."

New Jersey – John Witherspoon said "Aye."

New York – Robert Livingston said, "New York abstains because we have not been given specific authority to vote for independence, although I am sure that we will receive the power shortly."

North Carolina – William Hooper said "Aye."

Pennsylvania – Benjamin Franklin said, "With two abstentions, Pennsylvania votes Aye."

Rhode Island – Stephen Hopkins said "Aye

South Carolina – Edward Rutledge said "Aye."

One could hear a faint cheer by some of the delegates who were surprised by this vote.

Virginia – George Wythe said, "Virginia proudly votes Aye."

"Mr. President Hancock," Thompson said, "The ayes are twelve and there is one abstention. The motion to adopt the resolution carries unanimously."

The passage of Richard Henry Lee's resolution, declaring that the colonies were "free and independent States," marked a seismic shift in the political landscape of the Continental Congress. Though the idea of independence had been gaining traction, the formal adoption of the resolution was met with a mix of solemnity, urgency, and cautious celebration. Delegates understood the gravity of the moment—they were committing treason against the Crown.

An eerie sense of responsibility settled over the delegates. John Adams could be seen congratulating his fellow delegates from Massachusetts. George Wythe congratulated Thomas Jefferson as both lamented that Richard Henry Lee could not be with them on this pinnacle of success because of urgent problems in Virginia. At the Delaware table, numerous delegates sought Caesar Rodney to give thanks and support for his midnight ride.

Public reaction was swift and spirited. News of the vote was published that evening in The Pennsylvania Evening Post and the next day in The Pennsylvania Gazette, signaling to the public that the colonies had taken a decisive step toward nationhood. While celebrations erupted in some towns, others remained wary, knowing that war and hardship lay ahead. The resolution's passage also galvanized support among patriot leaders and gave ideological clarity to the military struggle already underway. An act of bold defiance had transformed colonial resistance into a revolutionary movement.

The South Carolina table was all smiles but with a serious look of anticipation as John Hancock gaveled the session back to order and called for Benjamin Harrison to report on the next matter of business: the declaration on independence. President Hancock described the process that would be used to review the Declaration: the Secretary would read from the document and delegates would be able to make motions to change portions that they deemed needed.

Rutledge and the other South Carolina delegates knew that the resolution that just passed was significant, but their main concern was to edit the declaration on independence to remove the slave trade section.

Hancock said, "We want to make sure that all delegates have an opportunity to pursue the best course of action on this most important document. I am willing to honor the special request of Edward Rutledge from South Carolina to review lines 16-29 on page three of the draft as the first item on the agenda."

The Hall responded in nervous chatter to this less than usual procedure.

President Hancock called on Edward Rutledge to be recognized.

Rutledge said, "I rise today to support the declaration on independence that was masterfully written, although I would like to ask for the Congress to make one alteration that I believe will make the document more streamlined and targeted for success. I refer to the four sentences that relate the slave trade on page three of the declaration."

"South Carolina believes that the declaration is direct and successful in making the argument that our colonies should be independent from Britain, but the inclusion of a discussion about the slave trade confuses the listener of our demands and provides a barrier for unanimous support for this declaration."

"Fellow delegates, South Carolina has been able to build a strong economic base in these American colonies using the plantation system. Our environment is particularly accommodated to grow food products and other saleable items, such as rice and indigo, and we have found that the system works best when field hands are utilized who have a special tolerance to the extremes in climate that are present in our area."

"Other colonies prosper also in the plantation economy such as Rhode Island and Connecticut who have built ships to carry this trade. Massachusetts and New York banks financed expeditions to Africa. Insurance for the plantation system has been provided through the good offices of banks in New York. Ports in New York, New Jersey, Maryland, and Pennsylvania process and profit by this trade through their businesses," Rutledge continued

"More importantly, the declaration is a political statement that we are issuing to England to address the harms that have befallen us over the last fifty years. Our focus should be sharp on those facts of independence: there has been taxation without representation, the King has dissolved our assemblies for no reason, he has failed to pass laws for our accommodation, he has obstructed our due process of law, and he has caused the cessation of trade for our products. The list goes on. There is no need to add the contentious issue of the slave trade to interfere with our true goal which is independence.

"Mr. President, I move that we strike from the declaration the section on the slave trade," said Rutledge.

"Do I hear a second?" Hancock asked.

Numerous voices said, "Second!"

"Who wishes to speak on the motion?" said Hancock. "The chair recognizes Mr. Dickinson from Pennsylvania."

John Dickinson rose from his seat and said, "Thank you, Mr. President and thank you, Mr. Rutledge. I am standing today in support of the motion to delete the section from the declaration regarding the slave trade. As many of you have already heard, I am not supportive of the declaration on independence because of its timing. I believe that we are acting precipitously and are damaging our opportunity to settle these affairs in a different manner. However, if we are determined to pass this resolution, it should be precise and focused clearly on the matter at hand.

"The plantation business, Mr. Rutledge refers to, is a highly contentious issue among many in this room. I find it ironic that the good delegate from Virginia who also owns slaves, is the person who raises the issue of slavery in his own declaration. The document that we address this morning should have articles that are limited to our discussion about liberty. Side issues will not assist us in winning support from others who may become our allies. I vote to strike this statement on the slave trade."

The room was filled with muttering among the delegates.

"Order in the chamber," said Hancock. "Are there others who wish to speak on the motion?"

At least four hands were raised, and Hancock said, "I recognize Mr. Hoskinson from New Jersey."

"Thank you, Mr. President," said Francis Hoskinson. "I rise to support the motion to delete the passages referring to the slave trade. I agree with the statements of Mr. Dickinson regarding the elimination to make a more efficient appeal, but I would like to add another matter."

"If one were to read these passages, it sounds as though the author thinks that we colonists have been hoodwinked by trickery to accept slaves within our midst. I believe that both colonists and the Crown are equally liable for the institution of slavery in the colonies. In certain regions of America, the use of slaves on agricultural farms is much more advantageous than others. Yet, I dare say that slavery exists in almost every colony represented here today. Our goal is to issue a doctrine to the King so clear and unmistakable that even George will see it with clarity, if he can find his glasses."

The room erupted in laughter as the King was an easy target of mirth as Francis Hoskinson took his seat and Hancock banged his gavel.

"The chair recognizes Mr. Gwinnett from Georgia," said Hancock.

"Thank you, Mr. Hancock," said Button Gwinnett. "I rise in support of the motion by Mr. Rutledge from South Carolina. We may be late to this Congress, but the future success of Georgia depends on seeing this language removed from the declaration. We could not be more excited about the prospect of throwing off the shackles from King George, but we shouldn't upset our chances for financial gain, before we have the opportunity. Our delegation votes squarely behind South Carolina."

Hancock said, "I recognize Mr. Adams from Massachusetts."

Edward sat straight up in his chair and hoped that Adams would not lay waste to his designs.

"Thank you, Mr. Hancock and thank you, Mr. Rutledge for raising this important issue," said John Adams.

"Slavery is, in my estimation, a moral flaw that eventually must be eliminated," Adams said. "While some colonies depend upon slavery for their financial success, many others operate without its use. The viewpoint on slavery is not similar from one colony to the next. Some people think that slavery will eventually disappear on its own merits. I have no opinion on the matter. My main concern is to unite the colonies to achieve independence from England, and if that means keeping the paragraph on the slave trade, then I would vote yea. If the elimination of that clause means that we can have unanimity in declaring independence, then I would vote yea."

A decided rustling of papers and low conversation could be heard from the delegates as Adams sat down without definitively stating how he would vote.

Hancock said, "The chair recognizes Mr. Stone from Maryland."

"Thank you, President Hancock," said Thomas Stone. "I do not speak for the entire Maryland delegation, but I would like to say on the record that I believe the request of the gentleman from South Carolina is appropriate for our effort to become independent from England. I agree with Mr. Adams when he says that if omitting these words about slave trade brings unanimity to our enterprise, then I would vote yes to support the resolution. Thank you."

"The chair recognizes Mr. Ellery from Rhode Island," said Hancock.

"Thank you, Mr. Hancock," said William Ellery. "I rise in support of the resolution to strike the language from the text of the declaration pertaining to the slave trade. The topic of slavery deserves a wider audience than we can afford while we struggle to declare our independence from Britain. In my colony, we have many voices on both sides of this problem. Our merchants and shipbuilders prosper from the trade while the freemen in our colony stand ready to see it abolished. Until we achieve independence from England and can rely on our own ability to thrive, I would recommend that we focus on independence and eliminating this clause."

"Are there any delegates who wish to speak against the resolution on the floor?" said John Hancock.

Eyes darted back and forth as delegates waited to see if anyone would raise their hand, lift their voice, or take an initiative. After an interminable thirty seconds, Hancock struck his gavel and said, "The chair will allow five minutes for each colony to caucus to decide on their vote. The chair also rules that for changes in the declaration; a simple majority will be sufficient to adopt the motion. The secretary will take the roll call of the colonies."

After five minutes, Charles Thompson said, "On the motion to eliminate the section in the draft of the Declaration of Independence pertaining to the slave trade, how do you vote:

"Connecticut – Yea
Delaware – Yea
Georgia – Yea
Maryland – Yea
Massachusetts - Nay
New Hampshire - Nay
New Jersey - Yea
New York - Yea
North Carolina - Yea
Pennsylvania - Yea
Rhode Island - Yea
South Carolina - Yea
Virginia – Nay"

"The vote is 10-3 and the motion is adopted," said Charles Thompson.

"So ordered," said Hancock as he struck his gavel.

"The Chair will now ask the Secretary to read the declaration draft from page 1," said Hancock.

Secretary Thompson started at the beginning with, "A declaration by the representatives of the United States of America." The reading proceeded until a delegate rose and was recognized by the chair to allow him to offer amendments to the original text. In the first thirty minutes the secretary was interrupted five times and had only managed to cover four items on the first page of four. Meanwhile, Edward Rutledge sat lost in thought about how he had managed to protect South Carolina from the possibility of a disaster by maneuvering the debate on the one subject that he felt was the most important – slavery.

The afternoon turned into evening, and the delegates spoke and argued about one point after another. All debate was closed off at 7PM to be continued the next day at 9AM.

THE AFTERGLOW

The light breeze of a summer day in Philadelphia was comforting to Edward Rutledge as he left Mrs. Yard's boardinghouse. After the events of the previous day, Rutledge had a restful sleep and looked forward to the morning session of Congress. Overhead, he noticed birds gliding in the air currents coming from the river with wings capturing the wind, causing them to soar and circle around. Maybe this was a good omen for the prospects of independence for the colonies.

Walking toward the Statehouse, Edward encountered delegate groups of twos and threes who were heading in the same direction. Thomas Stone was walking alone, and Edward quickened his pace to catch up to him.

"Good morning, Thomas."

"And a good morning to you, Edward. We really accomplished a great deal of work yesterday. Do you think it could be any more exciting?"

"We need to finish up the work on the declaration, and I will be very pleased if we complete that today. My review of the balance of the declaration doesn't foresee any major hurdles that we will have to overcome. Of course, if yesterday's beginning of the editing process means anything, we may be in for a long day."

The draft version of the declaration on independence had already been altered significantly with the elimination of the clause about slave trade. To Edward, the continued debate about smaller issues was taking longer than he thought necessary. Of course, that should be expected with a body of fifty-five men who are asked to render more exact a document with over thirteen-hundred words. In addition, there was the issue of heaping insults on to the British people for not coming to the aid of American colonists. Edward thought to himself, he should prepare for a lengthy debate.

Promptly at 9AM, John Hancock gaveled the Congress to order, and before the declaration on independence would be addressed, the delegates pressed ahead on the less exciting items to be decided, although all were critical to the effort for successfully becoming an independent country.

Included on the agenda were six reports and requests that needed the delegates' attention. They ranged from reports submitted by commissioners of the southern division of Indian affairs, to the redeployment of soldiers from one theater to another, and these topics needed the entire morning to complete.

Finally, at about 11AM, John Hancock recognized Benjamin Harrison to report on the progress for the final approval of the declaration on independence that had been submitted the previous day. Harrison called on the Secretary to read from the draft submitted by the Committee of Five. The secretary started to read from page two of the Committee's draft.

The pace of the amending process was just as slow this day as it had been the night before. Previously, the delegates made ten different edits. The delegates argued about style and word choices. They changed the word "expunge" to "alter." They argued about the spelling of "unalienable," or was it "inalienable"? In some instances, the language choice made the document stronger. More often, though, the changes were semantic and driven more by the individual's need to have an impact as opposed to creating a stronger document.

By 7PM, thirteen additional edits were made by the delegates while leaving one more page of the draft to be reviewed. They adjourned for the night.

All the while, Jefferson sat at the Virginia table in silence. He listened carefully to the debate while taking precise notes on the actions of the day. He never asked to be recognized to offer clarification on a topic. During the dinner break, Jefferson sat next to Dr. Franklin seeking solace from the complex affairs of the day. Dr. Franklin related a story.

"I have made it a rule whenever in my power to avoid becoming the draughtsman of papers to be reviewed by a public body. I took my lesson from an incident I will relate to you.

"When I was a young man, I had occasion to travel. I stopped at an inn and asked for a room. The innkeeper showed me one with a new sign hanging above the door. It read: John Thompson, hatter, makes and sells hats for ready money.'

A friend of his had suggested he get a sign to advertise his business, and so he did. But then came the edits.

One neighbor said, 'Why say John Thompson? Everyone knows you're John Thompson.' So he struck that out.

Another said, 'Why say hatter? It's obvious from the hats in the window.' So, he struck that out.

A third said, 'Why say makes and sells hats? If you sell them, surely you will make them.' So, he struck that out.

And finally, someone said, 'Why say for ready money? That's understood.'

In the end, the sign simply read: 'Hats.'"

No one is sure how well Jefferson related to the parable, but he did know that the editorial and drafting process was not yet finished.

The next day, July 4, 1776, the delegates filed back into Assembly Hall, and John Hancock began the meeting. Only one item of business needed to be addressed before the Secretary began the review of the declaration on independence.

Delegates continued to make more objections to small pieces of language. When the secretary read the entire document, and President Hancock asked the secretary to call for the vote, every colony voted yea, except for New York, which abstained, whereupon Hancock said, "The motion carries unanimously."

Numerous other pieces of business were adopted including how to have the document authenticated and printed. Additionally, plans were made for publishing the new declaration.

As the delegates filed out of the Statehouse, some delegates were celebrating while others showed a nervous exhilaration when they thought about the huge responsibility they had just shouldered collectively. None of the delegates could even begin to imagine how transcendent and revered these actions would be in years to come.

Freedom For Some

Pompey walked out of the hot steamy kitchen and into the humid alley as Mrs. Yard's servant girls were cleaning pots and drying dishes after the dinner for Edward Rutledge and his friends. Pompey finally realized why Master Edward wanted him to attend Congress, and he wanted to put all the pieces together. He wanted to talk to Caesar and Bob and to confer with Robert if he could find him. Pompey looked up and down the alleyway and didn't see anyone except for a few kitchen hands dumping items in the trash.

The hot day had evolved into a comfortable, breezy darkness that would soon allow the fireflies to emerge blinking in the night. Pompey rolled over in his head the comments Mr. Rutledge had uttered about freedom from the King and the pursuit of happiness for all. *Did the colonies seriously think they could fight the King for their freedom,* he wondered? He paced a few yards down the alley and then retraced his steps past Mrs. Yard's kitchen to the barrels of her neighbor. As he was returning, following a fourth circuit of the area, Pompey eyed Bob at the end of the alley. Pompey started walking faster toward Bob and met him before Bob could walk past the second house from the street.

"Bob, what have you heard lately that sounded unusual at Mr. Stone's table?"

"There has been a tension at the dining table the past two days, but it didn't register much with me. Why are you asking?"

Pompey leaned into Bob and said, "These delegates have decided they can declare independence from the King and instantly it would happen. Master Rutledge has been talking about freedom from the King and how we just needed to get rid of the Redcoats. I think he means the King's army, but then he recited the words I told you about life, liberty, and the pursuit of happiness. If I didn't know better, I would have thought that he was in his cups.

"Whoa! Are you fishy, too?"

"I'm serious, Bob. Something big has happened, and we should learn exactly what it is. Master Edward has been talking non-stop for the last two days about independence. Haven't you heard anything, Bob? You know that overheard conversations are how we get our information. What have you heard?"

"I do know that Mr. Francis Lee had dinner last night with Mr. Stone and they looked very proud of themselves – even more than usual. I do remember Mr. Lee said something about how pleased he was that all the delegates could agree on the declaration. He also said that he was happy that his motion for independence was finally adopted.

"That's what it must be. Remember last month when you told us that Mr. Lee's brother had made a proposal for independence, but then Mr. Rutledge blocked it and that made him upset? If Mister Rutledge and Mr. Lee are both pleased, that may mean that the delegates have decided to give themselves freedom from England."

"Can they just declare themselves free? Can we do that, too?"

"This is no time for trifles. I doubt if the King is going to just yawn and say, 'do what you want.' I suspect there is major trouble on the horizon. Remember what happened in Virginia when the royal governor left and told all the slaves that if they turned on their masters and joined the British Army, they would receive their freedom. I wonder if our masters will make a similar deal with us."

Just as Pompey and Bob were talking about the current events, Caesar, Francis Lightfoot Lee's valet, came around the corner of the alley and yelled out, "Did you hear the news? We're going to be free!"

"Slow up, Caesar, and keep your voice down. Do you want to get all of us in a pickle?" said Pompey.

"I was so excited that I forgot how far my voice is heard. Mr. Lee was having dinner tonight with Mr. Adams, and you would have thought that it was Twelfth Night come early. They were congratulating each other about a declaration on independence and how they hoped that King George would just come to his senses about their intentions. The other thing I heard was that Mr. Adams said Edward Rutledge had been responsible for getting the language about the slave trade out of the declaration."

Pompey said, "That sounds exactly like Master Edward. I was telling Bob that Mr. Rutledge and his friends were bragging about declaring freedom from the King and delivering liberty and happiness for all. Except, that doesn't include the three of us. They don't pay us any mind except when they want something done for them. I wonder how they would react if we agreed to declare our independence. I bet they wouldn't be too happy about that."

"What's all this talk about happiness? I can't remember the last time that I ever had any happiness," said Caesar.

"I'm not sure. It sounds nice, but what does it mean?" said Pompey. "It sounds like something you wish for as a goal but never expect to get. Happiness is not something I think about often as a slave. What joy can there be in polishing boots, running errands, and cleaning clothes? If I were given the opportunity to pursue happiness, the first thing I would do is say goodbye to Mr. Rutledge. After that, I would look for a plot of land to plant some crops to grow and provide for my family so we could be happy. I can't do that now."

"Sounds like you been thinking about freedom. Maybe Master Stone could give me a parcel of land where I could raise my own family. But I don't think he would be any happier than the King would be when he hears about their declaration on independence."

"Master Lee owns more property than he can manage now. Maybe he would benefit from letting me and my family open a small farm. I could perform some of these tasks I do now for him on the side," said Caesar.

Pompey eyed his friends with resignation. "Boys, I doubt if we are going to see freedom any time soon, even if our masters somehow convince the King of England to let them live without his help. Furthermore, even if the master does achieve some sort of independence, our relationship with our master will not change. They treat us like dogs, and like dogs, we live and work for them until we die, and then he goes out and gets a new dog. Have you ever seen a dog polish a boot? Have you ever seen a hound run errands? No, and it won't happen because our master will never let us go free. They own us as property, and they treat us like that. The only way we get our freedom is if we write our own declaration of independence. Our master doesn't understand how we really feel about our relationship with them. They look at us as if we are animals with no emotions or feelings. They believe that they have made a great life for us by bringing us from a backward Africa. They don't understand we had a good life in Africa before we were captured against our will and brought to America to be their slaves."

“You should write our declaration on independence, Pompey. You tell the truth, and we would all agree. How do we get all the slaves to meet and agree?”

“Bob, did you hear what you just said? How are we supposed to get the slaves together if they keep us all apart? That’s never going to happen.”

“Then, what should we do? Are we supposed to just bow and scrape and hope that one day the master will see the error of slavery?” Caesar said.

Pompey said, “Unfortunately, boys, that is precisely all we can do. Slavery will always exist while the master has the whip. The only way slavery will change is if the white folk start fighting among themselves, and I don’t see that happening any time soon, probably when all of us are dead and gone.”

“Maybe we need to start our own revolt. If the different colonies meet to face off with the King, maybe the slaves could do the same.”

“Now you’re really talking like a fool. First, we could never talk in public about starting a revolt. We’d be whipped or worse before the first meeting ended. Secondly, when there have been revolts, the master always becomes the executioner. Slaves had a planned revolt in South Carolina many years ago. They killed every person who even talked to some of the leaders, and they killed some others who only heard about the plan. The master will be ruthless and keep us at their beck and call. Furthermore, I am not convinced that those colonies who don’t have slaves – they don’t have very high opinions of us Africans. Have you talked to any of the Free Black men in Pennsylvania. Just like the Free Black men in New York, they have complained that they are treated with open and mean distrust when compared to white people. Our black faces have created a near unclimbable wall that is almost impossible for us to climb over.”

“Pompey, you’re talking like there is no hope for us. It seems to me that, if the colonies go to war with Britain, that might be the opportunity for us to unite and gain our own freedom.”

“And how do you think we are able to accomplish that? Look what they have done to the Indians. Those people were minding their own business when the ships from Europe started to come here. Look what they have done to them. Do you think they would treat us any better?”

Bob said, "All I know is that Master Stone treats me kindly, and I got no cause for risking my life on a dream that I don't see happening. If I were ever to step out of line, he would send me right out into the fields to cut tobacco. That would break my back as sleek as a shadow and twice as sly."

"You are the one who is speaking the truth now, Bob. The masters have all the power, and we are left to try to stay out of trouble as long as we are able. I saw another house slave that Mr. Rutledge did not like. He was sent out to the rice fields, and I have not seen him since. Freedom may happen for the white man, but I doubt if I will ever get the opportunity."

Caesar said, "That's another thing that I don't understand. Mr. Lee talks about how the King treats the colonists as slaves and how unfair that is. I hear this nonsense and think to myself, why don't you open your eyes and look at how you treat me. Now that's slavery."

"How do you think the British will react to this declaration? I don't think they will be very happy. Do you think that we might be better off with the British than with our masters?

"Whatever side you take in this struggle, we will lose," said Pompey. "Our masters are British-born, and they will be fighting the British. Whoever wins, they will continue to treat us with the same abuse and complaints. We're hemmed in on all sides."

"The master doesn't want to be a slave to the King, and yet he has no problem with being the master to me. He says one thing and means another, yet the meanings are as thin as gruel."

"Has anyone seen Robert Hemmings, Jefferson's valet lately?"

"I've seen him at the markets buying things for his master. But I think he stays very close to Jefferson."

"I've seen him on the docks buying fabric for Mr. Jefferson. He's younger than any of us, and he is shy. I have only had a couple of brief conversations with him."

"He would be a valuable source of information about this liberty and happiness that we are hearing. He probably knows a lot more about Mr. Jefferson than he has shared with us. The next time you see him, let him know about our meetings here in the Second Street alley. He would be a terrific addition to our conversations."

"I think that the master picks younger valets because he thinks that, if we are young, we won't catch what they are talking about among their friends."

"Caesar, you are wiser every time we meet. Master always wants the most for his money in slaves. He thinks that maybe I would be more valuable in the field when I get older and stronger. I want to be big and strong, but if it means working in the fields, I may want to rethink that."

Pompey, Caesar, and Bob were worried about their future, considering the news they had heard from their masters about the so-called declaration on independence. As the night got darker and the stars became more visible, the sliver of the moon cast a faint shadow on the threesome. Pompey motioned that he needed to return to see what his master needed after dinner was completed, and the others agreed that now was probably the time to, once again, recognize that their bodies were not owned solely by themselves, so they headed home.

AFTERWORD

The origin of this book came from researching the political debate between delegates at the Continental Congress about the topic of slavery. While many historic literature and critiques have been made about the debates at the Constitutional Convention in 1787 regarding the 3/5th Compromise that Southern and Northern delegates hashed out, little written research has been available to examine a similar process that happened in Philadelphia eleven years earlier.

Very few documents have survived from the day-to-day proceedings of the Second Continental Congress. The delegates at the outset of their deliberations decided to debate in secret with no note taking or minutes kept. One document many cite is Thomas Jefferson's *Notes of Proceedings in the Continental Congress*, often referred to as his "Notes on Debates." It was written retrospectively, not during the actual debates of 1776. Jefferson wrote these passages forty-nine years after the fact, during which time lapses of memory could imperil the accuracy of the transcript. Another book, *Journals of the Continental Congress, 1774-1789*, compiled in 1902 by the Library of Congress using original manuscript records, provides a daily review of existing documents.

While trying to understand why no mention of slavery was included in the final version of the Declaration of Independence, I came across two entries made in Jefferson's *Notes*, (1) Mr. Rutledge of S. Carolina then requested the determination be put off to the next day, as he believed his colleagues, though, they disapproved of the resolution, would then join in it for the sake of unanimity, and (2) the next day, when it was again moved, South Carolina concurred in voting for it. Furthermore, more than fifty edits to the Jefferson draft of the Declaration took place. The exclusion of 168 words that concerned the actions of King George in foisting the slave trade on the American colonies is the most widely edited document known among historians, though no notes, votes, or discussion exists that could provide a reflection of the debates.

When discovering these innocuous passages, I asked myself, *what happened overnight to change the votes of the South Carolina delegation?*

Why was Rutledge the only delegate mentioned by name regarding the postponement of the motion to pass the vote on a declaration for independence by one day? What conversations took place on the evening of July 1 regarding the slave trade section? What discussions occurred between June 28 and July 1 when the Jefferson draft became available to the delegates?

Despite all the research I've undertaken, I have found no definitive answers to these questions.

However, we do have a certain amount of information about the delegates through some of their writings that have been preserved. Unfortunately, the players in this drama did not leave many traces of their opinions or actions. The written record of Edward Rutledge is scant at best. Only one biographer has offered a book on his life, and that one mainly featured his brother, John. In addition, other delegates provide few historical archives in the form of letters or notes. Although it is impossible to know the exact dialogue between delegates, the historic records of the delegates to the Second Continental Congress provides background for some of the language that I have utilized.

The other issue I wanted to report is how slaves reacted to events in Charleston and Philadelphia. The slaves, who were employed to be valets and cooks, were readily available to overhear conversations and see who was coming to the meetings. George Washington most famously is known to have had his personal valet, William (Billy) Lee, at his side throughout the entire Revolutionary War. During the pre-Revolutionary times, students at William & Mary always had as companions their valets who served as part of their entourage when traveling to cities like Philadelphia. These plantation owners saw having a black valet at their side as proof of their wealth and power. Various pieces of evidence through ledgers and letters refer to the presence of valets who performed tasks for their owners in Philadelphia.

The other mystery that piqued my curiosity was why the slave trade section was proposed and then discarded. In the Continental Association agreement of 1775 concluded among the colonies during the first Continental Congress, when discussing the non-importation provisions, delegates endorsed a section that reads, "*Second.* That we will neither import nor purchase any Slave imported after the first Day of December next, after which Time we will wholly discontinue the Slave Trade, and will neither be concerned in it ourselves, nor will we hire our Vessels, nor sell our Commodities or Manufactures, to those who are concerned in it."

Although the Continental Association was an agreement among the colonies at the First Continental Congress, when the declaration was discussed at the Second Continental Congress, circumstances had changed significantly. Nonetheless, the inclusion in the Association document about the slave trade indicates that the slave trade was not an unknown subject for the delegates at the Second Congress.

Thomas Jefferson, who owned slaves, wrote the draft of the Declaration, and included a section berating the slave trade, a radical move to force the delegates, like himself, to face this issue directly. However, in the end, all language about slavery was abandoned – a victory for southern colonies who depended on the practice to fuel their economies.

Scholars and activists have tried to understand why the subject of slavery was not mentioned in the Declaration of Independence, specifically when the preamble of this document included the words "all men are created equal." Yet, the obvious counterpoint is the fact that men in the room, from Black valets to the signers of the Declaration of Independence, were not treated equally in any way. Samuel Johnson, the famous British poet, essayist, moralist, literary critic, biographer, and lexicographer stated during these debates, "How is it that we hear the loudest yelps for liberty among the drivers of Negroes?"

Many historians of the United State Constitution accurately report that the word "slavery" is not mentioned anywhere in the document The use of euphemisms reflects how difficult the topic of slavery was to discuss in a search to find common ground. This book was written to demonstrate and express how the discussions may have been articulated.

When doing research on Edward Rutledge, the lack of documents and correspondence made it difficult to come to any conclusive findings. No letters to or from his wife, Henrietta, were discovered. Correspondence with his brother, John Rutledge, was also difficult to come by. One person explained that Edward may have intentionally destroyed documents. There is little evidence to verify such actions, though the record suggests that some of his recovered papers were found in an outhouse.

One source, who was trying to trace her DNA among relatives, hinted that Edward may have been the father of a daughter by a slave woman, a practice that is well known to have occurred among slave owners, like Thomas Jefferson. The source claimed that one of her descendants had the same DNA as Dr. John Rutledge, Edward's grandfather. The ancestry of the Hemmings family from Monticello confirms that such occurrences were not rare. Similarly, Edward's participation during 1790 with the General Assembly of South Carolina showed that a petition was presented by four individuals asking that they not be considered slaves, but rather African Moors. Edward Rutledge was on a three-person committee that reviewed the petition and reported back to the Assembly that these Moroccan Blacks should be exempt from the Negro Act of 1740. A source claimed that one of the wives in this case was the mother of a child by Rutledge. No other evidence supports the claim.

The inclusion of the slave conversations in the *Valet's Witness* surrounding the passage of the Declaration of Independence provides a window into the minds of the enslaved. They were often literally in the room when many historical moments transpired in Philadelphia during the debates of the Continental Congress. Although the language that appears in this book is contrived, the facts are slaves were present and slaves spoke among themselves. Yet, hardly anywhere among the reconstructions of those debates was the presence of slave valets noted. It is difficult for people nowadays to have a sense of what it must have been like to see important decision makers have slaves at their beck and call. Certainly, among the slave owners from the South, it was a mark of distinction that they had slaves in their entourage. Rarely in paintings that depict these important historical events do you see the faces of enslaved Black people, except for the likeness of George Washington's slave, Billy Lee, in a work that was painted by John Trumbull, the painter of "The Revolution" which is currently exhibited at the Metropolitan Museum of Art in New York City.

As was made clear in the speech that Frederick Douglas gave in Rochester, NY, at an 1852 gathering of the Rochester Ladies Anti-Slavery Association, African blacks viewed July 4, 1776, from a totally different point of view than white people. Although the dialogue in this book is recreated, the tone and directness of Edward

Rutledges valet, Pompey, and his friends gives the reader another perspective to view the celebrated activities of the early Revolutionary period. The amount of information Black valets obtained may seem impossible to imagine, but many stories have been told about how knowledgeable slaves were present to the events of the day. Therefore, it is not difficult to guess that a few well positioned individuals could have had these same conversations.

EPILOGUE

In some ways, Edward Rutledge reached the pinnacle of his life on July 4, 1776, as his influence on major events waned after he left the position of delegate to the Second Continental Congress. Later in 1776, Edward joined a committee that included John Adams and Dr. Benjamin Franklin to negotiate with the British Admiral Lord Richard Howe. The Lord Admiral had requested a dialogue to explore a peaceful resolution to the conflict. After three hours the conference was adjourned. No other peace conferences took place again until Lord Cornwallis surrendered in 1781, and the Treaty of Paris was negotiated from 1782-83.

After his return to Charleston from Philadelphia, Edward restarted his law practice and became a member of the South Carolina General Assembly, while obtaining the rank of captain in the Charleston Artillery. During the months between November 1776 and May 1780, colonial and British military were in constant contact with ebbs and flows of dominance until British forces captured Charleston in 1780. Edward Rutledge was taken as a prisoner of war on August 27, 1780, although the British treated the prisoners in a manner that we might not recognize, as Edward took a manservant and a silver teapot with him.

During the occupation of Charleston, British forces took control over plantations and mansions for their own use. Some slaves enlisted in the British Army while others either disappeared or were taken for bondage by other local citizens. People were given the option of remaining as supporters of the Revolution or they could sign a loyalty oath to be treated better. Henry Middleton, delegate to both the First and Second Continental Congresses, and father-in-law to Edward Rutledge, decided to sign the loyalty oath.

John Rutledge was elected President of South Carolina and fled Charleston ahead of the British invasion. Later, he became a delegate once again to the Continental Congress and helped to deliver aid from Congress to South Carolina. In his role of President, he helped the South Carolina militia and the Continental Army, under the leadership of General Nathaniel Greene.

After the surrender of Lord Cornwallis to General George Washington, it took months to agree to a peace agreement. The British relinquished Charleston nine months after the Treaty of Paris was signed.

After eleven months of captivity, Edward Rutledge was released in a prisoner exchange in Philadelphia, reunited with this family, and returned to Charleston less than two weeks later.

John Rutledge held many key South Carolina offices from delegate to the Continental Congress, delegate to the US Constitutional Congress which produced the US Constitution, State Chancellor, Chief Justice of the State Supreme Court, and he sat briefly as the United States Supreme Court Chief Justice.

Edward Rutledge was a member of the South Carolina General Assembly from 1783-96 and became known for his astute political analyses. He was a key member of the Constitutional Convention that approved the United States Constitution. In 1798, he became Governor of South Carolina by vote of the legislature even though his health was poor. Edward suffered a severe stroke on January 10, 1800, and died January 23. John Rutledge died July 18, 1800.

Slavery continued in the United States until after the Civil War in 1865. During this entire period, most white Americans thought that Africans could not operate in society with whites because they supposedly had certain deficiencies and characteristics that made it impossible for them to compete in society on an equal basis. Many whites thought Africans were intellectually inferior, using pseudoscience and biased observations to justify racial hierarchies. These views were often reinforced by limited access to education for blacks, which perpetuated stereotypes and ignored the achievements of free and enslaved African Americans. Enlightenment thinkers and abolitionists challenged these assumptions, pointing to examples of Black intellectuals, writers, and orators as evidence of equal capacity. Regardless, widespread prejudice persisted, shaping laws, social norms, and educational opportunities well into the 19th and 20th centuries.

As an example of how Africans during the Revolutionary period could compete on an equal basis, I would suggest that four individuals are worth examining:

Phillis Wheatley was an African-born poet who was enslaved and brought to Boston as a child, where she was educated by her owners.

She quickly demonstrated extraordinary literary talent. In 1773, Wheatley became the first African American and one of the first women in America to publish a book of poetry, titled Poems on Various Subjects, Religious and Moral. Her work blended classical references, Christian themes, and subtle critiques of slavery, earning admiration from prominent figures like George Washington. Despite her fame, Wheatley struggled with poverty and racial prejudice throughout her life, dying young and largely forgotten until later generations reclaimed her legacy.

Ona Judge Staines was a mulatto slave who worked as the personal maid to Martha Washington, wife of the first president of the United States. Ona's parents were owned by Daniel Parker Custis, Martha Washington's first husband so Ona was considered as dowager for George. Ona was given no education or religious training. She escaped slavery by running away from The President's House in Philadelphia on May 21, 1796. As a mulatto with very light skin and freckles, Judge blended into the crowd and eventually made her way to Greenland, New Hampshire where she met a Black sailor, Jack Staines, and they became the parents of two girls and a boy. She learned how to read and write and converted to Christianity. Until Washington's death in December 1799, he worked feverishly to lure Ona back to his estate, but she refused all entreaties. Washington was angered because he believed Ona should have shown gratitude for the fact that she had been raised almost like a part of the family. After her husband died in 1803, Ona Staines lived in poverty while her girls became indentured servants, and her son became a sailor.

The son of a white woman and an African father whom he never met, Lemuel Haines was born in 1753 and was bound by indenture to a deacon at age five months until he turned twenty-one. Brought up in a religious home in Connecticut, Haines learned to read and write attending a common school. Theology fascinated Lemuel. He experienced a conversion and read sermons by other clerics, inserting one of his own into a service to the surprise of the deacon. In 1774, having completed his period of service, he joined the minutemen and trained on the village green. Soon after the skirmish at Lexington, he joined the army for the siege of Boston.

At about this time Lemuel wrote a ballad about the battle of Lexington. At the center of the poem is a clash of freedom and slavery:

For liberty each Freeman strives
As it's a Gift of God
And for it, willing yield their lives
And seal it with their blood
Twice Happy they who thus resign
Into the peaceful Grave
Much better these in Death Consign
Than a Surviving Slave.

In an unpublished, unfinished manuscript by Lemuel Haines titled, "Liberty Further Extended: Or Free Thoughts on the Illegality of Slave-Keeping.

His main argument is "That an African, or, in other terms, that a Negro may justly challenge, and has an undeniable right to his liberty: Consequently, the practice of slave-keeping, which so much abounds in this land, is illicit.

In 1775, Haynes marched on the expedition to Fort Ticonderoga that was captured by the Green Mountain Boys led by Ethan Allen.

Frederick Douglas was born in 1818 as a slave, taught himself how to read and write and escaped slavery in 1838. He rose to become one of the most powerful voices for abolition and civil rights in 19th-century America. His autobiography, "Narrative of the Life of Frederick Douglass, an American Slave," revealed the brutal realities of slavery and showcased his eloquence and intellect. As a speaker, writer, and statesman, Douglass challenged white Americans to confront their moral contradictions and advocated fiercely for equality, including women's rights. His life embodied the struggle for freedom and the transformative power of education and self-determination.

Asked to give the keynote speech on Fourth of July celebration in 1852, Douglas said,

"Fellow citizens, why am I called upon to speak here today? What have I, or those I represent, to do with your national independence?

Are the great principles of political freedom and of natural justice, embodied in that Declaration of Independence, extended to us? And am I, therefore, called upon to bring our humble offering to the national altar, and to confess the benefits and express devout gratitude for the blessings resulting from your independence to us?

Would to God, both for your sakes and ours, that an affirmative answer could be truthfully returned to these questions! Then my task would be light, and my burden easy and delightful. For whom is there so cold that a nation's sympathy could not warm him? Who so stolid and selfish, that would not give his voice to swell the hallelujahs of a nation's jubilee, when the chains of servitude had been torn from the limbs? I am not that man. In a case like that, the dumb might eloquently speak, and the "lame man leap as a hart."

"But such is not the state of the case. I say it with a sad sense of the disparity between us. I am not included within the pale of this glorious anniversary. Your high independence only reveals the immeasurable distance between us. The blessings in which you, this day, rejoice, are not enjoyed in common. – The rich inheritance of justice, liberty, prosperity and independence, bequeathed by your fathers, is shared by you, but not by me. This Fourth of July is yours, not mine. You may rejoice. I must mourn. To drag a man in fetters into the grand illuminated temple of liberty, and call upon him to join in joyous anthems, were inhuman mockery and sacrilegious irony.

"What, to the American slave, is your Fourth of July? I answer, a day that reveals to him, more than all other days of the year, the gross injustice and cruelty to which he is the constant victim. To him, your celebration is a sham; your boasted liberty and unholy license; your national greatness, swelling vanity; your sounds of rejoicing are empty and heartless; your denunciation of tyrants, brass fronted impudence; your shouts of liberty and equality, hollow mockery; your prayers and hymns, your sermons and thanksgivings, with all your religious parade and solemnity, are, to Him, mere bombast, fraud, deception, impiety, and hypocrisy – a thin veil to cover up crimes which would disgrace a nation of savages. There is no nation on the earth guilty of practices more shocking and bloodier than are the people of the United States, at this very hour."

Black valets to the signers of the Declaration of Independence in 1776 knew that the freedom that was sought by the colonists would not be rewarded to them.

ABOUT THE AUTHOR

Rohn Hein is a first-time author with fifty years of involvement in non-partisan community activism Starting as a VISTA volunteer in 1973, he worked for five different non-profit organizations working with welfare recipients, senior citizens, urban housing, racial justice, and environmental efforts in Wisconsin, Minnesota, New York and New Jersey. For the last 40 years Rohn was an investment adviser while volunteering with social justice activities in affordable housing, racial justice, and environmental issues. Rohn has written testimony presented in the Minnesota and New Jersey Legislature and appeared at numerous churches, city council, county, and regional government agencies.

He works with many New Jersey non-profit organizations on racial justice issue, such as The NJ Institute for Social Justice, Salvation and Social Justice, NJ NAACP, Fair Share Housing, and UU Faith Action. He has worked on landmark affordable housing legislation and on the enactment of a racial justice impact statement on legislation in New Jersey.

Learn more about Rohn Hein at
www.historiumpress.com/rohn-hein

www.historiumpress.com

www.ingramcontent.com/pod-product-compliance
Lightning Source LLC
LaVergne TN
LVHW041309150826
845673LV00008B/2817

9798950078941